HEART
OF THE
CROWN

DAUGHTERS OF PEVERELL

HEART OF THE CROWN

HANNAH CURRIE

WhiteSpark

This is a work of fiction. All characters and events portrayed in this novel are either fictitious or used fictitiously.

HEART OF THE CROWN

WhiteSpark Publishing, a division of WhiteFire Publishing
13607 Bedford Rd NE
Cumberland, MD 21502

ISBNs:
978-1-946531-87-2 (paperback)
978-1-946531-89-6 (hardcover)
978-1-946531-88-9 (digital)

To those who wonder if it's too late for a second chance,
It's not.

And to Becky, Beth, Brittany, Marielle, and Emily—
the teens, now adults, I had the privilege of walking alongside
during their high school years.
I might have been your leader but you impacted my life
more than you'll ever know.
Keep taking on the world.
I'll be here, same as always, cheering you on.

Bring on the tears
That fall down my face
As I realize I've blown it again
I try so hard to hold it all together
But all I'm holding is broken
I scramble and grab
Grasp and hope
But I have nothing
I've fallen short
Again

God, please
Make something good of this mess
You're the only one who can
Catch my tears in your hands
Restore my soul
Help me to forgive myself
And let the pain go

And by the grace I know you offer
Take these broken pieces
All I have to give
And use them to create
Something beautiful

ONE

When Alina asked me to come with her to meet Hodenia's new princess this week, neither of us had expected we'd be coming for her funeral.

"Princess Rachana was the epitome of grace, her last days and months filled with kindness, despite the end she knew was coming. She will be missed by all of Hodenia but especially by her husband, Prince Marcos, and son, Prince Ryan."

Marcos laid a hand on his young son's shoulder. The boy barely moved, his focus set on the glossy wooden casket as if any moment it might open and the only relative he truly knew come back to him. Everything in me ached to go over and place a hand on Ryan's other shoulder, let him know he wasn't as alone as he felt.

No, not on his shoulder. I wanted to pick the little boy up and cuddle him close. Sit right down there on the grass and pull him into my lap, smothering him with the certainty that he wasn't alone.

But, of course, that would hardly be appropriate in such a setting. Even if he did know me. Which he didn't. At all. Although, I had danced with his father. Once. What felt like a lifetime ago. When I was still naïve enough to think everyone had the option of marrying for love. And that a moment of defiance was limited to simply a moment.

Come on, Wenderley. God forgave you, remember? You've got to let it go.

I let my gaze stray to Prince Marcos again, as if the sight of the strong man weeping wasn't clawing my heart to pieces.

No, not weeping. Weeping intimated loud noises, hiccupping, a loss of control. Prince Marcos showed none of these. His broad shoulders didn't shake nor his hands tremble. His back was as straight as ever, showcasing every inch of his six-foot-plus frame as he stared somewhere beyond the shoulder of the man leading the graveside ceremony.

But those tears, the proof of pain sliding down his face. He must have truly loved his wife. Despite what the papers said. I wished he hadn't. It would have been easier on my heart if he'd stood there, stoic, emotionless, and still.

"Today, as we say goodbye to Princess Rachana—mother, wife, friend, and princess—let us hold on to the fact that she will forever be in our hearts, having left a grand legacy of love. Her life of twenty-four years was far too short, but she made a difference. Perhaps that is the greatest legacy of all."

Marcos squeezed Ryan's shoulder. I forced myself to look away.

I shouldn't have even been here. The funeral was one thing but this private graveside burial? It should have been close friends and family only.

Of course, friends were difficult to define when you were the rulers of a kingdom.

The sun hit the coffin at just the right angle to send a burst of glare into my eyes. Didn't the sun know it was supposed to hide behind clouds during funerals? Funerals were supposed to be dark and gloomy, preferably with enough drizzly rain to make everyone miserable and add enough wetness to everyone's cheeks to make it unclear as to who was really crying and who was there for the show.

But no, today the sun shone, as bright and clear as if it had just won a race to the sky's zenith—and wanted everyone to know. No clouds. No wind. Just a clear, beautiful day. Too beautiful. Were it not for the stone monoliths and flower-covered graves spotting the brilliant green hillside, one would have thought the group out for a picnic.

As if on cue, my stomach grumbled. I hurriedly placed a hand over it, hoping to muffle the sound. Would the man's speech go much longer? Not that I wanted to be irreverent or anything, but my stomach wasn't the only part of my body protesting the lengthy service. The balls of my feet had been arguing back and forth with my shins for an hour now over who had the worse end of the deal. Spindly heels weren't made for soft grass. Nor I for heels. Though Kenna and Alina, either side of me, didn't seem to have the same problem, standing tall without the slightest sway or fidget. Of course, heels came part and parcel with their royal roles whereas I only wore them when forced.

The boy lost his mother and you're complaining about heels?

It wasn't a booming voice from the heavens but the voice inside me might as well have been the way I flinched. My conscience was right though, I had no right to complain. Not considering all this little family had been through.

Please God, help them.

The prayer came almost as naturally as breathing, having prayed it daily over the past thirteen months. Sometimes there was more to it. Some days I prayed till the burden lifted and I felt as wrung out as if I'd waged a physical battle. Many times, it was simply those three desperate words. Over and over. *God, help them.*

Though I prayed for them both, it was Prince Marcos who lay heaviest in my heart. The day the story broke that Ryan was his son, it was as if God stepped into the dining room, where I sat eating breakfast, and poked me in the chest, telling me to pray for him. Right there, paper balanced in one hand and spoon in the other. I'd stared at Marcos's photo on the front of the paper as the words echoed in my mind. *Pray for this man.*

So, I had.

I'd prayed God would bless his and Rachana's new marriage as I pushed a chair beneath Alina's collapsing legs, the letter announcing Marcos's elopement fluttering to the floor beside her wedding gown. I'd prayed for strength the day Ryan was officially named heir to the throne of Hodenia and what looked like a few hundred reporters parked themselves on the palace's front lawn. I'd sat on my bed, head tucked against my knees, sobbing out barely distinguishable prayers the day the palace released the news of Rachana's terminal illness.

And in amongst those days, I'd prayed for courage for them. Strength. Hope. Love. Wisdom. Patience. I'd prayed for fun times and special memories. Most of all, I'd prayed that, even in this mess of media appearances, people's expectations, rash judgments, painful diagnoses, doctors' visits, and regrets, they'd know God and find peace. Somehow.

I hadn't known what to pray when Alina and I arrived at the palace, three days ago, to find out Rachana had died an hour earlier. I still didn't. Not really. How did one put grief into words?

Marcos took Ryan's hand as they stepped forward to lay white roses on the coffin, bowing their dark heads in a long moment of silent respect. I wanted to scream at the unfairness of it. To be brought to this. A final goodbye, after all they'd already been through. My hand went to my mouth, desperate to hold back the sob tearing its way up my throat.

Look away. Focus on something else. Their pain isn't yours. You didn't even know Rachana. You barely even know them.

But my heart listened about as well as the sob which finally made its way out of my throat, gaining a sympathetic glance from Alina beside me. I shook my head, silently refusing the tissue she offered. There would be no tears. I would hold it together. For the gathered dignitaries, because it was expected, but mostly for me. I'd already had enough sympathy to last a lifetime.

God, I know you're enough, but—

No. I wouldn't pray that. Not again. God was enough. He'd patched my broken heart back together and got me through this past year of more doubts than I could even put words to. He'd given me a second chance when no way did I deserve it. He had a plan in this too. He had to. Because if he didn't—

Don't go there.

Marcos turned then. I thought he might say something to the gathered crowd. Perhaps he meant to, only instead of words came simply a nod before he and Ryan walked to one of the waiting black cars and drove away.

By the time I made it back to the guest room the palace had allocated me, I was certain my ankles had swelled to three times their normal size and I couldn't even feel my toes, but at least I had my heart back in check. How on earth did Alina do this day after day? If torture were still an acceptable form of punishment, wearing heels for an entire day—or even a few hours—would be more than adequate. Especially if they were a size too small, as these ones I'd borrowed from Alina were. I should have asked Kenna to bring me some of my own when she came yesterday. The one-inch version. Certainly not the three-inchers Alina favored which threatened to topple me with each step. Thankfully, I'd only actually tripped twice. And only one of those had been all the way to the floor.

Needless to say, the thick carpet felt like bliss under my bare feet. Sitting down would have felt even better, but that wasn't an option. The post-funeral reception had gone for longer than I'd expected, meaning the car taking Alina and me back to Peverell was leaving in twenty minutes, rather than the two hours I'd thought I'd have, and my clothes were still somewhat strewn around the room.

Creativity was my strength. Tidiness? Not so much. Still, the maids were too busy with all the other guests to clean up after me, and I wouldn't have let them even if they had offered. I might have been the daughter of a dignitary rather than the daughter of a king, but I still had my pride. Tugging the caramel hair I'd spent half an hour this morning straightening into a much more practical ponytail, I got to work.

The room was almost back to its immaculate state eighteen minutes later when the door banged open and Alina flung herself through.

"I'm coming, I'm coming," I told her. "You said three-thirty and it's only twenty—" I checked my watch again, grimacing.

"—nine past." Was that one of my dresses on the chair in the corner? Oh, and shoes. I probably needed to put some back on before I left. Flats, of course. No way was I putting those torture devices back on. The ones I'd kicked out of sight under the bed. Although, I should probably rescue those too. Not that Alina would want them back with all the hundreds of pairs she owned. "Just a second. Almost ready…"

"Actually, I came to ask you if you'd consider staying."

The half-folded dress dangled above my suitcase as I tried to make sense of Alina's words. "Stay? Here in Hodenia? Why? Princess Rachana's dead." I cringed at the words, not realizing how blunt they'd sound until they were out of my mouth. Still, they were true. It was difficult to visit someone who was dead.

"But Ryan's not. And Mrs. Graham, the woman who was going to be Ryan's governess as of next week, just sent word that her daughter is pregnant and is so unwell that she is practically bedridden—with two kids under four already to care for. Mrs. Graham sent her profuse apologies to Queen Galielle but said that it's more important that she be there for her daughter at this time."

Which tugged at my heart, terribly, but still didn't explain why that meant I had to stay. Although, the guilty expression on Alina's face told me I wouldn't have to wait too long to find out. "And?"

"I told Queen Galielle that you'd consider being Ryan's temporary governess."

"You did what?" I dropped the dress into the suitcase before plonking myself down on the bed. Alina stayed standing, hands clutched in front of her as they'd been most of the day. "Why would you do that?"

"Because I was with her when the message came. You should have seen the look on her face. She was trying so hard to keep smiling and hold it all together, but that note was one thing too many after the past few days. The fact that she even told me what it said proves how distraught she was. Come on, Wenderley. You know you'd love it. I saw the way you were looking at Ryan at the funeral. You're in love with him already. Think of it as an all-expenses-paid holiday. At a palace. You love Hodenia. Weren't you saying last week how much you wished you could get away from Peverell for a bit?"

I huffed. "I didn't mean to a palace." Palaces came with rules, dress codes, expectations—and princes. Ryan was cute, sure. I'd love to spend time with him. But his father? *Gorgeous. Perfection. Striking. Prince.*

Yes, prince, *Wenderley. And don't you forget it. You fell for one of those once and look where that got you. A whole country looking at you in sympathy. The girl the prince rejected.*

Never again.

"It wouldn't only be Ryan. You could spend time with Lucie and Kahra too. Think how much fun you'd have with them."

Marcos's younger sisters? "But I don't even know them." No one did. Not really. The palace released an official portrait of them each year on their respective birthdays but, beyond that, the girls were kept well clear of any media.

"Since when has that stopped you? You're the nicest, kindest, warmest, most welcoming person I know. If anyone could befriend two hurting princesses, it would be you."

Queen Galielle, Ryan, Lucie, and Kahra…Alina was really throwing everything at this plea. Almost too much.

"You're not trying to set me up with Prince Marcos, are you?"

"What?" Alina looked horrified I'd even ask. "Of course not. The poor man's just buried his wife. Why on earth would you think I'd be setting you up with him? Today, of all days."

Because choosing me to be Ryan's governess seemed odd. I was too young, for one. Weren't governesses supposed to be old? Or mothers at least. Retired teachers. People who'd actually *had* experience caring for young children. And qualifications, of which I had none. I was a nineteen-year-old girl who'd spent her whole life planning to marry one man, only to watch him marry her best friend. Sure, I'd thrown myself into tutoring young children not long after, but all I did was help them with their schoolwork. I did spend quite a bit of time with my nephew, Callan, but that barely counted as experience since he was only six months old. Even the group of girls I mentored, I only saw once a week.

Although I did really enjoy that time I spent with the kids and my girls. And meeting new people. And exploring new places. And had spent enough time with royalty over the years not to be overwhelmed by them. And wouldn't mind at all having the chance to try to put a smile on little Ryan's somber face. And really did want to get away from Peverell for a while.

Perhaps it wasn't such a strange suggestion. And yet—

Alina dropped into a chair with little more care than I'd used packing my clothing. Her frown was more confusion than anger. "I thought you'd be excited. You keep saying you want to make a difference with your life. Why not here?"

I looked sideways and spotted the edge of my sketchbook, peeking out from between two blouses I'd carefully tucked it between. Why not here? Because there was more to my story than she knew. Because I was still paying for the last two times I'd let my heart overrule my mind. Because God might forgive and forget, but no one else did. Because of the mint green letters which kept showing up in my mailbox—one a month, for the past year, ever since that night I wished I could erase. Because Lord Campbell Waitrose held far more power over me than any evil man should have.

"I have commitments back home," I said instead. It was the truth, if only a small part of it. Anna, Max, and Aimee especially had tried to hide their disappointment when I'd postponed this week's catch-up to come to Hodenia, but I'd seen it. In the craziness of their young teenage lives, the constancy of our weekly meets was something they clung to. As did I. I'd promised them an ice-cream sundae party and sleepover with the rest of the girls next week to make up for it.

"I'll organize others to tutor your kids and *personally* fill in for you with the girls you mentor. I'm sure Kenna would love to help too. You know what she's like when it comes to disadvantaged kids."

"We were going to have a sleepover."

"I'll invite them to the palace instead. I'm sure we could find room for eight fourteen-year-old girls *some*where." Alina grinned, almost laughing. I couldn't quite find a smile to join her. Hang out with the princesses? Sleepover at the palace? The girls would love it, no question.

And never want me back again.

"But—"

Alina's teasing smile dropped. "Please, Wenderley? Thoraben, Kenna, and I have that breakfast tomorrow morning in Peverell we need to attend, or we'd stay longer ourselves. Queen Galielle has so much to deal with already with Rachana's death and all the visiting royals and dignitaries. And the girls and Ryan have already been through so much. Your staying could be the answer to so many problems."

So caught up in the drama of Rachana and Marcos's story, I hadn't even thought of what Lucie and Kahra would have been through. And they did seem nice. Whether of their own accord or thanks to the request of their brother or mom, they'd cared for Ryan during the reception following the graveside service, keeping him occupied in a corner of the room, as oblivious as a child could be to the sympathetic stares and wondering of too many adults with too little information. The two of them had even convinced Ryan to take his jacket off and untuck his shirt—much to my satisfaction—though his bow tie had stayed as perfectly placed as it had been that morning.

I'd have gone over and spoken with them if I hadn't, to my extreme embarrassment, forgotten which princess was Lucie and which was Kahra. It was one thing to ask the name of a stranger or someone you hadn't seen for decades, but quite another to forget the name of a royal.

"Please?"

I looked back at the suitcase on my bed, moved a hairbrush from one side of the case to the other, and back again. Mindless fiddling, something to occupy my hands while my brain went to war with my heart.

I wanted to agree. There was no point even trying to deny that. Prince Ryan's trembling. Prince Marcos's tears. Everything in me ached to make them better. To be the one who helped the two of them through this, showed them that there were still reasons to smile, that hope wasn't gone, that they could find peace even in the middle of this storm. Not only pray for them, as I'd been doing for the past year, but do something practical.

But that was exactly the reason I couldn't stay. My heart was already involved. Far too deeply. It had been ever since the day I started praying for them. I'd never be able to walk away. And God knew, I'd have to. I couldn't stay. Waitrose would make sure of that.

"I can't."

She was looking at me with those eyes again. The ones that could make me do anything. I closed mine and blocked out her pleading. And was instead accosted by the memory of Ryan's teary face.

No, just…no. Walk away now. You can't stay.

"What if I promise you won't have to wear a single ball gown?"

I ran my toes through the thick carpet, leaving behind a trail. Another sweep of my foot erased it. Alina probably thought that promise would be the thing that swayed me. If only my aversion to ballgowns was the only thing holding me back. Once—before—it might have. But now?

Decisions come with consequences. Forgiveness doesn't erase those. Someone has to pay.

"Surely, she can find someone else. It's the royal family, for goodness' sake. They must have people lining up to come work for them."

"You would have Queen Galielle go through a whole interview process again the same day she buries her daughter-in-law? Or is it Prince Marcos you plan to send out into town to find someone to care for his son?"

When she put it that way, it did sound rather selfish, but surely there was someone already known to the palace who could care for the young prince. A maid? An advisor? The mother of a guard? Marcos himself? Any of them would be better than me. At least Ryan already knew them.

"Please, Wenderley. It would be such a relief for Queen Galielle to have this sorted today, and Mrs. Graham too. She's already so worried about her daughter. I can only imagine how much letting down her queen must be adding to that stress."

Why had Alina even bothered asking me if she refused to accept my answer? Not that I was doing a good job convincing her. We both knew what I wanted to do.

"Why does this matter so much to you?" I asked instead, merely delaying the inevitable. "Prince Marcos isn't your fiancé anymore. After the way he left you at the altar last year, it's not as if you owe him anything."

"He's a friend. One who's just lost his wife. I would do anything to help him, and I felt—" She stopped. Frowned. Shook her head. Considered me as if she wasn't sure whether to finish that sentence or not. I was having none of it. If she was going to ask me to stay and take away every excuse I had for leaving, she was going to finish that sentence.

"You felt what?"

"It's probably wrong. I mean, you've been a Follower longer than me so would know better than me. It was probably nothing and—"

"Just tell me."

She wavered another few seconds before apparently realizing I wasn't letting her out of this room without an answer. "Fine. I feel like God wants you here. Now. It sounds crazy, I know, but the instant Queen Galielle finished telling me what the letter said, you came to mind, along with the words, clear as if the queen had said them herself, 'suggest Wenderley.' Now, maybe I'm wrong and it wasn't God at all, but what if it was? What if, as unqualified as you feel, you're the one God wants to do this? Help this family."

What if I was the one... *God, really? You'd pick me?*

There wasn't an instant thunderclap of answer. There wasn't even a tiny impulse pushing me one way or the other. But Alina's words tugged at the something inside me—the hope that I might be the one. That I might be enough. That God might use me, even despite the stupid choices I'd made in the past. That maybe, *maybe*, he could use me to make a difference in this world.

"Just temporarily?"

"Three weeks? Four? Maybe less. You'll be back in Peverell before you know it."

Back to being "that girl." The one Prince Thoraben hadn't chosen. I was so tired of the sympathetic looks thrown my way. And they only knew the half of it. They'd be sending far more than sympathy my way if they knew the rest. Anger, disappointment, the law itself… Maybe staying in Hodenia for a few weeks wouldn't be so bad. If nothing else, it would be a great distraction. I'd pay for it when I left but—

"I'll need a few more outfits. I mean, if Queen Galielle does want me to stay. I only packed with a short visit in mind. And I should definitely let my parents know."

Alina's smile could have lit an entire wing of the palace. "You'll do it?"

What I should have done was run in the opposite direction. Instead, I nodded. "For three weeks." Surely I could keep my heart in check for that long.

"I'll speak with your parents and send more clothing as soon as I get home. Thank you, Wenderley. Queen Galielle is going to be so pleased. This was just one more thing on top of everything else that's happened."

"So long as you know that I'm staying for Ryan, not Prince Marcos."

Alina waved a hand like the point wasn't even worth the air I'd expelled to argue it. "Of course. He's the crown prince of Hodenia, no doubt just as busy as Thoraben. With that kind of schedule, in a palace this size, you probably won't even see him."

TWO

A lina was right. I didn't see Prince Marcos. Not before I ran into him. Literally. A whole thirty seconds after I walked out of the guest room I'd been staying in for the past few nights. It was like walking into a brick wall. That caught my arms before I could fall, and smelled like sandalwood and soap and—

Wenderley! Heart in check, remember?

"Forgive me, I—"

"Sorry, Your High—"

Our rushed apologies stumbled over each other in the otherwise empty hall, bouncing off the ceiling and stuttering to a stop. I looked down at his hands, still gripping my forearms. He let go as quickly as he'd grabbed them, hands dropping to his sides, rigid as a rusted suit of armor. I took a step back, still feeling the warmth of his grip. Berating myself for wishing it could have lasted longer.

"Lady Wenderley, isn't it? Princess Alina's friend? We danced at Peverell's ball."

He remembered our dance. The thought shouldn't have thrilled me as much as it did, but I was surprised he remembered anything from that night, given how distracted he'd been. Being engaged to one woman while another very publicly claimed to be the mother of the son you never knew you'd fathered had a way of doing that to a man. And yet, he remembered me.

"Yes."

"You came for the funeral?"

19

"Actually, Alina and I came to—" I clamped my lips shut, belatedly realizing what I'd been about to say. Oh sure, tell the grieving prince that we'd come to spend time with his dead wife. Smart, Wenderley. "Yes. We did. I'm sorry for—" Again the words caught in my throat. *I'm sorry for your loss*, that was what I was supposed to say. What I should have said. Only standing in front of Marcos now, captured by the deep darkness of his eyes, still edged with red, I couldn't do it. They weren't enough. No words ever could be. "I wish it had been for another reason."

He nodded, breathed out. This close, I could see the stubble shadowing his jaw, the way he pursed his lips slightly like he was gritting his teeth, the dusky circles under his eyes. Was he sleeping at all?

"Are you okay?"

The question tumbled out of my mouth before I could think better of it, but I had no wish to take it back, despite having no right to ask. In all their condolences and bowing and simpering to the grieving prince, had anyone actually asked Marcos if he was okay? Surely someone had, but the tiniest bit of surprise on his face made me wonder. Or perhaps he was surprised it was me asking. Me, who was for all intents and purposes a complete stranger.

Those dark eyes took in my face before looking down at the hand I hadn't even realized I'd placed on his arm. Heat filled my cheeks as I took it back, folding my arms across my chest. I should have apologized when I ran into him and kept walking. This staring was a little ridiculous, even for me. But the question hung in the air, tethering me to the spot. Tethering us both, apparently, because Marcos hadn't moved either. Was he actually considering answering?

But, as quickly as the hope arose, it was dashed again. His chin went up and with it his defenses. "I'm fine," he said, like we didn't both know that was a total lie. "Excuse me."

Propriety was all that stopped me from running after him. Even if I had been a close friend—which I certainly wasn't—he was in no place to talk. But still, at least he knew I cared.

God, help him, I prayed again, wondering how many times I'd offer up the same prayer in the coming weeks. *Help me too.*

Was I really doing this? When the last thing I needed right now was to be within the temptation of a palace? It didn't matter how appealing or rugged or broken Prince Marcos was, he was still a prince. I'd learned my lesson the first time with that particular breed.

I hoped.

Grieving, remember? Just buried his wife?

"Lady Wenderley?"

And his mother was standing right behind me. "Your Majesty," I said, dipping in a slight curtsey. Queen Galielle smiled when I looked at her, something I hadn't been expecting. Not today. Although, it probably came as naturally to her these days as the grace with which she walked and the kindness in her eyes. She'd been a queen for as long as I'd been alive. "It's a pleasure to meet you."

"And you."

She looked me up and down as we stood there. I curled my bare toes into the carpet, belatedly realizing I should have put some shoes on before leaving the room. Though the thought of mashing my feet back into any kind of footwear right now made me cringe.

"Forgive me for getting right to the point, but did Princess Alina tell you about my dilemma?"

"She mentioned Ryan's governess has been detained, yes."

Queen Galielle shook her head and sighed. "It's just one thing after another this week. Not that I don't feel for the woman and her daughter, but it took months for Rachana to agree to even *consider* employing a governess to care for Ryan. She was so determined to see to all his care herself. It was only last week she finally settled on a candidate. Mrs. Graham was supposed to arrive in two days but, as you heard, won't be coming. I would never have even thought to ask you to fill her place had Alina not recommended you. It would only be temporary, of course, until we could find a replacement or Mrs. Graham's daughter is well again. Although, if there are any complications with the pregnancy—"

"I would love to stay and help care for Ryan," I assured the queen. It wasn't a lie, much as I wondered how much I'd regret it.

"Oh, you have no idea how much of a relief that is."

I hated to cause trouble, not when she was looking at me like I'd saved the entire nation, but it had to be said. "You hardly know me."

"Princesses Mackenna and Alina both speak highly of you. That's enough for me. Meet me in my office in two hours? We can discuss the logistics then, and I'll answer any further questions you might have."

She walked away then, much like her son had moments before. I stood in the hall just as stunned. *God…what just happened?* I'd prayed he would help them—both Marcos and his young son. Surely bringing me here wasn't part of that answer. Was it?

And if it was?

God, help us all.

With its spindly wooden chairs, embroidered throw cushions, and lace-covered tabletops, Queen Galielle's office seemed like a room far more suited to tea parties than business meetings. Not that I was complaining. While I preferred bold colors, and seats that didn't look so delicate they'd collapse if a butterfly landed on them, it was beautiful. Something I was starting to think I'd be describing the whole palace as.

"Lady Wenderley. Thank you for coming. Please, take a seat. Would you like some tea?"

I accepted the cup she was already handing me and sat, crossing my legs at the ankles and smoothing down my dark blue skirt. I'd spent far longer than called for trying to decide whether it would be appropriate to change out of my black dress before this meeting, but in the end, decided a slightly less formal and far less black outfit which was clean gave a much better impression than the dress I'd been itching in all morning.

Also, the heels which went with the black dress had been pushed back too far under the bed for me to reach. Thankfully, Queen Galielle had also changed.

"First, let me thank you again for agreeing to stay, especially with such short notice. The last few days have been—well, let us just say they have been trying. I don't know what I would have done had Princess Alina not suggested you when she did. Like I said, she and Princess Mackenna both speak highly of you. You grew up with them, I understand?"

"Yes. My family have been close friends with Peverell's royal family for as long as I can remember. Alina and Kenna were my two best friends until the day my family moved to Hodenia when I was twelve."

"You moved because of the religious persecution?"

I blinked, surprised by her frank words. They were true, but no one talked about it quite so bluntly in Peverell. No one talked about it at all. The uncertainty must have shown on my face for hers immediately softened.

"Forgive me, you have nothing to fear. This conversation will not go beyond the walls of this room, it is simply that Alina mentioned you were a Follower. When you said your whole family had moved, I wondered if that might have been why."

She took a sip from her teacup, smiling kindly at me over the rim. Clearly, her heart wasn't thumping as loudly as mine or she would have spilled her tea everywhere.

Alina told her I was a Follower? What else had Alina told her? And why had that come up in the first place? Sure, Alina was new to faith and wanting to share it with everyone but she, of all people, had to know how dangerous it still was to be a Follower in Peverell. Especially since she knew I was more than a Follower. If King Everson ever found out what I did, he wouldn't even need a jury to declare me guilty of the worst crime known to Peverell. Murderers were treated with more respect.

"I …we…" Was this a test? Not that it mattered, given Alina had already told her I believed, but still, this was more than just me. Not that my parents had done anything wrong, per se.

Queen Galielle waited patiently, taking quiet sips of her tea as she gave me all her attention. She didn't seem as if she was about to jump out of her seat and go running to report me to King Everson, and it wasn't as if I was telling her the full extent of my crime. Not like Waitrose would, if I dared defy him. The worst the king could do was exile me. Waitrose could destroy me.

"Yes," I finally answered. "That was why we moved. My parents wanted to raise us—my sister, two brothers, and me—to know God."

When Queen Galielle only nodded and took another sip of her tea, I continued. "We returned to Peverell a little over a year ago. The way the royal family welcomed us back, it was as if we'd never left."

"Wonderful. I love hearing other people's stories, don't you?"

That wasn't the response I'd been expecting. "Your Highness?"

"I became a Follower a few years ago now, my daughters along with me. Marcos and my husband, however..." She shook her head. "They're stubborn. They're happy enough for us to believe but refuse to listen or even consider anything beyond that. Marcos needs a good influence in his life." Her soft smile was thoughtful as she looked at me. "Maybe you're the one who'll get through to him. Although—"

She stopped, frowned slightly. I looked down at my skirt, wondering if I'd spilled tea without realizing, but no, it was clean. As was my blouse. Perhaps the weariness of the day had stolen her thought midsentence. "Although?"

"Never mind." The smile was back, as if it had never gone. "It probably won't matter anyway." She put down her teacup, picking up a stack of papers off the table instead. "Let's discuss your role."

Dinner was delivered to my room that night, something I was thankful for. Today had been so full and unexpected that I was still trying to get my head around it all. I hadn't met Ryan officially yet, the queen suggesting I wait until tomorrow morning to "begin work," such as it was. I was also moving rooms tomorrow, though I'd assured Queen Galielle that this one was more than adequate. She'd disagreed, claiming it functional but not appropriate for an extended stay. She'd been so adamant that I hadn't bothered to point out the fact that it was twice the size of my bedroom at home. If the queen decreed it then who was I to argue?

She'd also answered as many questions as I could think to ask regarding Ryan and his routine. By the time I'd left her office, I'd known his birthday, favorite toy, which rooms in the palace we were allowed to spend time in and which required permission, what time he usually woke and went to bed, that he preferred beans to peas but ultimately disliked both, had a sweet tooth, was particularly shy especially around other children, and loved his treehouse—something I couldn't wait to see given Queen Galielle's description of it. The only thing I didn't know was whether this was a terrible mistake.

Staying would help Queen Galielle, Ryan, potentially Lucie and Kahra, and maybe even Marcos, but at what cost to me? At what cost to my heart?

God, you planned this, obviously, and I hate to ask since clearly you did or I wouldn't be here now but…you have a plan in this, right? I mean, my heart's going to break, I know that, but it'll be for a reason, right? Please, tell me it's for a reason. Because otherwise, send me away now. Please. Before I even start.

I doubled over my pillow, bunching it up under my head as I rolled on my side. The questions were going to drive me to insanity if I didn't stop thinking about them. I was here. I was staying. Perhaps that was all the answer I needed for now.

One day at a time, remember, Wenderley? That's what you decided after Thoraben married. One day at a time. Don't think about tomorrow. Keep moving forward or get trampled by those who are. All will be well.

Yes, all would be well. I had to believe that. It was all the truth I had left.

THREE

Truth and belief didn't always sit well together. One terrible night's sleep later, having cleaned off the breakfast tray which had been delivered and devoured, I walked along another long palace hallway and wondered, for the umpteenth time, whether I should have dressed up a little more. Maybe invested in a pair of the nude-colored high heels Kenna wore so well. Or a pink pair even, like Alina favored. Put back on the black ones I'd suffered wearing through the funeral. Anything other than the lime green high tops I currently wore.

You're caring for a child. A boy, at that. Heels are, and always will be, completely impractical.

At least I wore my best jeans.

Although heels wouldn't have tried to trip me up like the grip of the shoes I currently wore. Or squeaked quite as much on the glistening white tiles.

Oh, forget it. The whole country is still in mourning. No one's looking at your shoes. Plus, you're here to look after a child. Not impress the prin—queen. King. I rolled my eyes at my silly musings. *Anyone.*

"If you'll follow me…"

Right. Follow the woman with the white hair and air of owning the place. Maybe she did. Being the Head of Operations Staff, Mrs. Henderson—no first name offered—probably knew more about the palace than King Dorien himself.

She'd been waiting at the door when I'd opened it with my

empty breakfast tray in hand, thinking to take it back to the kitchens myself and save some poor maid some work. She'd promptly taken it out of my hand and left it on the floor. She hadn't commented on my outfit but the cursory glance of it had left her frowning. Or perhaps it was me she didn't approve of. Did she think me too young to be caring for Prince Ryan? Not that it mattered what she thought given her queen had already hired me. For some crazy, as-yet-unknown reason. Every time I'd tried to bring up my suitability during our meeting, she'd changed the subject. Sometimes so subtly that I didn't even notice for several minutes.

I knew so much about Ryan, but as to why she'd chosen me? Nothing. Perhaps it really was simply that I was here and Alina had vouched for me.

My foot scuffed again, this time on the elegant blue runner stretching the length of the hall. I swallowed back the huff of frustration and determined to concentrate on lifting my feet. Although the grandeur of the palace was making that near impossible.

I'd spent a lot of time in Peverell's palace over the years, growing up alongside their royal family. It was grand but in an antiquated way. Stepping inside it was like stepping back in time. Four hundred years or so. This was nothing like that.

Where Peverell's palace was built of stone, its towering turrets surrounded by thick walls and an air of history, Hodenia's encapsulated both modernity and elegant style. Whitewashed walls, what felt like hundreds of large bay windows, staircases leading to covered porticos. Bright. White. Beautiful.

And just as stunning inside, if not more so.

I followed Mrs. Henderson up another flight of stairs, along a long hall and round four more corners, trying my best to remember the way. Six—seven?—doors down, she stopped and opened one.

"This will be your room for the duration of your stay."

The argument I'd been about to—again—offer regarding the ridiculous waste of energy it would take for me to move rooms when I was perfectly content in the guest one I'd been staying in died the second I stepped through the door.

The suite—since one could hardly call it a mere room—was stunning. A thousand times more beautiful than the pretty but functional room I'd been staying in. If they were offering it, I'd take it. Arguing was clearly fruitless anyway.

An oversized sitting room led to a bedroom with large skylight windows taking up much of the ceiling. The bright sunlight made it feel almost as if I'd stepped outside. But no, there was a balcony for that. Looking out over what appeared from this distance to be a series of gardens and the tops of some smaller outbuildings. I'd be going out there to take a closer look as soon as Mrs. Henderson left.

The bedroom was gorgeous. Bright to the point of almost needing sunglasses, the white walls shone, balanced out by the polished wood floor. A large mat covered half the room—deep purples swirled with blue, a perfect match to the royal blue of the cushions scattered across the window seats, couch, and bed. There were two sets of curtains at each of the windows. The first a white lacy underlay and the second deep blue again in a thick fabric. They were tied back with golden ropes which might have looked out of place had it not been for the narrow, waist-high line of gold drawn on each of the white walls and the gold rose accents intricately carved into the wooden bed frame. Simple. Elegant. Clean and white but with enough color and light to be absolutely beautiful.

And all pulled together by two paintings. A field of purple flowers and a bridge over a river. An orange bridge. Surprising. And yet, everything else in the painting was shades of blues, greens, and purples. Shocking, yet perfect. A girl could get used to this.

"I'll leave you to settle in. Your clothing arrived early this morning and has already been unpacked and put away for you. If you need anything else, please don't hesitate to let any of the staff know."

Not likely. I was staff too now, or didn't she remember that?

"When you're ready, Prince Ryan is in his room. It's at the opposite end of this hall, second door from the right. One of the maids is with him at the moment. Lunch will be served at half past twelve. Please don't be late."

Message and temporary governess delivered, Mrs. Henderson turned and left. Amused, I followed her to the door, closing it behind her. Half past twelve. It was only just past nine now. Plenty of time to look around.

True to her word, Alina had sent clothing—apparently almost everything I owned. It was all hanging, pressed and ready to wear, in the giant walk-in closet. How long exactly had she thought I was staying? Of course, this was Alina, who frequently went through five or six outfits in a single day, so perhaps this didn't seem like much to her. I grinned when I saw the four formal gowns carefully wrapped at the back of the closet. So much for her claiming I wouldn't have to wear a single gown. Clearly, she didn't believe it herself if she'd purposely packed some. Although, again, maybe she was simply ensuring I'd have one, or four, should the need arise.

I really hoped the need wouldn't arise.

To my delight, she'd also sent a sketch pad and pencils, the books which had been sitting on my nightstand, and all of my shoes. The note that went with them, bemoaning my lack of heels, made me laugh. Apparently three pairs of heels—black, silver, and bright green—didn't qualify as a proper collection. I rarely wore them anyway, much preferring the eighteen pairs of high tops I had for everyday wear and fourteen different colors and patterns of ballet style flats for when I had to dress up. Heels were overrated. *Sorry, Alina,* I thought with a grin.

Her note included a message from my parents, both of them agreeing that this was a great opportunity for me. I could almost hear their relief through the paper. They loved me, I had no doubt about that, but I hadn't been the easiest person to live with the past eighteen months.

But that was going to change. Alina was right, this was my chance to get away from all that. New people, new place, new job. While I was here, I could be whoever I wanted. Leave all that mess behind. Even if it was only temporary, I'd be a fool not to take the chance.

Starting right now.

"He's in here. At least, he was. Ryan? Ryan? Where is he? He has to be in here. I know he didn't come out."

I stilled the maid's frantic search with a hand to her arm and pointed to the child-sized bare feet sticking out the bottom of the bed's quilt, so easy to miss in a room of this size. Was he hiding? Sleeping? "Thanks for your help," I told the woman. "I'll go introduce myself, shall I?"

"You don't want me to stay?"

"I'm sure you have other things you want to be doing. We'll be fine."

With a final glance in Ryan's direction and an encouraging smile, she thanked me and walked away. I stepped into the room, leaving the door wide open behind me. Partly because I wasn't sure what the protocol was for me being alone with the young prince but mostly because I didn't want him to feel threatened. There was something about an open door which gave the illusion of freedom, even if that wasn't always the case.

"Ryan?" His feet didn't so much as twitch. I wished I knew what it was which had him hiding. A game of Hide and Seek? Possible. Sleep time? Also possible, although this early in the morning it was unlikely, and the maid would likely have mentioned that if it was the case. I hoped it wasn't that he'd heard I was coming and hid out of fear. "Ryan?"

I pulled the quilt back, just enough to see his face, mashed into the soft sheets. "Ryan?"

If I'd looked away, even for an instant, I would have missed the moment he turned his face toward me. As it was, I blinked and he'd hidden it again. But that moment was enough. He wasn't playing a game or hiding in fear. He was crying.

"Ryan? What's wrong?"

"Go away."

The words were muffled by the sheets but not enough that I didn't understand, or hear the heartbreak behind them. No way was I leaving him like this. "I could, or I could stay. No one should have to cry alone."

"I'm not crying. I don't want you to stay. I don't want another mom."

"Oh, honey." That was what he thought? That I was here to replace his mom? No one could do that, least of all me. Especially since that would mean marrying Prince Marcos. If trying to make Thoraben love me had taught me anything, it was that I'd make a terrible queen. Much as I'd spent my life till last year trying to be the perfect one. I'd never been happy. I'd grieved it for so long, overwhelmed with jealousy and bitterness toward Kenna who'd "taken my place," but watching her now? The schedule she lived, event after event, always having to look the part—something Kenna did effortlessly but I had always struggled with. That wasn't the life I wanted.

"I'm not here to be your mom."

The head lifted slightly, one brown eye peeking out at me through a mess of dark hair. "You're not?"

"No, sweetie."

"But Grandmama said you're here to look after me and make sure I'm okay and give me a bath and tuck me in if Papa's not home in time. That's what a mom does."

"It is, isn't it."

He nodded, a tear dripping off his nose and leaving a wet dot on his sheets. It was all I could do not to drag him into my arms and hold him till the fear was squashed away by love. But I couldn't do that. Not yet. Maybe one day, soon, when he trusted me.

"I'll tell you a secret. It's also what friends do. Do you think maybe we could be friends?"

He considered that for a moment, his forehead crinkling in consternation exactly like I'd seen his father's face do. "I guess that would be okay."

"I'm Wenderley. Do you think you can say that? I know, it's a tough name to say."

"Wenderley."

"Oh, you said it perfectly! Most people get it wrong the first time. And often the second too. Now I *know* we're going to be friends."

He almost smiled. I took that as a definite win.

"You know what else friends do?"

"What?"

"Make cookies."

He sat up, scrubbing the last of the tears aside with his sleeve. "Cookies?"

"Sure. Have you ever made cookies before?"

"Once. But I wasn't very good at it."

"Want to know another secret?"

He lifted his whole face, staring up at mine as if I held the secrets of the universe rather than one silly anecdote my mum had once told me. Bless his adorable little heart.

"I happen to know that cookies are the best thing to make for people who aren't very good at them because you can make them any shape or size you like."

"Really?"

"Sure. I was thinking of making chocolate chip ones. Would that be okay?"

"I like chocolate chip."

"Perfect! What do you think—little cookies or big ones?" I widened my eyes as big as I could. "Or *giant* ones?"

"Like, the size of my hand?" He held up his hand, stretching out all his fingers as far as they could go. "Do you think we could make them that big?"

I grinned. "Bigger. Let's make them twice that size. Maybe we could even put your handprint in them? You've heard of thumbprint cookies, right?" He shook his head. "Oh, well, they're round cookies which you stick your thumb into to make a dent on top which you fill with jelly. I think we should make *handprint* cookies. Your hand would be just the right size."

"Really? We could do that?"

"Sure, sweetie."

"But…can we still make chocolate chip ones?"

"Of course. Giant chocolate chip handprint cookies. We could even fill the handprint with chocolate."

If Ryan's eyes got any bigger, his eyeballs would fall out. The poor kid had clearly never made cookies with someone who didn't follow the recipe before. Good. Part one of his introduction to childhood was about to begin. Even royalty needed to know how to let loose. Especially when they were six years old. If he survived the giant chocolate chip experiment without the world exploding, maybe next time we'd add food coloring and make them green. Or blue. Or even rainbow.

"So, you're coming?"

He jumped out of the bed in lieu of an answer, putting his hand in mine. I thought about cheering but decided that would likely scare him back under his sheets so grinned instead and tugged him out the door.

FOUR

Seven minutes and four wrong turns later, we found the kitchens. If it weren't for Tari, Kate, Wilson, and Walter—indoor staff and my newest friends—we probably still would have been searching. Directions have never been a strong point of mine, and this palace was an absolute maze of hallways and doors. Thankfully, the staff so far had all been as kind and helpful as Mrs. Henderson had intimated, even if every single one of them had gawked at my green shoes. Maybe tomorrow, I'd wear my canary-yellow ones. That would give them something to talk about.

"Alrighty then, butter first. Can you put those two sticks in?"

I watched, my heart melting as quickly as the butter in his hands as Ryan painstakingly pulled off the paper without ripping even a single bit and placed both sticks in the bowl, side by side. He was so adorable.

"Right, now we cream them. Hold the mixer up straight now. That's right. We don't want butter all over the walls. That's it. Good, good. You're doing great."

I measured out two cups of sugar, taking the mixer so he could pour them into the bowl, again, even despite the mixer running, not getting a single bit out of place.

"It's so smooth!" he said after a minute. I looked down into the bowl, having been so distracted by the way the tip of his tongue stuck out the side of his mouth while he concentrated that I'd forgotten to pay attention to the mixture.

Focus, Wenderley. You gave your word to Chef Meyer that you wouldn't destroy the kitchen. And your word to Queen Galielle that you'd care for her grandson. Care, *not get his fingers caught in the mixer on Day One.*

"Perfect. That's how it's supposed to look. Do you want to do the eggs?"

"Um…" He eyed the two eggs as if they might suddenly jump out of my hand and attack him. Had he cracked an egg before and it had gone badly? Was that what was worrying him?

"It's okay if you get some shells in there," I said, taking a guess. "We can always fish them out."

"Maybe I could do one and you could do the other?"

"Sounds like a plan." I handed him one of the eggs. "Ready? Set? Crack."

Both of the eggs exploded. Onto me. Well, mostly on me. There were also a few pieces of eggshell in the bowl and a nice spray of yolk across the counter. I'm not entirely sure how it got there. Or how Ryan managed to miss it all. My younger brothers always ended up covered in flour, butter, and mess by the time they were finished baking, and Ryan had yet to even get a speck on his oversized black apron. I'd definitely have to see about getting him one in his own size. Not that he needed it, meticulous as he seemed, but little aprons on kids were so cute.

Ryan's lip trembled. "Oh no…"

I grabbed a towel, swiping egg off the counter before any more could drip onto the floor, sending him a grin as I did it. "Hey, no worries. That's what aprons are for." We'd come so far already. I couldn't have him giving up now because of a bit of egg. "And baths."

He didn't smile but he didn't look like he was going to burst into tears or run away anymore either. Good. Onward, then. It didn't take long to rescue the eggshells from the mixture, crack in two more eggs, and be back to beating in the remaining ingredients. I couldn't help but dot a fingerprint of flour on Ryan's nose, giggling as he went cross-eyed trying to see it.

"Do I look like you now?"

I was wondering what he meant when he reached up a finger

to gently touch my cheek. I brushed at the spot, surprised when my hand came away white.

"You've got some in your hair too."

I almost dropped the mixer at the sound of Marcos's voice, so deep and full compared to Ryan's childish one. What was he doing here? I'd thought I'd be safe for sure from him in the kitchen. My mind was such a muddle with trying to figure it out that it took a moment for his words to register.

Flour. In my hair. *And* on my face. And I hadn't done anything about the egg sprayed across the front of me yet either. Not exactly a vision of competency.

Before I could think better of it, I swiped a floury finger across Marcos's cheek. There, now he was as messy as me. It took a whole two heartbeats for my sense to catch up with me and wipe the grin from my face. Two heartbeats too late. He stared at me, shock written across his now floury face. What was I doing? *This isn't one of your brothers, Wenderley Davis. He'll think you're flirting. Wait, are you flirting? Wenderley!*

"Prince Marcos, I'm so sorry! I …uh…" I, what? I thought it would be funny? I forgot you're a prince? I'm a complete idiot? Yep, that last one pretty much covered it. "I'm sorry. I shouldn't have done that."

Shock morphed into confusion as he stared at me. "What are you doing here?"

"I'm…uh…" Oh no. His mother hadn't told him. When she'd been the one to interview me—such as it was—and ask me to stay, I'd assumed Marcos was too busy or distracted with grief to want anything to do with the practicalities of finding someone to care for his son. It was understandable. He'd been under a lot of pressure and the hiring of household staff wasn't exactly what I'd expect to be part of a prince's responsibility. Although, this was his son.

"We're making cookies," Ryan told Marcos, dragging his father's stare away from me and saving me from having to answer. I think I was thankful for the fact. Though there was a part of me that wished I could have stared into his dark brown eyes for a few more minutes. Hours. Days. So dark they were almost black, it was like looking into a well I couldn't see the bottom of. Deep, like the man himself. "Chocolate chip handprint cookies. Do you want to help?"

It was a good thing the mixture was done already because I'd suddenly forgotten the recipe entirely. Among other things. Like breathing. *He's a prince. Remember? You don't fall for princes. Their wives become queens.* Not that I was thinking marriage, of course. *Also, his wife just died.* I groaned.

"Wenderley?"

What was he still doing here? And why hadn't he wiped the flour off his face yet? "Sorry. Forgot the, uh—" I gazed frantically around our little corner of the vast kitchens, desperate for inspiration. "Trays. We need baking trays for the cookies, don't we, Ryan? I'll go get them." And hopefully a big dose of reality while I was gone. *Grieving, Wenderley. His wife hasn't even been dead a week. Give the guy a break.*

Marcos was still standing there when I came back. Still staring at me like I was short a few important brain cells. I probably was. "Prince Marcos?"

"Come to my office when you finish here," he said in a tone that brooked no questions. "There are things we need to discuss." With a nod to his son, he spun and left the kitchen. I put the trays on the counter beside the bowl of mixture and watched the door swing shut behind him.

Aye, aye, captain.

FIVE

I never did get to Prince Marcos's office. By the time we'd flattened the cookies, pressed them with handprints, filled the handprints with chocolate and baked them—cleaning up while they baked because even young princes should know how to clean up, and because we didn't want to leave the cookies alone in case someone else ate them before we could—waited for them to cool, proudly showed them around to every appreciative staff member in the kitchen, and eaten one, it was time for lunch.

And by the time we'd finished lunch, I'd forgotten about Marcos's request. Caught up with trying to keep Ryan occupied and finding my way around the palace, it wasn't until almost dinnertime that I remembered, and by then I was seeing to Ryan's bath and trying to keep him from falling asleep in the suds. If Marcos was at dinner, I'd apologize then but surely he had to realize that caring for his son came first. Unless that was what he wanted to speak to me about. Which—I cringed—it probably was.

"Time to get out, handsome."

I grabbed a thick blue towel from a nearby chair and wrapped it around Ryan with one hand while pulling the plug with the other. Thankfully, he was old enough to dry himself since I had to rescue first a rubber ducky, then a plastic boat and finally a rubbery frog from the plughole before the water finally disappeared. Next time, I'd have to remember to empty the bath of its toys before I let out the water. If there was a next time. After all, I had all but snubbed Hodenia's crown prince. After putting flour on his face. Something I still couldn't believe I'd done.

"You brought my pajamas in."

"I know. They're cute."

"We haven't had dinner yet."

"We'll go right there as soon as you get dressed."

"In my pajamas?"

"Were you planning on wearing something else?"

"Usually I wear proper clothes to dinner."

He did? What, did they dress up for dinner around here? Surely not. Not a child, anyway. What was the point in dressing him in new clothes now only to change him again in an hour? It made no sense.

"Well, you can wear pajamas tonight."

The uncertainty I felt was stripped bare by the excited smile he gave me as he pulled on his flannelette dinosaur-print pajamas. I mentally dared anyone to tell me he wasn't utterly adorable, if not the cutest kid ever, wearing them. And also begged the people I was already defending myself against in my head to not send me home my first day. Namely Prince Marcos.

"Ready?"

"Are you sure Papa won't mind if I don't wear proper clothes to dinner?"

Was "Papa" his father or grandfather? I'd have to find that out. Also a few more rules if I was ever going to look after Ryan again, like what was appropriate to wear for dinner. Today, I'd claim ignorance, and send enough glares in all the adults' directions to keep them silent one way or another until I could find out. Either way, I'd make sure none of them said anything to Ryan. "Not at all."

He finished the last of his buttons and looked up at me. "I could show you the way to the dining room, if you want."

Not for the life of me would I tell him that was the one room I actually remembered directions to. "You could? That would be wonderful. You'd better take my hand so I don't get lost on the way."

I couldn't help the smile that spread across my face at the feel of his little hand in mine. There was something so precious about a child's trust, and it had been hard won this afternoon. It still felt precarious, but only time would help with that. If I stayed.

He led me out of his room, along a series of halls, through the portrait gallery—where we stopped to look at the portrait of his mother, father, and him for so long that I thought we might miss dinner altogether—and finally down two flights of stairs to the dining room.

It took only one glance to have my suspicions confirmed. We were late. The entire royal family, minus one six-year-old boy, were seated, roast meat and vegetables already served onto their plates. I hoped it was at least still hot.

"Lady Wenderley, I presume," King Dorien said from his place at the head of the table. He wasn't frowning, though he certainly didn't look pleased.

"Yes, Your Majesty. Forgive our tardiness. I hope you weren't waiting long."

I walked Ryan quickly around the table, hoping I was correct in assuming the seat beside Marcos would be his.

"Did Ryan want to look at the portraits again?" Queen Galielle asked. If she'd picked up her dinner plate and thrown it at me, I doubt I would have been more surprised. She laughed at my shock. "He asks every night. I should have warned you to leave earlier. No matter. You're here now. Marcos, be a gentleman and pull out her chair."

I blinked from the queen to the prince, rising from his chair to stand behind an empty place setting on the other side of Ryan's.

Dinner? Me?

I wasn't dressed for dinner. Something that, looking around the table at the men in their buttoned shirts and women in their dresses, I definitely should have taken Ryan's word on. My jeans and t-shirt stood out like a stroke of red paint on a charcoal portrait. I pressed a hand against the palm-sized water mark near the hem of my shirt, a darkly obvious splotch against the rest of the lighter green. It wasn't as bad as the egg had been, but it wasn't a whole lot better either.

"My lady?"

Marcos was still holding the chair, waiting for me to sit. "Are you sure?" I couldn't help the whispered question that came out of my mouth. Nor the way my stomach rolled over like a happy puppy when Marcos shrugged.

"Mom decreed it. Let it be done."

I looked across the table at the queen again, hands clasped beneath her chin, gentle smile on her face as she watched me. It was the food in front of her that made me sit. They'd been waiting too long already due to Ryan's detour, it would be cruel of me to make them wait any longer, something which would definitely happen if I chose to argue this.

"Thank you," I told him quietly as I sat. There'd be time to sort out proper place settings later. When there wasn't a plate of roast beef and vegetables drizzled with some kind of burgundy liquid in front of me sending up an aroma that made me want to moan with joy. Every year, I chose a roast for my birthday dinner. Never once in my nineteen birthdays had it smelled this good.

As soon as I sat down, they all began eating. I pulled Ryan's plate toward me, helping him to cut his meat in an effort to make myself believe I had a place at this table.

The princesses sat directly across from me. Thanks to our extended walk through the portrait gallery, I now knew which was which. At fourteen, Kahra was the older of the two and, like her brother and young nephew, closely resembled the king in appearance. Strong, striking features, neat dark hair, dark eyes.

Princess Lucie, in almost direct contrast, took after her mother with green eyes, generous curves, and lighter hair, currently bordering in that awkward place between waves and frizz. Not that either she or the queen were overweight, even slightly so, but their body types looked softer next to the rest of their family. Perhaps that went with their personalities. The two of them seemed far more approachable too. Likely because they weren't quite so perfect.

"What do you think of the palace, Lady Wenderley?" Lucie asked, timing her question perfectly to the second I put a large piece of meat in my mouth. Thankfully, it all but melted as I quickly chewed it. Had it been any poorer quality of meat, it would have been almost dessert before I managed to answer her. *Note to self, take tiny bites, in case someone asks you a question.*

"It's lovely," I forced out. "All of it."

"The Lake Garden is my favorite," Lucie continued. "It's always so peaceful there beside the lake. There are all these pretty lilies on the water and on a clear day, the water is so still, it's like a mirror. Two worlds in one. Although Mom refuses to let any of us go there by ourselves."

"With good reason," Queen Galielle said, defending herself. "I almost had a heart attack that day you fell in."

"I was six! I can swim now, as can every other person in this family."

"Yes, well. You never know what might happen around water. I stand by my decision. You take a friend or you go somewhere else."

Lucie grinned. "Yes, Mother."

"Not that either of you are going anywhere without your security team anyway. Lucie, you really have to stop trying to lose yours."

Kahra and Lucie started squabbling about something to do with their security teams then, although with another conversation going on between Marcos and his father and the queen stopping a passing server to ask something, I didn't catch what it was. Why had I imagined dinner with a royal family being a quiet affair? This was almost louder than dinnertimes at my house growing up, which said a lot given my brothers liked the whole of Peverell to know their opinion on everything from how creamy the mashed potatoes were to who was the taller of the two of them. Emmett, still, although Eder would probably catch up one day soon given the growth spurt he'd just begun.

I put another piece of meat in my mouth, content to sit and let it all swirl around me, still trying to convince myself I was even here. Mom and Dad hadn't even asked for time to discuss it when I'd mentioned Alina's invitation to accompany her here to meet Rachana last week. "Yes, go. What an honor," Mom had said, Dad nodding his agreement. Had I been any less excited about the chance to come, I might have been offended at how easily they agreed.

Only I had been that bad. They didn't have to pack my suitcase for me to know that. I really had been. Moping around. Starting projects in a rush of manic energy only to walk away without finishing them. Spending hours wandering the Queen's Garden only to come home and sit in my room, filling sketchbook after sketchbook with my frustrated emotions. Getting angry over silly things which didn't warrant anywhere near as dramatic a response. Much to the annoyance of everyone in the family. Myself included. *I* would have sent myself away, if I could have.

Ryan chose that moment to knock over his glass of water, right into his plate, which gave him such a fright that he knocked the edge of said plate right into his lap. Gravy, potatoes, and what seemed like far more meat than he'd had to start with dripped down his shirt, puddling on the napkin placed across his lap. Water dripped off the edge of the table. The poor boy who'd been happy a few minutes ago now looked ready to burst into tears.

To my annoyance, but not surprise, the table went silent. I wanted to glare at each of them in turn and remind them that he was a kid, accidents happened, and it was just as easy to clean up as it was to make, only now wasn't the time. Right now, it was far more important that I get the poor boy out of here before the angry fireworks exploded. I stood as calmly as I could and nodded toward the king and queen, purposely ignoring the other royals.

"Excuse us, Your Majesties. I'll take Ryan to clean him up."

"Oh, nonsense," the queen said, rising from her chair. "I'm finished and you're still eating. I'll take him."

The queen? Herself? "Oh, but—"

"Here, sweetie."

They were gone before I could protest again, Ryan's hand tucked securely in his grandmother's, her head ducked down toward his, talking, as they walked out of the room together. I sat back down, feeling oddly guilty. Like I'd failed him, somehow. Even the mess had already been cleaned by an overzealous maid, nothing but a small wet patch on the white tablecloth proving it had even happened.

"You missed our appointment," Marcos said, as soon as Ryan was out of the room. "Cookies don't take six hours to make." Though his words were quiet, meant only for me, his voice held enough authority to raise those defenses of mine straight up again.

I frowned at my plate, thinking it a better option than turning said frown on the man beside me, though it was awfully tempting. He was seriously going to start this now? At the dinner table? The one I was quickly wishing I hadn't agreed to sit down at? A nice supper in the kitchens. That's what I should have done. Chef Meyer would have let me. She'd been all too welcoming this morning when I'd arrived with the young prince in tow and asked if we could make cookies. Tomorrow, I'd definitely be eating there, or wherever the rest of the staff ate. Tonight, there was a prince none too patiently waiting for my answer.

I pasted on what I hoped seemed like an apologetic-enough smile to hide my true feelings and faced him. "Actually, they did take a while, and then we had to clean up and eat and—" He didn't need to know the details, not judging by the glare he was sending my way. Right. Not interested. "I'm sorry. I should have come." Or, at least, sent word that I wasn't coming.

"Next time, see that you do."

I stuffed a large piece of meat in my mouth before what I really wanted to say to that came out. Somehow, I doubted even the queen could save me if I publicly accused her son of being highhanded, arrogant, and far more caring of his schedule than the needs of his son.

So I spent time with his son rather than him. That was my job. Exactly what I was here to do. It might have seemed like Ryan and I were only baking cookies to Marcos, but it was far, far more than that. First impressions went a long way to building trust with a child so young, which was exactly what the whole cookie idea had been about. Did I need to make cookies today? No. Should I have cut our time short in order to meet with Marcos? Maybe.

Okay, probably.

But, then again, maybe not. I'd chosen to stay with Ryan all afternoon rather than dropping him off with another maid. I wanted him to know I was here for him today. *Only* him. That, in the midst of his mother's death and his father's crazily busy life, he hadn't been overlooked. He was, and always would be, a valued, vital, cherished part of this family.

"And the pajamas?"

My fork stabbed at the meat on my plate a little harder than it needed to, my defenses already on high alert before Marcos's derisive comment. Yes, the pajamas were a definite mistake but there was no way I was admitting it with him glowering at me like that.

"What about them?"

"They're not suitable for dinner."

"I think they're cute."

"Whether they're *cute* or not is beside the point. They are inappropriate."

"No one else seems to have a problem with them." Why was I fighting him in this? It wasn't like I was ever going to do it again. No pajamas at dinner. Right. Got it. The way Marcos was reacting, anyone would think I'd dressed him in scuba gear or let him come naked. They were just pajamas.

"Do not dress him in them for dinner again. Do I make myself clear?"

As crystal. The kind I'd really like to throw at a wall right now. Just to have the satisfaction of seeing it shatter. What would the very proper Prince Marcos do then?

"Yes, sir," I all but saluted.

His eyes narrowed. Any more and he wouldn't be able to see. He waited. I dipped a chunk of potato in my gravy, swirling it around, put it in my mouth, chewed, swallowed. Still waiting. Oh, fine. "Yes, *Your Highness.*"

He didn't smile. Just went back to his dinner as if he hadn't stared me into respect. An outward respect anyway. Ryan came back, clean again, and sat between us, completely unaware of his role as buffer. I snuck a look sideways, grinning at the adorable little dinosaurs still tumbling across his legs, swinging under the table. Queen Galielle had changed his shirt but left his pajama bottoms. I no longer regretted putting them on him. Nope. Not one bit.

Not until two hours later.

SIX

If there was one thing I'd learned over the past eighteen months, it was that regret and retrospect were the closest of friends, and I hated going to their parties. Unfortunately, their parties didn't come with the option of declining. So, here I lay on a bed, yet again, staring up at the ceiling, wishing uselessly that I could turn back time. Not even the beauty of the stars visible through the sky lights above me could distract me from my self-directed fury. How could I have been so rude, fighting Marcos like that? Not only was he Hodenia's future king—something demanding of respect in itself—but he was grieving. Something I'd forgotten in my need to be right.

If I'd known where Marcos's room was, I would have walked right up to his door, knocked on it, and pulled out every apology I could think of. After banging my head on the door first. For a few minutes. As if that might take away my guilt.

Oh, for goodness' sake, Wenderley. The guy just buried his wife! Even if he was wrong, which he wasn't, give the guy some grace! People tiptoed around you for months after Thoraben's wedding and he wasn't even dead. It's only been a few days.

It was a good thing I didn't know where his room was. I don't know what would be less appropriate—me going to his room or me falling to the floor in front of him and groveling until the guilt was gone. Which might have taken a few hours, if not weeks. The poor man. It wasn't as if I hadn't seen him at Rachana's funeral, tears dripping down his face as his heart lay in the casket in front of him.

Still, it would have been nice to apologize.

It had been Ryan who reminded me. He'd started crying when I chose a book off his little shelf to read him. "That was Mama's favorite," he'd said, his trembling smile hitting me like a brick. In my eagerness to win over Ryan and defend my misplaced pride, I'd completely forgotten there had been someone else in this family last week. Even if she was dying, Rachana had been here. Since the day, just over a year ago, when Marcos married her. For Ryan, every day of his life so far.

To my best understanding, which came entirely from gossip rags rather than any reputable source, Rachana was the only family Ryan had had up until the day she married Marcos. Imagine, being introduced to a complete stranger and told he's your father. Moving to a palace, of all places. Watching your mother get sicker and sicker. Most kids got a doll or train for their fifth birthday. Ryan got an entire kingdom, and all the responsibility that came with knowing he would one day rule it.

"We can read something else," I'd offered, going to put the book back. Ryan had instantly shaken his head, jumping out of bed to take the book from me.

"You can read it," he'd said. So, I had. The story of a little penguin who was scared of the water and his mother whose belief in him gave him the strength to take a leap of faith and dive in. I'd read it to him, feeling like not one of the papers or gossip columns had come even close to capturing the essence of Rachana's heart as that children's book did.

As soon as the book finished, I'd tucked the covers around Ryan, said goodnight, and come back to my room, where, for the past two hours, I'd been lying on my bed, staring up at the glass ceiling, seeing nothing but my own foolishness.

I had to apologize. There was no way I'd sleep until I did.

Pulling myself off the bed, I tucked my feet back into my shoes, ran a hand through my hair and walked out the door, wondering where he might be. There was the obvious, of course, his room, but I very much hoped he wasn't there. What did royalty do after dinner? It was possible he'd gone out to an event or something but, so soon after Rachana's death, I doubted it. Anything except the most pressing engagements would have been canceled, at least for the next month or so. More likely he was in his office or…or… Well, I didn't have another option yet, but I'd find one. For now, I'd check his office.

As soon as I found where it was.

Unlike earlier, when there had been staff at every turn, the halls were empty. Not surprising, given the late hour, but not particularly helpful either. I took my time, wandering the passageways, hoping to come across a late worker, working out in my head what I was going to say. *Forgive me for my insolence* sounded like I was trying to be humble and coming across as arrogant, but *I'm sorry I forgot you were grieving* wasn't much better. Like I was a complete imbecile or something. Everyone in the entire kingdom and abroad knew Prince Marcos was grieving. *Forgive me?* Short. Simple. Covered all bases. *Yeah, and none at all.*

"Lady Wenderley?"

"Princess Kahra." I smiled at the girl walking toward me, wondering at the fact that I felt so much older than her when, in reality, there were only five or six years separating us. Funny how much a few years' life experience could change a person. Being dumped so publicly had a lot to do with that, although growing up outside the shelter of a palace did too. "I'm so glad I found you. Could you please tell me where your brother's office is?"

"Sure. Take those stairs down one flight," she said, pointing a little further down the hall, "and then it's the second door on your left heading in—" She thought for a moment before pointing again, "that direction. Look for the suit of armor. It's right outside his door. He thinks it's cool. I think it's creepy, but hey, I'm just a girl, right? What would I know?"

Her smile was infectious, as was the fact that she could laugh at herself. I appreciated her directions. If she'd told me to head east, I would have been totally lost. But a suit of armor? That I could relate to.

"Thanks."

"You're welcome."

She continued on her way, heels tapping out a muffled beat over the thin rug stretching the length of the hall. I was glad she hadn't asked me why I wanted to know where the office was. I don't think I would have been able to explain without guilt painting me red and needing far more explanation than I was comfortable giving.

One flight of stairs and two doors down, I spotted the tall suit of armor. I was with Kahra on this one. It was creepy how real it looked. Like there really was a knight standing guard at Marcos's office door. One who, with armor like that, would have been far more comfortable in a dank, brick dungeon hiding among the rats and spiders than here in this clean palace with its modern lines and white, art-covered walls.

At least it made the office easy to find. I wouldn't have to ask for directions here again. Even if I did forget which floor and hall it was in, I'd just search up and down till I found this fellow.

Sir Silver, I'll call you. No, Sir Brass. No, I know. Sir Merrett Tanner Coulson the Slightly Rusty. Perfect. Rusty, for short. Hello, Sir Rusty.

Oh boy. I needed to apologize to Marcos and get out of here before I totally lost what was left of my mind. Talking to statues when kids were around? Perfectly acceptable. But alone? Not so much.

I knocked on the door before my mind could lavish on the poor, creepy fellow a full backstory of all the family he'd left behind when he became a knight and the beautiful but slightly flawed woman he'd been fighting for in the battle which dented his breastplate. My mind did things like that. It wasn't always helpful.

"Come in."

Marcos was sitting at his desk, which was a relief. Until I saw, too late, that he wasn't alone.

"Lady Wenderley? What's the matter? Are you lost?"

What? No. Why would he think—Oh. He was wondering why I was here. Right at this moment, so was I.

"Good evening, Your Majesty," I said, curtseying toward King Dorien before turning back to Prince Marcos, "Your Highness."

What was I supposed to do now? I didn't want to apologize in front of the king, especially given I'd then have to admit how I'd disrespected his son. But then, what excuse could I make up for having come? Fictional stories about suits of armor were one thing but lying was quite another.

"There was something I wanted to speak to you about, Prince Marcos, but I can see you're already occupied. It doesn't matter." Except it did. "Forgive me for intruding."

It was warm in Marcos's office. Not only the temperature, though the fireplace saw to that, but the colors. The decor. Dark brown wood, deep green carpet, big windows, huge desk. Solid and severe, like the man himself but, also like the man, revealing hints of something else. A softness. The framed picture of him and Ryan, taking pride of place on the corner of his desk. Even though neither of them were smiling, they were holding hands. Ryan's tiny one overwhelmed by his father's much larger one. Safe. Secure.

Then there was the stained-glass window made up of golds, reds, and oranges depicting the Hodenian shield, but with blocks of color taking the place of details. The shelves full of books. The well-worn leather wingback in the corner by the fire. Was that where he sat to read?

"You can speak."

"Oh, I—" Distracted by Marcos's office, I'd forgotten to leave. My glance at the king must have given away my uncertainty. Marcos's face immediately hardened.

"Whatever you have to say, I'm certain it's nothing my father can't hear."

Apologize in front of both of the monarchs? Admit I'd been wrong not only to Marcos but to his father? The man who'd raised him? It would be…would be…humiliating. That's what it would be. Humiliating. Degrading. Mortifying.

And nothing more than what I deserved. *Wenderley, you were wrong. Just admit it.*

"I came to apologize." There. I'd said it. It was out. "I shouldn't have disrespected you like I did at dinner earlier. It was wrong of me. You're Ryan's father and your decisions regarding him, including his clothing, stand. I'm sorry."

The stunned expressions on both men's faces should have heartened me, but I was too wrung out suddenly to appreciate them. I'd done what I came to do. Now it was definitely time to leave.

I got a whole two steps out of the office before I heard my name.

"Lady Wenderley?"

Marcos walked out into the hall, closing the door softly behind him. The stunned expression was gone from his face, replaced with something bordering on confusion. Or wonder, perhaps. Or...actually, I had no idea what it was. The longer the silence stretched between us, the harder he was to read. The harder he was to read, the more I wanted to.

What was he thinking, his head slightly tilted like that as he stared at me? Was he wishing his mother hadn't invited me to stay? Wondering whether I was going to cause this much trouble the entire time I was here? *Probably.* Wondering if getting a second suit of armor would be a better deterrent to keep the riffraff like me out of his office since clearly one hadn't worked? *Wow, Wenderley, you really need to get out of here...*

"Was there something else?" I finally asked.

"Forgive me. I, that is, no one has ever apologized to me like that."

"Never?"

"Not without their life on the line."

Was that a joke? Did Prince Marcos joke? Probably not. He probably meant that literally. Thoraben often presided over judicial matters alongside his father in Peverell. Prince Marcos likely did the same.

"I meant it. I'm sorry. It was rude of me."

"Thank you for your apology. I hope you'll forgive me my words, also. This was your first dinner here. You didn't know."

Prince Marcos was apologizing to me? It took a man of real character to do that. And strength. My gaze went to his shoulders, admiring, picturing my arms around them, before I realized what I was doing and snapped my gaze guiltily back up. *Focus, Wenderley.* What were we talking about again? Oh, dinner. Clothes. *Ryan.*

"For future reference, what is appropriate for dinner wear?"

"Anything but pajamas."

Obviously. "So, scuba gear? A tuxedo?" I was giddy. Crazy with relief at having that apology over. Nervous being alone with Prince Marcos like this, even knowing his father was right behind that door. Likely overtired too, given the strain of trying to impress Ryan all day. "Fancy dress?"

Was that a smile? It was difficult to tell. His expression changed so slightly but I was certain I saw a softening to his eyes. *Oh, those eyes…* "Perhaps not the latter."

Latter… latter… look away from those eyes… latter… that was…

I blinked. Grinned to cover my distraction.

"Right. Scuba gear it is."

"Wenderley…"

I doubted the expression on my face was anything close to innocence, but I tried it all the same. "Yes, Your Highness?"

He shook his head before reaching back to grasp the handle of his door, though he didn't open it yet, instead staring at me again, that odd expression back on his face. *Was* it confusion? Intrigue? Or perhaps he really was just dumbfounded as to why his mother had invited a woman as crazy as me to stay.

"I hope you sleep well."

SEVEN

M y sleep was punctuated by a pair of impossibly deep dark eyes pulling me in, only to be tugged back by hands which wouldn't let go. It made for a restless sleep at best. I woke to the sound of my door opening, something which would have given me far more of a fright had I not spotted a familiar head peeking round the door about halfway up.

"Ryan?"

What time was it anyway? I squinted around the room, searching for a clock, finally finding one on the wall closest to the door. Eight twenty-two. What? Oh no.

"Ryan, what time is breakfast?"

"Um, I don't know. Maybe thirteen o'clock?"

Right. No help from him then. Clearly telling time would be on the list of things we'd work on. Bother. Why hadn't I thought to ask what time breakfast was? I'd barely made my way back into Marcos's good books. Being late for breakfast wouldn't do anything to help me stay there. At least it was Queen Galielle who seemed to be in charge of employing me. She was far easier to please. So far.

Telling Ryan to sit and wait, I dressed as fast as possible in the oversized closet. Given I'd never been one of those girls who bothered with makeup or even, to my mother's eternal frustration, brushing my shoulder-length hair, it didn't take long. Deciding which pair of shoes to wear with my jeans and favorite yellow blouse took the longest. The green ones I'd worn yesterday? Pink with polka dots? Plain blue? Striped green and purple? A mix of two pairs? I'd done that before—taken the left of one pair and the right of another. They were all the same type of shoe, just different designs. Ryan's expression of utter horror when I suggested it though made me grin and put them back. Yellow it was.

I took his hand and jogged down the hall toward the dining room. Tempting as it was to let Ryan lead, we were already late, and I didn't need another tour of the portrait gallery. Perhaps after breakfast.

We were almost to the dining room when a door opened right in front of us, missing my nose by inches. The man who walked through it was incredibly apologetic—and incredibly good-looking in his black formal suit which did nothing to hide the giant muscles in his upper arms. I froze, startled into a fight or flight moment before my brain could even register why.

Then it hit me. He looked like Lord Waitrose, from his combed but still defiant short brown hair to the slight cleft in his chin to his impossibly blue eyes looking at me in undisguised appreciation. The two of them could have been brothers. Maybe they were. This man and the one determined to ruin me. As if I hadn't done a good enough job of that already by myself.

"I...excuse...a..."

"Lady Wenderley, isn't it?"

Stranger, not a threat. Not Waitrose. You don't have to run. Or hide. Or wonder if you should have taken self-defense classes after all.

"Luka Wintergreen, at your service."

Not brothers then, thankfully.

He grinned, looking down at my young charge, either oblivious or ignoring my irrationally terrified response to him. "I also answer to Mr. Luka, as your young prince has dubbed me."

"Oh. He's not mine."

His eyebrows shot up into his hair, his wide eyes now filled with mirth. "I know."

Of course, he knew. Everyone in the palace and likely the world knew who Ryan was. His parentage had been the matter of investigation for weeks before Prince Marcos married Rachana and publicly claimed Ryan as his son. Personally, I thought it a bit ridiculous that they'd done so many tests to prove his parentage. The boy was a spitting image of his father, right down to the same eyes so dark a brown that they might have been black.

"Mr. Wintergreen—"

"Luka, please. At least inside the palace."

"Mr. Wintergreen," I repeated, stepping slightly in front of Ryan, as if someone my size would be able to protect the young boy against a man who probably weighed more than both of us. "You are…"

"He's Papa's boss."

This time, Luka's mirth overflowed into laughter. "Not quite, buddy." He looked at me again. I tried a smile and ordered my heart to calm down. It refused to obey.

"I'm Prince Marcos's Head of Security."

See, Wenderley? Trustworthy. Marcos wouldn't have made him the Head of Security if he wasn't someone who could be trusted. It's not his fault he looks like the man who frequents your nightmares.

"Prince Marcos mentioned at our meeting this morning that you were his son's governess until further notice. I thought I should introduce myself. Ask if you needed any assistance. We'll be seeing a lot of each other while you're here."

"We will?"

"The same team who protect Prince Marcos also look after his son. If you're wanting to go out of the palace at all, I'm the one who clears that for you." He handed me a card. "Here's how to reach me. Feel free to come by." He winked. "Anytime."

I took a step back, almost tripping over Ryan. He was flirting. It was Waitrose all over again. The fear was back. That sick feeling in my stomach. The voice in my head telling me to run as far away from him as I could. Unfortunately, it seemed, that wasn't likely to be all that easy. Nor was it a reasonable reaction. *Head of Security, Wenderley. High clearance on everything. So, he winked. Big deal. He probably does that to all the women. It doesn't mean you have to respond. You're stronger now. You made a promise.*

I took the card and tucked it into my pocket. Maybe there would be no reason to go out of the palace with Ryan. After all, I was only here for a few weeks and the boy had just buried his mother. No one really expected him to be out and about, did they? Queen Galielle had said his schedule was mostly clear.

"Well, I'll leave you to get some breakfast. Unless there's anything else you'd like to know?"

"No. Thank you." I grabbed Ryan's hand and walked a few steps forward. "Nice to meet you, Mr. Wintergreen. We're late for breakfast, which is—" I looked up and down the hall, counting doors, trying to force my skittish brain to remember which one the dining room was through. Not that it would have bothered me trying them all. If I hadn't had an audience of one particularly overconfident man watching me. And pointing to the door two down from where we stood. "That way."

I was halfway through breakfast before the sick feeling disappeared. At least the rest of the family hadn't been waiting for us this time. According to Morgan, the peppy maid who sent through to the kitchens what Ryan and I would like to eat, breakfast was served wherever and whenever the royal family wanted it. Marcos and the king tended to take theirs early in their suites, the princesses mostly ate in the dining room although they liked to sleep in whenever they could, and the queen took hers in her tearoom as she went over her daily schedule with her personal staff.

"Wenderley?"

"Mmm?" I poked another forkful of scrambled eggs and toast in my mouth, swallowing it fast enough to be guaranteed indigestion later. "What's up, buddy?"

"Were you scared of Mr. Luka?"

"No. Why would you say that?"

"Because you were holding my hand really tight when you were talking to him. It kind of hurt, but I thought you might need me to hold your hand because you were scared so I didn't say anything."

What was left of my heart melted. No wonder Rachana hadn't

wanted to give up a moment with Ryan to a governess. I wouldn't have wanted to either. He must have been such a comfort to her.

"I wasn't scared." Not of Luka Wintergreen. Just of a man who couldn't reach me here. "Thanks for holding my hand though. I'm sorry I squished yours."

"It'll be okay. What are we going to do after breakfast?"

"I don't know. Maybe you could give me a tour of the palace?"

EIGHT

By the time we finished breakfast, it was after nine-thirty. By the time we finished our tour, it was time for lunch. Something I now knew the time of, along with all the other meals, thanks to Chef Meyer. Ryan's tour had covered the gardens closest to the palace, the stables, the treehouse which had been built for Marcos and his sisters and renovated for Ryan, and most of the rooms inside the palace. Their doors, at least, since he wasn't allowed to open any that were closed. We'd spent most of the time in his treehouse and done a whirlwind tour of the rest.

I'd come to four conclusions. One, the palace was huge. Even going as fast as we had, it had still taken almost an hour to walk the length of all five stories of the palace. Two, the palace was incredible, as I'd suspected yesterday when I'd followed Mrs. Henderson to my suite. Three, I definitely had to find out what was behind all those doors. Far too many of them were closed for my curiosity. Maybe Lucie and Kahra could help with that. We hadn't seen them yet today, but Ryan told me, when he pointed out their rooms, that he often spent time with them in the afternoons.

And four, when the royal family called something a "treehouse," that's exactly what they meant. A house, up in a tree. Well, more built around a tree than sitting in one. A house big enough for a small family to live in. Huge felt like an understatement.

Winding stairs led to the first story, with a complete—if completely fake—kitchen, large couch-lined seating area, small "bedroom" complete with two child-sized beds, balcony and working telescope. Another set of winding stairs led up to the second story, a big open room with wooden storage boxes, a closet, and even a reading nook recessed into one of the walls. In case that weren't enough, one last set of stairs stretching up above the tree's canopy led to a final floor. This one only had half a roof, with the other half open to the elements. Hot during the day but I could only imagine how perfect it would be at night for star-gazing.

Ryan had shyly admitted that the treehouse was his favorite place here, something that didn't even come close to being surprising. It was every six-year-old's dream come true. Every ten-, twelve-, and nineteen-year-old's too. Who wouldn't want a hideaway like that? I could already see us spending hours playing there. We could be pirates, sailors, jungle explorers, writers...

Prince Marcos was absent from the dining table at lunch. To my great and utter relief. My plan to keep him well out of my head had been thwarted by his unmissable presence in every part of the palace. His portrait, or some variation of it, seemed to hang in every second hall, and those places where it didn't, it might as well have given how often he was spoken of.

In the stables. "And this is Prince Marcos's favorite mount, Storm. Cares for it himself, you know. Out here, every morning, exercising him for an hour before brushing him down. Then, again, at night. Couldn't ask for a better master."

In the vast kitchens. "Prince Marcos has always been so appreciative of our work. Comes down frequently to thank me and the other cooks for his meals."

In the laundry, of all places. "...of course, Prince Marcos always sorts his clothes before he sends them down. Never once found so much as a white handkerchief in the black pile. Saves us so much time, you know."

I wondered if that last one was as much his being particular about things being done right as making the laundress' jobs easier but kept that thought to myself. Also the itch to throw a white sock in his black pile, just to rile him up a little. Was Ryan as much of a control freak as his father? I certainly hoped not.

Not that I could blame Marcos, though, for thanking the

kitchens in person for their exceptional meals. Dinner had been incredible last night, and lunch wasn't far behind. I had a mind to go there as soon as Ryan finished his lunch and thank all the staff myself.

If he ever finished.

I'd never seen anyone eat so slow. It was almost like, between each bite, he forgot he was eating. He'd stare off into the distance, or simply at his plate, and just stop. My plate had been clean fifteen minutes ago, having given up on trying to pace myself with Ryan. Lukewarm pasta wasn't my favorite, but I'd done it for him. I might as well have eaten it hot.

"Ryan?"

He blinked twice before looking up at me.

"Are you going to eat some more?"

"I think I want to go rest now. I'm tired."

"But you barely ate anything." Six bites of pasta—*maybe*—and half a piece of garlic toast. Hardly enough to keep a boy his age energized. My preteen brothers ate three times the amount on Ryan's plate every meal, and usually snacked in between.

"I'm not hungry."

"Well, maybe after you have a rest, we can get some fruit or something from the kitchen?"

"Okay."

He sounded as excited as a lamb herding lions. Grief did that to a person though. Took away their appetite. I'd give him a few days, see if it returned. If not, we'd figure that out. Smoothies were always good for getting lots of nutrients into a person without an appetite. Juices. Popsicles, even. Although, he'd eaten all his dinner last night so maybe it was just today. Maybe he didn't really like pasta. I hadn't even thought to ask.

"Bed, then?"

He nodded, lip trembling as if he were about to burst into tears. Definitely time for bed.

"Come on, my little prince."

A tear dripped off his eyelash. "Mama called me that."

"Oh, honey."

This time, I did wrap my arms around him, kneeling there on the hard floor beside his chair. No, it wouldn't change anything, Rachana would still be gone, and I couldn't promise him it would get any easier but, at least today, he didn't have to face this alone. His teary face smeared snot across the front of my shirt, but it was worth it to feel his wiry arms clinging to my back.

"Your mom really loved you."

"I know. I miss her."

My throat was too clogged with emotion to answer so I just held him tighter.

When his arms loosened, I sat back on my haunches, still keeping hold of his hand but giving him a bit more space. "Will you tell me about her?"

His eyes widened. "Really?"

"Sure. If it doesn't make you too sad, thinking about her."

"I like thinking about her."

"Well, I like hearing about her. What was your favorite thing about your mom?"

He tilted his head as he thought, a smile coming to his face when he settled on an answer.

"I liked her laugh. It was really big and happy. I'd do something silly and she'd pretend to get all mad but then tickle me so hard we both laughed. Sometimes I did silly things just to make her laugh so I could hear it."

"I'll bet she loved hearing you laugh just as much."

"I think so. I liked her hair too. It was really soft. And how she snuggled me in at night. She'd tuck the blankets around me really tight and make me look like a caterpillar. Then I'd wriggle around like one and get myself out."

Whatever else the mysterious princess had been, she was clearly a great mom. For every moment she'd been there for Ryan, she'd truly been there.

"What was your favorite thing to do together?"

"That's easy. Read. She used to read to me all the time. She said we'd never be able to travel together for real but we could go wherever we wanted in books. She taught me how to read, and sometimes I read the books to her when she was too tired."

"I'll bet she loved that."

"I got a lot of words wrong but she said it was okay."

Would my heart ever stop aching for this boy? Six years old and already having been through so much. His first five years without a dad, seeing his mom get more and more unwell, being thrown into the royal family, watching his mom die, trying to find a new norm with the father he'd only just come to know.

"I'm sure she was incredibly proud of you."

He nodded. "She was. She told me. She said I was brave too, but I don't know about that. I keep crying, and that's not brave."

"Oh, honey. Crying doesn't mean you're not brave. It means you really loved her."

"Did Papa love her too? He cried at the funeral."

I fiddled with the edge of the tablecloth, searching for an answer. It felt wrong to answer for Marcos or put words in his mouth, especially if they weren't true, but then, there had been all those tears at the funeral. However their marriage had come about, he clearly cared about Rachana. Deeply, to be so moved by her death.

"Yes. I believe he did."

"She was really special."

Yes, I was beginning to see that. It was impossible to spend any time with this incredible boy without acknowledging how amazing the woman who'd loved and mothered him must have been.

Ryan yawned then, big enough to set free a couple of tears.

"Sleep time?" I asked.

"Just a little one."

"Come on. I'll get my sketch pad and sit and do some drawing while you rest."

"And show me when I wake up?"

"Sure thing."

Sketching had always been something I enjoyed. Since Thoraben's wedding, it had become my lifeline. The one place I could truly let my emotions out, without having to explain or justify them to anyone. Not even myself. There were pages filled with storms, the angry pencil lines so dark and convoluted that sometimes it was difficult to even see what the picture was. Other pages held flowers, some torn, some beautiful. Lighthouses and trees were frequent subjects too, although none of those were particularly good.

People were my favorite subject. Faces, hands, people standing, people doing, people simply being. The kids I tutored, the girls I mentored. Reminders that, though some days it felt like my life was over, God wasn't finished with me yet.

Today, I added Ryan to that mix, my heart breathing out prayers as my pencil slid across the page.

His face came first. Those dark eyes, framed with impossibly long lashes. His soft nose, the one part of his appearance which came from Rachana. A dark thatch of hair, falling over his face as he slept. A tentative smile. The one that wasn't quite sure whether he could trust but clearly wanted to.

I paused for a moment before drawing his body, considering what clothing to sketch him in. A button up shirt and shorts seemed to be his normal fare, but it was his dinosaur pajamas which found their way on to the page.

Which, of course, had my thoughts turning to Marcos, no matter how hard I tried to force them back.

Did Papa love her too?

Was Marcos crying in the silence of his room too? Somehow, I couldn't picture it. He seemed too...dignified, I supposed, for that. And yet, to bury his wife and never think of her again was too cold.

The papers had never mentioned any love between Marcos and Rachana. *Had* Marcos loved her? Ever? Did he now? They'd been married for a little over twelve months. Long enough to fall in love, certainly. But then, nothing about their marriage had been normal, from the way they eloped the night before Marcos was supposed to marry Alina, to Rachana's illness and the existence of

Ryan—what many considered the only reason Marcos and Rachana had married at all.

Marcos's likeness appeared behind Ryan on my page, one hand on the boy's shoulder, much like it had been for most of the graveside service. Unlike the service, he wasn't crying. He was smiling, as he looked down at his son. It was something I'd yet to see—even in their official family portrait, his expression was stoic—but very much hoped to.

God, please. Give Prince Marcos a reason to smile again. Give him and Ryan both reasons to smile. No, not just smile. Give them reasons to laugh.

NINE

My second night as governess, I dressed Ryan in a white, button up shirt—open at the collar since I refused to put a tie on him—and some clean shorts. I also took him directly to the dining room and pushed him through the door alone before scuttling down to the kitchen to see about finding some dinner for myself. Something I had no idea would be so difficult.

"What do you mean, I have to eat with the royals? I'm the governess, and barely even that given I'm only really filling in for a few weeks. Hardly a member of the family. Can't you make me a toasted sandwich or something? Better yet, point me to the bread and I'll make it myself."

"I can't do that," Chef Meyer said, for the fourth time. Or was it the fifth? It was difficult to tell exactly how many given the amount of mumbling she was doing under her breath. I chose to believe she was talking to herself about the dishes she was overseeing rather than how annoying Prince Ryan's temporary governess was.

"But why not?" I tried again. "I'm perfectly capable."

"Your dinner is waiting in the dining room."

Chef Meyer walked away again, dodging her way past steel counters and white-jacketed people, busily stirring and chopping all manner of concoctions. If she was trying to avoid me, she had a thing or two to learn about persistence. Something I'd spent my life perfecting. You didn't chase a prince for a decade without learning all about it. Lot of good it did me, but still, lesson learned.

She stopped beside a man pulling what looked like chocolate puddings out of an oven. Unfortunately, he put them back in before I could count to see whether there would be enough for me to claim one. Although, if I *was* supposed to be eating with the royal family, then there would definitely be one for me. I'd have to remember to come back for it. After my sandwich. Or whatever that delightful smell coming from the other side of the kitchen was. Beef? Pork? It was salty like pork, but there was something else. Pumpkin spice?

"Please, Chef Meyer, surely you don't expect me to eat with them."

She bustled around a few more counters before coming to a stop at the plating counter and running a practiced eye over the gold-trimmed white crockery lined up. "I don't see why not."

Apart from the fact that they were the rulers of this country? "I'm staff."

"Hardly."

"Excuse me?"

"You said it yourself, you're more a guest than staff anyway. Take the honor and be gone with you."

"But—"

Chef Meyer finally stopped bustling around long enough to look me in the eye. "Lady Wenderley, I understand. Truly, I do. But I have my orders same as you, and you're keeping us all waiting arguing."

I frowned. "What do you mean? They've started, haven't they?"

"Before everyone is seated? Of course not. That would be rude."

No. She couldn't mean… "They're waiting for me?"

"Yes, now are you going, or are the king and queen of Hodenia going to be eating cold pork tonight?"

They were waiting for me. For the second night in a row, I'd held up the royals' dinner. *Nice work, Wenderley.* Without another word I sprinted out of the kitchen, up three flights of stairs,

through two wrong doors—why were they all painted the same?
—and burst through the door to the dining room where, just like
Chef Meyer had said, the entire royal family sat waiting.

Queen Galielle was the first to smile. "Wenderley, there you
are. We wondered where you'd gotten to."

"Forgive—Sorry, I—" Had left my breath somewhere around
the second flight of stairs. "I didn't realize I'd be eating with you."
Sure enough, there, beside Ryan, as it had been last night, was a
full place setting and an empty chair.

"Of course," Queen Galielle answered again. "You're family."

It was on my tongue to argue again but a quick shake of the
head from Marcos had me biting it back. Now wasn't the time. I
nodded instead, thanking the queen as I took my seat. At least I
knew what all the forks meant thanks to all the formal dinners I'd
attended in Peverell. I might feel completely out of place, but I
wasn't going to embarrass myself.

What I was going to do was speak to the queen about this
notion of hers that I was somehow family.

Tomorrow.

After I guiltily enjoyed every single bite of my dinner tonight.
Including dessert.

Although, I did cut up Ryan's pork for him, even though it
was so tender he could have easily done it himself, to make myself
feel useful.

"Don't argue with her."

I'd just left dinner—walking despite stuffing myself so full I
could have rolled—when Marcos's words stopped me. He'd been
deep in conversation with his father when I'd excused Ryan and
myself and walked away. Now, he was standing behind me. How
had he gotten here so fast?

"Excuse me?"

"Mother has decided you're having dinner with us each night.
Don't argue it. You won't win."

"I can be very persuasive, especially when I'm right."

"You often argue when you're wrong?" He held up a hand before I could answer. "No, wait. I don't want to know that. Just come to dinner. Preferably on time."

I crossed my arms. He thought this was my fault?

"I would have been on time, if I'd known I was supposed to be."

"You need a schedule?"

"No, thank you." The schedule the palace had given me prior to Alina's first attempt at a wedding, when she'd named me as one of her bridesmaids, had been enough to last me a lifetime. Page after page of names, dates, times, numbers, who to talk to and who to avoid, what to talk about and what to avoid, family trees, historical feuds—some going back centuries—alongside fitting dates for the pink poof of a gown I was only wearing because Alina was such a good friend.

The day Alina announced she was marrying Joha Samson, I happily threw both the gown and the thickly-bound schedule in the bin.

"In my defense, I didn't know I was invited. If you noticed, Ryan was on time, and appropriately dressed."

"I noticed."

It was kind of embarrassing how much those two little words made me want to smile. Possibly throw my fist up in the air and cheer. Also, highly inappropriate. I settled for a demure nod. "Good."

"You'll be on time tomorrow, then?"

"If I must."

He frowned. "Most people would be honored to dine with my family."

Stop teasing the man, Wenderley. "As am I, Your Highness. I was joking."

"I see."

"Prince Ryan and I will be at dinner tomorrow night ten minutes early."

"Thank you. It will mean a lot to Mother. She likes you."

She did? Already? I'd barely met the woman, although her approval of me likely came more from the faith we shared than who I was as a person. The fact that she was a Follower, and not afraid to admit it, told me a lot about her too. We might not share a history, but we shared a heart. "Your mother is a wonderful woman."

"I think so."

Two maids ducked their heads as they walked around us, standing there in the middle of the hallway. Ryan was silent beside me as his father considered me long enough to race past flattering and awkward and land solidly in the realm of plain disconcerting. What was going on in that head of his? More, did I really want to know? Probably not.

"I should put Ryan to bed," I said after a minute or so of silence.

"Of course. Forgive me. Go. I'll see you tomorrow."

Right then. That was it. No more talk. "Goodnight, Your Highness."

"Goodnight, Lady Wenderley. Ryan."

Marcos made no move to embrace Ryan or do anything more than nod at his son, much as he had me a few seconds ago. It felt so cold, compared to the way my father used to piggyback my siblings and me into bed, and what Ryan had told me earlier about the caterpillar snuggles Rachana gave him each night.

A nod. Just a nod.

Everything in me welled up with the urge to call Marcos out on it. Demand he at the very least ruffle his son's hair or something of the sort. Instead, I took Ryan's hand and forced myself to walk away, reminding myself that this wasn't my battle. Everyone grieved in their own ways and every family was different.

Still, if Marcos continued to be so indifferent toward his son, I'd have something to say to him about it before I left.

TEN

Despite Marcos's admonition, I still went to find Queen Galielle first thing the next morning, creeping downstairs while Ryan was still sleeping. She wasn't in her office, but a helpful maid told me to try the library. With a grin, I set off in the direction she pointed. The library in Peverell's palace was a sight to behold. I couldn't wait to see Hodenia's.

One wrong door later, I found it, and it was well worth the anticipation.

It was around the same size as Peverell's with the same wall to wall, floor to ceiling shelves filled with beautifully bound books, but that was where the similarities ended. Where Peverell's was set up like a meeting room or extra office space, almost, with long tables and chairs across the middle of the room, the library here looked like a sitting room or a person's living room. In one corner, huddled around an ornate fireplace, were five or six couches, tables with leadlight lamps keeping them company. Two more larger couches sat in another corner, partially blocked off by a row of shelves which jutted out from the wall. For privacy, perhaps? Or simply because they had too many books. A happy problem indeed.

I could only imagine—and dream about—how cozy it would be to come in here on a rainy day and snuggle up on one of the couches with a good book.

Or sketch at one of the two desks.

Wandering farther in, I ran my finger along the desk closest to me. Solid wood, large drawers down the sides and tiny ones cubby-holed along the top just begging to be explored. Hutches and shelves above holding books, photos and all manner of knick-knacks. Every item, no doubt, with a story of its own.

Red felt lay across the top of one while the other was done in dark green. A complementary pair.

I tucked my hands behind my back and forced my feet to be still. Not my desk. Either of them. No matter how much I wished they were.

What would it be like to have permanent, unfettered access to such a place? To be able to come in and sketch late at night as the lamps threw colored light across the walls, or snuggle like I'd imagined by the fire. Sit and talk books for hours with a friend, or wander the shelves pulling out whichever book took one's fancy. Sneak a kiss behind the—

Wenderley!

No. No kisses. That was the vow I'd made after—

"Lady Wenderley, this is a surprise."

I spun guiltily to see Queen Galielle standing a few steps behind me.

"Is everything okay, dear? You're looking a little flushed. You're not unwell, are you?"

I put a hand to my burning cheeks before brushing away her concern with a smile. "I'm fine. It's warm in here, don't you think?"

Queen Galielle's mouth might not have smiled back at me but her eyes did. "If you say so."

Right. Well. No more thinking of kisses. Even if the ambience of this room was totally made for romance and—

"Do you like books?"

I blinked, my mind taking far too long to jump back from imagination to reality. Books? What? Oh, right. Library. Books. "Yes. Books."

If I hadn't been standing in front of the queen, I would have slapped a hand to my forehead. I sounded like a two-year-old. *For goodness' sake, Wenderley. Snap out of it. This is the queen you're talking to. Also the woman who hired you, believing you were mature enough to care for her grandson. Try to act like it.*

"Were you looking for anything in particular?" she asked, thankfully choosing to ignore my momentary ineptitude.

"I was hoping to speak with you, actually. One of the maids told me you'd be here. Forgive me for assuming I could walk right in."

She waved a hand. "Not at all. You're welcome to visit the library any time. I come here most mornings to sit but, as you can see, there's plenty of room." She gestured toward a pair of chairs. "Come, sit with me and tell me what it is that's worrying you. Your room, perhaps? Did you want to be closer to Ryan's? Further away?"

The chair she offered was as comfortable as a wooden chair could be. The couches by the fire would have been far more comfortable but, kind as she was, I couldn't imagine Queen Galielle curling up in one. Nor would it help my credibility any to ask to move there after claiming the room was already too warm.

"No, no, my room is fine. More than fine. It's truly beautiful. Stunning. Absolutely perfect. Really, I love it. What I wanted to discuss with you was dinner."

"Ah. You think you shouldn't be there."

She got it. This was going to be easier than I thought. "No, I don't. I'm honored you want me there, but I'm more than happy to eat with the rest of the staff. Dinner should be family time."

"I understand."

So much easier than I'd expected, given Marcos's dire prediction. Why had he cautioned me against talking with his mom about this? "Thank you, Your Highness."

I started to stand. Unfortunately, the queen wasn't finished.

"Tell me, Lady Wenderley, apart from feeling like you don't belong at the table, do you have any other reasons for not wanting to be there?"

The chair almost tipped as I landed awkwardly back in it. "Other reasons?"

"It's too noisy, you're intimidated by my husband or, for that matter, my son, you're worried Ryan is going to drop his meal in *your* lap next time, the girls' infatuation with you makes you uncomfortable, there are too many forks…"

She was kidding, right? She had to be. "No, not at all. Your family is amazing." And I was well-versed in which fork to use for each course.

"Good. Then I expect you to be there every night you're here."

What? No. That wasn't how this was supposed to go. "But—"

"Are you a queen, Lady Wenderley?" Queen Galielle interrupted.

"No, Your Highness."

"Well, I am, and I say you will be at dinner."

She raised one of her perfectly shaped eyebrows, daring me to continue arguing. It was enough to make me swallow back all the other arguments I had lined up. Marcos was right. I never even had a chance.

"Yes, Your Highness."

"Good. I'm having tea brought up in a few minutes. You're welcome to join me, if you like."

A glance at my watch told me Ryan would be waking soon but the thousands of books begged me to stay. Ryan enjoyed books. Maybe I could find a couple to read to him before I left.

"Thank you, but—" I looked around the library, wondering what kind of order the books were in, if any. Color? Genre? Size? Those close enough to read the titles of seemed to be historical, although, with titles like *The Lost Rock of Geris Island* and *Memoirs of a Kingdom Gone*, they could just as easily have been fiction.

"Would you like to take a book with you?"

"Actually, I was thinking of Ryan. He said one of his favorite things to do with his mom was to read together. I know I'm not here to replace Princess Rachana, but I thought it might be something Ryan and I could do together too. Of course, I have no idea what kind of books he might like. I don't think tales of fairies or ponies would hold his interest for very long."

Queen Galielle smiled. "Oh, I don't know. Marcos's favorite book when he was Ryan's age had a fairy in it, though the main character was a pirate. I lost count of the number of times I saw him reading it. I wonder if it's still…" Her voice petered off into silence as she walked along the rows of books, finger against her chin as she searched. "Yes, here it is."

It was near the bottom of a back corner shelf that she found it, a book about the width of my thumb, dark blue with a caricature of a crocodile on the front. *Pirate Pumpernickel Meets his Match.*

When she offered it to me, I happily took it, flicking through to the first page.

> *There once was a boy who dreamed of being a pirate. That is, until the day he met one. Tom was the boy's name, and the pirate? Pirate Pumpernickel. The grand, the esteemed. The somewhat-forgetful. And that, my friends, is how Pirate Pumpernickel met Tom.*
>
> *You see, Pirate Pumpernickel had forgotten where he'd docked his ship, and what he'd done with his crew. He and his daughter—Pirate Plum—had been wandering the town searching for it when they came across young Tom, who told Pirate Pumpernickel in no uncertain terms that not even the fiercest of pirates could hide a ship in a little boy's back garden.*
>
> *"Ah, but you see—" Pirate Pumpernickel said, "'tis an invisible ship. And it flies."*

I was grinning already, imagining Ryan's face lit up with delight and curiosity as I read him this. Imagining where we'd read it, the things we could do. The treehouse, of course, would have to be transformed into a pirate ship, what with the telescope and crow's nest already in place. We could make a flag, have a secret password, create our own code. Did pirates have codes? Maybe that was explorers. Or spies. Probably only spies. Still, it would be fun.

Oh, and we'd definitely have to take some ropes up there, to tie up any rogue crocodiles or prisoners which might come our way. Ryan and I could have a whole pirate-themed day! I could talk Chef Meyer into letting us take our lunch up to the treehouse and we could pretend to be pirates all day. Maybe on a day she served fish for lunch.

"Perfect," I said, partly to myself and partly to the queen still watching me. "Ryan will love it."

"I think so. If not, you're always welcome to come back and choose another. Come anytime. Or, if none of these work, let me know and I'm sure I can track down whatever you're after. Being a queen has its privileges, you know." She smiled, and I was struck again by how kind and welcoming she was—even if she was forcing me to come to dinner with the family. Although, I supposed, that was the highest form of welcome a queen could bestow.

Though I'd spent a great deal of time with the Peverellian royal family, I'd never had reason to meet Queen Galielle or her husband before. I'd barely even spoken with Prince Marcos before coming here. And yet, here the queen was, welcoming me into her home, treating me like a valued guest. Family, even.

"Thank you, Your Highness. You're very kind."

"How is Ryan?"

Queen Galielle's question came as a surprise—or perhaps, it was more the intensity behind it which surprised me. She'd said it so casually, and yet, the concern in her green eyes had me thinking through the answer before offering the quick "he's fine" which immediately came to mind.

"As well as can be expected, I suppose. He's quiet, much quieter than any other boy his age I've known, and he doesn't eat much...but he just lost his mother a week ago."

"Do you think he needs professional help? A counselor or such?"

I didn't know Ryan well, but I was pretty sure he'd clam up altogether if someone put him in a room with a stranger and tried to make him talk. Of course, that might also have been because I didn't want someone else to be the one who helped him. I wanted that person to be me. But was that selfish? Arrogant of me, even? The last thing I wanted was for Ryan to be emotionally scarred for life because I was too proud to let someone else help him. But it had only been a week.

"Honestly?" I asked Queen Galielle.

"Of course."

"Maybe, sometime in the future, but I think what he most needs now is time."

"And pirate stories."

I smiled. "Yes, lots of pirate stories. Time to be a kid. Time to adjust to this new life he's been thrown into. I know he's in line for the throne one day and there are tens of thousands of lessons that come with that, but could they be put off, for a little while at least? He's already had to deal with so much in his short life."

"He has, hasn't he. Poor child. If only we'd known, six years ago…"

Queen Galielle blinked several times. Was she trying to hold back tears? I'd been so focused on Marcos and Ryan that I hadn't even considered what this might be like for the queen.

Her first grandchild, and she'd missed his birth and the excitement leading up to it. Missed spending hours holding him and marveling over this miniature version of her son. Missed his first birthday and celebrating over his first steps. Missed being there to support him when he was sick. The first five years of his life, she hadn't even known he existed. I probably wouldn't have thought it would affect her this much even if I had considered it.

She was the queen. Refined. Beautiful. Separate from the people. And his grandmother. It wasn't as if she was Ryan's parent. She was Marcos's mother. The man who'd had a relationship with a woman and kept the whole thing a secret from his parents. From everyone. If anyone had a right to be angry at Marcos, it was her. She could have easily shunned Ryan and the circumstances of his birth, despite the fact that Marcos had claimed him.

And yet, seeing her trying to keep control of her emotions, thinking about all she'd missed, it was impossible not to see how much and how personally she cared. About her son *and* his.

"I'm sorry…"

She shook her head, as if trying to dispel the memories she'd been lost in. "Yes, well. We can't change the past, can we. We must just do the best with what we've been given."

Didn't I know *that* well.

Also, I really needed to change the subject before we were both crying.

"Are there any other books here you think Ryan might enjoy?"

"Well, now, let me see…"

When I left the library five minutes later, I carried seven other books alongside the Pirate Pumpernickel book. And a whole new respect for Hodenia's queen.

We started the book that night. I was right. Less than two pages in, Ryan was hooked. Three chapters in, I wondered if reading it to him before bed was as clever an idea as I'd thought. I was supposed to be the responsible adult here, reading "just one more chapter."

"One more chapter" had been four chapters ago. I was still reading.

> *The storm raged around them, tossing the ship this way and that. Every few terrifying minutes, the waves would push them skyward to sit atop what felt like the world. But then, making Tom's stomach lurch and his head spin, the ship would drop down again, surrounded on all sides by waves taller than Tom's house.*

A rustle at the door had me glancing over, stumbling slightly over my words when I saw Marcos standing there. Had he come to say goodnight to Ryan? Couldn't he have waited till Pirate Pumpernickel and Tom got out of the storm? *Wenderley, really? Show some maturity.*

"Ryan," I whispered, closing the book, my finger tucked safely inside. "Look who's here."

Ryan sat up immediately, his eyes lighting up with delight when he spotted his father. "Papa!"

Whether Marcos had planned on coming in or not, he had to now. I climbed off the bed and walked to the other side of the room, giving the father and son some privacy. Tempting as it was to keep reading, I kept the book shut.

Which meant I saw the way Marcos walked over to Ryan's bed and sat beside the little boy. I heard Marcos ask Ryan about his day and whether he'd brushed his teeth. The two of them were so close. Take a photo and all you'd see was the picture of a loving father and his son saying one final goodnight before bed—until you looked closer.

And saw the way Ryan squared his little shoulders and tried to be taller beneath tonight's truck-patterned pajamas.

And the strain on Marcos's face—not a smile, not a laugh, but not a frown either.

And the way Marcos tapped Ryan's knee, instead of embracing him when he said goodnight and went to leave.

They were close, yet, in so many ways, still strangers.

"Prince Marcos," I said before he could reach the door. "Did Ryan tell you we're reading about Pirate Pumpernickel? Your mother said you used to enjoy this story. Would you like to stay?"

I held up the book. He looked from it to me to Ryan and back again. For a moment, I thought he might actually agree. Then he shook his head.

"Another night, perhaps. I have a meeting."

Of course he did. He was the prince. Even while grieving, his life didn't stop.

"Goodnight Ryan, Lady Wenderley."

Though I asked Ryan if he'd like to finish the chapter, he lost interest the moment his father walked out. I didn't blame him. My heart was heavy too. I tucked Ryan in, kissed his head, and turned out the light.

ELEVEN

Five hours later, I wished I could switch my brain off as easily as I'd switched the light. No matter how many sheep I counted or silly alphabet games I played, my brain wouldn't stop. Doubts, fears, hopes, dreams, regrets, Marcos's face, Ryan's tears, Queen Galielle calling me family and admitting she thought I was the answer to her prayers. Over and over, they played in my mind in a dizzying cacophony. Every moment, every memory heightened by the darkness and silence around me. Regret fought against hope, Queen Galielle's delight against the truth of who I was. What I'd done. Would she have looked at me the same way if she'd known?

Law-breaker. Fraud. You can't hide from the truth forever.

No. But I could ignore it tonight. Or at least, try.

Had I done the right thing in agreeing to stay at the palace? Should I have gone home instead? I had no doubt Alina would follow through with her promise to be there for the girls I mentored, but would she know that Anna wasn't as confident as she pretended to be? That Aimee found it hard to trust? That Liz processed her emotions by talking and Parker by thinking them through? That Milly Rose loved to sing and dreamed of using that gift to lead others to God? That Rory's lack of punctuality had nothing to do with her own time issues and everything to do with her little sister's illness?

And how could I help Marcos to be the father Ryan needed? The way they'd said goodnight tonight haunted me. They were like strangers, rather than father and son.

I kicked the sheets and rolled onto my side, rolling back again a minute later, berating how ridiculous it was that I couldn't get comfortable on a mattress this luxurious. Lying on my back was no better. I growled into the darkness. It wasn't the bed. It was me.

Going for a walk helped settle my mind sometimes. Not that I had any inclination to dress again and wander about the palace after midnight but—

The balcony. Perfect. Spacious, outside in the fresh air but private enough that I didn't have to dress or wonder who I might meet in my travels and how to explain to them what I was doing.

I grabbed the twisted blanket off my bed and wrapped it around my shoulders as a barrier against the cold before slowly opening the balcony doors and walking outside. The brisk air had me smiling in an instant as I lifted my face to the breeze. This was what I should have done an hour ago. I tugged the blanket a little tighter around my shoulders and moved to the railing, leaning my elbows on it as I stared out into the night.

The balcony overlooked a garden, a series of small buildings and, in the distance, a tennis court, still lit though silent at this time of night. I wondered who played. Maybe all the royal family did. Maybe none. I'd ask Ryan tomorrow. Shy as he was, he seemed a wealth of information. I supposed when you were as quiet as he was, you heard a lot. I'd also write to each of my girls. That would help with the feeling of guilt that I'd deserted them. And to Alina, letting her know enough of their little quirks to ensure they still knew they were loved.

The door to the balcony beside mine opened, drawing my gaze. Every crazy, dizzying thought flew from my mind the instant I realized who it was standing there.

Prince Marcos. The man himself. Still dressed in his black suit, shoes on and everything. On the balcony. Less than ten feet away from where I stood. Was that his room? Surely not. Someone would have told me if his suite was right beside mine. And yet, why else would he be on that particular balcony—leading out from one of the suites—unless it was his?

Although, the bigger question was, should I stay on mine?

He hadn't seen me yet, leaning against the railing, staring out much like I had been only moments ago. Unless I moved, or said something, he probably wouldn't. I certainly hadn't checked to see whether the balconies either side of me were occupied when I'd first walked out.

But then, would that be wrong? To allow him to think himself alone when I was here? Oh, the dilemma.

As it was, he turned, right at that moment. Started, squinted, stood up straight.

"Lady Wenderley?"

I thought it strange he should ask, as if he wasn't quite certain it was me. Until I remembered all he could see with me wrapped in a blanket was the top of my head. At least I didn't have to wonder what he thought of my pajamas. Not that I cared what he thought of them. Of course.

"Yes. Sorry. I'll go back inside." So much for enjoying the breeze.

"You're up late."

I stopped shy of opening the door. "Couldn't sleep."

"Me neither." He turned back to the view, pensive again. "The air is so fresh out here at night."

Was he wanting to talk? He hadn't invited me to stay but then, maybe he didn't need to. After all, I was on my balcony, he was on his. There was no reason why we couldn't both enjoy the night air. I leaned back against the door, not quite certain enough to walk the few steps back to the railing but not quite ready to go inside either.

I tried to relax and forget Marcos was there, but it was like ignoring an elephant sitting on my chest. Though I didn't let my gaze go anywhere but the tennis court, I was all too aware of the prince ten feet to my left and the way he stood, so rigidly upright. Was he thinking about Rachana? Should I ask him if he was okay? How his meeting had gone? Why he couldn't sleep? Offer to talk?

Oh sure, that'll help you keep your distance. Not. Come on, Wenderley, give him his space and go inside.

But even if the few minutes outside had calmed my mind, I

knew I'd never sleep knowing he was still standing there. I stayed right where I was, blanket wrapped around me like a puffy caterpillar, back resting against the cold glass of the sliding balcony door, watching the stars. Pretending I wasn't also watching Prince Marcos, still as tense as he'd been when he first came out.

"I didn't realize your room was beside mine," I finally said, needing to break the silence.

"It's not."

It wasn't? Then why…?

"I like the view from this balcony."

"Yours doesn't have a view?" I would have imagined, being the prince and heir and all, that he'd have one of the best views in the palace. The only people ranked higher than him around here were his parents. Surely that meant he had prime choice of palace real estate.

"It does."

Oh.

"But also memories."

Oh. Rachana. Of course. He'd shared that suite with his wife for the past twelve months. His dying wife. For all I knew, it was where she'd actually died. Had they sat out on their balcony late at night chatting? Relaxed there together, doing their best to ignore the fact that every minute spent together was one minute closer to the moment they were pulled apart? Whether the memories at the time had been happy or sad, they'd all be tinged with grief now.

It seemed we were both hiding from our memories out here.

"So, you come here," I said.

"Sometimes."

"I'll go then."

"Only if you want to."

I didn't. Nor did I know what the protocols were—whether I should or not. He was the prince, usually surrounded by at least a few security guards if not a whole cohort. Here, it was just us. Albeit with the distance of a balcony between us. Even if both of us reached out, our hands wouldn't touch. No one could accuse us of anything untoward. Not physically, anyway. Emotionally, my heart had already skipped across the railings and wrapped it-self around the grieving prince much as I had Ryan in the dining room yesterday.

God, please help him through this. Give him the courage to keep going and the strength to want to. Help him to be the best father and prince he can be.

"Well, goodnight, Lady Wenderley. I hope you sleep well."

I murmured my own goodnight to Marcos as he walked in-side, closing the door behind him.

He was different than I thought, than anyone did, likely. Alina had gone on and on about him when they'd been engaged. So much so that a person would think they knew him, if not for the fact that Alina really only talked about his looks. Not that they weren't worth talking about. A girl would have to be blind not to appreciate them. But beyond that, he'd always been an enigma. Quiet, standoffish, but not in a rude way. More like he wasn't sure he had the right to join in. Which was ridiculous, given his title.

Even at the Midsummer's Ball, what had become his and Ali-na's engagement ball, he'd been a mix of quietness and strength. Strength when he'd come forward, surprising everyone by inter-rupting King Everson's longwinded speech and kneeling down to propose to Alina, but quiet again, when she'd surprised him by jumping up and embracing him in front of everyone. The two of them danced then, and Marcos had seemed happy enough, but I'd seen the way his expression dropped into politeness as they walked about the room, thanking the crowd of people who offered their congratulations. He still cared, he just didn't know what to do with people who came too close.

That awkwardness of Marcos's had confused me for weeks. He was the prince. He had been all his life. The public aspect of his life should have come naturally to him after twenty-something years of living it, yet it didn't. It was almost as if he was afraid to let himself breathe lest someone think badly of him and his coun-try. Even standing on the balcony before, when he thought he was alone, he hadn't been relaxed.

God, help him, I prayed, for the umpteenth time. *He needs you.*

There was a chair on the balcony, but I sat on the floor instead, content to snuggle the blanket around me as I leaned against the door and watched the night sky, hoping for a shooting star. My thoughts continued to rush past one on top of the other but, focused on the stars, they seemed detached from me somehow, almost as if they were someone else's. Like they were a show, and I watched from the audience.

Even that thought seemed too convoluted to consider, tired as I was.

I sat there, on the balcony floor, until my lids grew heavy and the temperature too cold to be comfortable. When I went back inside, I'd come to three conclusions:

One, I should have chosen the chair. It would have been far more comfortable and easier to get up from than the floor.

Two, shooting stars were clearly a myth. Or reserved for people far more patient than me.

And three, I was here. Now. Whether that was a mistake or not didn't matter. I would do whatever I could do to help this family in the time given me. And maybe, just maybe, I really could make a difference.

TWELVE

"Ryan?"

He was supposed to be in his room. That's where I'd asked him to stay, assembling his wooden train tracks while I checked the menu for the day with Chef Meyer in the kitchen. It had taken me almost two weeks, but I'd finally realized how much easier it was to convince Ryan to eat when I knew in advance what was being served. I'd only been gone a couple of minutes. Five at the most. Chef Meyer had had the entire week's menu written on a piece of paper waiting for me. I'd thanked her with a hug, tucked the list in my pocket, and run all the way back. Only to find the room empty.

"Ryan?"

He had to be here somewhere. I checked the bed, closet, curtains, under the bed, shook out the covers just in case he was hiding there again, pretended we were playing Hide and Seek for a minute or so just to see if he'd giggle, searched the bathroom, the closet again, tripped over a train which blended in with the floor mat, and finally admitted he wasn't here.

Which shouldn't have worried me as much as it did. He was a six-year-old child in a palace full of family and employees. Old enough not to get into too much trouble. At least, not the dangerous kind, and Ryan didn't seem like the kind of child to go drawing on walls or trying to aim a ball at a chandelier. I hoped.

I walked down the hall, checking in each room along the way, trying to keep my worry under wraps. So, he'd tired of playing trains. No big deal. He was probably in the kitchen, trying to talk Chef Meyer into some more pies, having taken a different route than me. Or in his treehouse, now the best pirate ship in Hodenia with its proper skull-and-crossbones flag flying from the roof. I was still waiting to see if I'd get in trouble for that. No one had commented yet.

He wasn't in the kitchens. Or in his treehouse-slash-pirate-ship. I probably would have found him already if I hadn't been too proud to ask for help. Somehow, admitting I'd lost the future king of Hodenia seemed a bit too close to failure when I was supposed to be his stand-in governess.

"Lady Wenderley!"

Uh oh. Marcos. Yelling. Well, thundering was probably closer to the truth. He who always sent an official summons if he had a problem and never raised his voice even then. He called out again, my name echoing furiously around the entirety of the palace. I smiled weakly at a passing maid, trying to pretend everything was fine when we both knew it was nothing of the sort. This couldn't be good.

"Wenderley!"

Oh, I'm coming. Calm down.

My shoe caught on the floor runner again, tumbling me into his closed office door, my left elbow banging against the door jamb as I tried to balance myself. Not that Marcos helped with that, flinging open the door just as I put a hand up against it. I fell forward. He pushed me back, clearly not in the mood to play rescuing knight.

"What is he doing here?" he demanded instead, pointing behind him.

I looked past the angry prince to the small boy sitting quietly on one of the office chairs, favorite train clutched in his hand. Ryan. He was here. "Visiting you?"

Wrong answer, if Marcos's fury was anything to go by. "He drew on my ledger. In ink."

"I was trying to write like him," Ryan said in a tiny voice. "I wanted to be like Papa."

My heart melted. Unfortunately, Marcos's didn't.

"He ruined my book."

"Surely, it's not that bad."

The glare he gave me could have set Ryan's treehouse on fire.

"Did he apologize?" I asked, trying desperately to catch up on the situation while my gaze went back and forth between the two princes—one glowering at me and the other looking as lost as he had the day of his mother's funeral.

"That's not the point. He shouldn't have been in here in the first place. He's not allowed. He knows that, and I would have thought you did too."

Surely, whatever Ryan drew on wasn't worth all this yelling. I crossed my arms and tried to keep my voice calm—for Ryan's sake. Certainly not for the sake of his overbearing father. "He made a mistake. He was trying to get your attention."

"Well, he got it. And now I have to spend the rest of the day paying for it."

Ryan looked ready to burst into tears. I wasn't far behind, although my tears came from anger rather than hurt. How dare Marcos be so blind as to miss how much his son wanted to be with him? How dare he shout at Ryan when all Ryan wanted to do was be like his dad? The boy was six years old, for goodness' sake.

I walked over to the chair Ryan sat in and knelt in front of him, taking his shaking hands in mine. It took clearing my throat twice for the words to come out. "Ryan, honey? How about you take your train back to your room. I'll be there soon." After I told Marcos in no uncertain terms what kind of a father he was currently being. Ryan definitely didn't need to be here for this.

With a tiny nod and an even tinier wince of a look in his father's direction, Ryan took my hand and let me lead him out of the room. I smiled and waved when he looked back at me from halfway down the hall. As soon as he was out of sight, I closed the door and let loose.

"How could you do that? You yelled at him. Your own son! Don't you care about him at all?"

Marcos, apparently not bothered in the slightest by my anger, walked calmly back to his desk. "He shouldn't have been in here."

I wasn't giving in so easily. "He wanted to see his dad."

"He drew all over my book."

Marcos held up a book, some type of ledger, with tiny numbers meticulously lined up in every column—and giant, slightly shaky numbers written over top. I might have cringed. And pushed down a little ill-timed pride at the fact that the seven and three were the right way around. I'd have to get Ryan to draw them again for me later so I could tell him what a good job he'd done.

As soon as I got through to his clueless father.

"He didn't mean to make a mess. We've been working on numbers. He was probably really proud to be able to show you how well he could write them."

"He should have done it somewhere else. This is my office and I don't want him in here."

I wanted to scream. Really, really loud. As it was, I barely kept my voice to an acceptable level.

"So, he's supposed to see you when? At dinner? When every other member of your family is there? Are you spending any time at all with your son?"

Marcos picked up a pen and slowly began transferring numbers from the marred page to a clean one. "I have work to do. I am a prince. I have responsibilities."

"Yes, well, so is he, and he needs his dad." I crossed my arms before the temptation to shake some sense into him got the better of me. How was he not getting this? "Have you even seen how much his face lights up when you walk into a room? Or how upset he is when you leave without a word to him?"

"Who made you his guardian?"

"Someone has to speak up for him. Clearly his father isn't going to."

That barb was supposed to hit Marcos in the chest and stick there. Burrow in, even, until the pain of it woke him up to his son's pain.

Either he was completely heartless—something I knew from the funeral wasn't the case—or it missed, because his writing didn't even pause for the space of a heartbeat. *Read number, flick page, write number. Read number, flick page, write number.* He might as well have been a robot.

"He has my mother, aunts, a dozen servants, and you, apparently. If you're going to set yourself up as his guardian, I'd appreciate it if you'd make sure he doesn't disturb me again. If he has need for me, he can contact me like everyone else does."

Yep. Completely heartless.

"He's your son!"

Marcos looked up just long enough to find my gaze. "Yes. He is. And you'd do well to remember it."

I was too angry to even think of a reply to that. I bit back, barely, the scream of fury welling up from my chest as I watched Marcos go back to writing out numbers. Stupid, heartless, arrogant, irresponsible, selfish, *cad* of a man. Yes, cad. He might have been handsome, but he was a cad. Poor Ryan just wanted his dad's attention. He wanted to be loved. My eyes watered as I gritted my teeth together.

"Was there something else? Because I have work to do."

Calm down, Wenderley. You'll never get through to him with shouting. Count to ten. Deep breaths. One...two...

Yes, there was something else. A million something else's. Like how could he not see how much he'd hurt Ryan with his yelling? And didn't he know how impressionable young children were? How dare he sit there as if he hadn't just crushed his only son. Had he forgotten he was the only parent Ryan had now?

But then, he was new to this. Maybe he didn't know. He'd never been a parent before meeting Ryan. What was it like to be told you had a five-year-old son and suddenly have to figure out how to become a father overnight? Sure, it had been a year since they'd become a family but from what Ryan, and Queen Galielle, had said, Ryan had spent much of that year with Rachana. Had Marcos been there too? Or had Ryan and Rachana kept to themselves, with Marcos always feeling on the outer? Was he really only getting to know Ryan now?

My anger began to seep out, pushed aside by welling compassion. He'd never done this before. Maybe Marcos was as scared and lost as his son. He needed help, not derision.

"I'm sorry. I'll talk to Ryan and make sure he stays out of your office. I shouldn't have yelled at you. You're right, he's your son."

Marcos looked up then, a frown across his forehead as he considered me. I gave him the most honest smile I could and walked out of the room.

THIRTEEN

Luka Wintergreen was with Ryan when I got back, to my annoyance. The walk from Marcos's office to Ryan's room was far too short for me to have calmed down enough to deal with another impossible man.

"What are you doing here?" I asked brusquely.

"Well, if it isn't the lovely Lady Wenderley..."

Definitely too short. "Forgive me, Mr. Wintergreen, but I believe I asked you a question."

He raised an eyebrow but otherwise didn't comment on my refusal to be overly familiar with him. Or familiar at all. Ridiculous, I knew, especially since the man had done nothing more than flirt a little on first meeting. But I was in no mood to be reasonable.

"I ran into young Ryan in the hall just now. He looked upset. I asked him why. He told me what happened and that you were speaking with Prince Marcos so I thought it best to keep Ryan company while we waited for you to return. We've been playing trains."

Ryan was smiling happily as he played beside his father's Head of Security. I'd thought he'd still be upset. Maybe, selfishly, I'd even wanted him to so I could be the one to comfort him. Instead, here he was, content again. All because of Mr. Wintergreen. I supposed I should have been happy. Maybe I was. Really, really, *really* deep down.

"Thank you. You can go now."

"So soon? But we're just getting started."

"I'm sure you have other things you should be doing." Like staying away from me.

"Nothing urgent. Not for the next few hours. I'm all yours," he waggled his eyebrows, "if you want me."

No. Absolutely, definitely, most assuredly not. The last thing I needed right now was another overconfident man trying to get my attention. Maybe I should have sworn off men altogether and not just princes.

"I'm here to look after Ryan."

"Well, would you look at that. That's exactly what I'm doing right now, too. We're having a great time, aren't we, Ryan?" He grinned down at Ryan, who smiled right back and nodded his head.

Wonderful. What part of "not interested" was Luka Wintergreen missing? Were all the men in this palace clueless? First Marcos having no idea how much he'd hurt Ryan, now Mr. Wintergreen missing the fact that I wanted nothing to do with him.

"Come on lovely Lady—"

"Look, I'm not your lovely lady nor do I want to be. I'm not interested, okay?"

His grin didn't even falter. If anything, he seemed even more amused, while I felt so guilty over how rude my words were that I almost apologized them into non-existence.

"Can't blame a man for trying." His gaze swung left, his face instantly serious. "Prince Marcos, did you need to see me?"

My stomach dropped to somewhere near my toes. I didn't turn. I didn't want to know. Marcos was standing behind me? For how long? How much had he heard?

"No, thank you. I came to see Ryan."

My stomach jumped back up, colliding with my thudding heart. He'd taken my advice? Or—Oh no. He hadn't come to berate Ryan again, had he?

"If that's fine with his guardian here, that is?"

At that I turned, caught Marcos's gaze. Stared at him as if I could read the intention of such a comment in his eyes. I could see myself reflected in them but not the answer I sought. Was he joking? Teasing me? Uncertain of his welcome? Completely serious?

"You're going to play with me?" Ryan asked. "Mr. Luka *and* Papa?" His eyes were wide as he looked back and forth between the two men, clearly having forgiven the one who hurt him all of ten minutes ago.

"Sure. I have some time until lunch," Marcos said, walking over and sitting right down, there on the floor, shucking his suit jacket as he did so. "I'm sorry I yelled at you," he told Ryan, putting a hand on the boy's knee.

"Mr. Luka said you didn't mean it. He said it's hard sometimes being a prince and that people get angry sometimes when they're tired and really busy like you."

What? That was what I was going to tell him. Jealousy ripped through me like a sharp wind. Followed quickly by a wave of guilt. *This isn't about you, Wenderley. It's about Ryan. What does it matter who comforts him, so long as someone does?*

Marcos nodded to Luka—a silent thanks?—before picking up a piece of the wooden train track and joining it to the one Ryan had been working on. "Luka's right. I was busy, but I still shouldn't have yelled at you."

"Did I ruin everything?"

"You—I—" Marcos shook his head. "No, you didn't ruin everything."

Ryan's nod was as serious as his father's.

"Now that's settled," Luka said, grin firmly back on his face. "How are we going to get Lady Wenderley to agree to come over here?"

What? No. Spending time with Ryan was one thing. Spending time and, more terrifyingly, such a small *space* with him and two men who were far too handsome and intimidating for anyone's good, was quite another. I'd be a muddle of nerves the entire time. Where would I even sit? Between the two of them? What if Luka continued to flirt? What if Marcos said something that riled me up again?

And, I further justified, Ryan needed this time with his father. Without me. I wouldn't be here forever.

But then, could I really leave Ryan? He seemed fine now, but he'd been crying ten minutes ago when Marcos shouted at him. Sure, Marcos had apologized, but what if Ryan was still scared?

He's fine. He has Luka, who he clearly adores. And Marcos is trying. Give him that. You told him—ordered him, really—to spend time with Ryan. Are you really going to be annoyed at him for doing it?

"Lady Wenderley?" Marcos invited, staring up at me from his place on the floor. I couldn't tell from his guarded expression whether he wanted me to stay or was simply asking because it would be rude not to.

"I—"

Marcos tilted his head, something changing in his gaze. Softening almost, though that could have simply been a trick of the light. Or the fact that he'd been glowering at me before and now looked all but calm. Either way, I wasn't staying.

"—have to check something with Chef Meyer."

The excuse itself was pathetic, and I think everyone in the room, bar one little train-distracted boy, knew it. I fled before any of them could see how I really felt. Which was such a messy combination of relief, guilt, jealousy, happiness, grief, and fury that I didn't even know where to begin to process it. Finding Ryan when I'd thought he was lost brought relief, but Marcos's anger made me furious, then sad, then Luka came along, and then Marcos was back being the father I'd begged him to be and—

Too much. Too many emotions. Chef Meyer could wait. What I wanted to ask her wasn't all that important anyway. Part way there, I switched directions and went to my room instead, pushing the way through my door before going straight out to the balcony, desperate for fresh air.

Only I found something else. A memory. Of Marcos, leaning against the balcony beside me. So tense he couldn't sleep. So determined to be everything to everyone, even when he was hurting.

God, I need to apologize again, don't I?

When was I going to stop blundering my way into other people's lives as if I knew the way? Mom warned me once that my soft heart was going to get me in trouble. She'd been right. First Thoraben, then Waitrose, then Mar—

No, I wasn't falling for Marcos. I just cared. And owed him another grand apology.

I checked my watch. One hour until lunch. One hour to get my heart and mind back in check. Marcos was Ryan's parent, not me. Marcos was the one who would be staying with Ryan forever, not me. I was merely passing through. Helping, along the way.

Yes, helping, Wenderley. Not cementing yourself into their lives. No matter how much your heart wants to. They're not yours to keep.

A bird hopped along the edge of what I now thought of as Marcos's balcony, singing its lungs out in a gorgeous melody. Below me, on the trees dotting the garden paths, the buds of yesterday turned into the flowers of today. Pink, white, and purple blossoms, more than I could count. Beyond the garden, there were people on the court today. The princesses? The king? I couldn't tell from here. It didn't matter.

Two more weeks and I'd be gone. Back to trying to figure out the mess of my life I'd left behind. This was a dream, an escape. It couldn't last forever.

None of it would.

It was ridiculous, really. Here I was, berating Marcos, when I'd made so much more of a mess of my life than he had. I could tell myself all I liked that I was here to help Ryan and do good, but it was still just delaying the inevitable. The truth would come out. Sooner or later, in some way or another, it would. Truth had a way of doing that. And Waitrose was not one to be trusted.

FOURTEEN

I was sitting at breakfast with Ryan, Lucie, Kahra, and Queen Galielle the next day when Marcos walked in with a pile of envelopes. I took a bite of toast and determined to ignore him. Something that would have been far easier if he had done the same.

"A letter, for you, Lady Wenderley."

The instant I saw the envelope, all the blood drained from my head. Mint green with my name written in bold, dark script across the front.

No...

I didn't have to open it to know who it was from. There was only one man who ever sent those letters. One a month. For the past year. Ever since that night. Far enough apart for me to start feeling free. Close enough together to know I never would be.

Waitrose had followed me. Not in person, thankfully, but he might as well have. He knew exactly where I was and how to reach me. It was enough to make me want to actually befriend Luka Wintergreen and ask for my own security detail. Not that there was anything they could save me from, unless they had a working time machine. And really, there was nothing for them to protect me from anyway. No sword or manner of weapon could stop words.

Yes, Wenderley. Words. That's all they are.

Even so, it took two attempts for me to take the letter from

Marcos's hand. I tucked it under my leg, wishing I could leave it there. Or, better yet, throw it in a fire somewhere. Turn back time so Waitrose never had reason to write to me at all. I should never have looked his way. I knew better. Stupid, thoughtless, moment of defiance.

"Thank you," I said, my voice not as confident as I would have liked.

"If you're going to have suitors write to you at the palace, you might tell them to use your own name rather than put it in an envelope with mine."

Waitrose was hardly a suitor, though I couldn't tell Marcos that without having to explain far more than he ever needed to know. Than *anyone ever* needed to know.

"He wrote to *you*?" I tried to hide my shock, but I'm not sure I succeeded. The words came out a little too fast, and a little too loud. Marcos frowned. Queen Galielle was looking at me too. Thankfully, the other three were too interested in their food to care about a simple envelope or the undercurrent of tension it produced.

"No, there was no letter to me. Just this envelope for you."

"Thank you," I said again, my mind rushing too fast to come up with anything but banalities.

"Is everything okay, Wenderley?" Queen Galielle asked.

"Yes," I lied. "Fine." I sounded as convincing as Marcos had the day of the funeral. I tried again, attempting a light laugh. "Surprised, that's all. I didn't expect to hear from him while I was here." Was hoping I'd never hear from him again, to be honest. Although he'd made it very clear that would never be the case.

"How about I see to the rest of breakfast and deliver Ryan up to you soon," Queen Galielle said. "Will that give you enough time to read your letter?"

Plenty, since Waitrose rarely wrote more than one line. Threats didn't take all that many words. Of course, it didn't take too many words to topple a weak woman either. *You look beautiful.* Three words. One poor decision. A lifetime of regret.

"Thank you, but it's fine. I'll read it later."

I already knew what it said. Or some variation of it.

"You're mine, Wenderley. And don't you forget it."

As if I ever could.

"You know who'd look good in this?" I asked, holding up a ridiculously large, floppy mauve hat.

When Queen Galielle had suggested to Lucie and Kahra that they spend some time cataloguing the Gift Room this afternoon, I'd jumped at the chance to help. I would have scrubbed clean every hallway in the palace on my hands and knees if it gave my mind something to focus on rather than the chilling words of Waitrose's letter.

You think moving countries will hide you from me? Think again. I know your secret.

"No one?" Kahra offered. Lucie just shrugged.

I grinned. "That suit of armor outside your brother's office."

Lucie burst into a fit of giggles. Kahra didn't laugh, I don't think she knew whether to take me seriously or not, but she did smile. Ryan kept trying on hats, most of them falling over his eyes.

Filled with all the gifts presented to the royal family for the past hundred years—and, by the look of it, a few more cases and boxes which had been in the family far longer—the Gift Room was a treasure hunter's oasis. Soft toys, flags, and books sat alongside carved bowls, furniture, jewels, and case after case of clothing. Some of it was labeled, much of it wasn't, meaning you never knew what you might find in a particular box. Queen Galielle had set the girls to work sorting it as part of their schooling. I wasn't sure exactly what they were learning from this experience, but we were certainly enjoying it.

"Let's do it," Lucie said, when she could finally talk. "Please? I can just imagine what it'll look like, all droopy and feathery with those ghastly colors."

"Are you sure Marcos won't mind?" Kahra asked.

I shrugged, trying to contain my own giggles at the thought of such a monstrosity sitting on top of the armored suit. And more, the look of surprise on Marcos's face when he saw it. It would definitely distract him from that letter I'd received. He'd wanted more of an explanation. I had no intention whatsoever in obliging him. "It's only a hat. He can always take it off if he wants to."

"It would make the suit look less creepy."

I raised my eyebrows, purposely looking from Kahra to the hat and back again. "Are you sure about that?"

This time, she did laugh. "Well, maybe a little."

"Can we do it now?" Lucie asked, bouncing on her toes with excitement. "He's not there at the moment. He visits his charity on Wednesday afternoons. We'll have lots of time to sneak down there and put it on. We could even add some other things. This scarf would do wonderfully, don't you think?"

She held up a pink, orange, and green scarf which, though it looked to be made of a beautiful silky fabric, must have been painted by someone with their eyes closed. The colors clashed so vividly that it was almost like it had a strobe effect woven in.

"Perfect."

"Don't forget a purse," Kahra offered, belatedly catching on to the fun and throwing over a clutch which might have been green once but had faded into a kind of puce color. "An outfit is nothing without a purse." She said it with a grin, like she'd heard it a few too many times already in her fourteen years. I had no idea how we were going to get the suit to hold a purse but I wouldn't have denied her it for anything. Maybe we could loop it over the armor's metal glove, or tie it on somehow with twine? Without wrecking the suit, of course.

It took a few minutes of convincing, and the assurance that we'd come back and play again tomorrow, before Ryan would leave the piles of clothing, but soon enough the four of us were traipsing down the stairs, loot in hand, trying our best not to look suspicious as we giggled our way toward Marcos's office. Which I was taking the word of a twelve-year-old would be empty.

The hat looked even better than I'd imagined perched on top of the suit of armor. I'd wondered if it might be too small to fit over the fellow's helmet, but whoever had worn this hat originally had clearly had a large head. Or perhaps that was the reason it was packed away in a forgotten chest in the Gift Room, because it had been too large for anyone to wear.

The scarf's colors were even more hideous in the bright light of the hall, the sun beaming through the windows opposite catching every horrible stripe. Kahra wedged the purse up under one of the suit's arms and pulled the other arm forward slightly, just enough to look like it was out for an afternoon stroll.

It was all we could do not to break into laughter loud enough to bring every person in the palace running when we stepped back to take in our masterpiece. The poor fellow never knew what hit him. I wished we could have stayed to see Marcos's reaction, but I don't think any of us were brave enough to risk that. Not even Lucie.

Of course, that meant we were all on edge from the moment he arrived back at the palace. A moment we were all well aware of, given we were happily playing cards by the girls' sitting room window at the time. The window which, providentially, overlooked the front drive of the palace.

Also, playing cards was somewhat of a stretch. They were there, hands dealt out in front of us, in case anyone happened to walk in and we needed an excuse, but none of them had been played. We were all too busy staring out the window, watching for Marcos, giggling at random as thoughts of the horribly dressed suit of armor drifted across our minds.

But not one sound came from Marcos's office. Not even when we found the courage to tiptoe halfway down the stairs and peek through the banister. Marcos's door was closed, but there was enough of a sliver of light showing beneath it to prove he was in there. Surely he hadn't walked straight past the fellow and not noticed. I knew Marcos was focused, but no one had that much focus.

Apparently, he'd just ignored it.

I probably should have too. Why did it always take so long for my brain to catch up with my mischievous side? This was a palace, for goodness' sake. That was probably a centuries old suit of armor we'd just all but desecrated. What if Marcos had meetings in there later today? A suit of armor dressed like this hardly left a good impression. And what if that hat, or scarf for that matter, was actually important? For all I knew, they'd been a valued gift, or a treasured heirloom. They could snag on a piece of metal when we tried to take them off, or be destroyed by the rust.

"Maybe we should take it off…" I mused, to the instant dismay of both girls.

"No way. We can't. It looks so…so…"

None of us could find words to describe what we'd done to the poor fellow.

"It stays," Kahra surprised me by saying before grinning. "Until we find something worse. Race you to the Gift Room."

FIFTEEN

Marcos didn't say a word about the knight or his unusual outfit, to the disappointment of every person at the dinner table under the age of twenty-five—though not for a lack of trying on Lucie's part. After a few comments that were far less subtle than she thought, I started to wonder whether Marcos was purposely being obtuse just to annoy her. Of course, that would take a sense of humor on his part, and I'd still yet to ever see him properly smile. Occasionally, his eyes would soften or look almost like they were laughing but his mouth never changed. The only time I'd ever seen him actually smile was his wedding portrait, the one they published in all the papers, and even that hadn't reached his eyes.

I'd become a professional at reading facial expressions in photos during the years I'd lived in Hodenia, while pining for Thoraben. Every photo of his I could find, I'd poured over, ensuring I didn't miss a thing.

"Marcos, we missed you this afternoon. How was your time at Fleming House?"

I narrowed my eyes at Lucie, who looked far too innocent for such a question to be as polite as it sounded.

"It went well, thank you. I had some good conversations with the men currently staying there."

"I'm sure they appreciated your presence. Did you wear a hat?"

"A hat?"

"Yes, you know, one of those things that sits on your head. Or perhaps a scarf?"

She was at it again. *Seriously Lucie? Subtlety, dear…it's an art.* Although…was Marcos smiling behind the glass he'd raised to drink from? Perhaps it was merely a figment of my imagination or a quirk of reflection, since, when he moved the glass, not even a hint of a smile was there. Probably not smiling then.

"No, no hat, and I don't believe I own any scarves."

"Of course."

Lucie went back to eating her dinner. For all of three bites.

"Wenderley," she began again. Oh no. She was dragging me into this now? "Have you seen my green clutch? I loaned it to someone recently, but I can't remember who. Maybe it was at *night*?"

I had to admit, she was pretty adorable. And she was trying so hard.

"I don't think I've seen—" I started.

"That's okay," she said, cutting me off before I could finish the sentence. "Marcos? Have you seen it? Or one of your *guards* has, perhaps?"

There. That was definitely a smile, for the tiniest of moments. I would have missed it had I not been watching so closely. He was totally playing with Lucie.

"What's a clutch?" he asked.

"Oh, you know. A little bag. Like the one on your—"

Kahra cleared her throat and sent a glare that could have turned the beef from rare to well done in an instant, had she been aiming it at Lucie's plate instead of her face.

"Um, actually, I think I remember where it is."

Marcos nodded. "Good. In that case, could you please pass the salt?"

She did, and then quietly ate the rest of her dinner. I might have felt sorry for her if not for two things—the determined expression on her face which told me this was far from over, and the very knowing and slightly amused look Marcos sent my way when I finally dared to meet his gaze. This definitely wasn't over.

I was just settling down with my sketchbook later that night, deciding who to draw, when a knock came at my door. The last person I expected to see there was Kahra.

"Kahra? Is everything okay?"

"Yes, of course." She smiled brightly, before letting it drop altogether and letting out a sigh instead. "No, not really. Can I talk to you?"

"Yes, of course. Come in."

She was still dressed as properly as she had been at dinner, complete with shoes, despite it having been several hours ago. She was like her brother in that way, though I doubted she worked late into the night like he seemed to each day. I, on the other hand, had changed back into jeans and ditched my shoes as soon as Ryan was tucked into bed. It was clear to see between the two of us which was the princess.

"Your room is pretty."

I smiled as I sat on the seat across from the one Kahra had chosen, tucking my feet up under me in the hope that it would make her feel more comfortable too. Maybe I'd even convince her to kick off her shoes, if she stayed long enough. Back home, I'd instituted a no-shoe policy when my girls and I met. It was impossible to share at a heart level when wearing shoes.

"I certainly think so. I love being able to see the stars from bed."

"I have skylights in my room too."

She marveled over the cushions on my bed next, then the picture on the wall, then asked about my sketchbook and whether I liked having a closet as big as most people's bedrooms. I answered each of her questions, happy to talk, knowing none of them were the reason she'd come. I'd spent enough time mentoring girls Kahra's age—and being a teen myself—to know it took time to build up enough courage to ask the tough questions. Soon enough, she'd run out of bedroom fittings to talk about.

"Do you think Marcos is mad at me?"

Her question was so quiet I almost didn't hear it, especially since I'd been expecting her to talk about the furnishings for a long while yet. After all, she'd yet to even start on the carpets or chairs. There was such a vulnerability in her expression.

"If you mean because of the outfit we dressed his suit up in then no. I think he actually found it pretty funny."

She almost smiled at that, her mouth tugging up for the tiniest moment. "No, I mean just, in general, I guess. He's my big brother, you know, and I really love him, but sometimes I don't know if he likes me back. He's so different from what he used to be when we were younger."

"His life hasn't been easy lately."

"No, I know that. But it's more than that. It's like—I don't know, it's hard to explain. Like I did something wrong and he doesn't want to be around me anymore, but I don't know what it was so I can't apologize or fix it."

Her words made my heart ache, or perhaps it was the yearning behind them. The yearning to be loved. A feeling I knew all too well. "I'm sure you've done nothing wrong."

"Then why doesn't he spend time with me anymore? Or Lucie?"

I didn't want to put words into Marcos's mouth. I still felt as if I barely knew him. But I did know he loved his sisters. No man would put up with what we'd done to his poor suit of armor today if he didn't utterly adore them.

"I don't know. Maybe it's all the added responsibility he's had lately or the fact that he's missing Rachana or—I don't know, it could be one thing or a thousand little things. What I do know is that he adores you and that will never change."

Kahra didn't seem particularly comforted or convinced by my words.

"Did you want me to talk to him?"

"No," she answered immediately. To my relief, since I wasn't entirely sure how I would have. "Please don't. It's fine." She shrugged. "Maybe he is just busy. I guess that's what comes with being the crown prince and growing up, right?"

"Unfortunately."

She nodded, a gentle smile finally making its way back onto her face.

"Thanks for talking with me."

Though I didn't feel like I'd been very helpful, I smiled back and assured her that as long as I was here, she was welcome to come and talk.

"Really? Because there was one other thing…"

"Sure. What's on your mind?"

"It's just—I thought maybe—that is, I can't ask Mom because that would be so embarrassing and she'd make a bigger deal of it than it is and, um…"

A blotchy red blush stamped its way across her cheeks and neck. If I was going to hazard a guess, I'd say this question had nothing whatsoever to do with her brother. I nodded in an attempt to encourage her to keep going.

"You can ask me anything. Promise."

She deliberated for a few more seconds, pursing her lips and taking in some deep breaths before letting her words out in a rush.

"Have you ever liked a boy?"

I smothered a smile. Now we were getting somewhere.

"Yes." Not that I thought her question had anything to do with me. "Have you?"

Kahra ducked her head, hands clutched under her knees. "Maybe."

"Oh?"

She sighed. "He works in the gardens. I don't know if he's an actual gardener or an apprentice or what exactly, but he's really sweet and…caring. I skidded on a patch of mud I didn't see the other day while walking in the garden. He caught my hand and stopped me from falling. He let go of it straight away, of course, but the way he asked if I was okay…I just—I don't know, I wanted to stay there and talk to him longer. Maybe even a lot longer."

"Why didn't you?"

She looked at me aghast. "Are you kidding? I was too scared to even ask his name. I don't know anything about talking to boys.

The only one I've ever really spent time with is my brother, and you already know how that's going. That's why I came to you."

"You want me to find out the gardener's name for you?"

"No! I mean, you could, I guess, but I thought maybe you could tell me what to say to him? So that next time I don't look quite so dumb?"

"'Hello' is a good place to start."

I said it as a joke. She nodded as if I'd given her the most valuable piece of wisdom anyone had ever bestowed.

"I could do that. Then what?"

Oh. Um…

"Given he's a gardener, maybe you could ask for some flowers for your room, or what plants or gardens he likes working with. How long he's been working here, even? Or, you know, his name."

Kahra nodded again, tilting her head slightly as if she were playing through how those questions might work in reality. "That could work."

"Let me know how it goes."

Her thoughtful expression gave way to a smile. "I can do that. Thanks, Wenderley." She stood, hands automatically running down her skirt to straighten it. I followed her to the door, wondering whether it would be appropriate to offer her a hug. It's how I always ended chats with my youth girls, but they didn't have the title "princess" in front of their name. I'd just opened my mouth to ask Kahra what she thought when she stopped and turned back.

"If you don't mind, I actually do have one more question…"

"Of course. Anything."

I should have known by the impish smile on her face—so much like Lucie's—to brace myself.

"Do you have a crush on my brother?"

SIXTEEN

The tea in my cup bobbled, almost spilling onto my hand and the small pile of books balanced in my lap. When Queen Galielle had requested that I leave Ryan with his aunts and come to the library directly after breakfast, not even my crazy imagination could have foreseen this. The crazy imagination which could come up with a story or wild explanation for any weird and wonderful occurrence or backstory for a suit of armor in an instant, but couldn't manage to come up with even one semi-believable answer to Kahra's question. Still. Three days later. She was probably still laughing to herself at the way I'd turned red and bumbled my way through some semblance of a denial.

"We call it the Holiday Party," Queen Galielle said. "I'm sure you've heard of it. The royal family holds it at the end of every year, inviting hundreds of children and their families to attend. This will be Ryan's first time, and I don't want him to be alone, but surrounding him with an entire security detail would scare away any of the other children who might potentially be friends. The girls, Dorien, Marcos, and I all have roles already and can't stay with him. I thought you might like to. I know Ryan would love to have you there with him. He trusts you already. He might actually be brave enough to talk to some of the other kids if you're there."

Hodenia's Holiday Party. I'd heard of it, though not much beyond that, given only children between the ages of five and ten were invited. When I was fourteen, Father had taken my brothers, Emmett and Eder, to the party. It was the first of only twice in my life when I'd wished I was younger. The other time had been the year after when they'd been invited back a second time. Both times they'd come home hyped up on sugar and fun but not been particularly descriptive about what happened there. All I'd been able to get out of either of them was that it was the most fun they'd ever had.

Peverell held a ball every year to celebrate the holiday season. It was one of their four major balls of the year. The people's ball, they affectionately called it. When everyone came together, commoners and royals alike. They'd hang thousands of gold fairy lights around the palace's grand hall and everyone came dressed in red, green, and gold. Did Hodenia do the same?

"It's not a formal event, is it?" From what I remembered, my brothers hadn't dressed up.

"No, not at all. Picture a child's party, with finger foods and cake and sweets. We usually get in a magician and a few roving performers. There are games set up all around the grounds with plenty of prizes. Last year, we had a performer come in who worked with bubbles, of all things. She had these enormous poles and strings and would make bubbles big enough for a child to stand inside. I think the parents enjoyed it as much as the children."

It sounded amazing. Just as I'd always imagined. Only—

"You're still holding it this year? Even though…" I didn't say it. I didn't need to.

"We did consider cancelling it, in light of Rachana's passing, but it's such a special tradition for children in Hodenia, and us as a royal family. Dorien, Marcos, and I discussed it with our advisors and decided it was important to keep the tradition going. The country has been unsettled lately by all that's happened. We could all do with a reason to smile."

It was something I'd always admired in Peverell's royal family, the way they cared about their people above all else. Even above their own comfort, many times. What I'd seen Kenna, Alina, and

Thoraben do for their people was astounding. Alina had been willing to give up Joha's love altogether to marry Marcos for the good of her people, for goodness' sake. If that didn't prove how much she loved them, nothing would.

And now, here it was, that same incredible care, in Hodenia's royals too. Looking beyond their grief to find ways to make their people smile. It took more than courage and duty to do such a thing, it took real love. A total sacrificing of one's self. It was what sorted the truly noble kings and queens from the good ones.

"You'll still be here in two weekends' time, won't you?"

"Yes, of course." Even if I had been planning on leaving before then, there was no way I was missing this, my one—and likely only—chance to attend. "I'd love to go and keep an eye on Ryan. He'll have a great time."

"I hope so. He's such a quiet child."

"He's had a lot to deal with."

"I know. I just worry. I've never seen a child so quiet."

I took another sip of tea as I considered Queen Galielle's comment. Ryan was quiet, but I'd also seen glimpses of the boy he might have been, before his world was tipped upside down. His grin when he tried his best to convince me that his train track really did need to stretch the entire length of his room, and under the corner of his bed, as if I wasn't already convinced. The creative stories he came up with during the long hours we spent up in the treehouse. His laughter as we read Pirate Pumpernickel, which neither of us were ready to end.

"My brother, Emmett, used to be quiet like Ryan," I said. "He's thirteen now and, while he's still quiet, he's also the one who'll come out with the best jokes and is really quick to make other kids feel welcome wherever he goes. I think it's because he's quiet. He notices more, and then heads straight for those people who need encouraging. Quiet isn't always a bad thing."

"No. I suppose not."

She was quiet herself, long enough for me to wonder if I should let myself out. I'd promised the girls Ryan and I would help them do some more sorting in the Gift Room today. They'd been all too eager to go back and do more work there, even though they'd only just been in there a few days ago. I was pretty certain the majority of their enthusiasm had to do with finding Sir Rusty a new outfit, after not getting much of a reaction out of the last one.

"Sorry, lost in my thoughts," Queen Galielle said, standing. "I'll get your name added to the invite list. Smart casual dress, by the way. Jeans are perfectly fine."

Jeans. Good. I hoped that meant heels were also out. Although I would have worn heels, if she told me to. I would have worn a clown suit if that's what it took to attend the Hodenian Holiday Party. The butterflies in my stomach were already doing somersaults of delight.

They reached the coast by midday, but not even the blazing sun could make the cave before them seem more welcoming. It was dark, bleak almost. Water and rock, stretching back into nothingness. No trees, no plants, no light, no markings of any kind to say whether this was a friendly cave or something far more sinister. In every story Tom had ever read, a cave was one or the other. Never simply a cave.

Some held treasures, some took a man in never to return, some were gateways to another land. Which would this be? Because, whether he had the courage to find out or not, Tom was going in. The entire ship was, steered ever forward by Pirate Pumpernickel.

The crew went silent around him, nothing to be heard except the gentle swish of water against the sides of the ship. And the loud thudding of Tom's heart.

"And that's the end of the chapter…" I told Ryan, glancing over to see if he was still awake. Only it was Marcos who caught my attention, standing listening in the doorway. Had he been standing there long? Caught up in the story, I hadn't even noticed.

I inclined my head, silently asking if he wanted to come in. In lieu of an answer, he walked away. Lying on a cushion, his back to the door, I doubted Ryan had even known his father was there.

"Can we read another one? Please? It's not *that* late yet, is it? I'll stay awake. I promise."

"Sure, but how about we move to the bed. It's a bit more comfortable than the floor."

Ryan did as he was told. I looked at the doorway, half hoping Marcos had come back and would pop his head in now I'd stopped reading, to say goodnight to Ryan. He didn't. If I could have replayed the last five minutes, I wouldn't have acknowledged Marcos at all. Maybe then, he would have stayed.

Ryan fell asleep during our third "one more chapter." I bookmarked the page as soon as I saw. Tom and the pirate crew had made it through the cave, thanks to the light of a tiny fairy—likely the one Queen Galielle had mentioned—and their ship now bobbed gently in an underground lake. Much as I was itching to know whether the fairy was good or bad, leading the crew away from their ship to find the treasure she claimed she knew the location of, it felt wrong to keep reading without Ryan listening. I left the book on his bedside table, kissed his forehead, tucked the blankets a bit tighter around him, and turned off the lights before walking down the stairs.

Perhaps it was the book, with its storm and cave of wonder and description of the lake so vivid I could have dived through the pages and found myself there, but I wanted to be outside. The treehouse tempted me, with its unhindered view of the stars, but I hadn't brought a light of any kind with me and attempting those winding stairs and ladder alone in the dark didn't seem like the smartest idea. Nor did I want to go back inside to get a flashlight or anything now that I was out here.

I wandered the garden paths instead. I'd seen them so many times from my balcony, but this was the first time I'd been in them. They looked so different from here. The trees which had looked barely taller than my waist towered above my head, for one. And I'd never seen the lamps which lined the main path, hidden by the trees' boughs from above, though I'd known the path had to be lit by something. I put my hand against one of them, its post cold to touch. Refreshing, on a muggy night like this. Refreshing and beautiful, the way the yellow light shining through the lamp's clear glass contrasted with the dark post.

I didn't know where I was going, but it didn't worry me. The trees were tall but not so dense that they ever blocked my view of the palace. Any time I felt myself getting disorientated, I merely had to look up and know which way was home.

Home. I breathed in the word, letting it out with a smile.

It did feel like home. A strange thing to feel for a place I'd only been in for three weeks. And a palace at that. They were supposed to be imposing and intimidating, but it had never felt that way to me. Likely because of Queen Galielle's insistence that I be treated like family rather than a guest.

"Lady Wenderley, what a pleasure. Enjoying your walk?"

My peace scattered like fireflies. "Good evening, Mr. Wintergreen." What was he doing out here? He wasn't planning to stay, was he? I really hadn't been counting on company. Especially being alone with a man I still couldn't convince myself to be comfortable around.

"Still insisting on Mr. Wintergreen?"

I kept my mouth shut and hoped he'd get the hint and go away. No such luck.

"I was doing a check of the grounds and noticed you out here," he said, leaning back against one of the light posts. I appreciated the space, if not the company.

"If it's a security issue, I can go back inside."

"Not at all. You're very welcome to walk out here. Might I have the pleasure of accompanying you?"

There was such hope in his voice that I almost agreed. Only it would have been a lie. I didn't want to walk with him. I'd be on edge the entire time, and the whole reason I'd come out here was to relax. Nor did he seem like the sort of man who'd appreciate being led on when there could be no future for us. The sooner he understood that I wasn't interested in a relationship with him—or any man—the better. "Thank you, but—"

He straightened, walking closer again. "Come on, Wenderley, don't send me away. I've been hoping since the morning I met you for a chance to know you better. Let me be your friend, if you're not ready for more. It's not as if you have a boyfriend back home who'll be jealous."

"How would you know?"

"I'm Prince Marcos's Head of Security. It's my job to know everything I can about the people around him." He grinned. "But it didn't take a security check to know you're beautiful."

I blanched, swaying slightly in the lamp light. He'd checked my background? What else did he know about me? How deep had he looked?

"Walk with me. Please?"

Those words. *Walk with me.* In an instant my mind swept back to another night, another man.

I was standing in a hallway, swirling music playing in the grand hall behind me, the skirt of my purple ballgown billowing out, its corset restricting my breathing as I stared at the tall man in front of me. He'd called me beautiful. He'd looked me in the eye, on a night when everyone else had sent pitying glances and looked away.

But there was no pity on Lord Campbell Waitrose's face, only admiration. His hand didn't waver as he held it out to me. "Walk with me," he'd said. Only his eyes said more. They looked at me with desire. Passion. He wanted me.

I'd looked through the door behind me, watched the smiles on the women's faces as they danced in their partners' arms, oblivious to my pain, for one long wistful moment more before making my decision. Turning back to Waitrose, I put my hand in his and walked away from it all.

"Wenderley?"

The ball was long gone, along with the innocent girl I'd been that night.

Luka touched my arm. I flinched as if his fingers were fire.

Instantly, his hands were up in the air, a million questions on his face. No, not a million. One.

Why?

SEVENTEEN

"W enderley?"

I wrapped my arms around myself. One breath, then two, forcing the memories into the past. Where they belonged. Where I wished they'd stay.

"Forgive me," I bit out, wondering whether it was so much Luka I was asking as God. Somewhere, deep down, I knew I could trust Luka. He wasn't Waitrose. He probably did only mean to walk with me. But I couldn't. Because, even though I could trust him, I couldn't trust myself. "It's not you. It's—"

A sob stole the rest of the sentence. I didn't stay to try again. Tears pricked at my eyes as I ran all the way back to my room, ignoring Luka calling my name and the confused looks of the several maids I passed.

My sketchbook lay on my bed where I'd thrown it earlier today. I picked it up, along with several black pencils, and opened to a new page. Within minutes, dark storm clouds thundered their way across the top of the page while giant waves crashed around a tiny lighthouse, stuck out on a rock at sea. The lighthouse stood strong against the storm, but would it always?

God, help me. I know you've forgiven me and I'm trying to let it go, but it just keeps coming back. It's been over a year. Will I ever be free of that night? How am I supposed to go on?

When my heart slowed to a dull thud and my pencils became too blunt to use, I put the paper away and went to bed. I should have known I wouldn't sleep. Every time I closed my eyes, I saw

Waitrose's hand reaching out, and me taking it. Felt the hot pain of regret, over and over again. And, on top of the regret, the anger. The doubt. The self-loathing. The loss. The grief. When I opened my eyes, it was no better, the dreams of months past playing in my mind so vividly it was like I was watching a film above my bed.

Selling a precious jewel only to realize after it was gone how much I loved it.

Watching my future float away, my desperately grasping fingers never quite long enough to pull it back.

Failing. A thousand different times in a thousand different ways.

People turning away when they saw me coming, pity in their eyes. The only words I ever caught, "she could have been so much more."

And the one I dreamt all too frequently which still wrecked me every time—a faceless man kneeling before me, holding my hands, professing love, proposing marriage, only to have my hands turn black and decayed, and his love turn to horror as he drops them and says the words which haunt me. "Oh, but you're not her. Not the girl I thought I loved. She was pure."

Was.

I kicked the sheets away from my legs. Not sleeping at all would be better than this torture. Not even bothering with a blanket this time, I walked outside, automatically checking to see if Marcos was on his balcony. He wasn't. It was a silly hope anyway, given he only came out a couple of times a week and rarely stayed long enough to do more than ask how I was and comment on the weather. I always felt guilty when he came anyway, as if I was invading his space, even though I was always there first.

A cool breeze had come up and swept away some of the day's mugginess since I was out in the garden. It played with my loose hair and danced across my face as I sat in the darkness and stared up at the stars.

God, thank you for not walking away. Thank you for being here, still, with me today. Thank you for the stars. Thank you for Marcos, and Lucie, and Kahra, and Ryan, and Queen Galielle, and King D—

The door to the balcony beside me opened, stopping my train of thought. Marcos walked out, looking straight over at me in my chair and pajamas.

"Wenderley."

Strange. Was that relief in his tone? Why would he be relieved? Maybe I was imagining it. After all, he'd only said one word. Hardly enough to be assigning emotions.

"I was hoping I'd find you here."

He was? *Don't read into that, Wenderley. There are a million reasons he might be looking for you. He probably just wants to ask you something about Ryan.*

"Did you need something?" I asked. His jacket was still buttoned, tie still in place. Shoes on, of course. Another late meeting?

"Actually, I wanted to check that you didn't." He walked over to the edge of the balcony closest to mine, one hand resting on the ledge while the other dropped to his side. "Luka was waiting for me when I got home just before. He said you were upset earlier. He wanted to come and check on you himself but said he wasn't sure you'd appreciate the gesture."

So Marcos had come instead? Part of me was charmed to think he cared. The other far larger and more practical part reminded me that I was the one caring for his son. Of course he'd want to ensure I was still well enough both mentally and emotionally to do so.

Had Luka told Marcos how I'd flinched when he touched me? How I ran away like Luka was the one who'd hurt me?

"Tell him I'm fine."

"Certainly but…are you?"

"Yes, of course."

He stared at me across the balconies, his gaze so intent that I almost gave in and told him everything. But what was the use? He couldn't change anything and who knew how much more mess it would cause if he tried?

"Please," I whispered. "It doesn't matter. Let it go."

"You'd tell me if you were in trouble though, wouldn't you?"

"I—"

"Because you can. That is—" His voice lowered, gentled. "I'd like you to."

Prince, Wenderley, remember? They're trained to be nice. It's not you personally he cares about. It's his country. The safety of his child.

"Thank you."

It wasn't what he wanted me to say. That much was evident in the way he continued to stare at me, as if waiting for something more.

"Please. Let's talk about something else."

My plea stretched from my balcony to his, drifting on the breeze, hanging like a line between us. I didn't want to beg but neither was I ready to go inside yet, and I couldn't talk about this.

"My suit of armor seems to have changed outfits again," he said finally. "Your doing?"

My eyes slid shut for a moment as I smiled, and thanked him profusely in my head for the topic change.

Lucie, Kahra, Ryan, and I had swapped Sir Rusty's latest outfit for a lime green scarf, blue jacket and pink glasses yesterday morning. Ryan had giggled when I'd lifted him up to put the glasses on. The sound had gone straight to my heart.

"Maybe." I wasn't admitting to anything, even though he clearly knew it was me.

"He was never dressed before you arrived."

"An oversight indeed." It was nice to see this more playful side of Marcos. I'd been starting to wonder if he even had a sense of humor. Maybe he needed the occasional break from reality as much as me. "Poor Rusty was feeling a little cold."

"Rusty, is it?"

"Sir Merrett Tanner Coulson the Somewhat Rusty, actually. Although he prefers Sir Rusty."

A sound that might have been a smothered laugh—or just as easily an offended huff—came from Marcos's balcony. "I'm not surprised."

I grinned. "Please don't tell the girls you know."

"Of course not. Although Lucie is likely going to tell me herself any night now."

He wasn't wrong. Poor Lucie was going to have a bruised shin if Kahra didn't stop kicking her under the table, but Lucie was determined to get a reaction out of her older brother. Last night, she'd gone all out, asking Marcos first if he thought the guards should have a new uniform—green scarves would be a nice touch, she suggested—then if he'd seen her friend who'd been wearing a blue jacket and glasses. According to her, said friend had been last seen near Marcos's office. A particularly swift kick from Kahra and its accompanying glare had silenced Lucie before she could come up with any other ways to ask. Marcos, as per usual, had kept a completely straight face the entire time.

"Do you mind?" *Please say no. Please say no. Please say no.*

He shook his head. "It's nice to have something to share with them."

His words were light—that almost smile still on his face—but there was a sadness to his words.

"You don't spend much time with your sisters?" Kahra had mentioned that, but it hadn't occurred to me Marcos might be feeling the same loss.

"Not as much as I should." He sighed. "I don't know what to say to them anymore. We have so little in common these days. They're so young."

I could have argued that the age gap between Marcos and his sisters wasn't all that large, only I knew exactly what he meant. I'd thought the same when I first met them. It wasn't a case of numbers. It was life experience. They were beautiful girls, but sheltered.

"And…I don't know…Maybe I've been avoiding them somewhat too, ever since that night with Rachana."

"You felt guilty?"

"I didn't want them to turn out like me. And I didn't want to be there when they realized their hero and the big brother they thought could do no wrong had disappointed them. I disappointed them all—Hodenia, my father, my sisters. Mom. Her especially. She's so happy to have a grandson and adores Ryan, but I know she wishes she'd gotten to know him under different circumstances."

A bunch of platitudes came instantly to mind—*you're not as broken as you think, it'll be okay, it is what it is, they're just pleased to have you back and know Ryan at all*—but that's all they were. Platitudes. True, but poorly timed, and likely to cause far more hurt than help.

"I'm sorry."

He nodded, lost in his thoughts for a few moments more before shaking his head. "What's worse is that I didn't even realize how much I missed Kahra and Lucie until you started dressing my suit of armor."

"They miss you too, Kahra especially."

"Maybe I should take her out for breakfast sometime this week. Just the two of us. Do you think she'd like that?"

I could barely answer past the sudden lump in my throat. "I think she'd love that." And if he kept saying things like that, I was going to burst into tears. Or something equally embarrassing and impossible to explain to him. Time for a redirection. "Just wait till you see Sir Rusty's next outfit."

Marcos smothered a smile. "You're not offending his manhood completely and dressing him as a ballerina or something, are you?"

"Nope. Although it is a costume. Ryan found this one."

"A sea captain?"

"Close." I grinned. "A pirate."

"Ah. Like Pirate Pumpernickel."

"Exactly."

Marcos leaned his shoulder against the wall, crossing his arms. Had I ever seen him this relaxed before? "I haven't heard that story for years. You read it well."

I pulled my legs up underneath me on the chair, thinking how nice it was to talk with Marcos like this. Marveling at the fact that he allowed it. "Thank you. Ryan gets so into the story. I love how big his eyes get and that little gasp of breath he does when something happens that takes him by surprise. It makes reading to him a lot of fun."

"I can tell."

How long *had* he been standing outside Ryan's door listening tonight before my attention drove him away? Long enough to hear me read and recognize the story.

"You could have come in."

"I thought about it."

I wanted to ask what stopped him, but it felt too personal. And for all I knew, he'd already been late for the meeting he'd clearly had. Not that I could even in the farthest stretches of my imagination picture Prince Marcos being late for anything. "Maybe tomorrow," I said instead.

"Maybe," was all the reply he gave.

The silence stretched again, with nothing to break it but the breeze. Although even that had lessened as if it, too, was calling it a night.

"Why you?"

Marcos's question came out of nowhere. "Excuse me?"

"Why did you become Ryan's governess?"

Oh. "Because your mother asked me to."

"You could have said no."

Many days, I still wondered if I should have, especially when I thought about leaving. "I wanted to help."

"Ryan?"

"Your whole family," I admitted. "You all looked so lost at the funeral. I thought maybe I could make a difference."

"You have, you know. Made a difference."

"A good one, I hope."

I felt like my presence here was making a difference, every time I saw Ryan smile or heard the girls giggle over the outlandish outfits we dressed Sir Rusty up in every couple of days. When Kahra had kicked off her shoes to tuck her feet up beside her last time we talked and I shared a smile with Queen Galielle across the dinner table. On nights like this when Marcos let go of his worries long enough to stargaze and philosophize with me. But was it changing anything, or was I only a short-term distraction?

His smile warmed its way past my fear and doubts. It was small, but definitely a smile. "Very good. Wenderley—"

He stopped. I waited for him to say more. He shook his head instead. "I should go and let Luka know you're okay. Good night, Lady Wenderley. I hope you sleep well."

I murmured my own goodnight back, watching as he walked inside and carefully closed the door. When I couldn't keep my eyes open any longer, I finally gave in and went to bed.

For the first time in months, I didn't dream about Waitrose.

I dreamed about Marcos.

EIGHTEEN

The rope wouldn't stay, no matter how many times I twisted it around itself and knotted all manner of tangle into it. Every time I let go, it fell again.

Bother.

"Wenderley?"

"Yes?" If I could just get that rope to stay tied, our treehouse-turned-sailing boat would be up and running. Or, rather, sailing. Unfortunately, my knot-tying skills didn't extend much further than the ones I used to tie my shoes each day. Still, I kept trying. At first, it had been for Ryan. It had stopped being for his sake twenty minutes ago. Now, it was purely for my own pride. I refused to be beaten by a stupid piece of rope.

"Do you think they'll keep me?"

The knot unraveled, falling at my feet along with the blanket Ryan and I had repurposed as a sail. I kicked them both aside, the past half hour of determination to make the perfect sail forgotten as I looked into the questioning eyes of the boy who seemed to find a new way every day to break my heart. Before fixing it with his smile. And then breaking it all over again.

Still, maybe he didn't mean what it sounded like. Maybe he meant in that particular room, or at the palace. Royals sometimes lived in places other than the palace, right? He could be asking that.

"I mean, now Mom's gone."

Or he could mean exactly what it sounded like. *Oh, Ryan.* I sat down cross-legged in front of him, hands clasped together.

"You're worried you'll be sent away?" My voice came out remarkably calm given how much the question—or rather, the worry on his face—had shaken me.

"A little bit. I'm trying to be good and quiet and do what I'm told, but there are so many rules and things to remember. Papa only took me because Mom asked him to. What if he sends me away now she's gone?"

Breathe, Wenderley. Hold it together. Answer now. Fall apart later.

"He'd never do that."

"But what if I break something again? Or draw on the wrong book? I know he said sorry, but he was really angry when I did that."

"Ryan, your dad really loves you. You're his son. You always will be. He's not going to send you away. I promise. You can make as much noise and trouble as you like." And if Marcos dared raise his voice again, he'd have me to answer to.

"Really?"

"Yep. You can jump on your bed and run down the hallways and wear crazy colored shoes—"

"Like yours?"

We both looked at my blue shoes. The ones you almost couldn't tell were blue given all the bright yellow sunflowers painted over top of them, with the occasional ladybug lazing on a petal. Sky blue laces finished them off. Much as they were among my favorites, I doubted this particular design would work for Ryan. "Maybe not the sunflowers."

"Yeah, they're kind of girly."

I forced out a laugh. "Dinosaurs would be cool though. Or paint splats or..." *Don't cry, don't cry, don't cry. Shoes, think shoes.* "How about we paint some black and then splatter them with shades of blue and white and maybe a tiny bit of purple? They'd look like a starry sky!"

His eyes widened. "We could do that?"

"Of course." I'd paint him a hundred pairs and find space in his room for every one of them if it made him feel like he belonged here.

"And I'd be allowed to wear them?"

"Well, maybe not everywhere, but definitely around the palace and in your treehouse. Especially while you're captaining our sailing ship. Which, I might add, still needs its flag."

He sent me a tiny smile before picking up a blue marker to outline the lopsided star he'd already drawn. "Almost done."

The worry was gone from his face. I wished I could banish the feeling as easily. My insides still felt as if he'd stuck his tiny hand inside me and squeezed a few vital organs. It would take a while for the bruises to disappear. Was he fine now? Did he believe me? Were kids that resilient that one single answer would be enough? Especially from someone who wasn't even family and, moreover, had been a complete stranger to Ryan three and a half weeks ago. Perhaps that's why he'd felt comfortable asking me.

I stood, going back to the rope, eyes too blurry with heartbreak to try to figure out how to even begin to try to tie it up again. Were my hands shaking? They were shaking. All this time, Ryan thought they'd throw him out if he made a mistake. He must have been terrified that day Marcos yelled at him. And yet, it wasn't as if he'd had a normal, safe childhood to this point. His mother so sick, being introduced to his father, finding out he was a prince. And where had they lived before all that?

A hiccup caught in my throat. He thought they were going to send him away.

Hold it together, Wenderley. He'll get even more worried if he sees you crying.

I had to say something else, if only for my own peace of mind, but what? Time would help, of course, but I hated the thought of him going through the next year or so worrying every moment of every day that he was one mistake away from being banished. *Ryan...*

Wait, that was it.

"Hey Ry? Do you remember your name?"

He stopped coloring and looked up at me with a tiny frown. "Ryan?"

"Prince Ryan Thomas Magnus Dorien of the Kingdom of Hodenia, second in line to the throne."

He nodded. "Papa gave me those extra names. I used to just be Ryan Thomas."

"Exactly. Those extra names were your dad's gift to you, one he gave you in front of lots and lots of people."

"At the big fancy building."

That was one way of describing the centuries old grand building of a chapel. "Yep. At that big fancy building, your dad told everyone that he was your dad and wanted to be forever. It's official, buddy, you're here to stay."

"Forever?"

"Absolutely."

"Oh. Okay."

With a single nod, he went back to his coloring, tongue sticking out the side of his mouth as he concentrated on keeping the yellow from smudging in the blue.

"Your dad really loves you, you know. We all do."

"Including you?"

There went my heart again.

"More than you'll ever know."

"Okay. I like you, too. Do you think this flag needs more stars?"

I knocked on Marcos's office door, silently begging him to be there. Ryan had worked on that flag for another hour after shredding my heart with his question. A full hour of being in that treehouse, doing every single thing I could think of to stop myself from throwing my arms around him and wrapping him in an embrace so tight he'd never worry again. I'd even swept the floor. With a handkerchief. The treehouse had never in its life been so clean. Nor me so worked up. The instant Ryan had sat down with his aunts for afternoon tea, I'd made up an excuse and fled.

"Come in."

He was here. My eyes blurred with tears. Was it relief? Sadness? The fact that, for the past hour and a half I'd been holding in the pain of Ryan's question and finally didn't have to anymore? Whichever one it was, my interrupted sleep last night hadn't helped. I pushed the door open, belatedly realizing Marcos might not be alone.

Thankfully, he was. He sat at his desk, a pile of paper in front of him, pen in his hand. He put it down as soon as he spotted me. "Wenderley?"

My forehead crinkled in an attempt to hold back tears. I didn't know what was worse—scrunching one's face up into a completely unattractive mess in an attempt to stop the tears or crying in front of a prince.

"What is it? Is it Ryan? Is he okay? Are *you* okay?"

"He's f—" I gasped back a sob. The falling apart was as mortifying as it was inevitable. Maybe I should have waited until I was slightly more in control of my emotions before coming to Marcos. But no, he had to know.

"He—He—"

Marcos took my arm, gently pulling me toward a seat, pushing me into it. A tissue appeared next. There was no way to delicately blow one's nose. I didn't bother trying.

"Wenderley, please tell me."

"I'm fine. I mean…okay, just…tired, which makes everything…worse and…" This hiccupping sobbing was the worst. I shook my head and tried to ignore everything but controlling my breathing, something made almost impossible by the fact that Marcos was now crouching in front of me, staring up into my face, his eyes filled with more concern than I could handle. I tried to smile in an attempt to make light of the situation, but I don't think it worked.

"Ryan asked…Ryan thought…"

"Yes?"

"He thought…you were going…send him away."

The words came out in a rush, followed by more tears than I could ever live down.

"He thought…now Rachana…him too…"

My explanation barely made sense but, by the thunderstruck expression on Marcos's face, he must have understood. He pushed another tissue into my hand before walking back to the desk, where he stood beside his chair rather than sitting in it.

"He told you this?"

"In the…treehouse. Just now."

"He thought I was going to send him away?"

It was easier to nod than force more words past the lump of tears I couldn't seem to dislodge from my throat. *Come on, Wenderley. Get a hold of yourself. This is the prince you're falling apart in front of.*

But Ryan…

The tears continued to fall, no matter how many times I wiped them away. The tissue grew soggy in my hand. It would take more strength than I had left to walk over to Marcos's desk and get another one.

Ryan wasn't only quiet because he missed his mom. He was quiet because he was terrified he would be the next to go. Had I done enough to convince him otherwise? Were there *any* words that could convince him?

"What do I do?"

Marcos's question was barely loud enough to hit the walls of the room but, somehow, I heard it. I just wished I had an answer for him. It was so quiet in the office that even the silence seemed to hold its breath.

God, help him. Help them both. Show Ryan how loved he is. Help him feel safe. Give Marcos the words to let his son know how much he cares. Make them a family again.

The tears finally ran out as I sat there silently praying. I should have left. I'd passed on the message, such as it was. And turned into a blubbering mess in the process, something no doubt Marcos wished he'd avoided as much as I did.

"Where is he now? Is he still upset? Should I go to him?"

"I think he's okay. I assured him you'd never send him away. He's with your sisters at the moment, eating afternoon tea. Maybe later, you could—" I stopped. What was I doing, thinking I could tell a father how to be one? It wasn't as if I knew any more than Marcos did about being a parent. "Never mind."

"No, go on. Please. I value your opinion."

"You do?"

"Of course, I do. You're the one who's with Ryan every day."

Yes, but he was Ryan's father. And the prince. And a man whose opinion I valued far more than I should. What if the advice I gave him was terrible? What if it made the whole situation worse? What if—

"Please."

The proud Marcos was gone, and in his place a grieving man. The sadness, the despair in his eyes, the way he gripped that chair, it tore at my emotions and every resolve I had to stay away. It was the funeral all over again, only this time, the person Marcos was grieving was still here. We could make a difference this time. We could help Ryan. We, together. I couldn't stay aloof any more than I could hold back the sunrise.

"I was thinking maybe you might like to come and read to him later. Before he goes to bed. Or have breakfast with him sometimes? Lunch even, if that fits your schedule better. I know you're busy, but the more time he spends with you, the more he'll feel like he really does belong here. With you."

Marcos didn't say anything. He didn't even nod. Just continued to stare at me as I sat there, trying to look confident, despite the fact that I knew my face must be a mottled mess of red from crying so hard. At least I didn't have to add running mascara to that mess. Never in my life had I been so thankful that I didn't wear makeup every day. A minute later, he was still staring, and even my fake confidence was beginning to feel shaky.

"Well…um…I should get back to Ryan," I said, standing.

"Yes."

"Thank you for—" What? The tissues? Not laughing or running in fright while I turned into a completely emotional girl in front of you? Staring at me until *I* ran in fright? "Listening." *Lame, but true enough.*

"Any time."

My traitorous heart read way too much into those two words. I didn't want him to promise me any time. I wanted him to promise me all time. Forever. But I couldn't ask that any more than I could accept it. We were too different. Or, perhaps in terms of regrets, too similar. Whichever it was, there was no point in wishing we could be any more than the two people we were now.

"I'll be there tonight."

"Tonight?"

"To read. To Ryan. Thank you for suggesting it. And thank you for telling me."

I nodded, told my heart to shut up, and fled.

NINETEEN

A week later, I knocked on the door to Marcos's office again, butterflies dancing alongside growing frustration in my stomach as I wondered what I'd done this time and hoping it wouldn't take too long to sort out. Especially since, when I left Ryan happily playing in his room, I'd assured him I'd only be gone a few minutes.

When I'd told Marcos he should spend more time with Ryan, I'd meant *with* him, not summoning me to his office every day to ask how his son was, and offer suggestions as to what *I* should do differently. I loved that Marcos was now coming to say good-night to Ryan every night before bed, but these summons were starting to get old. Marcos always seemed to have an opinion on something.

Monday, he'd wanted to know why I didn't force Ryan to eat his carrots. As if I hadn't spent fifteen minutes trying every trick I remembered my mom using on my brothers to make them eat food they didn't like. There was only so much a person could do when a child had no intention of touching them.

Tuesday, after asking what games Ryan most enjoyed playing, Marcos had mentioned the mess we left in Ryan's room and reminded me—"reminding" being a loose version of the term—that though there were maids who cleaned the palace, they weren't hired specifically to clean up after Ryan.

Wednesday, he questioned Ryan's bedtime routine and requested a list of books I'd both already read to him and planned on reading next. As if I thought that far ahead. I might have added in a few completely ridiculous ones just to be defiant. Including a three-inch thick classic with language in a style so old that most adults I knew hadn't even made it past the first page. Apparently, the joke was totally lost on Marcos, though, since he simply nodded and noted it down.

Thursday, I didn't get a summons. Although that might have been because Marcos was out for the day. For some reason, even though I knew that, I still wondered all day what he'd find wrong with our routine.

Friday, he wanted to know why I let Ryan sleep for so long in the mornings. I didn't even bother to answer that, walking straight back out before I said something which would get me not only thrown out of the palace but the kingdom too. Ryan was awake before seven AM most days. That hardly qualified as sleeping in.

"Come in."

I pushed the door open with a sigh. *Respect, Wenderley. He's the prince and Ryan's father. It's not you. He just wants to make sure his son is properly cared for and get to know his routine. Give the poor man a break.*

"Thank you for coming."

He was a prince. Would be king one day. One didn't exactly ignore a summons. Even when they came almost every day. At least not without a really good excuse. Which, sadly, I hadn't been able to come up with fast enough this time.

"You're leaving next week, I understand?" Marcos asked.

"Yes, Tuesday, all still being well with Mrs. Graham's daughter."

He nodded, his face giving nothing away as to how he felt about that. I was doing my best not to think about it at all.

"I have a proposal I'd like to run by you."

Here we go. Ryan should be spending three hours a day exercising. Why hasn't Ryan started learning multiple languages yet? Could you please start interviewing potential best friends for him? Two would be the optimal number. Six-years-old, like him, is preferable. And make sure they're children who eat their carrots and get up before seven AM. If they read, write novels, are proficient at horse riding, and speak several languages, that would be even better.

"What would you like to discuss this time?"

"Marriage."

"Excuse me?" He was trying to set Ryan up with a wife already? I knew his and Alina's betrothal had been discussed and understood since birth—for all the good that had done the two of them—but really? Ryan was six! Was the princess Marcos was planning on betrothing his son to even born yet? And really, I was only going to be his governess for another week. Hardly long enough for me to be involved in this discussion. Surely he had advisors for moments like this.

"I'd like you to consider marrying me."

"You? *Me?* Sorry…what?" Him? Not Ryan.

"I'd like you to consider marrying me."

He said the sentence exactly the same. As if somehow that would make it make more sense. Marry me. Him. Crown Prince Marcos of Hodenia. I almost laughed. Probably would have if I hadn't been trying to remember how to breathe.

Consider it. Like I hadn't a million times already. Like Prince Marcos proposing hadn't frequented my daydreams far more often than I ever cared to admit. Of course, I'd imagined it a little more romantically. Him being on one knee. Professing love. Something this clearly wasn't.

Not that it mattered anyway. Whatever the reason he was proposing, there was no way I could accept.

"Why?" I asked, dodging the question. "You don't love me."

Say you do and I'll fall to pieces.

And every single one of them will be yours.

"No, but you're a beautiful woman who's fit well into our family and the palace. You're titled, know Hodenia and Peverell equally well having spent your formative years in both and, most importantly, you are someone Ryan trusts."

"Then why not ask me to continue on as Ryan's governess?" Mrs. Graham certainly wouldn't mind staying with her daughter. I was certain she was only coming because she felt so terrible about pulling out in the first place.

"Because a wife better suits my needs."

"Your...*needs*?"

I couldn't help the blush that stained my cheeks, or the way I couldn't quite meet his gaze, though I refused to look away altogether. Something that would have felt far too much like cowering. If this was his idea of a marriage proposal, he had a lot to learn about women.

He frowned for a moment before widening his eyes. "No, not...that. I meant for Hodenia. With my elopement on the eve of the wedding they'd been anticipating all my life and the news of my...well, Ryan...Then Rachana dying, when they were just coming to terms with me being married to her." He shook his head. "Hodenia needs a show of security, something they can count on, to build their trust in me again, something marrying would provide. For that I need a wife, not a governess. You fit all my requirements better than anyone else I know."

How utterly romantic of him.

"Eighteen months ago, you proposed to Alina. Thirteen months ago, you married Rachana. Five weeks ago, you buried her. Don't you think it's a little soon to be focusing on another woman?"

Surely, he had to see how that would look. A relationship with another woman now—especially one as serious as an engagement—wouldn't gain him anything but the title of womanizer. Or worse. No one would believe with such a quick engagement that the two of us hadn't already been in a relationship while he was still married to Rachana.

"I wouldn't announce it immediately. I'd speak with my publicists and advisors to determine the best timing, but they all agree that what is most needed from me right now is a show of security."

"You've spoken to others about this?"

"No, of course not. I wanted to know your thoughts first."

This was crazy. Completely and utterly crazy. He knew that, right? Knew how completely ridiculous this was? Even if it was simply a marriage of convenience—which it would have to be, given the way he'd presented more of a business proposition than an actual marriage proposal—it wasn't right. You couldn't build trust on a foundation as shaky as a rushed marriage, simply for the sake of convenience. There was nothing convenient about grief, and he wasn't the only one mourning for Princess Rachana. Whether they knew her well or not, the whole country was grieving her death.

"Prince Marcos, I appreciate the offer and am flattered by your proposal but—" Was I really doing this? "No."

"You don't want to marry me?"

That wasn't what I said. At all. "I'm honored you would choose me, and I would love to care for Ryan and be there for him as he grows, he's a truly amazing child, but I can't. I'm sorry."

"I see. Would it change your mind if I told you I cared for you?"

Did he? My traitorous heart leapt for an instant before reality forced it back into place. He didn't. He'd already admitted that. And it would only make it worse if he did care, because then I'd be breaking not only my heart but his as well. One regret-filled heart was pain enough.

"It might have. Once upon a time. But—" Even if I could hide my failures from Marcos, even if the timing wasn't terrible and I believed it would work and one day he might come to care for me, Waitrose would never let it happen. It was as if he liked having that bit of control over me. He hadn't forced me into anything yet but those mint green letters each month never let me forget that he could. And I would never enter into such a sacred relationship as marriage without complete honesty, which would mean telling Marcos everything. No matter which way I looked at it, I lost.

"I wish I could help you," I told him. "I really do. But I can't."

"I'm sorry."

Me too. More than he could possibly imagine.

Would I walk out of this room and wonder for the rest of my life if I'd made the wrong decision telling him no? Probably.

Highly likely.

"I could stay, for another week or two, if it would be helpful. With Ryan's transition to Mrs. Graham, I mean."

What? Wenderley, really? Why would you offer that? Why would you do that to yourself? You've already stayed too long.

"You would?"

The emotion crossing his face was too brief for me to put into words exactly what it was. Relief? Care? Hope? It was there one instant and gone the next but enough that I couldn't take back the offer.

"Yes."

"I'd appreciate that. Thank you."

TWENTY

Ryan wasn't in his room when I got back. At least this time, he wasn't in his father's office. I knew. I'd just come from there. For better or worse.

Did Marcos really propose? Did I really turn him down? It felt too surreal to have actually happened, even though I knew it did. Marcos. Prince Marcos of Hodenia. Proposing to me. Even if he didn't love me. Even if I'd said no. It still happened. He still asked.

And you still can't find his son. Come on, Ryan, where are you?

After four days of dismal rain, I'd been so excited to wake to bright sunshine today. The grass had glistened with leftover raindrops, their jewel-like appearance likely hiding the mud beneath them, but I didn't care. The sun was shining, the sky clear of clouds and I'd been determined to spend as much time as we could outside today.

And then Marcos's summons had come.

"Ryan? Ryan?"

He was supposed to be in his room waiting for me to get back, but I should have known better than to think he would be. It was as if that assurance in the treehouse that he belonged had set something loose inside him. Instead of toeing the line this past week, he raced over it. Between Marcos's daily summons and Ryan's sudden enthusiasm for life, I'd barely had a moment's peace all week.

One of the days—I couldn't even remember which in all the craziness—in the time it had taken me to wash my hands, Ryan had helped himself to a delicate vase, dumped the flowers out of it, and used it all to make a hunting ground for his toy horses. Flowers became trees, leaves became tunnels, the water was quite obviously a river—through his carpet, no less—and the vase itself was laid on its side to become the ultimate cave. Much as I panicked at the thought of him breaking such a valuable vase, I couldn't fault his creativity, especially when he turned those dark eyes on me, handed me his favorite horse, and asked if I wanted to be the captain of the guard.

Two days later, I'd found him trying to saddle a horse in the stables. Much to the amusement of the grooms who he'd apparently ordered not to help. He was going to do this himself. I'd perched myself on a bench next to the grooms and watched as he'd dragged the heavy, full-sized saddle—almost as big as he was—over to his horse's stall, stood on a step stool, and reached up as high as he could to try to throw it over the very patient horse's back. The expression of absolute pride on his face when he got it was worth every bit of panic I'd felt while rushing around the palace, trying to find the boy. He'd been so focused on hefting up the saddle that he hadn't seen the groom on the other side, carefully pulling it into place. We'd all clapped and cheered when he turned around, thrust a fist into the air and said gleefully, "I did it!"

Another day, while Ryan, Lucie, Kahra, and I were in the Gift Room trying to find another outrageously ridiculous outfit for Sir Rusty, Ryan had told me he was going to the bathroom only to get distracted by the aromas coming from the kitchens, which, of course, he had to investigate. Chef Meyer claimed she planned on sending him right back, after a cookie.

Of course, that was before he'd talked his way into three cookies, a glass of chocolate milk, a piece of pie leftover from dessert the night before, and—to be healthy—an apple. Cut into the shape of an owl. I never did find out if he'd been to the bathroom. It was all I could do to keep up with him.

I peeked my head into the kitchen, an amused shake of Chef Meyer's head confirming he wasn't there before I even had to ask.

"Not today, although you make sure both of you come and get your morning tea in half an hour or so. I might have found time to make the apple pies young Ryan requested." I grinned and assured her we would. Ryan wasn't the only one who loved Chef Meyer's apple pies.

The school room was next, not that I expected him to be there. He wasn't. Neither was he in his playroom, the nursery, the treehouse, or back in the Gift Room.

"Ryan?" I called into his bedroom, wondering how much of the palace I would have to search before I found the little scamp.

There was no way he was hiding under his quilt again, straight as it lay, completely devoid of wrinkles—the maids must have tidied this room already—but I checked all the same. And in his closet. He wasn't behind any of the curtains either, something I'd learned to check.

"Ryan?"

I was just about to head to the stables when I heard his giggle, muffled but close. Was he in the closet after all? A second more-thorough search ruled that out. He wasn't in this room. But then, how could I hear—?

Marcos's room. He had to be in there. Marcos's suite was right next door to Ryan's—something I'd tried to avoid remembering from the day, three weeks ago, when I'd realized. That would explain the muffledness of the giggle but the fact that I could still hear it. The question was, did I have the courage to go find him? After all, that was the prince's bedroom. I mean, so was this one, but this was a little boy's room. And that was—Marcos's. The one place in the palace, maybe even the world, that was just his.

I walked out of Ryan's room and down the hall a whole two steps till I was standing in front of Marcos's door. Was I really doing this? Maybe I should find Luka to go in. Only I didn't know where Luka was, and who knew how much damage a six-year-old could do in the time it took me to find Luka? Marcos was, of course, completely out of the question. No way was I risking him finding out about this.

Another giggle came from within, along with the sound of

bouncing. *Oh no.* What was Ryan doing now? There was nothing for it, I'd just have to go in. With a knock which wouldn't have even startled a fly, I cracked open the door, peeking through the quarter of an inch gap to the suite beyond.

"Ryan?" I whispered.

No answer. Not that it surprised me with the full-blown laughter now bursting from inside. I pushed the door wider, just enough for me to slip through. "Ryan!"

Still no answer. I tiptoed through the suite's entry foyer and sitting area toward the sound, trying my best not to be distracted by the simple elegance of the room, so different from the mish-mash of colors in Ryan's. Whoever had designed this room had impeccable taste. Not that I was thinking about that, or anything. Certainly not the fact that I was in Marcos's suite. At least no one would have to know. I'd grab Ryan and we'd be out of here before anyone saw us.

There were three doors leading off the sitting area but only the one in the middle was open. I walked toward that one, hoping not to have to open any others. I'd already invaded as much of Marcos's privacy as my guilt could handle. The split second of relief I felt at finding Ryan there turned to horror as I saw he was jumping on a huge wood-framed bed which could only have been Marcos's. The little prince was going to be in trouble for this, no matter how sweetly he turned those gorgeous dark eyes on me.

"Prince Ryan Thomas Magnus Dorien of Hodenia, you get off that bed this instant! You know as well as I that you're not supposed to be in here."

"It's fine. I told him he could."

My head spun around so fast, my balance couldn't keep up, a blind grasp at the doorway the only thing stopping me from falling. "Marcos? What are you—"

I choked on the rest of the sentence as my gaze landed on the prince. The one who was supposed to still be in his office not *here*, despite it being his room. The one who'd been in a tailored black suit, as per usual, fifteen minutes ago. The one who looked heart-stoppingly good in jeans and a blue polo. The one who'd asked me to marry him not even half an hour ago, and I'd said no to. *Remind me again why you said no?* That color on him, those arms...*Oh boy*...

"Wenderley? Are you well?"

What, because I was so close to hyperventilating I might have actually swayed toward the man? Because I'd swallowed enough gulps of air to keep a submarine afloat? Because I was standing dumbly in the entrance to his bedroom, staring at him as if he was wearing just a towel?

Oh Wenderley, don't even go there...

"I was, just—" Blushing like a crazy person. I'd never seen the need for makeup before. Right now, I was wishing for every bit of it I could find to cover the telltale redness of my cheeks. Actually, forget makeup. A pillowcase over my head would be far more effective.

"I, uh—" He was still staring at me, even going so far as to walk a few steps toward me. Did I look like I was about to fall over or something? *Oh, kill me now.* I'd never felt this incapacitated around Prince Thoraben. *Get a grip, Wenderley Davis!* "It's, um..." *Words, Wenderley, useful things. Think of some. And stop blushing for goodness' sake.* "It's time for Ryan's morning tea. Chef Meyer made apple pies."

With a squeal of excitement, Ryan jumped off the bed and ran out the door. I wished my brain would work at even a quarter of the speed of his feet. *Oh boy, he's coming closer. Please, Marcos, leave a discombobulated pathetic excuse for a woman alone to her romantic disillusions...*

Even my subconscious could talk better than me.

Marcos stopped just short of me, gesturing to the door. "Shall we?"

I dropped my gaze in an attempt not to stare at the dark pieces of chest hair peeking out from his unbuttoned collar. Bad idea. Now all I could see was his trim waist, where the shirt tucked into his jeans. My hands jerked forward before I realized what I was thinking and forced them back again. *Embracing Prince Marcos?*

Seriously, Wenderley? You told him you couldn't marry him, remember? Waitrose. Think of Waitrose.

That took some of the blush out of my cheeks, but not even Waitrose could totally distract me. Muttering something even I couldn't understand, I ducked back out the doorway and fled.

"Wenderley?"

My eyes closed, the handle of the door to the hallway and freedom in my hand. So close. Here it came. The questions. The admonition for being in his room. The reminder that I was supposed to be caring for Ryan, not letting the imp run wild. The mortifying reminder that the only reason he wanted me for a wife was because I "fit" into his life. And I'd told him no anyway.

"Do you think Chef Meyer made enough pies for me to have some too? Apple pie is my favorite."

Like father, like son.

I pushed all emotion from my face except a careful smile. "I'm sure she has plenty."

Then I fled.

I'd run the whole way to the kitchen before realizing that Marcos was probably heading the same way. At least the kitchens were warm enough to account for the ridiculous blush still solidly stamped across my face when I looked up from Ryan to see the questions in Marcos's eyes. *Yes, you've let a complete imbecile into your house.*

Thankfully, he didn't ask. I wouldn't have had a proper answer to give him anyway. All the same, I kept my mouth full the whole time he sat there, just in case. It was only after he'd gone that I realized I'd eaten three and a half pieces of pie. No wonder my stomach hurt.

TWENTY-ONE

My heart thudded as I sat on my balcony that night, so loud I wondered if I'd even hear Marcos if he did come out. Which was ridiculous given he likely wouldn't and it shouldn't matter to me if he did. He was a prince, with so many more important things to do than stargaze in the post-midnight hours with me. Like sleep, for one thing. And yet, still, he came.

The first couple of weeks when he'd come out, we'd barely said a word to each other beyond social niceties, but since that night I'd run from Luka and Marcos came to check on me, he'd been staying longer. Coming more often. He'd been out most nights this week. Our conversations were never particularly deep. We'd talk about the weather, the stars, what Ryan had done that day, what he might do tomorrow. Simple inconsequential things, and yet, I always slept better the nights after I spoke with Marcos. He was a different person out here on our respective balconies. As if he left the title of prince in his room and came out simply as Marcos.

Every night he said the same thing as he left. *Good night, Lady Wenderley. I hope you sleep well.*

It felt like a benediction. A term of endearment, almost.

Oh, for goodness' sake, Wenderley. He's just saying goodnight. He doesn't mean anything by it. Remember, this is the man who asked you to marry him with a business proposition. You tick all the boxes. Yeah, he's really that romantic.

It was as ridiculous as me waiting out here for the man I should have been staying as far away from as I could.

What would I even say to Marcos if he did come out? He'd proposed, for goodness' sake. I still couldn't believe he'd done that. Or that I'd been strong enough to say no. Or that I'd made such a complete fool of myself in his room afterwards, and then the kitchen, after that.

Pray for him, God had asked, not fall in love with him.

But the more I prayed, the more I cared. Had God known this would happen? *Duh Wenderley, of course he did.* But then, why? Why me? Or were there others like me, all across Hodenia and maybe even Peverell, praying specifically for Prince Marcos, and it was only me who'd been weak enough to fall for the man, despite myself?

I flicked at a bug which landed on the arm of my chair. It buzzed over to the potted plant and crashed wildly into the window before landing back where it started, right beside my hand. This time I left it, getting up myself. Not because I was scared of bugs but because I was too nervous to sit anyway. Would Marcos come? Should I want him to? I'd already told him there could be nothing between us. Not while Waitrose held that night over my head. And yet, here I stood, waiting. Wishing. Wanting so desperately for him to come.

You're torturing yourself. You know that, right?

Yes. Of course, I did. But who knew how much longer I'd be here? An extra week and then what? I'd leave. That's what. Go back to being Lady Wenderley Davis, most sympathized and public broken heart in all of Peverell. Would I ever live down the title? It had been over a year. Or would I forever be known as the girl Prince Thoraben didn't choose?

The balcony door opened before I could muse myself back into depression, Marcos letting himself out before closing it behind him. He looked straight over at my balcony, nodding when he spotted me there. I told my wildly skittering heart that it didn't mean anything, but the line of communication between my mind and heart was most definitely down. Severed, no doubt, the moment I'd agreed to stay.

"Wenderley…"

My name had never sounded so beautiful.

"Marcos, hi…hello…that is…it's good to see you."

Nor had my mouth ever failed so spectacularly to function. Well, with the exception of this morning. Clearly, I was having a bad day. I shook my head at my own foolishness and pretended to look at the stars, even though none of the clouds I'd been staring up at for the past hour while I waited had moved enough to let any peek through. *Just a man, Wenderley. Forget he's a prince. You're a woman, he's a man. You can just be two friends talking. Plenty of people manage it every day. It's perfectly normal. This doesn't have to be awkward.*

Only nothing about Marcos or this situation seemed normal. Even this late at night, he still stood straight, the rules of posture so ingrained in him that I doubted he could slouch if he tried. But it was more than posture. More than the suits he wore or the hair which never strayed out of place or the depth of his glances. There was something about Prince Marcos of Hodenia that screamed royalty. A power about him. As if even the air around him bowed when it saw him coming.

God, thank you for this man. Thank you for letting me know him, even this smallest bit. Give him courage and wisdom and strength to be the best prince—and one day king—that he can be. Bring him to you. May he know you and the—

"You're quiet tonight."

I was? Really? Oh, of course. He couldn't hear the frantic thudding of my heart or the way my brain skittered from anxiety to excitement to fear to happiness. Neither did he hear my prayers, so loud in my ears.

"Just thinking."

"About?"

You.

"Hodenia. Stars. Posture. Sympathy. The palace. God. The future."

"An interesting list."

"Welcome to the female mind." He didn't know the half of it. All that merely masked the fact that I was still debating whether I should have said yes to his proposal. Even though I knew that no was the right—and only—answer I could have given. "What were you thinking?"

"Honestly?"

"Of course."

"Nothing."

"Oh."

The corner of his mouth tilted upward, not quite a smile but certainly amused by my response. "Sorry. I guess you were hoping for something more."

"It would have been more interesting, yes."

"How about what I was thinking just before I came out? Would that satisfy your curiosity?"

"Yes."

He looked over at me, smiled that half smile again and looked away. "I was thinking about you."

Oh. *Oh.* I let my heart feel that. Every tingly, beat-skipping, giddily-dancing, guilt-inducing word of it. He was thinking about me.

Of course, that didn't mean it was a good thing. He could have been thinking about how annoying it would be for him if I'd invaded his personal balcony time again, or how he should really get on to me about that teaching Ryan four more languages thing, or how overly bright and inappropriate my clothing was for a royal household, or how I ruined his grand plan of redemption in the eyes of H—

"I was hoping you'd be out here tonight."

"Any particular reason?"

"Is enjoying your company enough of one?"

Definitely a good thing then. "Yes."

We lapsed into silence then, him because that's what he did

and me, because my brain was too giddy to even contemplate putting two actual words together. He liked being with me.

Hear that, little bug? I said silently to the bug which had now decided the chair wasn't as exciting as crawling beside my hand. *He likes me. Well, being with me. Which is probably a good distinction to keep in mind since…* Since I wasn't staying.

If not for Waitrose, would I have let myself hope?

No, I'd decided the day Thoraben married Kenna that I'd never fall for another prince. They came with too many people watching. Fall, fail, and the entire kingdom knew. Plus, marry a prince and I'd forever be relegated to nude heels and demure pantsuits. No more jeans. No more clashing beaded bracelets. Certainly, no more brightly colored high-tops.

Only, on nights like tonight, when the two of us stood on our respective balconies and stared up at the sky, so content in each other's presence that words weren't needed, it was all too easy to forget Marcos came with all that.

"Did Mother ask you about the Holiday Party?"

"She did, yes."

"And?"

"And I agreed to accompany Ryan, of course." Like I would have said no. Even if it was the most boring event in the history of the world, I would have agreed. For Ryan. The fact that I'd wanted for years to go to one only added to the delight.

Marcos tilted his head slightly, staring at my face until I was certain he could see right through to my mind. "You're excited about it."

I leaned a hip against the balcony's ledge, turning to face Marcos. "And you know that how?"

"You're smiling."

Really? That was his justification?

"I smile all the time." Unlike him.

"True, but this one is different. Childlike almost."

"Are you calling me a child?"

"No, of course not. Forgive me, Lady Wenderley. I didn't in any way mean to insinuate that—"

"Prince Marcos?"

"Yes."

"I was teasing."

"Oh." He frowned. "You were?"

I cringed. "Sorry. That's probably inappropriate, teasing the prince and all that."

"No, it's fine. No one has teased me for years."

"Are you certain about that?"

"Are you teasing me again?"

I grinned. "Yes. Sorry, again. You're just so serious all the time."

"Ruling a country is serious."

"I know, but don't you ever just laugh? Let yourself relax?"

He looked away. "You say that like it's an easy thing. People always want something from me, wherever I go. A wave, a photo, a speech, a signature on their proposal." He shrugged. "A paragon. Now, more than ever, I can't let my guard down."

"But being perfect all the time? There has to be one place you can let down your guard."

"There has been lately."

"Oh?"

"Here. With you."

His words hit me like a hammer to the gut. *I* was the one person in the world he could relax around? I felt so honored, and, at the same time, saddened. One person. And I was leaving.

"What about with Rachana? Could you be yourself around her?"

"Maybe, if we'd had more time, I might have been able to, but I didn't even know her last name until the day we married. She tried. *We* tried, but it's difficult to really get to know a person when you know any day they might be gone. Preparing Ryan for what was to come seemed far more important than getting to know each other."

Oh Marcos.

God, I—

I couldn't even form the words to pray for him. My heart ached with all he'd been through but, more, the strength he'd had to show. When they were engaged, Alina had frequently complained about Marcos being so uptight—or was it upright? —that he refused to even kiss her until the day they married. How long had he been holding himself together?

Since that night when he was seventeen?

I had to change the subject before my heart broke beyond what could be repaired.

"Um…"

Of course, coming up with a topic before opening my mouth would have been a good idea. Hindsight was a killer.

"I'm not going to ask you to marry me again, if that's what you're worried about," he said wryly.

"No, I…uh…" *Love you. Forever and always. I'll be here for you. I'll be your safe place.* So many things I felt. None of them I could say.

"But yes, I've come to truly value your friendship."

Marcos…

Topic change. Now.

"You spent part of your childhood in Hodenia, didn't you?" Marcos asked. "Did you ever come to one of our Holiday Parties?"

There went Marcos, saving me from my own foolish heart, yet again. Yes, the party was definitely a good choice of topics.

"I was too old by the time we moved here. So, no."

"No wonder you're excited."

It must have seemed so silly, for an adult to be so excited about a children's party. An adult who'd grown up attending fancy balls and all manner of royal events. Especially to Prince Marcos, who'd probably been to twenty or more. "Is that weird?"

"No. It's refreshing. I've been to so many of them that sometimes I forget how much fun they can be. It's nice to be reminded."

"Your mother said you were involved. Dare I ask how?"

"The dunk tank."

I let out a short laugh. "Really?"

"Every year. My father and I take turns."

"You're serious?" Thoraben, I could imagine doing such a

thing. He would do anything to make his people smile, but Marcos? *King Dorien?* "No way."

"You don't believe me?"

"No." Although if he kept smiling that mischievous smile, I might be convinced to change my mind. "You'd get your suit wet."

"You do know I have other clothes, right?"

As of a few hours ago, I did. The pair of jeans and blue polo shirt which I was still trying to get out of my head. But he didn't need any reminder of that. I gestured to the suit he was still wearing. "Case in point."

"I had a meeting. I haven't changed yet."

"It's after midnight."

"The meeting went late."

"You didn't change after?"

"I didn't want to miss you."

And we were back to me trying not to melt into a puddle. Everything in me wanted to ask why he was so eager to see me. If I could have accepted whatever answer he gave without it changing everything, I would have. But a question like that had far too much potential to change everything. Or nothing. In which case, I'd leave disappointed, because these balcony chats, and the man I shared them with, meant everything to me.

"How was your meeting?" I asked instead, listening as he answered vaguely like I knew he would. He couldn't tell me details. He never did, and I didn't expect them. But I still asked, because every night he came out looking like the weight of the world lay on his shoulders alone. And every night, I wished that I could help him carry the load.

God, open Marcos's eyes to you. Let him see how much you care. Give him someone to stand with him and love him so he doesn't have to do this alone.

And, God?

I sighed out into the night. *No, forget it.*

I had no right to ask and dared not even think the words—especially after declining Marcos's proposal—but I couldn't deny there was more to that prayer. Deep in my heart. Beyond all logic and rational thought and what I knew could never be. The yearning as I looked across at Marcos on his balcony in the quiet of night.

Let that someone be me.

TWENTY TWO

The day of the Holiday Party arrived. Ryan wanted to know why I was so excited. It's a kids' party, he reminded me. As if that wasn't exactly why. Yes, it was a kids' party and, at the very heart of us, weren't we all kids wanting to throw off our responsibilities, fears, and too much knowledge, and simply be children again?

The morning had been long, Ryan's nerves mixing with my excitement to make every minute drag into an hour and the hours feel like days. But, finally, it was five o'clock and time to leave.

Taking Ryan's hand, I skipped down the hallway. This was the girl I'd missed being for too many years—the one who skipped and laughed without wondering who was watching and how loud. For the first time, maybe ever, I wasn't just okay or resigned to Thoraben marrying Kenna but actually happy. Relieved, even.

"Far too many ballgowns," I muttered, thinking of yet another photo spread I'd seen this morning of Kenna in five different outfits from two events.

"What did you say?" Ryan asked.

"Far too many steps," I said. "We should slide down the banister."

"Won't we get in trouble?"

"From whom?"

"Papa."

"He's not here."

"Yes, he is. He's right behind you."

What? I spun around, half laughing, half choking when I saw Marcos was, indeed, right behind me, that inscrutable expression back on his face as he waited to see what I'd do. Well, not even Prince Marcos and his stuffiness was going to ruin my fun today. "Even better," I told Ryan, shooting a grin at Marcos. "He's going to go down first."

"He is?"

"I am?"

Marcos, back in his customary full black suit, tie, and mirror-shiny shoes, was looking at me as if he wasn't sure whether to thank me or throttle me.

"Sure." I stood to my full height—which still only got the top of my head to about Marcos's nose—and crossed my arms. "You've done it before, right?"

He hadn't. That much was obvious in the way he frowned at me. Nor did he have any intention of doing so tonight. Only I couldn't back down now.

"I used to do it all the time at home," I said. "Although never with a banister so long. This is going to be so much fun." The enthusiasm I put in my voice did nothing to Marcos's frown, which was quickly turning into a glare. Uh oh.

"Can we really, Papa?"

Marcos looked down at his son, then at me. I begged him with my eyes to give it a go.

Come on, Marcos. Don't leave me on the ledge here. Be fun. Show Ryan that being a prince isn't all boring speeches and uncomfortable suits.

"You're certain it's safe?" he asked me, quietly. "What if he slips over the other side?"

I looked over the edge. It was quite a drop. Still, "I'll be beside him. Stop procrastinating. Are you scared or something?"

I said it teasingly, before looking at his face. He was scared. Or, at least, apprehensive. *Nice going, Wenderley.* "Sorry, you don't have to…"

"Let's give this a go, shall we?"

Anyone who said Marcos wasn't a good father had no idea

what they were talking about. Any father who'd put his own fears aside for the good of his child was the best father possible. I could have kissed him.

He was gone before the thought could turn my cheeks red, sliding down the rail and dropping right off the end with a thud on the floor. I probably should have warned him to hold on tighter at the end so that didn't happen. Poor guy was going to have a sore tailbone for the rest of the evening. But, to his credit, he jumped right back up again, smiled, and called out to Ryan that it was his turn—and stayed right at the end ready to catch his son before he suffered a similar fate.

I helped Ryan up, told him to hold on tight and grinned as he let himself fly. That smile. It was worth every bit of embarrassment, work, and lack of sleep to see it.

"Your turn, Lady Wenderley."

Oh. Right. My turn. Of course it was. I'd had every intention of sliding down after Ryan a few minutes ago. Before Marcos took up his position right at the foot of the stairs. I was wearing jeans so the whole lack of modesty with a dress wasn't the issue but… well…the view of me which Marcos would get from there wasn't exactly flattering.

"Don't worry, I'll make sure you don't fall," Marcos said.

As if that was what had me hesitating.

"Come on, Wenderley. You were right, it *was* fun," Ryan called up.

Every bit of embarrassment…

I turned my back on both of them and lifted a leg over the banister, trying to find a semi-comfortable position. This had been a lot easier when I was a child. Before I had, uh, shape. *Oh, just get on with it, Wenderley. You were the one who suggested it.*

My descent was far slower than my two predecessors' had been, my hands so suddenly clammy that I had to push myself down rather than gravity doing all the work. I jumped off before Marcos could offer to catch me.

"Well, then, that was fun," I said to Ryan, refusing to look in his father's direction. "Shall we go?"

"Actually, you're coming in my car," Marcos said. "Luka is going to drive the three of us." He gestured to his Head of Security, standing near the door. Luka, who did nothing to hide his amusement at what he'd clearly witnessed. *Wenderley, you really need to check who's around you before you decide to let your childish side rule your common sense.* So much for avoiding Marcos until my embarrassment gave way to the amusement of retrospect. Now, I'd be sitting in a car with him for the next half hour. And Luka too.

At least my backside won't be on display.

It was a small win, but I'd take it. The big win was the delight on Ryan's face as he took one of my hands, one of his father's, and skipped in between the two of us to the waiting car.

Definitely worth it.

The Holiday Party was everything I'd imagined—and so much more. The location was like a secret hideaway all of itself, a giant open field, surrounded by tall trees and only accessible by a tunnel covered with lights. Thousands more of the tiny lights spun around every tree in the field, making the entire place feel like a magical fairyland where anything could happen. Add to that the live music, joy-filled laughter of children, swirling ribbons of rainbow-garbed stilt-walkers, gingerbread-style life-sized cottages scattered around, and the smell of roasted apples, cinnamon, and some type of roast meat hovering over it all, and I was one happy camper. I could have stood in one place all day and night with my eyes closed and just breathed in the delight.

"What do you think?"

Marcos's voice was close to my ear, the only reason I could hear his quiet question over the noise. Not that I could answer said question.

"It's..." I breathed in the wonder and breathed out a sigh. "Incredible. Absolutely incredible."

There was definite pride in Marcos's expression this time, as if he'd set up the entire thing himself. Just for me. No, what was I thinking? This had nothing to do with me. The only reason I was here was for Ryan since I was well beyond the age of ten. Marcos was proud because Ryan had that same look of delight on his face, not because I felt like I'd been given the world and as much time as I liked to explore it.

"Well, I have to go and get ready."

"For the dunk tank." I raised my eyebrows at Marcos, daring him to tell the truth.

"You still don't believe me."

"No." Although I would have paid quite a bit to have a go at dunking him if he was telling the truth. But there was no way it was. That was something I'd do, not the esteemed Prince Marcos of Hodenia. Even if he was trying to redeem his reputation.

"Bring Ryan to the far side of the field in an hour. You'll see. In the meantime, there's a circus performance starting soon in the main tent, the royal zoo has some amazing animals or, if you're hungry, the best food is that way." He pointed to our left. "Enjoy yourselves."

He left then, off to—apparently—man the dunk tank with his father. We'd be there for sure. But, until then… I grinned down at my young charge. "So, Prince Ryan, what do you want to do first?"

"Ryan?"

Where was he? My heart beat frantically as I spun around, searching every face in the crowd for the little prince. *Calm down, Wenderley. He was beside you seconds ago. He can't have gone far.*

Maybe he'd walked back to look at the animals. He'd liked them, the parrots especially. Or the glass-blowing stall? I would have been happy to watch that man work for hours, the way the molten glass rose and fell in swirling colors. But Ryan would have told me, wouldn't he? *Ryan, where are you?*

I walked slowly back past the animals and the glass blower, checking every person. He wasn't there. Nor was he near the magician or among a crowd of children marveling at the man juggling ceramic plates while balancing on a table, three planks, two balls, and a triangle. The whole place was filled with plain-clothes security teams. I could ask them and have Ryan found in minutes, but I wanted to find him myself. And not only because Marcos was heading toward me.

Uh oh. I could just see how this was going to go. *Where's Ryan?*

I don't know.

You don't know?

He was right beside me.

He's not now.

I know…

Yeah, maybe not. What was Marcos doing back here anyway? Call me a doubter, but I'd checked with Queen Galielle when we'd seen her near the circus tent, and Marcos and his father really were participating in a dunk tank. Ryan and I had been heading in that direction to have a go when I'd turned to notice him missing.

God, help? Please? You know where he is.

I ducked around a man passing two pink balloons to his daughter and a woman pushing a stroller. Wait, was that…

"Ryan." Finally. Sitting tucked in between two stalls, it was no wonder I hadn't seen him. He was sitting on the grass, his face tucked in to his knees. He raised it when I said his name. His face was streaked with tears. "Oh honey, what is it?"

Ducking between ropes and tent sides not quite wide enough for two people, I folded myself in beside him, wrapping an arm around the trembling boy. His tears only increased, wetting the side of my shirt as we sat there together. Marcos peered in. I answered his silent question of whether his son was okay with a shrug. He walked into the small gap and sat himself down, suit and all, on the grass in front of us. His hand went to Ryan's knee.

"Ryan?"

Ryan looked up then. The instant he saw Marcos sitting there, he tried to stop the tears, to no avail. They kept coming. If I'd been a real governess, I would have had a tissue to give him. The best I could do was the napkin I'd scavenged from one of the food tents to write the time of Marcos's dunk tank appearance on.

"Ryan, what's the matter?" I tried again, deciding to do my best to ignore Marcos. Again, better said than done, given the sweet way he was trying so hard to be there for his son.

"Mom would have loved this."

"Oh, honey." Rachana. Of course. I hated how easy it was for me to forget her existence. When I was with Ryan and Marcos, I often forgot there'd been another person in their lives.

Which was completely ridiculous given all of Hodenia knew her name and was still grieving her, as much as one could a relative stranger.

But she hadn't been a stranger to Ryan. She'd been his mother. His only family until just over a year ago. His entire world.

"She liked fairs?"

"She liked anything that made me smile."

Of course she did. Just seeing Ryan smile made my entire day, and I'd only known him for four weeks. I could only imagine what it did to his mother. "She'd be happy you're enjoying yourself."

"But she's not here."

"No." It wasn't a profound answer, an encouraging one, or even all that helpful, but it was the truth. "I'm so sorry."

People walked past the stalls we sat between, some looking in at the three people sitting there, most simply passing by. I don't know how long the three of us sat there, listening as the noises of the party swirled around us. Laughter, music, chatter, crying babies, giggling children, the occasional pop of a balloon and the screech of fright which inevitably accompanied it.

But between the three of us, only the hiccupping breathing of a child trying to hold it together.

"Did you want to go home?" Marcos finally asked.

"Could I?"

I was wondering the same thing. This was the Holiday Party. Most kids' dream come true. Everything they could have wanted, and all for free. If nothing else, Ryan was expected to be here. Queen Galielle had been so excited to share it with her grandson.

Marcos too. Ryan had barely been here forty minutes. Hardly long enough to be seen, let alone see everything.

"Of course. There will be plenty of these parties for you to go to over the years. Let me get Luka and we'll take you home."

TWENTY-THREE

Marcos got up, brushing grass off his suit as he ducked through the gap and out into the crowd. He was barely gone a minute before gesturing us out. He walked all the way back to the car and, when I thought he'd leave, got in beside Ryan.

"You're coming?" I asked in surprise.

"It's fine."

He was supposed to be on the dunk stall. And making a speech at the end of the party to thank everyone for coming. And likely hadn't had time to eat or speak with any of the people he was supposed to be hobnobbing with. It probably wasn't fine, but I couldn't ask the truth with Ryan tucked in between us. Maybe he was just accompanying Ryan and me to the palace before coming back to the Holiday Party. Yes, that would make sense.

Only he didn't do it.

"How about dinner?" he asked, as soon as we were inside. "The kitchen staff either have the day off or are at the party, but I'm sure we could find enough food to do something ourselves. You know how to cook, right?" He looked at me. I must have been looking as dumbfounded as I felt, because he frowned. "Or we could eat raw carrots or something…"

The thought of Prince Marcos of Hodenia sitting on the kitchen floor eating raw carrots pulled me back to reality. "I can cook. Bake. Scavenge. Whatever."

"Perfect." He looked down at Ryan. "Wenderley will be our

chef and we'll be her assistants. What do you say, Sous-Chef Ryan? Sound like a plan?"

"I am a little hungry."

"Good. Then let's go."

The next thing I knew, the three of us were in the huge kitchens, turning on lights—I chose not to let the surprise get to me that Marcos even knew where they were—and opening fridges and pantries, finding supplies. Marcos found three aprons, helping Ryan with his. It was adorable how it stretched almost to Ryan's feet. Of course, also adorable were the two of them trying to figure out how to tie it so it wouldn't drag along the ground. I watched unashamedly as they fumbled around for a minute or so before taking pity on them and helping, folding the excess into the middle before tying a tight bow. A third apron hung from Marcos's fingers as he held it out to me. Only he didn't let go when I reached for it.

"Please?" I tried, thinking maybe he was waiting for some manners.

"Turn around."

"What?" Oh no. There was no way I was letting him put my apron on for me. It was way too personal. I mean, sure, it was just an apron, but really? He'd have to touch my hair. Maybe my back. No different from dancing but, well, actually, that would be bad enough. I'd danced with him once already. Over a year and a few lifetimes later, I could still remember the feel of his warm hand against my back. The fact that I'd never feel that again had been, in part, what had driven me to Waitrose.

My night with Waitrose hadn't even partially dimmed the feeling.

"I'll do it," I said, holding out my hand.

"Turn around."

He wasn't going to give it to me. Ryan was watching, waiting with a bowl in hand for us to be done so he could help mix or stir or add or—what were we even making? I couldn't remember. Had we decided?

"Just turn around."

Fine. I'd turn around. It was just an apron. Just an ap—

Marcos's hands were on my hair, gathering it into his hand as he pulled it free of the apron's tie. *Breathe, Wenderley.* It was just hair. Just warmth. Just his fingers, brushing my neck. Just me falling into a puddle on the floor. *Which he'll have to clean up. And I'll not feel the slightest bit guilty about it because it'll be all his fault.*

I tried to turn. His hands, now at my waist, held me in place. My waist? What was he doing touching my waist? All he had to do was tie a bow. No touching required. Definitely not—

They were sitting there. One of his hands on either side of my waist. Had he tied the bow yet? Did I care? Why was I still standing here? He'd cast a spell on me. That was it. Cast a spell and taken every breath I had. Every rational thought, swallowed up in the warmth of his hands.

He leaned in, close to the side of my neck exposed by his moving my hair. Far too close. I could smell his cologne. It swirled around me, pulling me down, stronger than any spell could have been.

"Beautiful," he whispered.

I spun out of his reach then. It was either that or swoon at his feet, something that would have taken far less effort than the laughter I forced out.

"I hardly think an apron is the latest fashion accessory."

He wasn't laughing. Far from it. He was staring at me, as if he'd never seen me before in his life and was stunned by the view. It was intoxicating. Thoraben had never looked at me like that. Waitrose certainly hadn't. Although I'd seen the same expression on Ashe's face when he looked at my sister, Jade. And Thoraben's when Kenna walked into the room.

"Papa?"

What was Marcos thinking? I wished I knew. And, at the same time, really didn't. Because he'd never looked at me like that before. And I didn't know what to do with it now. Although, neither did he, if the way he was frozen in place was any indication.

"Can we make something now?"

Ryan was waiting. And Marcos was still staring at me. And not leaving. And looking particularly endearing in his white apron. Maybe he wasn't so far off calling a person in an apron beautiful. It would never catch on as a fashion accessory but—

"Don't you have to go back to the party?" I asked, before my mind could go anywhere further in that direction. There would be no coming back.

"My parents know I left. They'll cover for me."

"What about the dunk tank?"

"Guess you won't have to worry about me getting my suit wet after all."

"And here, I'd been looking forward to seeing you wet."

His eyebrows shot up. I blushed. "You...wet...your suit, that is...I mean..." I grimaced. "I'm not helping this, am I?"

He smiled then, the way his eyes crinkled at the edges drawing my gaze into their depth doing nothing for my fragile control. "No."

"Right, well. You're staying. Got it. Cooking. Baking. Um, cookies."

"For dinner?"

"Sure, why not? They have eggs. Eggs are healthy. And chocolate. That's dairy covered. And uh—"

"Flour?"

"Sure, wheat. Just like bread is made from. Tick for another food group."

Ryan tugged on the edge of my apron, finally managing to break the magnet hold of Marcos's gaze. Not that Ryan didn't have the same eyes. Such a dark brown, I could see myself reflected in them. Looking as befuddled as I felt.

"Wenderley. I like cookies but could we make spaghetti?"

"Bolognese?"

"No, just spaghetti. It was Mom's favorite food. Sometimes she put cheese on top but mostly just a little bit of olive oil and some green stuff. Could we make that?"

As if there was any way I'd be able to say no to this boy, especially while his dark eyes were still rimmed with red. "Sure, honey."

"And then cookies."

I don't think I'd ever concentrated so hard on cooking in my life. Between Marcos and his intoxicating nearness, and Ryan, who kept asking every two minutes if the pasta was done yet and if he could stir it—something which I might have let him do, if he'd been slightly taller and less excitable—it was taking every bit of focus I possessed to not send all three of us to the medical wing. Assuming the palace had one of those. Probably not, but the alternative—an actual hospital—was more mortifying than I wanted to consider.

"Almost done." Thankfully.

"Can we sit on the floor to eat it?"

I glanced at Marcos, silently asking his opinion. I was more than willing to agree but he was the one in a suit. Likely one that cost more than my entire closet. He nodded. I smiled.

"Sure, buddy."

Marcos went in search of some bowls to ladle the spaghetti into while I drained it and Ryan laid a tablecloth down on the floor. Right in the middle of the kitchen. Was this something he and Rachana used to do as well?

I had to admit, as the three of us sat there cross-legged on the floor, so close our knees touched, eating our bowls of plain pasta, I was enjoying myself. More than enjoying myself. It was one of those random, completely spontaneous, simple yet all-too-meaningful moments I loved. The kind every kid deserved, no matter what his title or how many charities and schools had his name on them.

Thank you, God, for this moment.

We should have been at the party. No doubt it would still be going for a couple of hours yet, before the cleanup began and staff slowly started filtering back into the palace. But this moment? I would treasure it forever.

"Want to play in the treehouse?" Marcos asked Ryan, putting his empty bowl down in front of him.

Ryan looked up at his dad, eyes filled with hope. "At night? With you?"

"Sure."

"Yes, please. But we have to clean up first."

"Don't worry about that," I quickly said. "I'll do it. You go."

Ryan immediately shook his head. "No. The cook always cleans up their mess. You said."

"It's fine. Really." It wasn't a big deal. Sure, it was a good rule to live by, but there was nothing that said it couldn't be broken, especially for a rare father/son moment like this.

"We can help, right Ryan?" Marcos said.

"Yes. And then Wenderley can come to the treehouse too."

They picked up their bowls and walked to the sink. I followed a little slower, not sure what to do with this change in Marcos. He wasn't supposed to like me. Certainly not call me beautiful. Pushing him away was hard enough as is. If he cared? Started being more of a friend than he had been? Joking even? I'd fold. I knew it.

I thought back to the most recent letter Waitrose had sent me, sitting beside my bed as a much-needed reminder of what I had to lose. And not only me.

God, help me.

Marcos came back to take my bowl and glass from me. I held on to them.

"You could still go back to the party," I tried, one more time.

"And miss this? Not a chance. Come on, Lady Wenderley. We have some dishes to do."

TWENTY-FOUR

When Queen Galielle knocked on my door early the next morning, I thought I was in trouble. I'd finally pushed the sweet queen too far, letting Ryan leave the party so soon after he'd arrived. For all I knew, this was the young prince's official introduction to the world. His chance to make friends and prove he was more than the boy in the photo few people ever met.

She wasn't angry. Not at me anyway, though it took me ten minutes to figure that out as she stalked back and forth across my room.

"You're not mad I brought him home? Or that Prince Marcos stayed with us?"

Queen Galielle finally stopped walking, surprise on her face as she turned to look at me, fiddling with my hairbrush near the dresser. I'd barely had time to stand before she walked through my door, her knock apparently more for the appearance of politeness than the reality of it since she hadn't waited for me to answer.

"No, of course not. I'm thrilled Marcos put you and Ryan above his responsibilities. As to Ryan, I asked you to keep an eye on him and you did exactly that. How could I be angry for doing exactly what I asked?" She sighed, and started pacing again. "No, I'm upset I put all of you in the situation to begin with. I should have known it would be too difficult for Ryan. I shouldn't have forced it. The poor boy will never trust me now. And here, I thought we were making grounds."

"You are," I said, even though I was pretty sure she was too busy berating herself to hear me.

"He's so quiet all the time. So polite and content to do whatever he's told. It's hard to know what he's thinking."

"Your Highness, please," I tried again, putting my brush down and waiting until Queen Galielle focused back on me. "Ryan is fine. It takes time to grieve as an adult. It's no less because he's a child. Please don't blame yourself. He adores you. Truly. He thinks the world of your whole family. And he was excited to go to the party. Couldn't stop talking about it all day yesterday and was struck mute with wonder when we got there. He loved seeing all the animals at the mini zoo and touching the tortoise's shell. And the parrot! I wish you could have seen the delight on Ryan's face when the parrot talked to him. You were right to invite him.

"He was upset because he wished Rachana could have been there to share it with him, not because he wasn't enjoying himself. He misses his mom. Sadness is part of that. Having his dad leave the party to spend time with him helped a lot." I smiled, thinking back to last night and the time the three of us had spent together.

Marcos had lugged three chairs up to the top level of the treehouse, even though Ryan had been too excited to ever actually sit on his. We'd stayed up there, talking about everything and nothing, long after Ryan had fallen asleep on Marcos's lap.

"It was so sweet seeing the two of them together in the treehouse with the telescope finding stars. I assure you, you haven't ruined anything."

Queen Galielle sat down then, on one of the trio of comfy chairs in my room's sitting area. For a few moments, I relaxed along with her, happy to have finally convinced her to stop worrying. It didn't take long, though, for that relief to turn to uneasiness as she looked at me, a wistful smile on her face.

"You're good for him, you know."

"Ryan?" *Please mean Ryan. We're talking about Ryan. She means Ryan. She has to.*

"Him too, but I meant Marcos. You'd make him a wonderful wife."

I stared at Queen Galielle, mouth open, all manners flung from my head the instant her comment reached my ears. It wasn't just what she'd said, strange as it was to hear it, it was the fact that she'd said it at all.

"I've surprised you."

I couldn't even manage a nod.

"No doubt you're wondering why I'd say such a thing."

Only with every fiber of my being. She truly thought I would make Marcos a good wife? Why? I wasn't a princess or even all that good at pretending to be one. And while Marcos had been particularly attentive last night—something I was still feeling guilty for—*and* had already proposed once, it wasn't as if he cared. At least, he hadn't the day he proposed. *Had* that changed? Did his mother know something I didn't?

"Come, sit with me." Queen Galielle patted the chair beside her. I walked over, almost as if in a daze. *Marcos's wife?* I mean, sure, I'd considered it, but I was Wenderley the Daydreamer. I'd also considered finding a wife for Sir Rusty, and whether bugs had funerals for family members who got stood on.

"Was it something I did?" I finally managed, forcing the words past the heart thudding in my throat.

"No, not at all. At least, not while you were here."

"I don't understand."

"No, I imagine you don't. No doubt your actions that night were simply an extension of your beautiful heart and nothing out of the ordinary."

That didn't help. What actions? Moreover, what night?

Queen Galielle smiled as she crossed her ankles and tucked them beneath the seat. "I have a confession to make."

She was confessing now? To me? Would the shock never end?

"I knew who you were before we met at Rachana's funeral. When Princess Alina mentioned your name, even before she vouched for you, I knew you'd be perfect for Ryan."

What? "Why?"

"Because you'd already touched the heart of my son."

I sat up straight, adrenaline bursting through my body. "What?

I never—I didn't—haven't—" Was she talking about our balcony chats? They probably weren't entirely appropriate but if Marcos made no move to stop them then I certainly wouldn't. But no, she'd said it was something I'd done *before* I came to the palace. So then, when? "I don't—"

"Wenderley, stop. You haven't done anything wrong."

Oh. Then why—?

"At the King's Ball in Peverell, back when Marcos and Princess Alina were still engaged and none of us had met Rachana yet, you asked him to dance."

"Of course. Someone had to." It had been the best and last good idea I'd had that night. If only I'd left right after.

"Yes, but *someone* didn't. You did. Marcos didn't even want to attend the ball that night. The news that he'd fathered a son had just broken and the last place he wanted to be was out in public. Unfortunately, when you're a royal, things like that are taken out of your hands. For his own good and the good of the kingdom, Dorien and I asked him to go. Marcos agreed, seeing the wisdom of it, but I knew he wasn't happy and all night I worried.

"When he came home, I was surprised to see him smiling and asked how it had gone. He mentioned his dance with Alina but then, for the next few minutes, he talked about you. He told me all about how you'd walked over to him and asked him to dance, pulling him onto the dance floor before he could find a reason to say no."

"It was just a dance," I countered. Even if it had been the highlight of my night. And likely still would have been even if what happened after our dance turned out to be the greatest regret of my life.

"You accepted him when everyone else offered only judgment."

She was making me seem like a saint. Something that couldn't have been any further from the truth. "Alina danced with him too."

"I know, but the two of them were engaged. It was different with you. You didn't have to. Wenderley, you love with all your heart. You care without thought for what it might cost. And it's truly beautiful."

I was silent for a few moments, taking in her words. Feeling as if they weren't quite mine to accept, even though she'd offered them so kindly. I did know what loving with my whole heart cost. I'd been paying the price for the past year, in more ways than one. Still, she'd given me a compliment and it would be rude not to at least acknowledge it. "Thank you?"

"But that's exactly why I don't want you to marry my son."

She was giving me whiplash. "You don't?"

First she wanted me to be Marcos's wife, now she didn't. Not that I had any intention of being his wife, but it was hard not to take it personally that she didn't think I was good enough. "I mean, not that I plan to or anything. He's just lost Rachana and he's grieving and I'd make a terrible princess and even worse queen so of course I'm not going to. At all."

Queen Galielle leaned forward, putting a hand on my knee. "No, Wenderley, you misunderstand me. This has nothing to do with your suitability. Like I said, you'd make him a wonderful wife. The more I get to know you, the more certain I am of that. You are exactly the woman he needs. But I don't want you marrying him. Not yet. Not until he finds God for himself."

I'd barely processed her words when she took her hand back and rushed on.

"You have no idea how painful it is when the man you love most in the world doesn't share your faith. I adore Dorien and know without a doubt that he loves me, but until the day he comes to know God for himself, there will always be a part of us that doesn't connect. We're one in body and heart but not spirit, and when the spirit is the very soul of who you are, we might as well be from different worlds. It breaks my heart over and over and over again to watch him merely accept my faith without knowing God's incredible love for himself. When the most important thing to you—the one you'd give *everything* for—means nothing to him—" She blinked, swallowed. Was she fighting back tears? "There are nights I've cried myself to sleep from the ache of it.

"I don't want that for you. I wouldn't wish it on anyone, but seeing your beautiful heart and the way you love both God and people so fiercely—it would break you. You would forever be trying to choose between your husband and your God."

She looked down at her lap. Either composing herself or trying to find words, I didn't know. Nor did I break the silence. What would I have said anyway? "You're wrong, I could be strong enough?" When she was the one living this every day? When she looked back at me, there were tears in her eyes, though they didn't fall.

"I hope you marry Marcos one day. I really do. I would love to call you my daughter and watch the two of you live and love and serve this kingdom of ours side-by-side. You're so good for him and I can't think of anyone I'd love more to be Hodenia's next queen. But please, *please* Wenderley, promise me you won't agree to marry him until he believes. I couldn't bear to see your heart broken by his indifference."

I wanted to laugh at her words and brush them aside as a complete overreaction, but it was impossible to miss the agony on her face or the way her voice shook with emotion. She wasn't making this up. And really, was it such a hard promise to make when I could never agree to marry Marcos anyway?

"I promise."

She nodded, taking my promise but seeming as if it gave her no joy. I could understand that. It didn't fill my heart with hope either. What if Marcos never believed?

"Wenderley, I hate to ask, given what I just made you promise…"

A large part of me wanted to walk away and ignore any other requests the queen might have for me. Wasn't that one promise enough? Did she want me to leave Marcos alone altogether? I wasn't certain I could do that, even if she asked. He'd become more than a prince. More than Ryan's father even. Somewhere along the way, he'd become a true friend.

"Yes?"

"Mrs. Graham's arrival has been delayed again. Would you mind staying another week?"

I smiled. Nodded. That I could do.

I agreed to stay another week a week later, and the next, and the two after that. I think we all knew I was only prolonging the inevitable, and making the actual leaving more difficult. I told myself I was helping Queen Galielle, and Mrs. Graham, and Ryan, who was comfortable around me. It wasn't as if I had any pressing reason to go home. Mom was quite happily taking over my role as Callan's favorite babysitter, Alina had sent fully qualified teachers to tutor the kids I fumbled my way through helping, and she and Kenna were having a wonderful time befriending my girls. I told myself it was safer if I didn't spend much time with the girls these days anyway, with Waitrose's threats hanging over my head.

They were excuses though, all of them. Good ones, easily justified, but excuses all the same. The truth was, I didn't want to leave.

I loved our not-so-secret trips out to the Gift Room with Lucie and Kahra to find outrageous outfits for Sir Rusty, and the way Lucie almost burst trying to keep the "secret" inside. I loved reading to Ryan in the treehouse, or whatever our imaginations made it that particular day. I loved the kitchen staff and how willing they were to let me invade their space and do some baking when I needed time to think. I loved Queen Galielle and her quiet but unflinching faith. And, much as I shouldn't have, I loved those moments—sometimes stretching to an hour or more—out on the balcony with Marcos at night, just being. No pressure. No judgment. No expectations. Just two people, watching the stars.

I wasn't ready to go home. Truth was, I didn't know if I ever would be.

TWENTY-FIVE

"Your mail, my lady."

I wondered at the barely suppressed amusement in Marcos's voice, until I turned from my breakfast to see the pile of envelopes he was holding out to me. They were all mine? I'd never received so much mail all at once. There had to be fifteen or twenty, at least.

"Thank you," I said, taking the envelopes from him and setting them carefully beside my empty glass—a long way from Ryan's still full one. After his spectacular mess my first dinner here, I was taking no chances. "You don't have to personally deliver them to me, you know."

The mint green ones I would have liked to have hidden from him altogether. Waitrose had upped his game since I'd moved here. They used to only come once a month. Now, it was one a week. Every time I saw Marcos holding one, my heart all but stopped in my chest at the thought of him knowing what was inside. As if he could see through the paper, or would ever stoop to being so discourteous as to open another person's mail. But even without Waitrose's letters, it felt wrong to have Marcos bring me mail. He was the prince, after all.

"It's no trouble."

Somehow I doubted that, and raised an eyebrow to let him know. He gave me a sheepish grin.

"Fine. Not much trouble. You have a lot of admirers, Lady

Wenderley Davis. Perhaps I'm curious as to who's on the other end of your letters."

My heart thudded with dread. I turned to check on Ryan, taking the moment to compose myself. Still eating. One piece of cereal at a time. Still completely ignoring the conversation I was having with his father. I turned back to Marcos in time to see him grin.

"Especially the pink one covered in hand-drawn hearts."

Hearts? Waitrose didn't—

Tearing my gaze away from the all-too-captivating twinkle in Marcos's eyes, I looked down at the pile of envelopes, flicking through them until I found the one he meant. It didn't take long. It was the brightest one there. Also the biggest. A vivid magenta envelope all, as Marcos had said, covered in hearts. I turned it over, smiling at the return address on the back. Liz, complete with another heart dotting the *i* in her name. Apparently, even with two princesses and their offer of sleepovers at a palace, she still loved me.

A quick glance through the rest had my smile stretching further. It looked like all my girls had written to me. As had Kenna and Alina.

"Someone special?"

"One of my g—" I clamped my lips shut, cringing at the thought of what I'd almost given away. That was more than he needed to know. "Friends," I said instead. That would do. "The pink one is from one of my friends. A good friend. Liz."

"You should invite her to visit."

"Liz?"

"Sure, and all those other people who keep writing to you. The green letter writer seems particularly ardent. He writes to you every week, if I'm not mistaken."

My smile dropped, my excitement along with it. If only Marcos knew how markedly *not* ardent Lord Waitrose was. And how much I wished he'd stop writing. No, I wouldn't be inviting Lord Waitrose to visit. Nor, because of him, would I invite the girls. Some things weren't worth the risk.

"Wenderley? Are you okay?"

I forced a smile back on my face. "Yes, of course. Who wouldn't be when they're this popular?" I held the letters up, hiding my pain behind their joy. One night. One stupid decision. One regret which would mar every happy moment for the rest of my life. If only I could have turned back time.

"I could cancel my meeting this morning and take Ryan so you can write back to all your admirers, if you like."

He was so sweet, but I couldn't do that. He did, after all, have a country to help run. "Thank you, but I'll write back later. Ryan and I have big plans this morning." When Ryan finished his breakfast. *If* Ryan ever finished his breakfast. Was it really so difficult to use one's spoon to pick up more than one piece at a time? At this rate, I might as well send word to the kitchens not to bother with lunch. He'd still be going with his cereal well into the afternoon. "We're going on a treasure hunt."

Ryan looked up then, delight on his face at the mention of our plans. I handed him his spoon.

"*After* you finish breakfast."

Our plans were almost derailed when I walked outside to see ominously dark clouds overhead. Where had they come from? There'd been barely a cloud in the sky when I sat sketching on my balcony early this morning. Of course, Ryan had taken almost an hour to eat his bowl of cereal and changed his mind three times about what he considered proper clothing for a treasure hunter, meaning it had been almost three hours since I'd been outside.

Still, it wasn't raining yet. I handed the map I'd made over to my little treasure hunter—dressed head to toe in black, since apparently that meant no one would see him coming and steal the treasure before him—and watched in amusement as he scrutinized the paper, turning it round and round until he finally managed to match up the map with our surroundings.

"This way!"

He ran off to our left, very easy to follow in his black clothes, which didn't even remotely blend in with the bright green grass or trees. I took another look up, judging the clouds, before running off after him.

We were still running half an hour later when the sky let loose, drenching us in an instant. The map fared even worse, the color I'd used running in rivulets down the creases and leaving too much of a mess to make sense of. Poor Ryan looked devastated.

I crouched down to his level and waited until he looked at me. "Want to know a secret, Treasure Hunter?"

He nodded slowly, pushing wet hair away from his eyes.

"The treasure's in the kitchen. Chef Meyer has been guarding it all morning. If we can get past her, it's all yours."

His eyes widened, an excited smile taking over his sadness. "I can eat the treasure?"

"How about we get dried off and then go find out."

Ryan was off running again in an instant, muddy footprints leaving a trail through the palace's grand entry and up the stairs. I stood in the entry for a moment, paralyzed by the decision between following Ryan and making sure he didn't make more mess, and cleaning up the one he'd already made before anyone saw it. It was the almost muffled laugh of the doorman behind me which had me cringing as I turned. The doorman already gesturing a maid over.

"Go," he told me. "It's fine."

"Are you sure? I can help. Really. It's my fault. I shouldn't have let him in here like that."

The doorman and the maid both shook their heads. "Truly," the man said. "A little mud is nothing to seeing that boy smile."

It was more than a little mud, but they were adamant, so I pulled my shoes off and followed Ryan's trail in my socks. Maybe I should have taken Marcos up on his offer to look after Ryan this morning after all. Or invited Marcos on our treasure hunt. Apple pies were his favorite kind of treasure too.

Although, apparently, Prince Marcos didn't need an invitation to our treasure hunt. He'd found the treasure himself. He and Ryan were in the kitchen, playfully tussling over Chef Meyer's prized apple pie when I caught up a few minutes later. I stood there, just out of sight, a lump in my throat as I watched them. I'd never seen either of them so happy or carefree, as if the two of them were just boys. Not princes. Not in charge of kingdoms or buckling under the weight of too many people's expectations. Just two boys. My boys.

What? No. Wenderley…

Luka walked up beside me, Chef Meyer not far behind. Defenses jumped to my mind as I braced myself for their reproach. After all, the two princes were distracting the rest of the kitchen staff from working, Marcos was probably supposed to be somewhere else, and Ryan had obviously forgotten to change his pants along with his shirt and was now leaving muddy patches across the pristinely clean floor. *Leave them be, they're happy. Give them a few more moments, they don't get many. Can't you see they're—*

Luka put a hand on my shoulder. "Thank you, Lady Wenderley."

I turned to face him then, my gaze going back and forth between Luka with his humble gratitude and Chef Meyer, nodding. They hadn't come over to share their disapproval. They'd simply come to thank me.

"You're welcome."

My words were swallowed up in a cry of victory from Ryan as Marcos fell dramatically to the floor, arms flung out in surrender. Ryan plucked the mini apple pie off the plate and ran over to me.

"I found the treasure and won the battle against the dragon, Wenderley! Can I eat it now?"

The lump in my throat seemed to be growing bigger. I nodded, smiling as Ryan took his edible treasure to the closest chair and started eating. Chef Meyer asked if he'd like ice cream with it and went off to find some when he said yes. Luka walked over and tried to coerce Ryan into sharing. I stayed exactly where I was, caught under Marcos's spell.

He'd raised himself up on one elbow and was staring at me, like he had the last time we'd been in here, when he'd tied my apron and called me beautiful. It was a gaze that went far beyond mere warmth, scorching heat into my cheeks as I stood there, unable to look away. No, not unable. Unwilling. In that moment, in the middle of an industrial kitchen full of people stirring and calling to each other and getting back to work, something changed between us. And, for more reasons than I could count or name, it terrified me.

TWENTY-SIX

That night, the balcony drew me more than ever.

No, that wasn't right. The pull had nothing to do with the balcony, nice as it was. It was the man out there. The man whose presence I was attempting to avoid. It was for the best, I told myself over and over. It was also one of the most difficult things I'd ever done.

He'd gone out on to his balcony twenty minutes ago. I'd heard the door open and shut while I hadn't been listening. At all. Nor had I had my door open, so I could hear whether his did or not.

While I lay on my bed.

Fully dressed.

Not listening.

Wenderley, Wenderley, Wenderley, when are you going to stop lying to yourself? You're head over heels for him. Lost in a cloud of love. Weak at the knees. Starry eyed, smitten, wrapped around his finger. And all those other ridiculous sayings that suddenly don't seem so ridiculous anymore... You, Wenderley Davis, are in love with Prince Marcos.

The question is, what are you going to do about it?

But that was the thing. I shouldn't do anything. Couldn't. There were a million reasons why spending more time with Prince Marcos was a bad idea. I'd made a list of them while ignoring the voice of reason in my head telling me that if I really planned on staying inside, I would have changed into my pajamas.

The promise I'd made to his mother took out the top of the

list with Ryan and his grief only a whisker behind. Then there was Waitrose and my obligations to him, the fact that I'd sworn off princes, the fact that I didn't own—or care to *ever* own—a pair of the nude-colored heels which came as a prerequisite with the princess title, and the list went on. And on. And on. Which was why I was going to walk over to that door, close it, and go to bed.

Really?

I walked to the door. Put my hand on the handle. Laid my head against the cold glass. He was out there. And I wanted to be. That was the simple truth of it.

God, what do I do? I can't marry him. It's impossible. And I know you're the God of the impossible but this is, like, impossible impossible. Marcos isn't a Follower. I can't change time. Peverell will never change their hundred-year-old marriage law. King Everson hates Rebels. Waitrose will never let it go. Ryan is grieving. Queen Galielle made me promise—

"Wenderley?"

It had to have been the clear night which carried Marcos's whisper across the distance. If there had been even the slightest wind brushing through the trees below us, I would never have heard it.

"Are you there?"

No. I wasn't. I shouldn't. I couldn't.

I walked out on to the balcony, gently closing the door behind me. "I'm here."

God, I don't know what to do with this attraction I feel for him and I don't know why you won't take it away but please…please… do… I sighed into the darkness, not even knowing what I was asking. *Something. Do something.*

"Hi."

Marcos had taken his suit coat off already, his white shirt almost glowing in the half-moon's light. The way he stood there at the railing, arms outstretched along it, he looked like a captain surveying his ship. All he needed was a hat and he'd be set. He would have made a good sea captain. Although it would mess up his hair.

"I thought you might not be coming out tonight."

"If I were stronger, I wouldn't have." I muttered the words, forgetting how well sound carried tonight, knowing as soon as he tipped his head that he'd heard them.

"Why?"

I looked down, even though I knew my expressions were all but hidden from him in the muted light.

"Because you're attracted to me?"

He knew? "What? No! I—"

"It's okay, Wenderley. I'm attracted to you too."

The railing I held was all that kept me standing. He hadn't just said that. He wouldn't. And yet, that way he was looking at me. Waiting.

"We should talk about something else," I said.

"I've frightened you."

"No." I was frightened, but not of him. Of myself. Of the strength of my own feelings. While I'd believed my attraction one-sided, it had been easy enough to convince myself it was only my foolish heart. But now? "I don't think this is a good idea. For either of us. For Ryan. I'll be here for you, as a friend, for as long as you need me but more than that? It's not possible."

"Because of the man who writes you letters."

Much as I hated letting him think they were from a suitor, it was for the best. "Yes. And because of Rachana."

"Rachana."

"Your wife," I said, as if, somehow, he'd forgotten. "The woman you loved."

He sighed. "I barely knew her."

"But, I thought… At her funeral, you were crying."

"Because I'd failed her. She'd come to me, so hopeful and trusting. And here, she was dead."

"You're a prince. Not God. You couldn't have healed her."

"No, but I could have helped her. I could have been there when Ryan was born. Supported her all these years. Maybe if I'd been there when she first got sick, she might not have died."

"You didn't know." At least that's what the papers had said.

And the look of stunned shock which had still been on his face the night we'd danced at the King's Ball last year.

"But that's just it. I should have. If I hadn't walked away from Rachana in the first place... I should have waited to see if...that night..."

His voice ached with regret. I knew the feeling well.

"I met Rachana one night at a friend's house. She was seventeen, I was barely much older than that myself. Father had spent the past three days trying to teach me the history behind many of the laws of the kingdom and their nuances, and I was tired of it. Not only the laws but all of it. The rules, the expectations, the continual having to think of everyone else before myself. Not only my own family but an entire country full of people. I wanted out in the worst possible way. I went to my friend's house to blow off some steam, knowing that he was having a party that night. Rachana was there with some of her friends. We got talking and—" He shrugged, but there was no apathy to it, only sadness.

"It should never have happened, we both knew that. So, we agreed to part ways and never talk of it again. And we didn't. Not even when she found out she was pregnant. I wonder if she would have contacted me at all if she hadn't known she was dying and needed someone to take Ryan.

"I married her because it's what I should have done all those years ago. I respect her greatly and certainly learned to care for her in the short time we were married, but there was never anything romantic between the two of us. We didn't even share a room." He looked up at the sky, shook his head. "How can you love someone when every time you look at them, all you see is how you ruined their life? When I think of all Rachana might have done with her life if not for me, it just...wrecks me."

"She adored Ryan. He was her life." He had to see that. Even out of their mistake, God had given them a gift to treasure in Ryan.

"It doesn't change what I took from her."

"You don't think she would have forgiven you?"

"I wouldn't have accepted it if she did."

"Why not?"

He threw a hand out in frustration, stopping short of slamming it onto the balcony's ledge. His words were quiet but no less bitter. "I ruined her life, Wenderley. I don't deserve forgiveness."

"None of us do. That's what makes God offering it such a precious gift. We ruined his life too. We killed his son. But he still forgave us. Not only forgave us but loves us. Absolutely, wholeheartedly, would do it all over again *cherishes* us. Do you think you're better than him?"

Passion thrummed through my veins with a physical rush. It always did when I talked about God to others, but there was something more to it tonight, starting in my pounding heart and racing to my tingling fingertips. I wanted to say more, and less, all at the same time. Take on the impossible and put into words that didn't yet exist the greatness and overwhelming awesomeness of what God had done. Present it in such a way that it struck right to Marcos's heart.

"You're a Follower."

"Yes, and—?"

"I'm not even sure I believe in your god."

"Well, you should."

He raised his eyebrows at my bluntness. "Oh yeah? And why is that?"

"Because he believes in you."

The words hung in the air, suspended in time and hope. Later, I'd probably replay every one of these words I'd thrown at him, wondering if I'd been too brash. If I should have been gentler, like Kenna, or more patient, like Jade. But I wasn't them. This was me. And I couldn't get out of my rushing mind that this could be Marcos's moment. The very reason God had brought me into Marcos's life.

Would he believe my words? More, would he accept them? Could he? I wanted him to. The strength of desperation clawing at my insides was like nothing I'd ever felt before. Was this the ache Queen Galielle had been talking about? It was more than a want, I *needed* Marcos to believe. That God loved him. That God wanted him. That God forgave him.

God, please…

"Maybe."

It wasn't much. But it wasn't a no. My thrumming emotions slowly made their way back to some semblance of normal.

"Do you have any idea how beautiful you look, all riled up like that?" Marcos asked suddenly. "If there wasn't a balcony between us, I'd be seriously tempted to kiss you right now."

I froze, gripping said balcony so tightly my fingers hurt, incredibly thankful it was between us. "You can't."

"Obviously, since there's a balcony between us."

"No, because—"

This was ridiculous. I couldn't believe we were even having this discussion. There was no way I was telling him about the vow I'd made.

With God as my witness, I choose to live a life of honor, both of God and my future husband. I choose to live a life above reproach. I choose to make my witness glorifying to God, that others may see it is possible to live God's way.

"Because?"

He'd think I was all pious or something, especially coming after what I'd already so bluntly told him. Or immature maybe. Naïve at best. It was just a kiss. Plenty of people kissed. Even complete strangers. Would he understand why this was so important to me? Could I bear it if he didn't? If he laughed?

I choose to live a pure life, in every way, not even kissing any man ever again except the man I will one day marry. No matter what others think or say, I choose God's way, with God as my help, my guide, my motivation, and my strength.

"Why, Wenderley?"

We were too close already for me not to tell him. What if next time Marcos and I talked, there wasn't a balcony between us? I might not have the strength if I didn't tell him now.

"Because I made a promise that I wouldn't kiss a man unless I was engaged to him."

Silence met my timid declaration. Silence, and then low laughter. "You didn't."

What was that supposed to mean? Was he laughing *at* me? Thinking I was kidding? I wasn't. I was as serious about that vow today as I had been the week after the King's Ball, when I'd sat on the floor of my bedroom and written it, signing my name at the bottom. Feeling the weight of the moment as if God himself signed his name beside mine as witness. Marcos didn't have to understand it for it to be true.

"Yes, I did. I know it sounds childish, but I want my kisses to mean something. To not only show affection but truly honor the man I choose to marry. It's a way for me to honor God too."

"I promised myself after that night with Rachana that I would never again kiss a woman who wasn't my wife. I haven't broken it yet."

This time it was my turn to be shocked. He'd been seventeen that night with Rachana. Eighteen maybe. All that time? He hadn't kissed one single girl? He hadn't been laughing at me. He'd been relating. Commiserating, even. "That's why you never kissed Alina."

His eyebrows shot up. "You knew that?"

"She might have mentioned it. A few times. She was quite enamored with you. Before Joha came along, of course."

He shook his head, although he was smiling. "No, I never kissed Alina, though not for a lack of her trying."

I could imagine. "But even now? You're still keeping it?"

"What good is a promise if not kept? I won't kiss any woman but my wife. It's too hard for me to stop at kissing and—" He looked me in the eye, intensity etched across his face. "Some things are worth waiting for."

And here I'd thought he was laughing at me. I couldn't have been further from the truth. Not only did he not think my vow silly, but he'd been keeping one of his own even longer.

"Like you."

I looked over at Marcos, wondering if I'd heard him right.

"You're worth waiting for, Lady Wenderley Davis. Just because I don't kiss you doesn't mean I don't want to."

I shook my head, the hopelessness of our situation weighing too heavily to appreciate his sentiment. "Marcos—"

"You're attending Princess Alina's wedding tomorrow, I understand?"

The topic change was shockingly abrupt, but also tinged with relief. Marcos had a habit of changing the topic when a conversation started getting too serious. Sometimes it irritated me. Tonight, I took it for what it was—a much-needed reprieve for both of us.

"Yes," I answered, forcing my brain to think about tomorrow's plans instead of the way Marcos had looked at me earlier in the kitchen. The same way I imagined he was looking at me now. "Paige, one of the maids, will be caring for Ryan for the day. I've already told him and introduced them and let her know his routine and—"

"Wenderley?"

"Yes?"

"You're not going to worry about Ryan the whole time you're gone, are you?"

Was he teasing *me* now? I looked over at him, just in time to catch the smile he tried to hide. He was!

"No, of course not." Probably. Highly likely. Although I was looking forward to seeing my friends again and, surprisingly, wearing the ice-blue gown Alina had sent for me. Her eye for fashion was incredible. The geometric patterns of crystal beading on the bodice alone had sold me even before I pulled it from the box and saw the way the layers of chiffon fell so freely. Feminine, without being overly girly. Glamorous, without being immodest.

"Good. I'm glad. I should retire now but...Wenderley?"

"Yes?"

He waited until I looked over, capturing me in his gaze. "I hope you sleep well."

It was the way he said them—the gentleness of his voice, the way he stood there for a few moments more, holding that connection—that made those words so much more than simply good-night. This time I knew. They were his way of saying he cared.

Maybe even loved me.

TWENTY-SEVEN

When Alina had dreamed out loud about her wedding as a child, it had never looked like this. Not even close. Her dream wedding had been huge, to start with. Thousands of people watching her walk up the red-carpet-laid staircase of Peverell's grand cathedral, hundreds more watching her walk along the seemingly endless petal-scattered aisle inside. Flowers by the bushel lining her way, curving into grand arches above her—pink roses, mostly, with the occasional lily to break up the monotony. A white gown, trailing out behind her for at least twenty feet. Eight attendants, all in pink. A full symphony orchestra, tucked away who knows where. A stunning ball of a reception, attended by royalty the world over, come to pay their respects. Tables full of gifts. A cake fifteen layers high, white with pink roses and highlights of gold.

Stunning, elegant, royal, huge—a wedding talked about for decades to come.

Nothing like the tiny chapel I sat in now, pretty as it was.

Here at The Well—also known as Joha's family's farm, complete with cows, horses, and no shortage of ducks—there were no cameras, no celebrities. The only royals attending at all were King Everson, Ben, and Kenna. There were no red carpets, no attendants, no symphony orchestras. Only a guitar, quietly playing in a corner.

"Anyone sitting here?"

"Marcos! I mean—" I looked around guiltily, hoping no one had noticed my slip, or the complete shock I felt at seeing him here. Thankfully, everyone seemed to be in their own little excited bubbles of anticipation while they chatted and waited for the bride. "Prince Marcos. What are you doing here?"

"Attending a wedding, I believe. Same as everyone else, I suspect. Am I not allowed?"

He sat in the empty chair beside mine. I pulled the overlap of the split in my long skirt even further across my knees, ensuring not a single bit of skin showed through and pretended I was perfectly fine with him sitting there.

"No. I mean. Yes, of course you are. I'm surprised. That's all. Alina didn't mention you were coming." Neither did he, for that matter, when he could have so easily last night. He hadn't mentioned it, had he?

"I'm royalty. We're all invited."

"Yes, usually, but—" I looked pointedly around the room, from one non-royal to the next.

"You mean because I was once engaged to the bride?"

Not the point I was making but a good one all the same. "Something like that."

"Mother suggested I come. She thought it would be good for me. It wasn't all that difficult to procure an invite."

Was Queen Galielle matchmaking now? Surely not. She'd been the one to caution me against marrying him. I was probably thinking too much into this, as per usual. Was it really so strange that the royal family of Hodenia—Peverell's closest allies—would send a representative to Alina's wedding? It should have surprised me more if they hadn't.

Although, if Marcos had to come, couldn't he have at least brought Ryan to act as a buffer between us? This, us sitting together in a chapel surrounded by flowers and music, felt a little too intimate. Sure, it was only the two of us in our late-night balcony chats, but that was different. Dream-like almost, another reality, and with a whole ten feet and two railings between us.

He'd left barely an inch between us today. Something the hairs on my bare arms were all too aware of.

"You look incredible."

He wasn't helping me feel more comfortable with compliments like that. "Thank you." Especially accented by the appreciative expression on his face as his gaze skimmed down my gown, and landed on the yellow sunflower-patterned ballet shoes the dress wasn't long enough to hide while sitting. He didn't ask. I didn't offer an explanation. Not even when I caught the way his mouth tipped up at the edge in that infuriatingly adorable way of his.

"Where's your entourage?" I asked.

"Luka? He's around. Probably talking to the Peverellian security details. I told him I'd be fine in here on my own." He nodded toward the décor. "This is different. I expected…" He broke off, likely trying to figure out how to describe the over-the-top opulence Alina used to favor in a nice way.

"More?" I said with a quiet laugh.

"Yes."

Loving Joha had changed Alina. Or perhaps it was coming to know God. They'd happened around the same time. I was still trying to find out exactly what had happened during Alina's time at The Well. She'd been surprisingly close-lipped about it. All I knew was that she'd gone to The Well bitter, angry, and refusing to wear anything but designer clothes and three-inch-high-heels—as pink as possible—and come home a different woman entirely. Calmer, more centered and certain of herself, the proud owner of a pair of pink boots, and in love with the perpetually dirt-stained farmer Joha.

"She's different. Being at The Well, finding Joha, becoming a Follower—she's really changed in the past year. You'd barely recognize her from the girl you proposed to."

"That feels like so long ago."

"I know what you mean."

The man with the guitar stopped playing. Joha and his father walked to the front of the chapel. Conversations came to a sudden halt as everyone craned their necks toward the back of the chapel, waiting for that first glimpse of the bride. When the guitar music started up again, it was different. I couldn't help the delighted smile that tugged my lips up as I saw it was Joha playing. Alina had mentioned how well he played once or twice. Or maybe a thousand times. I'd put it down to infatuation, given she'd also raved about his skill with horses, his work ethic, his wisdom and insight, and his patience. Among other things. Listening to him strum and pick at chords, I was willing to rethink that assumption, if not throw it out the window altogether. She hadn't exaggerated at all. His playing was beautiful.

The quiet strumming turned to a song as Pat gestured for us all to stand. I didn't know whether to look at Alina, entering at the back of the chapel, or Joha, singing to his bride from the front. Both made my heart swell with pride and contentment.

Alina walked down the tiny aisle toward him, a single white rose held in her hand. Her gown was beautiful but simple. White, off the shoulder with an A-line skirt skimming the ground. It was as far from the dream of a wedding as it could have been. And yet, I'd never seen her happier. She glowed from within, almost radiating light onto the thirty or so of us who'd been invited to this special occasion.

> *I asked God for a princess*
> *A friend to walk beside me*
> *Someone for me to love*
> *And here she is…*

Joha's voice cracked as Alina came closer. I was surprised he could sing at all the way he was staring at her, as if his whole world was summed up in her. Perhaps it was. When the song finished, Joha handed the guitar to a friend and took Alina's hands in his, bringing them up to kiss her knuckles. Every single one of them. People around them tittered with laughter. A few joy-filled tears dribbled their way down Alina's face as she held Joha's gaze. Further proof of how much she'd changed, and how desperately she loved this man. It was beautiful. And beautifully heartbreaking.

Because as thrilled and proud as I was for Alina, I knew deep down that that would never be me. Short of Waitrose dying.

I looked away, unable to bear the pain of watching such an intimate moment.

God, you didn't forget me, did you?

Marcos turned to look at me, questions written across his face which I had no answers for. I smiled and hoped he'd let it be. Thankfully, he did. Although when we sat again, the inch between us had shrunk to half that amount.

"Welcome, friends, to the wedding of Princess Alina of Peverell and my son, Joha Samson…"

"The wedding was beautiful."

It seemed to be the only thing people were saying around here. Not that I didn't agree. It would have been impossible not to. Simple, elegant, short. Nothing like the lengthy public event I'd heard Kenna and Thoraben's wedding had been. Not that theirs wouldn't have been beautiful also, but there was something so poignantly sweet about the simplicity of Joha and Alina's. In taking away all the fuss, their wedding had been a reminder of what a wedding was—the commitment of two people to love and be there for each other for the rest of their lives.

Yes, beautiful was the perfect description for it.

And for the reception that followed.

Dinner, served outside underneath a giant white tent slung with golden fairy lights. Everyone sat around white tables, grass beneath their feet, smiles on their faces. It was loud, and it was beautiful. There wasn't a single place card in sight. People sat where they wanted, talked to whomever they wanted. It was a celebration like none I'd ever been to. Intimate, yet welcoming. Status, class, titles, beliefs—all left at the door. Under the wings of the marquee, there was only celebration.

Except for one table. No. One man.

King Everson sat alone. Not unusual but strange, all the same. Or perhaps it was the expression on his face that seemed so out of place. Thoughtfulness, regret, sadness? Both his children married. Was he missing them already? Or perhaps it was Queen Ciera he was missing. Yes, missing his late wife was more likely the case. I knew Alina was missing her mother, though having Adeline and Malisa here helped. Adeline, Kenna's mother and the woman who'd raised Alina, and Malisa, Joha's mom and the woman who had been Ciera's best friend. Alina might have grown up without her mother, but she'd still been surrounded by women who cared.

As I watched, Malisa walked over to King Everson and offered him something to drink. He looked at her without speaking for some time before taking it with a nod. With a wave of her hand and the gentle tipping of her head, Malisa invited King Everson to sit with her and Pat. For a moment, I thought he might agree, he certainly looked as if he wanted to, but then he shook his head. Malisa said one more thing and then walked away. Part of me wished she might have tried harder, until I realized she was the only one who'd tried at all.

"You and Marcos are together now?"

"What?" I spun to face Kenna, water flying out of the glass in my hand and leaving a spray of tiny dots across the front of her silvery gray dress. It was a good thing it was only water and would dry soon enough. Perhaps the surprise of it would wipe the delighted grin off her face.

No such luck.

"He's not here with me."

"No? You seemed quite close in the chapel, and he hasn't stopped looking at you the entire time he's been out here."

He hadn't? I'd been too busy avoiding him to notice. It was a good thing the ceremony had been short because I'd been struggling to breathe by the end of it. Holding your breath so you didn't drown in your own puddle of delight at your seatmate's cologne did that to a person. Marcos had somehow managed to completely close that half-inch gap between us by the end of it. Much to both my delight and terror. All I could think about was his words on the balcony last night.

I'm attracted to you too.

"I didn't even know he was coming," I said, completely ignoring Kenna's hints. If she wanted to know more about the relationship—or lack of—between Prince Marcos and me, she'd have to ask him. *No, wait, that's a terrible idea. She wouldn't, would she?*

"Are you going to dance with him?"

No way. "Actually, I was about to leave."

"Before the reception finishes?"

No. I looked over at Marcos, catching his gaze without even trying. He tilted his head toward the dance floor, raising his eyebrows in question. My heart thudded as a wave of longing swept through my stomach and tingled my toes. *Like you. You're worth waiting for...*

I couldn't dance with him. Not tonight. My heart would never recover. I had to leave now.

Before I give in.

The balcony was calling my name when I arrived back at the palace. Or, rather, the peace it offered.

Between the attraction I'd fought sitting beside Marcos for the entire ceremony, the exhaustion of avoiding him at the reception, the equal parts pain and pride watching Alina pledge her life to the man she loved, and Kenna's unwanted observations, the wedding today had been far more emotional than I'd expected. All I wanted was to sit in the quiet and breathe. No people, no expectations, no questions, no holding my breath so I didn't breathe in Marcos's intoxicating cologne. Just the clear night air.

There was no way Marcos would be out on his balcony yet, not given how early I'd left the reception and his particular penchant for propriety. He'd stay right till the end, as was expected, and then there was travel time to factor in. I figured I had at least an hour, if not two, before he'd even arrive back at the palace. I'd go back inside earlier than that, in case.

Picking up my sketchbook and pencils, I wandered outside, kicked off my shoes, and curled myself into one of the chairs.

"Wenderley."

And promptly dropped the sketchbook on the ground, pencils scattering across the balcony's floor as I tried to catch it. So much for my assumption that I'd be alone. I'd been so certain he wouldn't be there that I hadn't even checked.

"Marcos, um, hi." *What now? Go back inside? That would be rude. He clearly knows you just arrived. Stay? With him right there?* "You're back early."

"I left right after you."

"Oh." Seriously? He hadn't stayed until the end? But…but… that was the right thing to do. And Marcos always did the right thing.

"I only went because you did."

Oh.

"I'm interrupting you," he said, gesturing with his head to my sketchbook, still on the ground. "Did you want me to leave?"

Honestly? Yes. I loved our balcony chats, as I'd come to think of them, but tonight, I needed space. "Would you be offended if I said yes?"

He was. It was there in that instant of shock on his face before he managed to hide it. I'd hurt him. By caring too much.

"Was it something I did?"

His voice was as clear and polite as always but there was a vulnerability in it I'd heard before. In the treehouse, that day with Ryan when he'd asked if Marcos was going to keep him. I swallowed back a painful lump in my throat. I had to tell Marcos the truth. That much was clear. But how he'd react? How much everything would change between us if I did? Whether I was ready for that? I had no idea.

God, help me. Help us both.

It didn't matter what he thought of me. For my sake, as well as his, I had to tell him.

"Marcos, what you said last night, about me being attracted to you?" He nodded. I took a deep breath, bolstering my heart while I fell apart inside. "It's true. I am. I look forward to every moment I get to spend with you. You've become one of the most important people in my life. Maybe even *the* most important."

He smiled. I hated myself for knowing I was about to wipe it away.

"But that's the thing. You can't be. I can't love you like that. You're still grieving Rachana and I have…someone. Maybe in another time and another place, this might have worked, but we're not there. We're here. Now. And neither of us are free."

Though he nodded, his face was so purposely blank that I couldn't tell what he was thinking. Maybe that was for the best.

"I'll still care for Ryan, I promised your mother I'd stay for two more weeks, but I think it best we avoid each other."

"And if I don't want to?"

"Then I hope you'll respect that I do."

I don't know if he left like I'd asked him to. I didn't wait to see.

TWENTY-EIGHT

"I t's raining. Again."

I tried not to laugh at Ryan's lack of enthusiasm and the way he threw himself across the settee with far more drama than necessary. It wasn't the rain that had him bothered as much as the fact that I'd promised him I'd teach him how to climb trees today, something possible but not advisable in the pouring rain. I would have taken him for a walk in the rain anyway, but he'd been sneezing a bit the past couple of days and, much as I didn't think there was anything to the old wives' tale that being out in the rain caused illness, I also didn't plan on trialing it on my young charge.

"There's always tomorrow."

"I suppose."

"So, what shall we do today? I was thinking building a fort might be fun."

He sat up and looked at me, his eyebrows pulling in as he tilted his head slightly to the left. I'd never seen that expression on his face before, although I'd seen similar on his father's. Usually right before telling me what I should have been doing rather than what I was.

"Unless you don't want to," I quickly added, forcing Marcos from my mind yet again. "We don't have to."

"A fort?"

"Do you like building forts?"

"I used to do it all the time with Mom, especially the days she was too tired to get out of bed. I'd build it around her and we'd hide in there together."

"Oh." That would explain the strange expression on his face, like he wasn't certain whether to be upset or amused. Grief mixed with hope. "We can do something else."

"No, I want to build a fort. Could we make one big enough for both of us and then read inside?"

"Sure. How about in the nursery? I know you're way too old for a nursery, but it's a big empty room where we can make as much noise as we like. Also, it's not filled with antiques, or at least, not any we could break. Sound good?"

Ryan nodded, a smile slowly starting to show.

"I'll get the blankets, you get the pillows. Meet you in the nursery."

Twenty minutes and enough laughter to have me still holding my stomach in pain later, the fort was done. Until one of us— most likely me—touched it the wrong way again, sending the whole thing to the floor. Clearly it had been far too long since I'd made a fort, and Ryan was too busy giggling at me to be much help.

"Pull it tighter, Wenderley."

"This is as tight as it goes." I made a face, sending him into another round of giggles. I had to admit, I may have let the blankets drop a few times purposely, just to make him laugh. His giggle was far too infectious not to take full advantage of the moment.

"Move the chairs in closer then," Ryan suggested.

"But then the fort will be too small."

"But it will have a roof, instead of being a pile of blankets and pillows."

"Hey, I like those blankets. They look particularly comfortable. In fact…"

I threw myself down on the blankets, arms and legs flung out, smile on my face. It was actually pretty comfortable. Of course, piling up eight or nine pillows on top of two blankets and a comforter with another three blankets on top had no option really *but* to be comfortable.

"Do forts really need roofs? I declare this fort to be roof-less. This way, we can see the stars."

Ryan looked up at the nursery's plain white roof. "There aren't any stars."

Kids at this age were so adorably literal.

"Come on, young Prince Ryan. Pull up a pillow."

He didn't quite flop on the pillows as I had, but he did lie down. "You're right, this is comfortable."

"Told you. Open air forts, we've started something, Ryan. Everyone is going to be wanting one now. Right then, still want to read?"

"Yes."

"Good. Only one problem."

"What?"

"I forgot to get the book. Sorry, you stay here. I'll be back in a moment."

Unfortunately, getting out of the pile of comfort was far more difficult than getting in. There was nothing to push myself up on and all attempts at trying to roll to my side seemed to only get me more tangled.

"Uh, Ryan?"

He was giggling again. Humiliation? Worth it. So long as no one else came into the room right now.

"I'll get it. I know where it is. I'll be right back."

He was gone before I could argue. He'd also had no problem whatsoever getting up again. Why was it I suddenly felt like an old woman?

The upside of Ryan being gone for a moment meant I didn't have to be quite as ladylike attempting to rise. Not only did I have more room to move but I could stick my arms and legs wherever I liked. With a completely ungraceful heave, I finally managed to get enough momentum to roll myself off the pile onto solid ground. And not a moment too soon. I stood up as Ryan burst back through the door. *Thank you, God, that I'm not wearing a skirt. Silly, impractical things.*

"Got it. Oh, and a letter for you. I told Mr. Hamill I would give it to you since you were all the way up here and sometimes his knees hurt climbing stairs."

It was all I could do not to snatch the mint green envelope from Ryan's hand. Seeing him holding something that reprobate Waitrose had touched had my stomach churning. Ryan was so pure and Waitrose so...not.

"Thank you." I took it, folded it, and put it in my pocket.

"Don't you want to read it?"

Burning it sounded like a far better option.

"I'll read it later."

"But I brought it all the way up here so you could read it now. I thought you'd be excited."

Terrified and nauseated were far closer to what I was currently feeling.

"Don't you want to read your story? Pirate Pumpernickel has been stuck on that cove for three days now. We have to rescue him. Or, at least, find out what happens next."

To my delight, and that of the boy beside me, Pirate Pumpernickel had far too many adventures to fit into one book. We'd found another three in the library. This third one was turning out to be my favorite.

"It's okay. I can wait. It didn't feel like a very thick letter."

They never were. A few lines, that was all they'd ever been. Just enough to ensure I didn't forget what Waitrose held over me. Not that Ryan knew that. Why would he? He was too young to know about threats and blackmail and the pain that came from making a stupid decision you could never reverse.

As well he should have been. He already knew far too much about pain and grief for someone so young.

Fake it, Wenderley. You don't have to read it. Just open it and make it look like you're reading. Keep him happy.

I fished the letter out of my pocket, slid open the envelope, and pulled out the matching green piece of paper, flicking my gaze across the blocky black words long enough to pretend.

"See, all go—"

No, not good.

No…

The letter shook in my hand. One word. One name, having caught my gaze.

Anna.

He couldn't. He wouldn't.

> *Wenderley,*
> *Remember, you tell and I will. Won't your girls love being exiled? You know their ages won't matter. Neither will their innocence. Who would I start with, I wonder…Anna? She seems like a nice girl. Able to handle the indignity of a criminal record.*
> *W*

He had.

The paper shook in my hand. Anna was an orphan who'd spent most of her young life being sent from relative to careless relative. When the relatives ran out of what little familial obligation they felt, they tossed her out. The Bakers had found her trying to break into a school library one night because it was the only place she could think of that might be warm and empty. They'd taken her into their family. Made her their daughter. It was the best family she'd ever had, and the first real home. I couldn't take that from her.

"Wenderley? Are you okay? Is it bad news?"

My smile was as forced as my words. And just as much a lie. "I'm fine."

"You look angry or something. Was it something I did? Should I not have brought it to you?"

"No!" He jumped back a little. I softened my voice. "No, not at all. You, my handsome prince, could never make me frown."

"Even if I jump on my bed?"

"Nope."

"Or eat my dinner really, really slow?"

"Definitely not."

"Or hide all your shoes and replace them with those pointy ones?"

"You wouldn't…"

He shook his head, grinning. "Never. I like your colorful shoes."

"Me too, Ryan."

Anna did too. I'd painted her a pair of her own last year for her birthday with butterflies perched on red spotted toadstools. She'd worn them so much the toadstools had faded to a pale pink.

God, please, protect her. You can't let her pay for my mistake. Please, please don't let her be the one to pay. Or any of the girls, please…

I slid the letter back in my pocket and pulled Ryan into a hug, before tickling his sides until he was giggling again. It was a long time before I could banish the letter from my mind long enough to do the same.

I was folding the last of the blankets when Marcos came storming into the nursery two hours later.

"What is this?"

I blanched, holding the blanket to my chest, as if it could save me from the wrath on his face and the conversation to come. Marcos had my letter. One of them anyway, I didn't know which one. I might have thought it was a new one, except the envelope was open, the mint green page waving in his hand. He might like to be in control, but he would never open someone else's mail. Not unless the fate of Hodenia was on the line.

"Where did you get that?"

"Ryan brought it to me just now. He said it made you sad and wanted me to fix it for you."

Today's? But— I reached back to my pocket. Empty. The letter must have fallen out when I'd been tickling Ryan and he'd picked it up when we were packing everything away. He'd said he was going to the bathroom. He'd gone to Marcos instead?

"Did you read it?" It was too much to hope that he hadn't. He wouldn't have been thundering mad about it if he hadn't.

"This is blackmail."

"It doesn't matter."

"You told me they were from a suitor."

"No, you assumed they were."

He crossed his arms. "You should have told me."

I dropped the blanket, finding I had some fight in me after all. "Told you what? You might be the prince, but my correspondence is none of your business, and I hardly need to remind you that I asked you to respect my need for space. So, please, give me my letter and leave. This has nothing to do with you."

"Not a chance."

"Marcos—"

"No, Wenderley. There's respect and then there's stupidity, and I care about you too much to let you be stupid about this. If someone is hurting you, I want to know."

"No one is hurting me."

"Maybe not physically. Come on, Wenderley. How can I help you if you won't tell me what's going on? You let me believe these were from a suitor, which is clearly not the case. One a week, since you've been here and how many before that? What does this—" He glanced at the letter, still clutched in his hand. "—W person have over you? What secret is he making you keep?"

Did Marcos really think I was going to tell him? He'd read the letter. Even if he didn't know who Anna or the girls mentioned were, the letter made it clear they were important to me. Not worth the risk. Even for Marcos. "I can't."

"I'll protect you."

"You can't."

He scoffed, as if my saying that was a direct affront to his manhood. Perhaps it was.

"I have entire squadrons of guards and security teams at my beck and call. You'd be safe. I promise. Tell me, Wenderley. Please. I want to help."

The concern in his voice, on his face, it almost undid me. But I couldn't let myself be swayed. Too many lives depended on my silence.

"I'm sorry, I can't."

"Who is Anna?"

"A friend."

"You're not even going to tell me that?"

I shook my head. Why had I ever let a compliment seduce me? *Stupid, foolish girl. You knew better.*

"Tell me this then, is Ryan safe from this man?"

"Yes, of course. Ryan has nothing to do with this."

"But Anna does."

"Not directly. She's…in danger because of me. Because I made a dumb decision."

Marcos was silent for a moment, maybe remembering a few of his own decisions he'd rather not have made. When he spoke, his voice was quiet, the accusing edge gone.

"Is this why you said no?"

I didn't have to ask what he was talking about. The moment was likely as etched in my mind as it was his.

"I'll pack my bags."

"Stay."

"You want someone like me caring for your son? Hodenia's future king? What if W—*he* does threaten Ryan?"

"Do you think he will?"

Honestly? "No." There was nothing about Ryan that hadn't already been splashed across every gossip column. Waitrose would find no leverage there, unlike with my girls, who just by spending time with me put themselves in danger. *God, why? Why did you let me be so stupid? Why didn't you stop me?* And more, why did they have to pay? It was my mistake.

"Wenderley, please. Let me help you."

"I'm sorry. I can't." I picked up the pile of blankets. "Please don't ask again."

TWENTY-NINE

"Lady Wenderley, the queen wishes to speak with you."

I held back a groan, but barely. Ryan and I were in the middle of an epic treasure hunt in the garden. He still had five more things to find, in three different colors, before we read another chapter of our current book. He hadn't been the only one looking forward to finding out what happened next. It had taken every ounce of self-control I possessed—and a whole lot of distraction—to stop me from pulling out the book after Ryan went to bed last night and reading ahead to find out if Pirate Pumpernickel found his way home or got stuck in Crocodile Lake for all eternity. But when the queen calls…

"I don't suppose she'd wait an hour?"

Paige's mouth quirked in what probably would have been a smile if she hadn't been working. "I'll see to Prince Ryan while you're gone. She's in her tearoom."

"Thank you."

I handed over the list of things to find, selfishly kept the book's location to myself lest Ryan convince Paige to read it and I miss out, assured Ryan I'd be back soon—I hoped—and started the familiar trek to the tearoom.

"Your Highness?" I said, standing at the open door. Although she'd invited me, I thought it still best to wait for her direct invitation to come in. Also, I couldn't see her. Had Paige got the location of this apparently important and urgent meeting wrong? Or perhaps Queen Galielle had been called somewhere else?

"Over here."

I walked in a little farther, craning my head from side to side, trying to pinpoint the direction her voice had come from. Obviously, she wasn't sitting at any of the lace-covered tables or I would have seen her instantly. Nor was she watering the miniature rose plants over near the windows. It was her skirt I finally spotted, poking out from behind a large silk-painted screen I hadn't noticed before in the far corner of the room. Had it always been there? Probably. I'd have to check it out later. The painted design was exquisite.

Of course, I could go see it now. Though the queen's dress swayed like she was rummaging around behind the screen, she didn't seem to be coming out. What was she doing? She wasn't stuck, was she? I walked closer, winding my way around spindly white tables and chairs until I was right beside her.

She was rummaging. Through cardboard boxes? That wasn't what I'd thought would be hiding in the corner of an elegant room like this. Even if they were hidden by a beautiful screen.

"Can I help you, Your Highness?"

"I thought it was here."

If I didn't know any better, I would have thought she'd lost her mind, muttering to herself like she was, searching through box after discarded box.

"You're looking for something? Can I help?"

"No, no. I'm sure it's in here. I could have sworn it was in the chest in my room and if not there, then in the closet, but it was in neither of them. Then I thought of these, which have been packed up here since my mother's somewhat ill-advised but certainly profitable spending spree, but I still can't find it. Move those two boxes a bit further out, will you please? I'll have the maids pile them up again properly later but it's going to bother me until I find it."

"Find what?" I asked, tugging the two boxes she'd pointed at toward the wall. One seemed to hold boxed teacups—replacements for the ones used in here, perhaps? Though why they weren't stored in the kitchens with the rest of the crockery, I didn't know. The second seemed to be layers and layers of colorful fabric, the top third of which needed re-folding. I picked up a gorgeous purple and gold piece made from some type of iridescent thread which almost glowed in the light and set to work. It might have been dull work, folding sheet after sheet of cloth, had they not all been vibrant shades every color of the rainbow, and all made of the same glistening fabric. And had Queen Galielle stopped muttering, something which was becoming far too intriguing.

"Not there either. And here I was certain it would be here. Where else…? I know I didn't give it to Rachana but…ah…yes… perhaps…" She stepped back suddenly, an excited grin on her face. "Leave those. Come with me."

Before I could ask again what was going on, she'd pulled the emerald, blue, and silver piece from my hand, dropped it with far less respect than its magnificence demanded on the floor, and tugged me out the door.

I would have thought, given her age, Queen Galielle might have slowed by the third flight of stairs she ran up. But no, she raced up that one as fast as the first two. It was all I could do to keep up with her. She tossed over her shoulder at me what could only be described as a mischievous grin when she walked past Ryan's door and stopped in front of Marcos's. I was starting to realize why curiosity had killed the cat. What on earth was she doing?

She barged right through the front door like she owned the place, which, I supposed, you could do when you were the queen. I stayed at the door. I'd been in here once before. It hadn't gone well.

Queen Galielle was already opening another door—thankfully not Marcos's bedroom—when she noticed I wasn't beside her and looked back. "Coming?"

To an as-yet-unknown room in Marcos's personal suite? For all I knew, it was a bathroom. Or his dressing room. No, thank you. "I'll wait here."

"It's not his room."

It was like she could see right through me.

"It was Rachana's."

Intriguing. You could tell a lot about a person from their bedroom, and there was so much I still wanted to know about Rachana. But still, privacy and all.

"Oh, come on. She's not here and I might need you."

Fine. I'd go. But only because Queen Galielle would lay the guilt on thicker until I gave in. I already had enough guilt in my life without voluntarily picking up more.

My breath caught as I walked through the door. I'd thought the room I'd been given was beautiful, but this…

A mix of blues, teals, gray, and white woods, and more of the giant windows I'd come to love in my guest room, it was as if I'd stepped into a day at the beach. Minus the sand and sunburn and crowds that came with it. Pure relaxation. Pale blue walls, white edgings, gray driftwood frames on all the pictures, shades of teal across all the furnishings. Some dark, most light, all stunning.

"It's…wow." All manner of eloquent description caught in my wonder as I stood there, slowly turning in the center of the room. "Rachana had great taste."

"Actually, I decorated this room. It was mine, once. Many years ago."

"Really?"

"I told her she could change it, but she never did. I wonder if she didn't think she'd be here long enough to make a change worth it."

Oh. That took some of the joy out of my delight. Though certainly not all of it. Far from all of it. I ran my finger gently along a white wooden table, thinking how pretty a vase of tulips would look there. And another over in the corner, on that buffet, perhaps in a blue vase? Clear—maybe even blue—glass pebbles scattered across the top like bubbles spilling out.

Queen Galielle put a finger to her lips as she turned a slow circle, her eyes not quite focused, as if she were looking at something beyond the physical. A memory, perhaps? A bright smile tugged her lips upward as she pulled open another door, this one leading to a big, albeit completely empty, closet. Had all Rachana's clothing and personal items been packed away so quickly? Had Ryan kept anything of his mother's? I'd never thought to ask.

"A chair, if you please, Wenderley."

I pulled into the closet the first one I spotted, the one from the dressing table. She wasn't going to—

Yes, she was. This time it was me with a hand to my mouth as the very proper Queen Galielle of Hodenia stepped up onto the chair, balancing on the tips of her toes to reach the back of a shelf. "Queen Ga—"

My offer of assistance—or was it protest?—was stunted by her victorious cry as she pulled down a wooden box. Was this what she'd been searching for all this time? An entirely forgettable, unpolished, barely even painted wooden box? It must have been missed when the maids were clearing out Rachana's things. Not surprising, given it was the same color as the shelves. It would have blended right in. I rushed forward to offer the queen a hand down.

"Finally." She held the box in front of her like one of the crown jewels. "Come see."

Once again, I followed her. This time, we only went as far as the sitting area of Rachana's suite. Which was a relief, given I was growing more curious about this box by the second—and could have quite happily spent a few hours simply relaxing in this room. The treasure hunt I'd made up for Ryan had nothing on this. I sat across from Queen Galielle, watching as she stared down at the box, tracing a thin line on the top with her finger.

"Wenderley, I want you to have this."

With an air of great importance, she passed me the box. I tried to look appropriately appreciative, but up close the box was even uglier than I'd first thought. Not only was it unvarnished, but the paint had dulled with age, a large crack stretched along one of the sides, and there was a dent on one corner, as if it had been dropped on it.

"Thank you."

I smiled back at her, holding the box on my lap, trying to look grateful. Not that I wouldn't treasure it. I mean, how many people could say a queen had personally given them a gift? Even if it wasn't particularly pretty. I would keep it forever.

"Open it."

Oh. I blushed slightly. Of course. It wasn't the box she was giving me, it was what was inside, though what would be kept in such an unremarkable box was—

My mouth dropped open, making Queen Galielle laugh. This couldn't be right. She'd given me the wrong box, surely. She hadn't even opened the box to check what was inside it before giving it to me. If she had, she certainly wouldn't have—

"My mother's favorite tiara."

By some feat of superhuman strength, I pulled my gaze away from the stunning piece of jewelry nestled on a pillow of purple satin and looked at the queen. "But why—? How—? I can't—"

"If you're going to tell me you can't accept it, then don't bother. It's yours. I'm giving it to you. Don't you dare spoil my gift by refusing it."

"What about your daughters?"

"They have plenty of jewels."

"But—"

"Do you like it?"

Was she serious? "It's...it's..."

"I'll take that as a yes."

Too scared to touch it, I fingered the edge of the satiny pillow as I stared down at the tiara. It was gold, made up of intertwined hearts, the biggest in the center with those either side becoming gradually smaller. Though three white diamonds punctuated the three largest of the hearts, it was the pattern on the gold which made the tiara sparkle, cut in such a way that it caught the light whichever way I tilted it. Glittering, almost. Showy without being over the top. Elegant.

And mine, apparently.

"Don't royal jewels have to stay in the family?"

"Mother gave it to me. It's mine to do with as I please."

I closed the box, fingered the bordered lid, tried to figure out what to do with such a gift. What it meant.

"Of course, I'm still hoping one day you'll *be* family, but whether you marry Marcos or not, the tiara is yours. Please, take it. You've made such a difference in our lives these past two months. I wanted to give you something to let you know how much I've appreciated you. Something as precious to me as you've become."

I nodded, humbled by her words even more than the gift I held. An official thank you would have easily been enough and even more than I needed. I'd loved every moment spent with Ryan and counted it an absolute privilege to have been given the chance to know the whole family. Even knowing how much it would hurt to walk away. "Thank you."

"I'd be honored if you wore it to the ball next weekend. It'll go wonderfully with the gown I took the liberty of ordering you. Though, I might make a change..." She nodded, talking almost to herself. "Yes, that would work."

My mind must have been more clogged with emotion than I realized. I stared at Queen Galielle, searching every memory of the past two months—and further back—for any mention of a ball. Nothing.

"Sorry. What ball?" *Furthermore, what gown?*

"Oh. Forgive me. I assumed Marcos would have mentioned it to you. It's for his birthday. Normally we host a formal dinner, but this year he requested a ball. A small one, of course, given the timing of it. Close friends, other royals, several dignitaries, a chamber orchestra for dancing."

I must have looked as shocked as I felt because Queen Galielle laughed.

"I know. I was as surprised as you when he asked me. I'd thought for sure he would want to keep the celebrations minimal this year—if he chose to celebrate with anyone outside of the family at all—but he was quite adamant. I thought it might have had something to do with you, actually."

"Me?" *Marcos, what have you done?*

"I asked him to write a list of the guests he wanted invited. Yours was the first name on it. I know you've been spending more time together lately. Has something happened?"

For one long moment, sitting there in that serenely beautiful room, her extravagant gift held in my hands, I considered telling Queen Galielle everything.

About that night with Waitrose.

My girls and how unworthy I felt to be leading them.

The balcony chats with Marcos.

How, in spite of everything, I'd fallen in love with him.

How, even though I'd promised I wouldn't marry Marcos until he believed, I wasn't so sure about that anymore. It had been so easy to promise at the time, when leaving had still felt so far away. But now? Were the differences in our beliefs—or his lack of—really such an issue? I know Queen Galielle thought so, but what if it was different for Marcos and me? What if I was the one God used to change Marcos's heart, and my faith grew his? For over a year, I'd prayed for him, fought for him, wept for him. I loved him. Deeply. Was I really supposed to now walk away? Wasn't love supposed to stay?

Because I'd realized one thing, as I lay far from sleep in bed last night—I couldn't continue living with Waitrose's threats forever. Sooner or later, whether I stood up or he stood down, this was going to end. And when it did, I'd either be married to Waitrose, exiled, or free. And the latter two changed everything.

"Wenderley? Did something happen?"

I shook my head. "No, Your Highness." I couldn't tell her. Any of it. I was the one who'd gotten myself into this mess, and I was the one who was going to get myself out of it. Somehow. "There is nothing between your son and me."

THIRTY

"Wenderley, wake up!"

I blinked into the half-lit room, wondering where the sun was. A couple of seconds later, my eyes having adjusted enough to see the clock, I was wondering what the emergency was, and whether it was dire enough to actually force me out of bed since it hadn't been till sometime after three that I'd finally fallen asleep. The endless ticking of the clock had taunted me as I lay in bed, telling myself to let the fear go and sleep, while begging God over and over to spare Anna and the girls and agonizing in circles over the feelings I had for Marcos.

Sitting out on the balcony would have helped, if Marcos hadn't been doing the same. He'd been out there every night this past week. I'd sketched in my room and pretended he wasn't there. And that I wasn't thinking about him. Even if every page in my sketchbook proved otherwise.

"Come on, Wenderley," Kahra said from her place on the end of my bed. "We've got work to do."

Work. At 5:48 AM. With a girl so excited she could barely sit still. Not an emergency then.

"Lucie is waiting in her room. We've found the suit of armor the perfect outfit for the ball. You're going to love it."

Rusty? That's what this was all about?

"Sir Rusty is going to the ball?"

Kahra giggled. "Of course not, but everyone else is getting dressed up for it so why not him?"

I supposed there was some semblance of logic in that statement. Maybe. Somewhere. If I was slightly more awake.

"It's early." And I'd gotten, two—maybe three?—hours of decent sleep.

"I know," she said, completely unrepentant. "It's the only time we can be sure Marcos isn't going to be in his office. He makes a point of never going there before breakfast. And Ryan will sleep for another hour or so. Now is the perfect time."

Right. Time...clocks...breakfast...

Wake up, Wenderley. Kahra's going to think something is wrong if you don't get up soon, and the last thing you need is someone else asking questions you can't answer.

My head pounded as I sat up. I got up anyway.

"Marcos isn't in his office?"

"No, of course not."

She seemed offended that I'd ask. Strange, given how many times over the past few weeks she'd tried to push the two of us together.

Wenderley, could you take this to Marcos please? I told him I'd bring it to him but I'm too tired to walk up those stairs to his office right now. You understand.

She'd gone directly from speaking with me to jogging the garden paths for the next hour.

Wenderley? I told Marcos you'd show him those roses you liked in the garden this morning. You know the ones we looked at yesterday? He mentioned last night that his office could really do with some flowers.

And here I'd thought Kahra had more subtlety than Lucie.

At lunch yesterday...

Wenderley? I'm so sorry. I know Lucie and I were going to go on the picnic with you and Ryan tomorrow but we've got, um, things to do and can't anymore. Marcos is free though. We asked him. He said he'd love to come.

I was surprised she hadn't planned our wedding yet. I also needed to remember to come up with an excuse to skip the picnic. One a lot less obvious than Kahra's.

"You have an outfit for Sir Rusty?"

"Yes, Lucie has it. Are you coming?"

It was impossible not to be drawn into her excitement, even with my body protesting the lack of sleep. It was also really nice to see her smiling. This was why I'd stayed.

"Give me a second," I told the bouncing girl, walking into the giant closet I was becoming far too accustomed to having. Jeans, blouse, bracelets, and—I looked around—purple shoes today. They matched the lavender of the as-yet-sun-filled sky. My hair actually fell pretty well across my shoulders, so I left it down. Ready in under a minute, but still too long for the princess who tugged my hand the instant I reappeared and dragged me down the hall, up a flight of stairs, past too many doors to count, and into Lucie's room.

It was worth it. The second Lucie flung the sheet off their find, I burst into laughter.

A tuxedo. Sunflower yellow and covered with bright, multi-colored shapes like paint splotches which clashed horribly against the yellow. And a tie covered in sequins. The whole thing was so bright it almost made up for the lack of sunlight.

"I doubt we'll get the shoes on," Lucie said, holding up a pair of matching shoes, "but the hat should make up for it."

I looked around. "Hat?"

Both girls grinned, then pointed. I followed their fingers to the profusion of color and sequins sitting on a stool in the corner of the room. It was a wonder I hadn't seen it the second I walked through the door, large as it was.

It was a top hat, of sorts, though I'd never seen one so tall. Made of the same yellow, splotched fabric as the suit, it would have swallowed Ryan, should he have tried to wear it. Flopped right down over his head and settled somewhere around his toes. It well and truly overwhelmed the poor wooden stool it was precariously perched on. I felt sorry already for whoever had had to wear it in the first place.

"Perfect," I proclaimed, much to the princesses' delight. "Where did you get it?"

Lucie grinned. "Mr. Wintergreen."

Luka? "You're kidding." I looked from one girl to the other. Though they were both grinning now, it was Kahra who answered.

"No. I think he might have had it specially made, though he *claimed* he found it in his closet. He brought it to me yesterday, but said if I tell Marcos he had anything to do with dressing the armor, he'd tell Marcos the real reason I've become so fascinated with plants lately."

Her cheeks went red as I tried not to laugh. Her crush on the young gardener was so sweet. "Find out his name yet?"

She nodded shyly. "Damien."

"Nice name. Strong and noble."

Kahra ducked her head, fiddling with a button on the suit. Tempting as it was to continue teasing her, I didn't think her heated cheeks or the button's thread could handle any more. And we had a knight to dress.

"I suppose I'll take the, uh, hat?"

"You're in, then?"

"Of course. Sir Rusty is going to look spectacular. But you're certain your brother won't be there?" There was no way we were going to be subtly hiding this behind our backs if he happened to walk down the hall or—worse—be in his office already. Forget spotting it from a mile away. Someone sitting on the moon would be blocking the glare from this outfit. I'd have to thank Luka later. It really was perfect.

"He won't be. Promise."

With far too many giggles for such a secretive mission, the three of us grabbed the outfit and hauled it down the halls and stairs, hiding as best we could when we saw any maids or staff coming and running whenever the way was clear. We were all out of breath by the time we reached Marcos's office.

It didn't take too long to divest Sir Rusty of the clothes we'd previously put him in. I kept shushing the girls though when putting him in a suit jacket and pants proved far more difficult. In the end, I had to put my arms around Rusty's middle and lift him off the floor entirely to get the pants on. Thankfully, the suit was a few sizes bigger than Sir Rusty or we'd never have managed it. Embracing a rusty suit of armor—one I'm certain was probably an antique or, at least, not supposed to be touched—wasn't exactly how I'd planned on starting the day.

He almost toppled over entirely at one point when one of his arms stuck and I lost my balance. The thought of how loud the clang would be if he hit the marble had me scrambling to put myself between him and the floor. Kahra somehow managed to pull us both up.

The hat wouldn't stay straight but we finally got it balanced enough to take a step back and admire our work. It was all I could do not to burst out laughing. I refused to look at the girls either, knowing if I did, we'd all lose it. With a final nod to our handiwork, we grabbed the clothes and hat he'd been wearing and sprinted all the way back to Lucie's room where, of course, we all burst into laughter.

"That hat!" Lucie said, tears springing to her eyes as she tried to take a breath. "It... It..." She couldn't get the words out around the laughter, but she didn't need to. I knew exactly what she meant. I'd start giggling again every time the sight of that crazy hat sitting atop such a dignified knight came to mind today. Which, no doubt, would be frequently. I definitely needed to thank Luka.

"I should check on Ryan," I finally bit out, realizing the time. Had it really taken us almost forty-five minutes to dress Sir Rusty?

My amusement lasted another whole minute—the time it took to walk from Lucie's room to mine. The girls had been right. Marcos wasn't in his office. He couldn't have been, because he was standing in front of my door.

For an instant, my heart jumped but then, just as quickly, thudded back into place with enough force to leave a bruise.

He was holding a letter. A mint green one.

God... Another one? So soon? It's only been two days.

Had he read it? Surely not. And yet, I would have, had our situations been reversed.

He handed it to me as soon as I was close enough. It was still sealed.

"You didn't read it."

"Of course not. It's your letter."

"Thank you."

"I should have."

My hand shook, as much from exhaustion as from fear. He wanted me to open it now but he had to know I wouldn't. No matter how long he stood there, blocking my door. It wasn't that I didn't think he could protect me, as he seemed to think, it was that I loved him too much to let him get involved. He'd want to save me and, short of breaking several laws, he couldn't.

Hopeless frustration dragged my shoulders down. "What do you want me to say?"

"You know what I want."

For me to tell him everything.

He put a hand on my arm, much the same as I'd done to him the day of the funeral when he, like me now, had been doing his best to pretend everything was fine. We were both liars.

"You don't need to carry this by yourself."

"I'm not. I have God."

"Then why are you still terrified?"

I didn't have an answer for that. Maybe he didn't expect one because with a gentle squeeze of my arm, Marcos left. I wanted to call after him and assure him that my faith was big enough to weather this, that God was big enough, that all would be well. But I didn't know anymore.

What if God was big enough but his answer wasn't the one I wanted? What if—despite being forgiven—Waitrose still won, and my girls were all indicted, and I was left with a reputation no amount of time could ever heal?

God—

What? What could I even pray? Help me? Fix this? Turn back time? Don't let your best be my worst?

I let myself into my room, pulling my feet up under me on the couch nearest the big bay window as the questions continued to tumble around my mind. I could have stopped Waitrose months ago. All it would have taken—all it *would* take—was me telling King Everson what had happened. Maybe not even the king. Maybe only Thoraben. Kenna, even. Any one of them had the power to force Waitrose to obey the law and marry me. And yet, I'd let it drag on.

The fear, the threats.

I'd told myself over and over that it was for the girls and their safety that I kept my silence, but was it? Or was it simply that I was too afraid of the consequences to accept them? Too afraid what people might think of me.

No. I pushed that thought aside almost immediately. That was my tiredness talking. It wasn't me. I was strong. I was brave. I'd stopped caring what people thought of me a long time ago. Who I did care about was my girls and their lives. I wouldn't let Waitrose near them.

The envelope felt thicker than usual. When I opened it, a photo of Marcos and me leaving the Holiday Party came out alongside the letter. Grainy, as if zoomed in from a great distance with a poor quality camera, but unmistakably us.

> *Wenderley,*
> *Apparently one prince is as good as another where you're concerned. I don't know whether to be offended or impressed. Does he know he's getting a girl as used as himself? Or perhaps that's why you went for him. In which case, my congratulations. Although what I said still stands. Tell him, tell anyone, and you'll pay. You and those girls.*
> *-W*

My heart thudded as, with shaking hands, I tucked both the letter and the photo back in their envelope.

God, I know I'm forgiven but—

I shook my head. I was forgiven. I knew that. Once and for all. But just because I was forgiven didn't mean the pain went away. Nor the fear. Would Waitrose follow through with his threats?

Please, God. Those girls didn't do anything wrong. Don't let them be punished for my mistake. And please, show me how to fix this mess I've made. I know I don't deserve it but please, make something good of this.

Somehow.

THIRTY-ONE

When Queen Galielle said she had a gown for me, I hadn't thought it would be this. If I'd been able to design my own gown, it still wouldn't have come close to being as perfect for me as this one.

It was a ball gown, certainly, but like none I'd ever seen. The style itself was common enough—fitted, sleeveless bodice with a sweetheart neckline, ball gown skirt. But the colors! All I could think of was jewels. The fabrics I'd re-folded while she was searching for the tiara, the jewel-toned, glisteningly rich greens, golds, magentas, purples, and blues, she'd used them in this gown, I was certain of it. The bodice was gold but the skirt made up of panels of color.

It should have looked gaudy. Likely it would have, if not for the tiny black flowers embroidered in a spray across the bodice, gathering at the waist and fluttering down the skirt. They tied it all together. Brought elegance to the rainbow.

I'd been stunned into silence when I'd seen it for the first time, something I couldn't remember ever happening before in my entire life.

"This is mine? Truly?" I'd finally found the words to ask the five maids the queen had assigned to help me prepare.

"Yes, my lady," one of them had said. "But first, hair and makeup."

Hair and makeup. Gold tiara. Gorgeous gown. Maids at my

bidding. Well, I supposed I was more at theirs given the way they'd been bossing me around since they arrived in my room a few hours ago, stating that the queen had sent them to help me get ready. Five maids. I'd never had so many people help me get ready before.

And now, here I was, standing in the ballroom in the most gorgeous gown I'd ever seen, my hair by some miracle staying in the loose bun my maids had put it in, all topped with a gold tiara which might have made me feel self-important if not for the fact that every woman here was wearing one. Of course, almost every woman here except me was a royal of some version so that might also have had something to do with it.

The ball was extravagant. There was no other word for it. Even pared down as I knew it had been, everything was just a bit more than I'd expected—and I'd been to plenty of balls before. Every year, Peverell's royal family hosted four. I'd attended them all, lavish as they were. And yet, none of them had prepared me for this.

Muted lights set the scene, basking everything in a glow of magic almost. Bright enough to see, dark enough to dream. The music, too, was clear but not overwhelmingly loud, the bows of the violins, violas, and cellos synchronized in a dance all of their own. The only decorations were chandeliers, both hanging from the roof and suspended along the walls. With so many glass doors around the ballroom reflecting back the grandeur of both the lights and the sparkling people, there was little need for anything else.

Alina and Joha were still on their honeymoon trip so hadn't come, but Thoraben and Kenna were here. I'd spoken with them briefly out on the terrace earlier before another couple had drawn them away. I'd waved them off with a smile, promised Kenna we'd talk later, picked a small chicken skewer off the plate of a passing waiter, and thanked God once again that Thoraben had married Kenna instead of me.

"Wenderley."

My heart skipped at Marcos's soft address. I knew he was behind me. There hadn't been a single moment tonight when I hadn't been aware of where he was, who he was talking to, how dashing he looked in his formal tuxedo. I'd been all too content to cheer him on from a distance, praying God would protect him from any well-meant but hurtful words, and me from the force of my attraction to him. There was something about the enchantment of the night which made it all too easy to forget all the reasons I should stay away. But I couldn't let myself. Not even for one weak moment.

"Prince Marcos. Happy birthday."

Up close, he looked even more incredible. I still hadn't figured out what cologne he wore or if he wore one at all but every inch of him exuded power. Confidence. Strange, coming from the same man I'd seen cry at the funeral. He wore it like armor. But, like knights of old, he wore it well. A symbol of status and pride as much as protection. Beautiful in its strength.

"Thank you. Will you dance with me?"

I spluttered the sip of drink I'd taken to stop myself from making a fool of myself saying how strong he looked. I shouldn't have bothered. Now I'd simply spat all over him. He smiled slightly as he wiped a few wet specks off the front of his not-quite-so-immaculate suit.

"I take it you find such an invitation from me abhorrent."

"No! I mean, not at all." Far from it. "I'm honored you'd ask but I don't think that's a good idea."

"Because?"

He couldn't really be this clueless, could he? He was the guest of honor and this would be his first dance of the night. Whether anyone admitted it out loud or not, there was significance in who he chose to be his partner. After the first dance, it wouldn't matter so much, but this first dance? It mattered. Even more, this being the first and largest social event he'd attended since Rachana's death. Everyone would be watching.

His partner of choice meant something—to every woman here, if not the realms of clueless men. And, simply stated, there were plenty of partners far more desirable than me.

Princess Celeste, for one. She'd been trying to get Marcos's attention since she arrived and he still hadn't even so much as looked in her direction, although she was glaring a hole in the back of his jacket right now.

He was still looking confused. Maybe he really didn't understand. I'd have to try to make it easier.

"You haven't danced with anyone since Rachana."

"I'm aware of that."

"Dance with me and everyone here will think there's—" I cringed, ducking my head to stare at my hands, suddenly unable to look him in the eye. "—something between us."

"There is."

He was not making this easy. "Something more than friendship."

He waited a beat before putting a hand on my chin and lifting it until I had no choice but to meet his gaze. "There is."

I closed my eyes. It was too much. Every dream I'd selfishly cherished. Marcos, staring at me like I was everything he'd ever wanted in life, singling me out, humbly asking me to dance. Even with my eyes closed, I could feel him there. Waiting. For me. Just like he'd said he would that night on the balcony.

God, please…

"You've never struck me as a person who particularly cared what others thought of her."

My eyes opened again as I raised my eyebrows. "It's not their opinion of *me* I was considering."

"You're worried about my reputation?"

"Someone should be."

"You don't think I thought this through?"

Not in the slightest. "Did you?"

"Yes."

"Then—"

He dropped his hand. "Are you embarrassed to be seen with me? Is that it?"

"What? No, of course not."

"Then dance with me."

"I can't. I'm the help." Also, a titled lady, but desperate times called for desperate measures. Somehow, I had to make him understand what an inappropriate choice I was. Preferably before Princess Celeste walked within firing range with that glare of hers. Any other night, I would have been thrilled for her to scorch my gown or even destroy it altogether, but I really loved this gown. "I'll dance with you later. Promise."

"You're not the help. No, that's not right. You are, absolutely. A huge help. I don't know how I could have gotten through these past two months without you. But that's not all you are. You're a lady. Nobility. And," he took my hand, "my friend, even if you refuse to be more yet. Please. Dance with me."

"My title means little." Except to people like Celeste, who'd take it as a personal affront that the crown prince danced with a mere lady before a princess like her.

"But you mean everything."

His words stunned me almost as much as the fervency behind them. What did he mean by that? I meant everything to Ryan? To the others in the palace? He couldn't mean I meant everything to him. Could he?

"Please, Wenderley. Just one dance."

I must have nodded, though I couldn't remember deciding to do so, because with a gentle tug on my hand, he led me into the middle of the dance floor.

You mean everything.

You. Mean. Everything.

His arm came around my back, turning me in to face him. I kept my gaze at his collar, afraid to look any higher. If I looked up, I knew my face would instantly give away how much I wanted this, despite my claims otherwise. I'd loved dancing with him the first time we'd danced, at the King's Ball, all those months ago. But this time?

He wasn't my friend's fiancé.

He wasn't someone I'd pulled from the shadows to force into a dance for his own good.

And he certainly wasn't distracted, the way he stared at me.

"Thank you, Lady Wenderley. This means a lot to me."

His voice near my ear sent goose bumps all the way down to my toes, but it was his tone and gratitude that warmed my heart. He might look and be every inch of a prince tonight, but underneath it all, he was still just the man I'd stared at the stars with on those nights when it was torture to be alone. The man who knew what it was to have an entire kingdom judge and find him wanting, yet still had the courage to try again. This was just Marcos.

At some level, I was aware of the whispers and attention we were attracting as we danced—a steady mix of frowns, surprise, and delight—but it didn't bother me as much as it should have. I'd deal with the repercussions of what this meant later—no doubt Marcos and I both would—but for now, I wanted to enjoy this moment. Stolen, but treasured. Cherished, yet bittersweet. For one dance, I'd let myself forget our past, ignore our future, and bask in the warmth of Marcos's embrace.

"Thank you for asking me," I said.

"You're the only one I considered."

"Not Princess Celeste?"

"Who?"

Was he teasing me? He'd written the invite list. He must have put her on there. "The beautiful woman over there in the lavender gown." I nodded my head in her direction. He didn't look, even for a moment.

"I only see one beautiful woman here tonight, and she's not wearing lavender."

Marcos leaned forward, brushing a kiss against my temple. Flustered, I stepped left instead of right, almost kicking him in the process. He grinned. I considered kicking him for real.

Focus Wenderley. Left, two, three, right, two, three, forward, two, three, twirl—

"Although, she does seem to be taller than I remember. Not wearing your sunflower shoes tonight? Or the tulip ones?"

This time I did stumble. He'd noticed my shoes? Not that they were subtle or anything, brightly painted as they were, but he was the prince of Hodenia, with more important things to do than keep track of my shoes. Or my height. Was he really so observant that he'd noticed the inch and a half difference?

"I thought these heels more appropriate."

"Probably."

Marcos spun me out and in again in an elaborate series of twirls. My skirt flared into a kaleidoscope of colors, every shade intensified by the golden lights overhead. For a moment, my back landed against his chest, his arms tight around my waist. I heard his quick intake of breath, before—three beats late—I was facing him again. It was a wonder I could dance at all the way my heart thudded from his nearness.

A dance, that was all it was. Something I'd done a hundred times. But this felt like so much more.

A request. A hope. A promise.

"Wenderley…" He breathed out my name, part in question, part assurance. They were both there equally, though I couldn't have said how I knew. "Can I come and see you? When you go home. I know you've said a relationship between us is out of the question but I'm not ready to say goodbye."

"I'm not leaving for another week at least."

"I know, but I wanted to ask now in case I didn't get another chance. When I'm with you—" His voice cracked, forcing him to clear his throat.

"Yes?"

He cleared his throat a second time before trying again. "You're a good friend, Lady Wenderley. And I don't have many of them. I don't want another regret to be letting you go."

Perhaps it was the direction of his gaze, more than his question or tone of voice which had my heart trying to escape my chest. He was staring at my mouth.

If it had been any other man, at any other time, I'm certain in that moment he would have kissed me. But we were far from alone, and I wasn't his wife, the one woman he'd said he'd kiss. Nor would he break my promise.

The reminder was stark but effective, like I'd been the one dunked in a tank of cold water. This wasn't real. It couldn't be.

"I'm sorry, Marcos. More than you could ever know. But I don't think that would be a good idea."

When the song finished a few twirls later, I clapped along with the other dancers before thanking Marcos and walking out onto the ballroom's large balcony alone.

He didn't mean those things. Not like you wish he did. And even if he did, it doesn't matter. You have made a difference in their lives, but it doesn't mean anything has changed in yours. He's still a prince. And no matter what you or he feel, you're still not free.

"Lady Wenderley, we meet again…"

I froze. I'd heard that voice too many times in my nightmares not to be instantly chilled by it.

Waitrose.

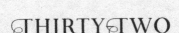

THIRTY TWO

Waitrose walked out from where he'd been standing, all but hidden behind a tall potted plant. What was he doing here? I hadn't seen him out on the terrace earlier or inside the ballroom at all. Had he been out on this balcony the whole time? Waiting for me?

God, help me...

His smile sent my heart thudding with fear as he closed the gap between us. I took a step back, wishing I'd stayed in the ballroom. There was nowhere to run on the balcony. Of course, we were also well within hearing distance of everyone in the room, should I scream, and anyone who looked our way would see us clearly, so it wasn't as if he could threaten me in any way physically. Not that he needed touch to threaten a person...

"What, no kiss? Not even a smile for the man who might one day be your husband?"

"I told you I'm not marrying you."

"You act like you have a choice."

"You promised..."

"And you believed me?" He let out a short laugh, completely devoid of amusement. "Silly question. Of course you did. You're Lady Wenderley Davis, Peverell's greatest fool. You even believed Prince Thoraben would marry you."

Another dance started inside, couples all over the ballroom bowing to each other before coming together. I couldn't see Marcos anymore. Couldn't ask for his help even if I'd wanted to.

Good. He should be enjoying himself with someone else. Much as it pained me to even think it. I could deal with Waitrose myself.

I hoped.

"Go away."

He didn't move. Not even a step. "Oh, but I'm a guest of the royal family tonight. I don't believe you have the authority to throw me out. Or have you wiled your way into this prince's bed too? I saw your dance. Lady Wenderley, the depths to which you've fallen. Wouldn't all your lovely little students love to hear about this? *Follow God. Do what's right. And excuse me while I do the total opposite...*"

"Don't—I didn't—You wouldn't—" My words didn't come out like I wanted them to, not that it mattered to the sneering man in front of me.

"Of course I would. Not all of us have your strict moral code, or any code at all."

"Maybe you should."

"Where's the fun in that?"

He was laughing at me, while I tried my best not to shake with equal parts fury and fear. "Why are you doing this? You don't want to marry me any more than I do you. Why can't you let it go?"

"My poor, pathetic Wenderley. Are you really so naïve? How do you think I've stayed on the palace's good side for so long? A rogue like me? That's what you called me, wasn't it? A rogue? Yes, well, I might be a rogue and a criminal and a poor excuse for a man, but I have the ear of the king, and his money."

He couldn't mean—"King Everson pays you?"

"For every single Rebel I turn in. It's a wonderful little agreement. He gets his Rebels and whatever other intelligence and, shall we say, items of questionable legality he requires, I get money and the freedom to do whatever I like while he turns his head."

I blinked, stunned into silence by his blithe confession. *He* was the one turning Rebels in? And not only that but, what? A spy? A thief? A thug? "You're a criminal."

He raised an eyebrow, seeming amused, rather than offended,

by my accusation. "Actually, my dear, I believe *you're* the criminal. Not only a Rebel but a Rebel leader? Grooming the next generation to oppose the crown? What is it, *eight* girls now, you have under your wing? How many more will you corrupt before the king discovers your treachery? What he would pay for you…"

"Don't do this."

He ran a finger up my arm. I shook it off, determined to show only anger, rather than the disgust and fear I felt. Anger, he'd merely deal with. Disgust, fear, or anything other than strength on my part would simply fuel his sick sense of power.

He grasped my hand, refusing to let go when I tried to pull away, tugging me so close I could see the tiny hairs along the bridge of his nose, the only place I planned to look.

"You know, you're looking quite beautiful tonight, Lady Wenderley." His hand was crushing mine. Purposely, of course. Anything he could do to exert power. I refused to let the pain show any more than the disgust. "Quite regal in your golden crown. A whole room full of royals and you're the most striking woman here. Maybe I'll tell King Everson of our need to be married after all, before Prince Marcos attempts to claim you. After all, I had you first."

"I'd choose imprisonment before I ever agreed to be your wife."

"Oh, don't be so dramatic. You might not have the title of princess if you married me, but I can assure you, I have enough wealth to keep you very happy for the rest of your life."

"You think wealth would sway me to give up my morals?"

He leaned in closer, his breath brushing against my neck, my ear. "Didn't even take that last time…"

I flung my head back, trying to get out of his reach. I would have slapped him if he hadn't grabbed my hand first, twisting both up between us. "You— You—" I couldn't even think of a name to call him this time.

"Wenderley?"

I froze. Marcos. Standing in the doorway between the ballroom and the balcony. How long had he been standing there? Had he heard? *No, surely not.* No one could have heard our low conversation over the noise of the ball inside. Though the fury on his face made me wonder.

Waitrose stepped back, calmly letting go of the hand he'd all but crushed. I gingerly tried to straighten it out, wincing at the pain.

"Prince Marcos, may I offer my condolences on—"

"Leave. Now."

Marcos's voice was like ice. Tall, razor-sharp shards of it. Big enough to kill a man stupid enough to stand under one. Even one as heartless as Waitrose. Luka stood a few steps behind him, every inch the Head of Security.

"As you wish."

With barely a nod of acknowledgement, Waitrose swept past the prince and back into the ballroom. Luka followed right behind him. I hoped Luka made him leave altogether. I might have acted strong in front of Waitrose but all the fight drained out of me the second he left. I put a hand to the railing to stop myself from falling, wincing as I realized too late it was the one Waitrose had injured.

Marcos was by my side in an instant, leading me over to a bench against a wall, sitting beside me.

"May I?" he asked, gesturing to the hand I held in front of me. His face was still gritted in anger, but the way he took my hand was gentle, cradling it in his as he ran his fingers along it, gently massaging the bones and joints back into place. Round and round, his thumb went in the palm of my hand. Up, down, up, down, smoothing skin and leaving trails of heat in its wake.

Music spilled out onto the balcony as we sat there—me, trying not to shake with post-adrenaline letdown and him, jaw clicking and gaze locked on our hands as he tried to keep whatever it was he wanted to say inside. Obviously, he'd been angry enough at Waitrose to send him away, but was he also angry at me? For all I knew, he thought he'd witnessed a lovers' quarrel or something of the sort and his anger had been jealousy.

"Marcos—"

"That was him, wasn't it. The man who's been sending the letters."

The ice was gone from Marcos's voice, but in its place was steel. Though his words were quiet, barely even able to be heard over the music, they demanded answers. And expected honesty. I couldn't hide it from him any longer. I didn't want to. It would cost me, I had no doubt about that, but I had to tell him the truth.

"Yes."

He nodded, as if the words didn't bother him at all. The way his hand skidded across mine told a different story. He began his massage again almost instantly, but it was enough. He might have seemed in control of his emotions, but there was far more going on below the surface than he was showing.

"You're afraid of him."

"Yes."

"Why?"

One word. One question.

One answer that would lose me everything.

THIRTY-THREE

The night was too beautiful for the story I had to tell. Over my left shoulder, the full moon flirted with wispy clouds in a celestial dance across the skies. Over my right, giant windows and the open door showcased the swirling gowns and twinkling lights of a royal ball, still in action. Beside me, cradling my hand in his, my voluminous skirt spilling out over his shoes, sat Marcos. Prince, friend, and the man I loved. It couldn't have been more perfect if I'd read it in a fairy tale.

"I can't throw him out if I don't know what he's done wrong."

Too bad I wasn't the heroine.

"You assume he's the one to blame."

"He's threatening a woman. Of course he is to blame."

"Yes…" I could do this. I had to. "But so am I."

I pulled my hand out of his before he could beat me to it and tucked both in my lap. The words were there, right on the tip of my tongue—the explanations, the excuses, the shifting of blame. Ready should I choose them. I didn't.

"I slept with him."

"No…"

The single word came out in a whisper, a gasp of pain almost, ripping my heart. I stared down at my hands, determined to get the story out. He deserved that much.

"It was the night of Peverell's King's Ball, back when you and Alina were still engaged. I was lonely. Maybe even a little angry. Everyone around me had someone. Kenna had Thoraben. Alina

236

had you. My sister, Jade, and her husband had just announced they were expecting a baby. Alina casually mentioned that Nicola and Arden were engaged. Even my younger brother, Emmett, had asked a girl to be his date and was shyly dancing with her. The only attention I was getting was sympathy—'the girl Prince Thoraben didn't choose,' 'the girl who thought he was going to marry her,' 'the girl who'd had her heart broken in front of an entire country'—and I was so incredibly sick of it.

"And then Lord Waitrose came up and told me I looked beautiful. Asked me to dance. I knew he was bad news—Kenna and Alina had both warned me about him—but I just didn't care. At least he saw me. When he asked if I wanted to leave with him, I went. It was a heady feeling to think someone wanted me. I gave him everything he asked for."

"Wenderley." There was so much pain in the way he whispered my name, but not condemnation. No pity either. Was it because he knew how easy it was in that moment to convince yourself it was just a kiss? Just a hand. Just an action. Was it because he'd been there? Made the same mistake? Carried the same regret? I wasn't the only one out on my balcony each night, long after I should have been asleep. "I'm sorry..."

I'd known it was wrong. And even if I hadn't, the thudding of my heart would have given it away. The overwhelming guilt, sitting like a weight in my stomach. I'd known it was wrong, but I hadn't cared. Not that night. That night, I'd wanted to feel something. Other than the anger and rejection I was so tired of dutifully pushing aside. Let it come in all its force. I'd thought I'd dealt with it—and maybe I had—but it kept coming back.

Every time I saw Kenna and Ben share a secret smile.

Every time Alina mentioned Marcos.

When Mrs. McCloud offered to give me a box of chocolates half price because chocolate was "the best cure for a broken heart." I'd put the box back on her grocery shelf.

That was the day I'd lost all interest in chocolate.

I hadn't wanted their sympathy. I was tired of pushing aside my feelings. The hurt, the ache, the anger. Maybe I'd gone looking for Waitrose. Maybe it had been a complete fluke that he'd been standing there when I'd walked past, but when he'd held out his hand, I'd taken it. And when he'd opened his door, I'd walked straight in, closing it—and the angst of the palace—behind me. I knew he was using me, just as well as I knew it was wrong. But I was using him too.

"I regretted it, of course. But not until it was too late. According to an old Peverellian law, he's obligated to marry me now, but I could never marry him. Nor does he want to marry me, or be tied down to any woman, for that matter, so he found a way to 'ensure my silence,' as he so eloquently put it in the first letter I found. I don't know how many women he's been with and blackmailed into silence. I doubt very much that I'm the first."

I curled a leg up under my dress, resting an arm on my knee as I stared at the people inside. They were so happy, every one of them smiling. How many were just for show?

"What does he have over you?"

"Enough."

I stretched my leg out again, too worked up to stay in one position for long but too committed to the conversation to stand up and pace.

"Why don't you tell the truth? You're friends with the royal family and he's clearly a criminal, especially if you're not the first woman he's tried this on. Tell the king."

"I can't." Even if I had wanted to risk it before, I couldn't now. Not knowing who filled Waitrose's coffers. Did Thoraben know that? Kenna? Was that why she hadn't reported Waitrose already? "If it was only me it affected, I could have lived with that. My mistake, my consequences, and I agree with you, Waitrose needs to be stopped. But it's not only me. Back in Peverell, I'm a—"

I stopped suddenly, swallowing back the words. Remembering where I was, who I was speaking with. Somewhere amidst Marcos's quiet listening and the connection I felt with him, I'd forgotten this was a prince. A ruler. A man obligated to do what was right, no matter the cost.

"You're a...?"

I shook my head, looking down at my hands as I tried to find words to backtrack. He reached out to hold one of those hands, cradling it softly. Offering his support. He wouldn't pressure me, not now, not ever, but that didn't mean he didn't care.

The song inside finished. People clapped. Another one started. Dancers took up their positions. A couple walked toward the balcony door before deciding to head in a different direction.

"Wenderley? What does he have over you?"

"Isn't that one stupid mistake enough?"

"It's not what keeps you up at night."

No. It wasn't, and he'd know, given how many times now he'd seen me out on the balcony staring at stars when I should have been asleep.

"Please, Wenderley. I want to help."

"You can't."

"I'm Prince Marcos of Hodenia. Pretty sure I can take on a mere lord."

"But can you take on the king? The law of Peverell?"

"What?"

I should never have said that. Now he knew far too much. I should have thanked him and sent him back into the ball after he saved me from Waitrose. Instead, I'd let him comfort me, hold my hand, sit right beside me in a place that was just private enough to speak openly and just public enough to feel safe. The words, held too long inside me, tumbled out.

"I'm a Rebel leader. I teach kids about God. Something that— as I'm certain you know—is against the law in Peverell. Anna, Liz, and the other girls who've been writing to me, they're my girls. For over a year now, I've been meeting with them each week to encourage them in their faith and teach them about God. Waitrose found out. If I tell anyone about that night or anything about Waitrose at all, he'll tell King Everson all our names. They'll be tried as criminals, them and their families. I can't do that to them. They're just kids. Your sisters' ages. It would be taking away their lives."

"So, instead, you'll live with this for, what, the rest of your life?"

A week ago, I'd been ready to confront Waitrose, tell the truth and end this. But now? Waitrose was more than a criminal. He was a criminal on the king's payroll. I'd never win.

"If I have to."

"Wenderley, this is blackmail. A criminal offense. He needs to be stopped."

"He will. One day. I hope. But not by me. Not at the risk of those girls' lives."

"He doesn't own you. That old law probably wouldn't even stand these days."

If only. "Kenna and Thoraben were forced to marry because of that exact law, and they hadn't even done anything wrong. Believe me, the law will be upheld." Although, would it? If King Everson really did look the other way where Waitrose was concerned, would Waitrose be forced to marry me? Likely not, especially if it was my word against his.

But then…the kids. Anna, Milly Rose, Max, Evanse, Liz, Parker, Aimee, Rory—none of them deserved this.

"What if you were already married?"

I shook my head. Wishing it were that easy.

"No one will marry me. Not after what I've done."

"I would."

What? My gaze collided with his, so calm in the face of my shock.

"I will. I meant it, that day I asked you. I still do. Marry me, Wenderley. Let me protect you."

"You want to marry me?" Me, who'd confessed to being not only a criminal but used goods, as Waitrose had so bluntly called me in his letter? Marcos couldn't want me.

"I don't propose to just anyone."

"I'd be the third woman in under two years."

"Yes, but you'd be the only one who's been my choice."

Oh.

Wow.

"Proposing to Princess Alina was expected of me. Marrying Rachana was the honorable thing to do. I cared about them both and would have been truly committed to them until death did us part—please, don't doubt that—but if the choice of a wife had been mine alone, neither of them would have been it.

"No one's forcing me to marry you, Wenderley. Not Mother or Father, or any of my advisors. You're the one I choose, not because I have to but because I want to. I proposed because I wanted you to stay. You calm me, you love my son, you give me reasons every day to smile."

Marcos put both his hands around mine, his hold so different than Waitrose's had been.

"Come with me to the jewel vault and choose a ring. We could walk right back into the ball, call for everyone's attention and announce our engagement right now."

I pulled my hands out of his, tucking them back between my knees, overwhelmed by his words. And the fact that I couldn't accept.

"Thank you—truly—but it's not your place to fix my mistakes."

"Maybe I want to."

"Why?"

"Because, like you said, we all have regrets."

For the briefest of moments, I actually let myself imagine agreeing. Allowing him to sacrifice his future to save me from my regrets. Letting him hold me, protect me, promise everything would be okay. Walking back into that ball with him by my side and being unashamed of it. Knowing not only that all would be well but that I'd be marrying a prince. Marcos, the man I'd not only prayed for, fought for, and admired but who, somewhere along the way, I'd fallen in love with.

But I couldn't do that to him. I couldn't do it to myself either. He'd already married once for honor. He deserved to marry for love, and not some misguided attempt to save me.

"Thank you, Marcos. I appreciate it, more than you know. But I won't be another one of your regrets."

THIRTY-FOUR

A handwritten note was sitting on a breakfast tray outside my door the morning after the ball.

> *Wenderley,*
> *I've cleared my day today and would love to spend it with my son. Take some time for yourself. You've had very little of that since you arrived at the palace, something I've been most remiss in realizing. Forgive me. I hope the time helps.*
> *Ryan and I will see you at dinner.*
> *Marcos*

I dropped the note back on the tray, standing in the doorway for some time before I remembered where I was and took the tray back inside. A whole day to myself. A whole day I could spend in my room without wondering what mischief Ryan would get up to or where Marcos either was, or was most likely to be, so we could be somewhere else. No pressure. No stress.

No one to distract me from the doubts I didn't want to have.

I'd been here before, in this doubting God game. The first time I'd ever talked to God had been a bargain. I told him I'd believe in him if he let me go home to Peverell and, going hand-in-hand in my mind, Thoraben. Choosing to give God control of my life turned out to be the best decision of my life, but I didn't get Thoraben. In some ways, many ways even, I felt like God had let me down. He'd failed me. But then, crying my eyes out every night, wandering around in a fog of weariness and hurt every day, I'd come to the realization that God hadn't failed me. He was still true.

Even after that night with Waitrose, I'd found God's forgiveness. He'd been faithful, just like he promised. It was me who'd failed, not him.

But now, it wasn't that I couldn't trust him—I knew I could—it was whether I was willing to accept where that trust might take me.

For the next four and a half hours, I slept, sketched, and wandered from task to task in my room, giving my hands something to do while my brain tried to sort through more questions and doubts than I knew what to do with. God was God. He was. I knew it. It was the same reason I knew all would be well. I lived it. I believed it. So why was I having so much trouble believing he could fix this now?

And was I right to say no to Marcos? Maybe marrying him was the answer. The law could hardly force me to marry one man when I was already married to another. Marcos knew my secrets now, and my shame. I loved him and he, at the very least, cared enough to still want to be with me. As to the issue of him not being a Follower, Thoraben had married Kenna before she was, so clearly it wasn't forbidden. Of course, his had been a completely different situation altogether but still, Kenna had come to believe not long after. Who was to say Marcos wouldn't also?

Back and forth, I went. Arguing against myself. Logic versus emotion versus faith. Each one's argument as strong as the other until I felt exhausted from the battle.

I was finishing lunch in my room when I heard the terror-filled scream. Even from a distance, it pulled me like a puppet. I was already halfway down the first flight of stairs when a maid came running.

"Wenderley! Come quick. It's Ryan. He's fallen."

"Where is he?"

"Near the lake."

"He fell in the water?" He couldn't swim! I shook my head against the instant terror of him drowning. If he was screaming loud enough for me to hear him from this distance, he wasn't drowning.

"No. From a tree."

"How high?"

"High enough."

I sucked in a breath and started running, leaving the maid behind, following the screams to the base of a mid-sized tree overhanging the water. It wasn't as high as I'd been picturing so the fall mustn't have been too far, but if he'd fallen awkwardly…

What had Ryan been thinking, climbing it? Anyone could see it wasn't strong enough to hold a child. Anyone but a child himself. Hadn't Marcos been watching him? He was supposed to be. I bit back the words I felt like berating him with only because the man already looked flustered enough trying to calm his screaming son.

"Ryan."

I knelt down beside the boy, wincing as a pebble bit into my knee. I brushed it aside and held out my hands. Tears streamed down Ryan's face, but it was the arm he cradled which worried me the most. It seemed straight enough but already swelling. Had he landed on it? Was it broken?

His good arm came around my neck as he pulled himself into my lap, swiping a grubby nose across the front of my shirt, curling himself into a ball of tears. At least he'd stopped screaming. A car pulled up a few feet away, Luka and a man with a medical kit stepping out of it. Marcos rose immediately, holding out his arms to take Ryan. The boy gurgled another cry and tucked himself closer against me. Which was fine with me, except for the fact that I couldn't get up still holding him. Nor could the doctor make any assessment. I tried pulling him out slightly.

"Ryan, honey, the doctor is here to check your arm."

"No. No checking. It hurts."

"I know it hurts. That's why he needs to look at it." The man came closer. I tried again to get Ryan to move. "Come on, just turn around a little?"

"No."

"Come on. You can do this. The doctor will be able to make it stop hurting so much."

That got his attention. "You'll stay with me?"

"Of course. We'll sit here together, shall we? How about we count how many birds we can see while the doctor looks at your arm."

"I can't see any birds."

"No? Have you got your eyes open?"

"Yep."

I gently pried the arm away from Ryan's chest, keeping him looking in the other direction while the doctor ran his fingers down it. Luka barked directions at two of his security team who'd arrived in another car. Whether out of courtesy or protocol, they all stayed back from our little huddle.

"Is it broken?" Marcos asked. Ryan's whimpers grew louder as the doctor probed the swollen part.

"Hairline, I think. Not a bad break, but we're going to have to splint it. Ready for a ride to the hospital, young prince?"

"No! No hospital!"

"Ryan..." I tried, my mind racing to think of something—anything—to sway the frightened child. Had his mother spent time in hospitals? Was that why he was afraid of them? Because the terror was instant. It could have been the pain, but he hadn't been shaking before the doctor mentioned the hospital. Although, as far as I knew, Rachana had spent all her time at the palace with medical care being brought in. At least, she had since marrying Marcos.

"No hospital," Ryan whimpered again.

"I could bring equipment to the palace," the doctor offered. "Though it'll take some time. You'll need to keep him calm and that arm as still as possible until then."

I looked at Marcos, wanting him as Ryan's father to make the decision, but the poor guy looked so flustered and out of his depth. Much as I wanted to blame him for Ryan's injury, my common sense poking its tentative way through the anger reminded me that kids were kids, and Marcos had hardly snapped the boy's arm himself. If anything, he looked like he'd rather have chopped off his own arm rather than watch his son moan in pain.

I took pity on him. "Yes, please. That would be good. Prince Marcos and I will take Ryan back to the palace and wait for you there."

"Very well. I'll be there as soon as I can." The doctor reached into his bag, pulling out a small vial of liquid. "When he's calmed enough to do so, get Prince Ryan to drink this. It will help with the pain."

"Thank you."

I cuddled Ryan close while the doctor climbed back into the waiting car and left with one of Luka's men. Thankfully, Ryan took the medicine without any issues, having calmed down immensely as soon as the doctor was out of sight. Marcos, on the other hand, still looked particularly green. I probably should have sent him to the hospital with the doctor. It was going to be difficult enough to get Ryan back to the palace. I certainly didn't need the extra pressure of trying to keep a grown man conscious.

"Marcos?"

He stared at the wake of dust the car's departure had left, slowly floating to the ground. Had he even heard me? Luka started forward. I shook my head and he stopped. This wasn't the moment for a security team. It was a moment for a father.

"Marcos."

I laced my voice with confidence this time, not shouting his name but putting enough force behind it to make his head spin toward me. Good. He was still with me.

"I need you."

THIRTY-FIVE

My words finally got a reaction from Marcos, though not exactly the one I was after. His eyes flicked up and down me, as if suddenly realizing I was there. In his space. Cradling his son. Begging for something much more lasting than a hand to pull me up. If I'd planned it better, I definitely wouldn't have used those words. Much as they rang true.

"Okay, men," I said, using my best drill sergeant voice. "This is going to take all of us. Ryan, I need you to stand up since I can't get up while you're on me. Marcos, can you help him? He needs to keep that arm as still as possible. Mr. Wintergreen and his man will drive us back to the palace, and we'll see if we can't find some nice hot chocolate and talk Chef Meyer into making cookies."

"I'll carry him," Marcos said immediately.

"You'd——" I bit back the question before Marcos took it the wrong way. It wasn't that I didn't think he could—with muscles like that, he could probably carry me all the way home, not that I was thinking that, despite the sudden blush racing past my ears—but Ryan was covered in dirt, still sniveling and doing his best to turn my shirt into a sodden, snot-decorated handkerchief. None of which would do Marcos's designer polo any good.

But before I could argue further, Marcos swept Ryan up in his arms, carefully balancing the injured arm across Ryan's stomach.

Luka had the car door open. Marcos slid into the back seat,

Ryan still cradled against his chest. I took the other side. Ryan immediately reached for my hand, gripping it tightly.

It was a slow drive back to the palace, Luka not wanting to bump either of the princes unnecessarily on the gravel road. Word had clearly spread because Lucie, Kahra, and the queen were waiting at the door along with several maids and more of the security team. Marcos ignored them all, intent on his goal of getting Ryan to his room. I smiled apologetically and tried to answer their questions while keeping up with Marcos since Ryan whimpered and started to cry every time I dropped out of view.

"It's okay, honey," I assured Ryan again, "the doctor will be back soon to fix your arm."

"It hurts."

"I know. You're being very brave."

"I fell."

"I'm sorry."

"Can I have some ice cream?"

"Sure."

"And two cookies?"

"We'll have to see if the kitchens have any ready."

"And apple pie for dinner?"

Wow. He was really milking this. Not that I could blame him. I would have too. "Let's wait and see what the doctor says first." I would have deferred it to Marcos, but he still looked as if he'd hand over his father's crown to Ryan in an instant if he requested it. Along with as much ice cream, apple pie, and cookies as the boy could possibly eat. The poor kid likely already had a broken arm. He didn't need a stomachache as well.

Thankfully, the rest of the entourage crowded into the room and distracted both princes before Marcos could promise his son anything else. Lucie ran back and forth around the room, finding Ryan's favorite toys for him, Kahra brought a wet cloth and wiped his face clean, all while Luka regaled us with stories of the bones he'd broken in his younger years and the—gradually becoming less and less believable and more and more humorous—ways he'd broken them.

When the doctor returned with his equipment forty minutes later, it was confirmed. One hairline fracture. The man was partway through splinting and bandaging it when Marcos walked out of the room. He didn't come back. He wasn't at dinner either which, thanks to his subdued but happy son, really was apple pie and ice cream. It wasn't until Ryan went to bed and Marcos still didn't come to see his son that I started to worry.

"Is Papa at a meeting?" Ryan asked as I propped his arm up on the cushion we'd tucked in beside him.

"I think he must be," I said.

"I thought he'd say goodbye before he left."

Me too. Though I could hardly say that in front of Ryan.

"Did you have fun this morning? Before you fell from the tree, I mean."

He nodded. "Yes. Chef Meyer made us a picnic, and Papa let me eat *all* the cookies, even though I think there were supposed to be two for each of us. Then we took our shoes off and splashed our feet in the water for a while, and Papa tried to teach me how to throw a rock across the water so it bounced, but mine kept falling in. They made good plops though, especially the big ones."

"That sounds wonderful." I leaned forward and kissed his forehead. "Do you think you can sleep now?"

"I think so. I'm a bit tired."

"You've had a big day."

"Yep. Goodnight, Wenderley."

"Goodnight, Ryan. Sleep well."

I smiled, waving one more time as I turned off Ryan's light. The smile dropped as soon as I stepped into the hall. The door to Marcos's suite was partially open—and the light was on. Either a maid was doing some late-night cleaning, or Marcos wasn't at a meeting. In which case, he was in big trouble. And I was going to be certain he knew it. How dare he leave his son alone at such a time?

"Prince Marcos?"

The door to his suite swung open easily when I pushed on it. The lights might have been on, but Marcos wasn't sitting out here.

I was about to leave and head to his office when I heard it. The crying.

Sobbing.

From Marcos's bedroom.

The sound wrenched through me much like it had at Rachana's funeral. Only worse, because this time, I knew him. I loved him. His pain was mine. My fury disappeared under a wave of compassion.

I knocked quietly on his door. "Marcos?"

Though the voices in my head almost deafened me with their long litany of reasons this was a terrible idea, I ignored them and went with my heart. The lone voice reminding me that no one should have to go through that much pain alone. Not even a prince.

I knocked again, growing more anxious when he didn't answer. I should go away. A man should be allowed some privacy but—

"Marcos?" I leaned forward, pressing my ear up against the door, almost tumbling forward when it swung open under the pressure.

Near darkness met my startled gaze, the only light in the room a small lamp on the desk where Marcos sat, slumped forward, head on his arms as his whole body shook with the force of his sobbing.

My heart thudded as I walked slowly toward him, reminding me of another night I'd walked into a man's room. But this was nothing like that. That had been about me. About my need for validation and someone—*anyone*—to notice me. This was about Marcos and his heart, which was clearly breaking.

"Marcos?"

The tears came then, streaming down my cheeks. I didn't even know why I was crying except that he hurt, so I did too. My heart, already weakened by his silent tears at Rachana's funeral, cracked right along the center seeing him now like this. The man who commanded armies, authorized laws, had earned the respect of a kingdom full of people—with never a hair out of place. Now sobbing. Shaking. Curled forward, head on his arms, his whole body wracked with the pain of it all. There were no words. Nothing I could say to comfort him.

God, help him.

The cry wrenched from somewhere deep inside me. Barely coherent let alone inspiring, but enough.

I knelt down in front of Marcos, touching his shoulder, taking his hands in mine. They were so much larger than mine and yet, I was definitely the one in control here. Even if tear after tear fell down my face.

"Hey." I ran a trembling hand over his hair, much as I frequently did with Ryan. Only this was nothing like touching Ryan. My heart throbbed painfully with a mix of anguish, excitement, and fear. Was I really doing this? And why wasn't he pushing me away? Could I really comfort him like I ached to do? "It's going to be okay."

He lifted his head, looked at me through bleary, red eyes.

"Wenderley. I can't do this. I'm not Rachana."

Marcos... How had I thought, even for a moment, that this man didn't care about his son? And why hadn't I, or anyone, for that matter, come to check on Marcos earlier? Had he been in here since that moment he walked out of Ryan's room? In agony, all this time?

It took a few swallows before I could get any words at all past the lump in my throat.

"Of course you're not. Nobody expects you to be. But you're his father."

He shook his head, hopelessness radiating like heat around him. "Am I? Really?"

"The tests proved—"

"I don't care what the tests proved. A father is more than a bunch of genetics. Sure, I'm his father by blood, but what do I know about being a dad? I wasn't there when he was born. Didn't see him take his first steps or know what his first word was. I can't tell when he's worried or upset or just tired, like Rachana could. I wouldn't have even known he was scared I'd send him away if you hadn't told me.

"I thought I was doing the right thing by marrying Rachana and bringing him to the palace, but what if I was wrong? How would I know what he needs?"

"What he needs is his father."

"He broke his arm."

"It was an accident." He had to know that. Accidents happened. No one could control everything, especially not Marcos, as much as he seemed determined to try.

"There were rocks around that tree. Big ones. What if he'd hit them instead? I shouldn't have turned my back, even for a moment. He could have died."

"But he didn't." I moved my hand to Marcos's shoulder, forcing him to look at me and see the truth in my eyes. "Ryan's arm will heal, and he'll grow into a strong prince who'll rule this kingdom with honor and strength, just like his father."

Marcos shook his head, sending more tears cascading down his cheeks. I tried to catch his gaze again, but he wouldn't look at me. "I'm not strong. If I was, I would have sent you away by now."

"I wouldn't have gone." Him being alone right now was a terrible idea. Who knew how deep he'd sink himself in depression? He was a man who thrived on order and control, and he'd been hit over the head with the realization that he held no power over either. He needed me.

"Wenderley…"

"Ryan really will be fine, Marcos. I promise. We'll get through this. Together."

"I don't know if I can."

I stroked his hair away from his forehead. A tear fell on the back of my hand, the one still clutching his. I bent down to kiss it before I'd realized what I was doing. I wasn't trained for this. I shouldn't have been in here. Not alone. Not at night. Not ever. And yet, I couldn't help but be thrilled, somewhere deep inside me, that I was. And that I was the one here to help him through this. Not because I wanted to tell the world that he wasn't as strong as he seemed but because I loved him. I wanted him. I'd fought against it for too long. Told myself it was purely because he was a prince and clearly they were my weakness, but that wasn't it.

It was the way his hair curled. His eyes. The half-smile he tried to hide while Lucie talked on and on at dinner about her mysterious friend we all knew was Sir Rusty. The full smile he wore when he looked at Ryan. The way he was so careful to do everything right, not because he was afraid of being wrong but because he wanted to be a good example. The way he played with the signet ring on his right hand when he was stressed. The way he'd been so determined to fight my battles for me, even when I refused to tell him what they were.

No matter what decisions he'd made in the past, he was a man of honor. One of the last remaining royals of old. I loved him for his heart.

The heart which was clearly breaking at this moment.

"Marcos?"

He lifted his head, finally. His face was wet with tears, his eyes bloodshot, his eyebrows heading in every which direction, his hair a mess of black. "Oh, Marcos." I ran a hand across his cheeks, brushing aside the tears. Cradling his face. He couldn't have been more precious to me, nor more handsome, than he was in this moment. I wanted to take all the broken pieces of him and make him whole again. Instead, I raised myself to my knees and did the only thing I could. I kissed him.

Gently. Softly. Achingly. His lips were soft and tasted of salt. When he didn't push me away, I came closer, the hand on his face dropping to the back of his neck. The thudding of my heart in my ears drowned out every sensible voice inside me telling me to leave as fast as I could. Perhaps it was weakness that kept me there, perhaps it was strength and the desperation I felt to give him something.

Anything.

Everything.

His hand came around my back, pulling me closer still. His other hand tangled in my hair. I kissed his cheeks, the last of his tears. Was he on the floor? Was I in his lap? Curled up in his embrace, time and space were lost to me. All I could feel was his warmth. His arms around me. A rightness. This was what loving someone meant. Being there for them when they broke. Helping them find the pieces. Kissing them back together. This was right.

"Wenderley…"

I tucked my head in against his shoulder, thrilling at the sound of my name on his lips. Lips which were finding mine again. Lips which traced a line across my cheek, down my neck, along my collarbone.

"Wenderley…"

"I love you."

He groaned into my neck. "You shouldn't."

I put my hands either side of his face, pulling his gaze to mine. Staring directly into those eyes I loved so much. "But I do. And I'm here. I'm staying. Tonight, forever, if you want me to. You're not alone anymore."

"Wenderley, we shouldn't."

His protest was swallowed up in another kiss. My hands skimmed his waist, found his back, muscled and as strong as I'd always imagined it. This was right. This was good. This was—

With a hand on each of my shoulders, Marcos pushed me away, so quickly I lost my balance and fell backward onto the floor. It was the thud which brought me to my senses.

"Marcos, I—"

My hand flew to my mouth, holding back the sob threatening to destroy me. The revulsion racing up my throat. What had I done? Kissing Marcos? Saying those things? Holding him like—I groaned against the pain of regret. A wife. That's how I'd been holding him. Like he was mine. In the eyes of God, the church, Hodenia.

Oh, God…

He didn't reach out a hand to help me up, both hands covering his face as he fought his own version of hell. A version I'd made. He'd tried to send me away. More than once. But no, I'd stayed. Broken his vow. Broken mine.

God, what have I done?

I fled then, scrambling to my feet and out the door before either of us could make it worse. My room wasn't far enough. No part of the palace would have been. He was in every inch of it. The palace, Hodenia, its people. I couldn't stay. Not after tonight. Not knowing how deep the passion ran between Marcos and me. And how fallible we both were. I'd thought I was so strong, which proved how much of a fool I really was. I wasn't strong at all.

The Pirate Pumpernickel book tumbled off my bedside table as I reached out a shaking hand for my sketchbook. It might as well have been Ryan himself. I slumped on the floor beside the bed, holding the pirate book to my chest as yet more tears fell.

I couldn't leave. Not now. Ryan had just broken his arm. He trusted me. He needed me. And Queen Galielle? Lucie? Kahra? What would I tell them? I was leaving because I couldn't even be in the same palace as Marcos without compromising every commitment I'd ever made?

Queen Galielle had been right to warn me. I'd thought I could be strong enough to hold on to my faith and convictions no matter what Marcos did or believed but here, not even married to him, I'd given them up for a moment of his affection.

I will not kiss another man unless we're engaged.

I'd been so filled with conviction as I'd written those words and signed them. A promise between me and God, as holy as the covenants he'd made with people to love them, no matter what. I'd felt his approval as I made it.

The piece of paper was worthless now. As worthless as the vow I'd broken.

I won't kiss any woman who isn't my wife.

I'd forced Marcos to break his vow too. The one he'd kept since he was seventeen. For over a year, I'd lived with the regret of that choice to go with Waitrose. How was it this pain was even greater than that? How could I have been so stupid? Thinking I was so strong. I'd ruined everything.

I couldn't leave, but how could I stay?

A knock at my door had my heart instantly thudding in my throat. *Marcos. He's come back. Or King Dorien, come to throw me out. Queen Galielle, come to tell me how much I've disappointed her. Oh God, please don't let it be Queen Galielle… Or Marcos. Or King Dorien. Or…*

I shook my head against the pounding pain of too many thoughts and emotions trying to take dominance. Maybe tomorrow, I'd be able to better deal with all this but not tonight. *God, don't make me have to see them again tonight. Any of them.*

The knocking sounded again. "Wenderley, I know you're in there."

It *was* Marcos.

He was at my door. Only minutes after I'd fled his room. He'd probably come to apologize and take all the responsibility as if it was his alone. When we both knew it was mine. He'd tried to send me away enough times. I'd been the one who stayed. Who instigated that first kiss.

I'm sorry, Marcos. Not tonight. Go away. Please, go away.

Tomorrow, I'd let him assuage his misplaced guilt and apologize. But not tonight. Not while I could still feel the impression of his arms around me and smell the scent of him on my clothes. I was too weak. Far too weak. If I opened that door, I'd never be able to walk away.

"Wenderley, please. It's important. You need to know."

The plea in his voice pulled me to the door. I stood behind it, leaning my head against the wood, silently begging him to leave. *Not tonight. Please, Marcos, not tonight.*

"There's news. From Peverell."

It was the way he said it which broke my resistance. He sounded so shaken. Shocked. Out of control. The Marcos I knew made a point of never being out of control. At least, the Marcos I'd known before tonight.

The door felt leaden as I pulled it partially open.

Marcos was standing there, Luka beside him. Both men were dressed as impeccably as if they were about to leave for an official engagement, despite the hour. I touched a hand to my throat, knowing how much of a mess I looked, wondering if it was too late to go back and change time. Never open the door. Never come to Hodenia at all.

Luka looked from me to Marcos and back again, the tension between us tangible. The tear-ravaged eyes we both had even more so, though Marcos had at least combed his hair. By some miracle—and to my eternal gratitude—Luka kept his mouth shut, though I had no doubt he'd question Marcos later.

"What is it?" I asked, the thudding in my throat making it difficult to speak.

"It's King Everson," Marcos said. "He's stepped down. Abdicated."

The door swung out of reach. I'm sure for a moment I stopped breathing. What? King Everson? The proud man and king everyone in Peverell held in such high esteem he was close to feared? Surely Marcos had it wrong. My mind argued that Marcos was getting back at me. Retaliating, trying to hurt or shake me like I'd shaken him. But even as the thought crossed my mind, I knew he'd never do that.

I grabbed blindly for the door, steadying my suddenly shaking body. Abdicated. But that would mean—

"As of this moment, Prince Thoraben is the new king of Peverell."

My mind went blank.

"Wenderley, are you—"

"I have to sit down." The words sounded like they came from someone else. Before I'd even registered they were mine, Luka had come forward and looped my arm around his shoulders, ushering me back into my room toward one of the chairs there, pushing aside random pieces of clothing and shoes. If he was looking for somewhere to put them, the floor was as good a place as any.

Marcos stayed in the doorway.

"What can I get you?" Luka asked, crouching down in front of me. "Water? Something else? Tell me what I can do to help."

I shook my head, embarrassed by how much the news had shaken me. Kenna was the one who cried, Alina the drama queen.

I was the strong one. The optimistic one. The one who saw hope in every situation. The one who never fell apart. Usually.

Think, Wenderley.

But I didn't want to think. I'd done too much of that already. My kingdom was crashing. My worlds colliding. First Marcos, now Peverell. My emotions far too raw to be trusted. It wasn't water I wanted, or even Marcos. It was my mom.

"I want to go home."

With the kind of efficiency only found in a palace, my bags were packed, a car and driver summoned, and I was on my way back to Peverell within fifteen minutes. Much as it wrecked me to leave without saying goodbye to Ryan and the royal family I'd come to love, the alternative was so much worse. I couldn't bear the thought of their trusting faces when, in so many ways, I'd betrayed them.

Especially since I had no intention of ever coming back.

THIRTY-SIX

Fourteen hours later, I lay on my bed and stared at the ceiling. My mind, barely able to think in a straight line at the best of times, felt like it was being pulled here, there, and everywhere, and taking my heart along for the tumultuous ride. Any moment my whole body was going to explode.

I'd been a wreck of emotions by the time I'd arrived at my parents' house in the early hours of the morning, and burst into gut-wrenching tears the second I'd seen my mom. Fallen into her arms while the ever-practical guard who'd accompanied my driver explained that King Everson had abdicated and that was the reason I'd come home. If my mom thought my reaction a little excessive for something that could have waited for daylight, she didn't say anything, simply holding me until I was too tired to even cry. Then she and my father had herded me into bed, ordered me to sleep, and said we'd talk in the morning.

It was now afternoon. I'd slept that long. Somehow, I was fairly certain my parents would still be around waiting to talk. Which was exactly why I was still lying here in bed. I didn't know what to say.

My feelings toward Marcos were still far too tender to dissect, so I pushed them aside to consider Peverell instead.

King Everson had abdicated. Why? How? Kings didn't do that. Not kings like King Everson. He was the type of person who would have made his way into royalty even if he hadn't been born into it. He liked the power. The absolute control. He set the rules and expected them to be followed.

Abdication wasn't only out of character, it was out of any realm of comprehension. Being overthrown was one thing but voluntarily stepping down? It made no sense.

Unless…

Alina had asked Kenna and me to pray for him one of the times we'd caught up, for wisdom especially. It had been eight, maybe nine months ago now. She hadn't given a reason, saying only that he had some important decisions to make. I'd promised I would, and had, once or twice. What king didn't have important decisions to make? But…was this what she'd been talking about? She'd never said. I'd never thought to ask again.

What must she be thinking right now? If I was this shocked… Me, loyal subject but hardly family. The staff would be in uproar. The whole kingdom…

Ben. What was going through his mind right now? Had he seen this coming? Surely he hadn't expected to be king any time soon. He was only twenty-two years old, for goodness' sake. Not that I didn't believe Ben would make a great king. He would be amazing, exactly the steadily devoted presence Peverell needed in the days to come, especially with Kenna by his side, but…

Oh, God. What's going on? What are you doing?

So many changes. Not only portraits and currency and all the practical things but laws and—

The Rebels.

Thoraben was a Follower. Not only that but he'd been helping those his father condemned as criminals and exiled for over a decade, finding housing and work for them. Ensuring they found friends and the support they needed as they began their lives over.

As king, Thoraben could change the laws. He could abolish altogether the law which made speaking about God illegal. He could build churches again. Reinstate spiritual leaders. Colleges. Bring the hidden gatherings into the light. Whether it happened immediately or in time, I had no doubt it would happen. Peverell could believe again.

It was almost too fantastic to even consider.

And that was just the beginning.

By the time I finally found the courage to get out of bed, the news had been confirmed. Front page of the paper my father held and likely every other one in Peverell. Maybe even the world.

KING EVERSON ABDICATES.
PRINCE THORABEN TO BE PEVERELL'S NEW KING.

Thoraben was crowned a week later. The whole Hodenian royal family came for the coronation, Ryan included. They stood in the second row of the grand cathedral, directly behind Kenna, Alina, Joha, and Kenna's parents. I stood with my parents several rows back as the elaborate golden crown, only ever taken out of its vault for coronations, was taken from King Everson's head and placed on Thoraben's. I know I wasn't the only one so proud I couldn't hold back the tears. Kenna probably couldn't even see the smile Thoraben sent her through the handkerchief she kept dabbing her eyes with, and many others were the same. Thoraben looked so regal, standing there, crown on his head, scepter steady in his hand as he recited his pledge to honor and serve the Kingdom of Peverell with peace, loyalty, courage, and hope. The title of prince suited him. The title of king defined him.

But alongside the pride that seemed to lift every head in the grand cathedral, there was an air of confusion. No one knew why King Everson had abdicated, even a week after the event. In a move as strange as the abdication itself, not one single paper had even offered a guess. No one dared. As a country, we held our breath, waiting to see what would happen next.

The answers didn't take long coming. Barely even twenty-four hours after Thoraben—now *King* Thoraben—had taken his oath, the newly demoted Prince Everson took his place on the palace stairs in front of a swarm of reporters and what felt like most of Peverell. To anyone watching, it might have looked like another press conference—the same lectern, same reporters, the same advisors and family members standing behind him. Only nothing about this was normal. Least of which the way Peverell's former king so clearly gripped the lectern, as if it alone could hold him upright.

He was a different man today, nothing like the confident king I'd always known him to be. Today, he seemed so broken. Not quite as tall. Not quite as certain.

The abdication rocked Peverell. I couldn't help thinking that what came next might break us.

With every business closed and barely a car on the road, Peverell stood waiting.

"My people—"

Prince Everson stopped, stared out over the crowd, tried a smile before quickly dropping his gaze back to the lectern and the notes there. As if they could give him the courage he was desperately trying to find. When he looked up, the sun caught the tear he couldn't quite blink back in time. The mob of reporters and their camera crews leaned forward as one, desperate to capture it.

"I was wrong."

In front of a crowd a few thousand strong, Prince Everson dropped his head and wept. It was several minutes before he could speak again. Not one person in the crowd left, transfixed as I was, to see what he would say next.

Alina walked forward and laid a hand on one of his shoulders. Thoraben took the other. Kenna and Joha stood beside them. Their show of support brought tears to my eyes. If Prince Everson could have cried any harder, he would have. I don't know where he found the strength to begin again—likely due to thirty years of being king and being prince before that—but with a nod and a steadying breath, he continued.

"The day I was crowned, I promised before a room full of witnesses, exactly like my son did yesterday, that I would lead this country with peace, loyalty, courage, and hope. Only I haven't. I failed it and I failed you. My people. Instead of peace and courage, in fear I ruled with a hand of terror. Instead of loyalty, I sowed discord. Where I should have cultivated hope, I did my best to remove it from the kingdom altogether."

He looked down at his notes, though I doubted he could read any of them through the tears still wetting his eyes when he faced the crowd again.

"Nineteen years ago, I knowingly condemned an innocent woman, whose only crime was caring enough to speak the truth. I branded her a criminal, labeled her an insurgent, and exiled her from Peverell for life. Perhaps, if I'd not been too full of pride back then to admit I was wrong, I wouldn't be standing before you today. Only I was, and instead of admitting it, I passed a law making every person who believed as she did a criminal. I called them Rebels and told you all they were a danger to the kingdom, fighting to destroy the royal family and what we'd built Peverell up to be.

"I lied. To every one of you."

The front line of reporters stretched their arms and recorders out as far as they could, almost toppling the barrier which marked the space between the royals and their people. A row of guards put their hands to their weapons, before relaxing to attention again. Desperate as everyone was for the story, no one dared make a scene lest the king stop speaking altogether and the story of a lifetime be lost.

"They weren't criminals. They were innocent of everything except believing in a God who cared, and wanting others to know him too.

"I told myself it was for the good of Peverell. That Peverell was too strong to believe in something as whimsical as an invisible God. I tried to cover up one wrong with a thousand others. And, for almost twenty years, Peverell has been the one to pay for it.

"But that God—the one Ciera believed in, the one that woman, Malisa Samson, mother of my daughter's husband believed in, the one I myself now know—he's not invisible. He's in the lives of everyone around me—including both of my children, their spouses, and several of my closest advisors. And he's not whimsical. He's been at work, all this time, using what I was doing not to stamp out faith but to grow it. It's taken me far too long to see the truth, and for that, I beg your forgiveness, even though I know I've done nothing to deserve it."

Murmurs around the crowd split the sympathetic from the realists but still, no one called out. With a glance at Thoraben, who was offering an encouraging smile and a nod, the former king continued.

"I used to argue with Ciera that God was a crutch for people who couldn't stand on their own two feet, and that surrender, as she called the faith she lived out each day, was an out for the weak. She'd smile and tell me that it took an amazing amount of strength to surrender. I never understood that until now.

"Yes, God is a crutch, and one we desperately need because none of us are strong enough to walk this life on our own. My son, Thoraben, knows that. As does his wife, Queen Mackenna. It is for that reason, and the consequences due me, that I have stood down and passed the leadership of Peverell to King Thoraben and the wife who will ably support him. I believe wholeheartedly that they will be far better leaders for this great kingdom than I ever have been."

Tears streamed down my face as I listened to Prince Everson speak. Every Follower I knew had prayed for him, that he would come to know and believe in God for himself. Every meeting we had finished with a prayer that his eyes would be opened to how much God loved him and how desperately he needed God.

Though I'd continued to pray, like everyone else, it had become rote over the years. I'd given up on ever seeing the miracle. And yet, here it was. Greater than I could have ever imagined. The former king, standing in front of his entire country, confessing not only his doubts and wrongs but his faith. He believed. Prince Everson, the man who'd condemned every believer he'd ever discovered and single-handedly ridded Peverell of any talk of or building representing God. Now standing, all pride gone, as he admitted he'd been wrong.

"Thank you, people of Peverell, for twenty-nine years of belief in me. I wish I'd lived up to that belief. I might have stood before you today a king instead of a criminal. As it is, I freely admit I was wrong and hand myself over to Peverell's judicial system and the sentence they pass down."

He turned and walked away then, directly back into the palace, without waiting to answer any questions from the press. Not that any of them called out after him. Where, before the speech, there was a silence filled with expectation, now, it was simply stunned. Prince Everson had admitted he was wrong. He'd turned the tables, claiming himself the one who'd committed treason, rather than the hundreds he'd condemned, and handing himself over to be judged.

Kenna was the first to turn and follow the former king. Thoraben, Alina, and Joha were quick to follow. I couldn't help but wonder what was happening on the other side of the door which closed behind them. Had they continued on to their respective rooms? Put Prince Everson under house arrest, such as it was? Or were the five of them clustered, a few steps beyond that door, comforting each other? Praying, even.

Thoraben had been praying for this day for almost longer than I'd been alive, desperate for his father to believe in God's love and rule as his mother had all her life. Was Thoraben sobbing behind those doors? Filled with wonder at his father's very public confession of faith?

A brave reporter from somewhere near the front finally called out a question, one that might as well have been on behalf of the assembled crowd and beyond.

"What happens now?"

One of Prince Everson's two closest advisors, both still standing on the erected platform, came forward and started answering. As best he could anyway. I don't think even they in all their wisdom had a precedent for this.

"As you might expect, the trial will be a long and drawn out process from this point on. A panel will be formed and the truth of King, excuse me, *Prince* Everson's claims evaluated. The exiles Prince Everson claims innocent will be contacted, retried, and

given the opportunity to lay charges. It may be some time before an outcome is reached. We will do our best to keep all of Peverell advised as to each step of the judicial process."

"Do you believe he's guilty?" someone called out.

The advisor didn't answer right away, clearly wanting to formulate his reply before giving it. I didn't blame the man. What many people here didn't know was that this man had been a Follower all his life. For those of us who did know, Mr. Grant-Hartley's answer would set the tone for our own opinions. How did a Follower react to this? What were we supposed to think? Not that one man held all the answers, or even any of them, but he was respected among us. Someone worth listening to.

"I believe he told the truth."

THIRTY-SEVEN

A letter from Marcos arrived while I was eating lunch the next day. I held it for some time before setting the envelope aside, unopened. It wasn't that I didn't care what he had to say. It was that I cared too much. I'd let my fickle emotions get in the way of my sense one too many times. It was time to grow up.

Sorry, Marcos. It's better this way.

Another letter came from him two days later. I put them both in an envelope, addressed it to him at the palace, and sent them back. It didn't matter what he said. Whether he apologized or not. Berated me or not. Whether, out of honor, he again proposed. It didn't make a difference because I didn't want to hear it. Any of it.

I'd made a mistake with Waitrose. A willful one, but a mistake all the same. It hadn't been that with Marcos. I'd known exactly what I was doing, and I would have done it again. Which proved what kind of a person I was. To let my heart and emotions get the better of me once? That could be forgiven, but twice? I couldn't even forgive myself.

So, I sent the letters back.

I should have known Marcos wouldn't stop at letters. The next time a knock came at the front door, it wasn't a postman as I'd expected but Marcos's Head of Security himself. I leaned against the doorframe and wondered whether to be annoyed or amused. Embarrassment also vied for a position, given the last time I'd seen

Luka, I'd been a complete mess. What had Marcos told him about that night? It had to have been something. But was it everything?

"Shouldn't you be protecting your prince?" The question, meant to be a joke, came out far more annoyed than I planned as I struggled to pull my scattered emotions into place.

Luka didn't grin. He didn't flirt or tease me. There wasn't even the slightest twinkle in his eyes as he looked at me. Instead, there was simply respect.

"Sometimes, protecting the prince means protecting what he loves most."

For a breath of a moment, I let his words sink into my heart—before carefully pushing them away with a shake of my head. "Luka…"

"Don't worry, I didn't come to give you another letter or a lecture or tell you how much Prince Marcos wants you back—although that last one is true, in case you're doubting. I won't even stay long. Prince Marcos just wanted to check you were okay." He offered me a wry smile. "I must admit, I did too."

Was that what Marcos's letters had been? Not apologies or anger but simply checking on me? Suddenly I felt guilty for not reading them.

"I'm okay," I told Luka. He narrowed his eyes as if he didn't quite believe me. I wouldn't have either if the last vision I'd had of someone was them all but collapsing in my arms. "Not great, I'll admit, but okay. Keeping myself busy."

Tutoring kids mostly—when I wasn't hiding in my room, filling sketchbook after sketchbook with angst.

Where, before my time in Hodenia, I'd been tutoring struggling kids five days a week in the mornings, now I did it six days—morning, noon, and night. I'd taken on more kids with more difficult learning challenges too, desperate to fill the silence. The teachers Alina had hired to fill in for me while I'd been away had been happy to have the extra time back.

"Lord Waitrose hasn't been bothering you again, has he?"

I shook my head, surprised to realize that I'd barely thought of

Waitrose once since coming back. Proof of just how distracted I'd been by everything else. "He hasn't written either."

"Good."

Something in the way Luka said that one word had me wondering exactly what had been said between the two men when Luka escorted Waitrose away from Hodenia's ballroom. If the satisfied expression on his face was anything to go by, I doubted Waitrose had been doing much of the talking.

"I'll let Prince Marcos know."

"Thank you."

Luka moved to leave then. I found myself suddenly wishing he'd stay longer. Not to protect me—it seemed he'd already all but eliminated my greatest threat—but as a friend. Of course, I couldn't actually ask him. With my next tutoring session in twenty minutes, I didn't have time to sit and chat, for one. And, if his uniform was any indication, he was still working. Despite what he'd said, protecting Prince Marcos was his first priority. Not sitting down to tea with me. Still—

"Luka?"

"Yes?"

"Thanks for coming."

He smiled then, his shoulders dropping as he visibly relaxed. "Thank you for talking to me. I honestly wasn't sure you would."

I sighed, hating that he thought that of me. Hating even more that his uncertainty was completely justified, given the way I'd always treated him. "Forgive me?" I asked. "I was so rude to you. You just—your flirting, your attitude, your looks even, reminded me of—"

"Waitrose?"

I cringed. "Yes. Sorry. But I couldn't have been more wrong. The more I get to know you, the more I realize you're not like him at all."

Luka grinned. "I'll take that as an absolute compliment, my lady."

"Please do."

He left then. I watched him go before walking back inside to make myself a cup of tea. I should have been preparing for tutoring. Instead, I sat at the table and stared out the window, lost in a maze of thoughts.

I knew what a broken heart felt like. Mine had cracked right down the center the day Thoraben married Kenna. Peverell's palace had a grand and extensive garden planted in honor of their late queen, and I'd walked every path in it at least four times over the weeks that followed as I'd begged God for answers. I'd wanted to come home so desperately that I'd made a bargain with God. If he'd bring me home to Peverell—and, more precisely, Thoraben—I'd believe and pledge him my life. He'd brought me home to Peverell. Only to see the man I thought I loved marry someone else.

I hadn't turned my back on God—where else would I have gone?—but the doubts were overwhelming. Why had he brought me home if not for Thoraben? Why had he let me fall in love in the first place? Why let it go on for so long? I'd felt broken. Betrayed. Lost in a swell of grief. I doubt there was a single plant in the whole three hectares of gardens that I hadn't watered with my tears.

It was different this time. My heart didn't feel broken. Not wrenched or torn or bleeding. It didn't ache. It felt dead. Empty. Like that moment in Marcos's bedroom had pricked a hole in it and all the hope and life drained out.

I'd been angry after that night with Waitrose. Bitter. Full of regret. It was so different with Marcos. I regretted what I'd done not because it was wrong but because I wished I could have been a better person. Stronger.

Marcos loved me. I was almost certain of it now. He never would have kissed me like that if he didn't. He wouldn't have even let me close. Nor would he have sent Luka to check on me. But it didn't matter, because I'd failed him. Him *and* God. I'd tried so hard to show Marcos what love really was—a love that went beyond feelings and fickle emotions, a love like God's—and here I'd done the exact opposite. So much for being an example. What would Marcos think of God now?

My throat throbbed with the pain of trying to hold back tears. I wouldn't cry. I had no right to. I'd made my decision back there in Hodenia. Now, I simply had to deal with the consequences. Move on, or be trampled by those who were.

Kenna and Alina were waiting at my house when I arrived home from tutoring. Apparently when, in the course of a week, one ignored six invitations and three official summons to the palace, the troops arrived in person to stage an intervention. None of my attempts at getting out of it worked.

I'm not feeling well. We have access to the best doctors at the palace.

I told Jade I'd look after Callan. Your mom has him this afternoon. She's so excited about spending time with her grandson. Your dad too.

I have tutoring later. We'll send someone else.

I don't want to dress up. Come as is.

It's a palace. We'll sit outside. No one will care what you're wearing.

It might rain. We'll take umbrellas.

Mine is lost. That didn't even deign a response bar a slightly amused expression from Kenna. Fair enough though. Callan was acting more mature than I was right now, and he was all of six months old.

"Go with them," Emmett yelled out from his room two doors down the hall.

"Mind your own business," I yelled back.

There was a thump from his room, footsteps down the hall, and then he pushed himself through the two royals to stand directly in front of me.

"You are my business."

I might have been offended, if the expression on his face hadn't been so caring. When had my little brother grown up?

"I didn't say anything till now because I didn't think you'd want to hear it, and you probably still don't, but I'm going to say

271

it anyway. I want my sister back. The fun one, not the sad one who looks like she's about to cry if anyone looks at her the wrong way. I was so excited when I heard you were home again. I really missed you. But this Wenderley? No thanks. Send her back. Even when Thoraben dumped you, you weren't this bad. I don't know what happened in Hodenia, but can you please figure it out?

"Also, if Prince Marcos hurt you, you'd better tell me because it's my job as your brother to make sure he pays. I can do that, you know. I might be younger than him, but I'll totally fight him for you. If you want."

It was Emmett's words which tipped the scale. Brothers. They always could make me do anything. Even face my two best friends and the questions I knew were coming. Prince Everson's trial would likely be easier than what I was about to face.

"So?" Kenna asked.

I went and got my purse. And changed my blouse to a nicer one, to both Alina's and Kenna's amusement.

We talked about the weather on the way to the palace. Then we ate afternoon tea, gushed over Alina's wedding photos, walked all the way to the kitchen to ask whether they had any macadamia shortbread, thanked every person in there for their work, wondered over what was going on in the closed rooms of the former king's trial, discussed various artworks on the walls of the halls between the kitchen and Princess Suite, conferred over whether sitting on Kenna's giant bed or the couches in the suite's sitting room would be more comfortable, decided on the sitting room, called for more tea, decided chocolates would also be helpful, and finally sat. Silent. Waiting.

I could have come up with more reasons to procrastinate but what was the point? We all knew why I was here.

"What happened?" Kenna asked softly. "And, please, don't tell us it was nothing. You've been avoiding us, and you never do that."

I looked out the window at the garden below, watching several leaves dance away on the breeze. It wasn't that I didn't want to answer their questions. I did. I just didn't know how. I mean, I knew the facts—I'd fallen in love with Marcos, kissed him, offered far more, fled—but the why? The what? The how? I'd gone to comfort him. That's all I'd wanted to do. But somewhere between kneeling in front of him and ending up in his arms… I'd lost all sense of right and wrong. All I'd wanted to do was heal him.

But therein lay yet another of my many mistakes that night. Only God could heal.

"I failed him," I finally said.

Alina frowned. "Ryan?"

"Marcos."

Maybe I should have called him Prince Marcos. Maybe I should have brushed their questions aside and kept the whole disaster to myself. *Yeah, and maybe I should have stayed in my room that night.*

"You love him."

Not that it mattered but, "Yes."

"Are you worried about Rachana?"

I shook my head, more out of anger toward myself than in answer to Alina's question. I hadn't thought of Rachana for weeks. Which was ridiculous given I'd been caring for her son, sitting in her place at the dinner table, falling for the man she'd married.

"She didn't want Marcos to be alone after she died," Kenna mused. "Nor Ryan. The day she found out she was dying, she started praying that God would send someone special to love her son and his father and take the place she couldn't in their lives."

Oh, Rachana. The heartbreak… "She told you that?"

"In confidence, yes."

"Why are you telling me?"

Kenna sipped her tea, carefully putting it back on the saucer before answering. "Because she's gone and you need to hear it. You could be the one she was praying for."

I let out a short, bitter laugh. "If I'm the answer to her prayer, then there's something seriously wrong with the world."

"You think God makes mistakes?"

I wanted to say no. I almost did. But lying on top of everything else already wracking me with guilt? The truth was, I wasn't certain anymore.

I believed it, once. Stalking the Queen's Garden, right outside Kenna's window, I'd fought it out until I felt wrung dry but at peace. Yes, Thoraben had married Kenna despite my wholehearted belief that God had chosen him for me. Yes, that hurt like nothing I'd ever felt before. Yes, the very human, still relatively new Follower part of me felt like God had let me down. But yes, *yes*, he was still God. Still worth believing in. Still faithful. Still in control. Still cared about me.

But now?

Being alone with Marcos that night had been my mistake. There was no one else to blame for that. But Rachana getting pregnant the one time they were together? Her dying? Me being invited to the funeral, hired out of virtual obscurity by the queen herself, having a heart too big to stay objective? All things beyond human control. Which meant they were in God's department. And if he didn't make mistakes, then…what? He *meant* them to happen? He *wanted* to ruin Marcos's life? Rachana's? Mine?

Emotion after emotion came flooding back as I stared at the floor, not even noticing I was crying until Kenna pushed a tissue into my hand.

The physical pain that had ripped through my chest at the sound of Marcos's tears. The hope I felt, that maybe I could comfort him. The ecstasy of holding his hands in mine and not being sent away. The thrill that shot from my stomach to my toes when our lips met and only intensified as he held me. The moment I knew not only that I loved him but that he loved me back. The wanting, the giving…the regret.

The guilt when I realized what I'd done. The disappointment tearing me to shreds. The voice of failure which wouldn't let my self-turned anger die. Hope draining away.

"It doesn't matter anyway. I can't marry him."

"Why?"

Where did I start? I crushed the tissue into a ball solid enough to bruise the palm it was pressed against. I'd held back the words for so long, keeping the shame inside, hiding the truth behind a carefree smile. These were my best friends. The women who'd befriended me as a child and welcomed me back into their lives as an adult. I could trust them. Surely.

And yet, they were so good. So pure. So innocent of my mess.

"Wenderley?"

Kenna put a gentle hand on my arm. Alina knelt on my other side, taking my hand in hers.

"Why can't you marry him?"

My breath shuddered as years of friendship battled my shame. I wanted to think I knew Kenna and Alina well enough to know they would react with grace and forgiveness, but what if they didn't? What if justice was stronger and they made me marry Waitrose? I knew the law as well as they did, and there was no question what consequences my actions should have.

"Because I made the same mistake Rachana did."

"You *slept* with Marcos?"

"No." I sighed. Even the truth felt like a lie. I hadn't slept with him. But I'd come close. It was easy to stand detached from it all now and claim that nothing really happened, but in that moment, wrapped in Marcos's arms, my mind overwhelmed with heady emotion, I would have given him anything.

So different from that night with Waitrose, when all I'd felt was defiance. There'd been no love between us. I might have known Lord Waitrose's name and reputation but, for all intents and purposes, we'd been complete strangers. Using each other to block out the happiness of everyone else around. For all the happiness it had brought us.

"With Waitrose."

A flash of color caught my eye through the door I'd forgotten was open, the split second of recognition making me feel sick. I knew that shock of red hair. Aimee. How long had she been standing there? What had she heard?

With a barely-there whisper of apology to the two princesses, I ran out the door.

"Aimee!"

She kept running. Down the stairs. Out the door. Into the Queen's Garden where I finally caught her. I'd wandered these paths far too often for anyone to have a chance of hiding from me here. I put a hand on Aimee's shoulder, begging her to stop. To let me explain, even though I had no idea how.

"Aimee, please."

She turned but shook off my hand, crossing her arms as she glared up at me. "You lied to us."

"I never lied."

A pair of gardeners walked past, ducking their heads in acknowledgement before continuing on. Aimee waited until they were out of earshot before continuing, her words barely kept in check.

"You told us to wait until we were married. That night we talked about relationships and you talked about even a kiss being a precious gift. We promised each other. We trusted you. You showed us the commitment you'd made and signed, and it inspired me so much that I spent the next month praying and writing my own. You said it was worth it, even if the law hadn't been there."

"I meant that."

She let out a short, derisive laugh. "Clearly, you didn't."

"Yes, I did." I softened my voice. "And now you know why. I didn't wait."

Aimee bit her lip. Holding back tears or more accusations? Not that I didn't deserve them. No, I hadn't lied to her or the other girls, but in withholding the truth, I might as well have. I certainly hadn't been honest with them. Had she really gone home after that night and written her own commitment? I'd had no idea my words meant so much to her. I'd gone home that night and wondered if I should have kept that particular lesson until they were a little older, given how much they'd giggled over the idea of even holding hands with a boy they liked.

"Aimee, I—" What? What could I even say? The short of it was, I'd failed her. But I couldn't leave her like this, looking so forlorn. "Have you ever wished there was a word bigger than 'sorry'?

If there was, I'd be saying it to you now because with everything in me, I wish I could take back that night and what I did. It happened before I met you all. And I've regretted it every day since. If only you knew how much. I wrote that commitment as a promise to God and myself that I'd never do that again."

Two weeks ago, I'd broken that promise too. So much for being a good example. Why had I ever thought I was strong enough? It should have been Kenna mentoring my girls. Or Alina. Or my sister, Jade, who'd faithfully waited years to marry the man she loved. Anyone but me.

I loved these girls fiercely—had ever since our first Rebel youth meeting when Anna shyly admitted that she'd always been bad at making friends, and Milly Rose had immediately put an arm around her and promised she'd never have that trouble again— but what if love wasn't enough?

"Why didn't you tell us?" Aimee asked, looking up at me. "We wouldn't have turned you in. You wouldn't have even had to tell us his name."

And there was the question. The one I'd struggled with every time the girls and I had talked about boys or relationships. I'd told myself it was for their protection. For their own good. That it was none of their business. They didn't need to know or be dragged into my mess. But even while telling myself, I'd known they were lies. Acceptable excuses but not the truth. I hadn't wanted to admit the truth then. I didn't want to now either, but something about the way Aimee still stood there—not running, not accusing, waiting to see if she could trust me—I had to.

"Because I was ashamed. I was your leader. You girls all looked up to me like I was someone worth imitating. I wanted to be that example for you of what a Follower looked like."

"You thought we wouldn't look up to you if you weren't perfect?"

"Would you? You can't say it hasn't changed your opinion of me, knowing what I've done."

She frowned a little, considering that question before answering. "It has."

I nodded, having known that one day it would come to this.
"See?"

"It's made me respect you more."

THIRTY-EIGHT

"Now, if two plus three is five, then three plus two is?"

Hallee scrunched up her nose and closed one eye as she considered the math equation in front of her. "Six?"

"Close. Want to try again?"

"Seven."

"Not quite. It's five."

"But you said two plus three was five."

Yes, I had. Quite a few times now. "They *both* make five."

"Oh." Hallee sorted all her pencils again, putting them into rainbow order this time rather than size. "Are you sure?"

I would have used her pencils to illustrate the equations, but she was quite particular about anyone touching her things. I'd brought colored buttons last time we worked on math, but she'd been so distracted by sorting them into colors, shapes, sizes, and patterns that I'd barely been able to teach her anything. Maybe food would work?

Or we could give up for the day. We'd already been at this for forty minutes, and my mind was almost as distracted as Hallee's, still trying to get my head around what Aimee had said. She respected me more. Not *because* of what I'd done, as she'd gone on to clarify, but who I'd *become* because of it.

I'd been shocked into silence. "I'm not saying what you did was right or that you should have lied to us about it," she'd said, "but it's like, I don't know, if God can forgive you for that, then I know he'll forgive me for the bad things I do too. There's…

hope…I guess you'd call it. If I make a mistake or fail or something, it isn't the end. God can still use me and my life, like he's used you to impact mine and the other girls' lives, you know?"

Yeah, I knew, but I was having as hard a time accepting it today as I had three days ago. For over a year, I'd been hiding my shame from the girls, convinced it would be the thing that lost me every bit of trust in their eyes, only to find the exact opposite occur. It hadn't been my perfection that impacted Aimee the most but my regret. Would the other girls think the same?

"Wenderley."

I blinked back into reality at the sound of my mom's voice. "Mom? What are you doing here?"

"The queen of Hodenia is at our house wanting to speak with you."

All thought of buttons, pencils, and mistakes flew from my head at my mom's words. Queen Galielle was here in Peverell? At my house? This couldn't be good.

"But I'm helping Hallee. And her mom won't be home for another half hour." It was a flimsy excuse, but it was all I could think of. I couldn't face Marcos's mother. Not yet. I needed more time. A month. A year. Maybe a lifetime.

"I'll stay with Hallee." All but pushing me out of my chair, Mom took my place at the table and smiled at Hallee. "Hi. I'm Wenderley's mom. You can call me Emmalyne."

Hallee nodded and set to rearranging her pencils again.

Mom looked back up at me. "Now, go."

So much for time. Not that any excuse would have worked, given the queen was apparently at my house.

More precisely, as I found out ten minutes later, the queen of Hodenia was in my bedroom, calmly sitting on my unmade bed. If I hadn't been so shocked to see her, I might have laughed. Or cringed. Were they my pajamas poking out from underneath her skirt? They were definitely my shoes strewn across the floor.

"Queen Galielle, before you say anything else, please let me apologize for leaving Hodenia without telling you. I—"

The queen held up a hand, somehow managing to still look as

regal as ever while sitting on my pile of mess. "Ryan is fine. Paige and some of the other maids have been keeping him entertained, and Mrs. Graham will be arriving tomorrow. I didn't come for an apology."

I'd been replaced already. It shouldn't have hurt as much as it did. I'd only ever been a stand-in in Ryan's life. "Why did you come?"

"I wanted to see if you were okay."

She'd come all this way for me? Not that I wasn't both flattered and touched that she cared so much about me, but there was a healthy dose of guilt and a little embarrassment in there too. She'd really come all this way for me. "I, uh, I'm fine."

I scooped up two pairs of shoes and threw them in the direction of my closet before walking over to my desk. Somewhere under the four outfits I'd vetoed this morning was a chair. It was no wonder Queen Galielle hadn't been able to find it. Or perhaps she'd thought it too much of an invasion of privacy to touch my clothing. So had chosen sitting on my bed instead? That didn't seem right.

"Wenderley, I know why you left."

I sat on the chair with a thump, her quiet words like a starting gun to my racing heart. She knew.

No, wait. You are so paranoid, Wenderley. She meant the abdication, nothing more. It had coincided with my leaving. All of Peverell had been in upheaval, and she knew how close I was to their royal family.

"Thoraben will make a great king. Peverell is in safe hands," I told her, parroting what I'd heard my mom tell a friend yesterday as I pulled clothing out from beneath me. The floor seemed as good as any a place to put it. Not exactly the refined image I wanted to portray to the queen sitting a foot away, but it was a little too late for that now with her having been in here for who knew how long already. I hadn't exactly rushed home.

"He will, and it is, but I meant what happened between you and Marcos."

My gaze flew to the queen's for an instant before dropping in humiliation. "How——?"

"Marcos told me."

Oh. So, she did know. How far I'd fallen. How badly I'd failed her. That I'd pulled Marcos down with me. Shame lodged in my throat, a lump I couldn't swallow past.

"I'm sorry…"

Just like with Aimee, I knew even as I whispered the words that they weren't enough. How could mere words change what I'd done?

"Wenderley, please look at me."

She waited until I found the courage. It wasn't that I was afraid of her, nor unwilling to face her condemnation, well-deserved as it would have been. It was that I didn't want to see the disappointment I knew would be in her eyes.

Only it wasn't there.

"I didn't come to accuse you," she said quietly. "No doubt you've done a good enough job of that all on your own. I came to see if you were okay and——" She stopped for a breath, tilting her head slightly to the right as she looked at me. "I wanted to ask you not to give up on Marcos. Or yourself."

What?

"What's between you and Marcos is real, and I truly believe you are the woman God has chosen not only for my son but to be the next queen of Hodenia. I know I asked you to wait on marrying him until he becomes a Follower—and I still stand by that—but I don't think it will be long. This thing with Everson, it's shaken Marcos. Dorien too. They've been asking questions about God. Questions that make me think they're not far from choosing him.

"I honestly admire you for leaving the palace like you did that night. I can only guess how difficult that must have been, having seen how unreservedly you love. But Wenderley, please, don't give up on what could be out of guilt or some misplaced sense of unworthiness. God has so much more for you than a lifetime of regret."

I was shaking my head even before she finished speaking. Though I admired her opinions and appreciated her belief in me more than I could say, she was wrong. A queen needed to be strong. Trustworthy. The king's greatest supporter, not the one who pulled him down and made him forget who he was.

"Thank you, but—" I shrugged.

"You don't believe me."

"I failed him once. What's to say I won't do it again?"

"Then you'd be as human as the rest of us." She held up her hand again, silencing me before I could argue that. "Wenderley, none of us are perfect. Not even royalty. We fail all the time. We go with fear rather than faith, choose selfishness over caring for others, listen to lies instead of the voice of truth. It's part of being human. But it's what we do with those mistakes that proves who we really are."

"I wanted to show him faith, and integrity."

"Now you have a chance to show him grace."

"You don't want someone like me marrying your son."

Queen Galielle laughed. "Quite the contrary, I assure you. You're exactly the woman I've always prayed he'd find."

"What about Alina? Rachana?"

"I would have supported and loved Princess Alina whole-heartedly, had Marcos married her. You can be absolutely certain of that. She's gorgeous, giving, compassionate, a truly wonderful woman. But there was always something in me that riled against their partnership, though I couldn't have pinpointed exactly what it was. I hate that she was hurt in the process, but I'm thankful she and Marcos didn't marry. Even more, after seeing how happy she is now with Mr. Samson.

"And Rachana? She, too, was beautiful, caring, easy to love." Queen Galielle leaned forward, placing a hand on my knee. "But Wenderley, Rachana wasn't a born princess. Not like you. I knew you were the one the instant I saw you trip at Rachana's funeral."

"You saw that?" And here I'd thought I got away with that one. How embarrassing. "But you barely even knew me then. How could you have known?"

"Because I saw something of myself in you."

I couldn't think of a higher honor, even if I didn't agree. Queen Galielle was beautiful and everything a queen should be. Kind, demure, passionate. She made heels look as comfortable as slippers, something that couldn't have been further from reality.

"But I don't want to be a princess. I've tried. The heels, the gowns, the simpering, and saying the right things. I can't do it."

"Personally, I think heels are overrated."

"But—"

"Did you ever see a photo of the gown I wore to my betrothal ball?"

"No."

"It was made from thick blue satin, the full skirt overlaid with sunflower-painted silk. And I wore green shoes. Without heels." She looked pointedly at the flower-patterned shoes I wore.

"But—"

"Despite how it might seem, being a princess doesn't come with a whole lot of unbreakable rules. Just a prince. And I can't think of anyone more perfect for my son *or* Hodenia than you. You have the heart of a queen."

"Even if all that is true, I just…can't. Not after…" I looked away, too embarrassed to hold her gaze.

"Do you hold Rachana against Marcos? Hate him for what he did with her?"

"No, of course not." How could I, when I'd done the same?

"How about King Everson? Do you hate him for making criminals of Followers?"

"I—" Did I? What he'd done was wrong in so many ways. He might not have murdered anyone, but he'd ruined lives. His decree was the reason I'd been wrenched from my friends as a young teen to live in another country.

But then, it was also because of his misguided decree that I'd come to know God, come to know and love Hodenia, deepened my relationship with Alina, Kenna, Jade, and my parents, found a passion for working with and mentoring kids, and been chosen by Queen Galielle to care for Ryan. The king's criminalizing faith had made me the woman I was today more than anything else.

"No. I don't hate him."

"Then why do you hate yourself? Why can't you forgive yourself this? One mistake doesn't condemn you for life."

"It's more than one."

The moment I said it, I wished I could take the words back. It was too dangerous. Even with Everson's public admission regarding the true nature of the Rebels, I would still be forced to marry Waitrose if the truth of that night ever came out. It was the law.

"I know about the man sending you threats."

"What?" How could she?

"Marcos told me about those too."

Marcos had been doing a lot of talking.

"Then you know how impossible my marrying Marcos is."

"You've already seen one miracle this month. Is it really so hard to believe God might give you another?" She put a gentle hand on my arm. "Do you love my son?"

Far too much. "Yes," I whispered.

"Hold on to that. Nothing is impossible. All will be well." She smiled, as if that were the end of the story, before patting me on my shoulder and leaving. I waved her off before wandering back to my room, still somewhat astounded by all she'd said, all Marcos had told her, and the fact that she still wanted me for a daughter-in-law. Really, the fact that she'd wanted me at all.

An envelope on my bed caught my attention. I picked it up, thinking to run after Queen Galielle and return it, only to see my name on the front in Marcos's now familiar handwriting. I held it for some time, staring at my name, before finally opening it.

There was only one page inside, and only one line apart from our names on that page, and yet it sank me to my knees.

Wenderley
  I forgive you.
  Marcos

THIRTY-NINE

I forgive you. I forgive you.

The words echoed in my head, bouncing from doubt to hope to fear to guilt to hope again as I sat out in the garden, staring at the stars. It was late and I was tired, but sleep wouldn't come. I wanted to believe the words in Marcos's letter, and those Queen Galielle had said yesterday. I wanted to let them sink deep into my heart and be free of the regret, once and for all.

But how? Just let it go? It was too easy. I shouldn't have gotten off scot-free. Marcos hadn't. His mistakes had been thrown around for both Hodenia and Peverell to see and judge for themselves. He'd married a woman who was all but a stranger to somehow try to make something good of them. Rachana hadn't gotten off easily either. Not that Ryan wasn't an absolute gift, but I don't think getting pregnant at seventeen was part of Rachana's life plan. Nor dying at twenty-four. And Kenna and Ben had been forced into marriage for a mistake they hadn't even made. The one I had. The world might never know my shame, but I did.

But then, maybe that's what made it so difficult. I wanted to *do* something to atone for my mistakes. Fulfil a punishment or something. Not just let it go.

God…what do I do? I can't… I don't want to… Don't know how to…

A noise at the side gate had me on instant alert. It was probably only a dog or stray cat sniffing around at this time of night but still.

"Lady Wenderley?"

My eyes closed as a wave of emotions crashed over me. Longing being the strongest of them all.

Definitely not a cat.

I could just make out Marcos's face peering into our garden above the gate. "You're still awake. Can I come in?"

First Queen Galielle, now Marcos. What was he doing here? I hadn't been prepared to see Queen Galielle. I was even less prepared for Marcos. What if he asked questions I had no answers to? Or told me Ryan needed me? The thought of Ryan's face had me wanting to go inside and pack my bags to leave tonight, but I couldn't do that. Until I had answers, I couldn't give the boy hope. Nor his father. But to send Marcos away when he was standing right there? It was one thing to send his letters back, but the man himself? When he'd come all this way?

I looked behind me, checking to see whether the light was still on in the living room. It was, meaning Mom was still awake, reading in her favorite chair, justifying a late night with the excuse of one more chapter. My love of books had come from her. And my night owl tendencies.

"Please, Wenderley. I know it's late and I'm probably the last person you want to see. I promise, I won't ask you to come back or to marry me or anything like that—I won't even come near you, if that's what you want—but I have to talk to someone. No, not someone. You. I have to talk to you."

He was a bumbling mess. With a prayer that this wasn't another thing I'd live to regret, I let him in.

It was Marcos, but nothing like I'd ever seen before. Even his suit was a mess—jacket open, shirt half out, black tie clutched in his hand. And that hair! It needed smoothing down in the worst way.

Keep your hands to yourself, Wenderley.

I walked back to my chair, picking up a ball one of my brothers had left behind on the way to keep my hands busy, rolling it between them. I would have sat on them, but they were too restless to have stayed. Marcos was here. In my garden. But as far from the self-assured Marcos as I'd ever imagined he could be.

Suddenly, it wasn't him and what he might say that I was afraid of. It was me. What if he cried again? What if Mom went to bed and I lost her presence as my security blanket?

"It's fine. Take a seat." I gestured to the seat across from me, hoping he'd take it rather than the one beside me. He took the one beside me. I moved over one. He didn't even offer a rueful smile. *God, help him. Help me.* "What's bothering you?"

He rubbed a hand through his hair, clearly not the first time he'd done it tonight given the way it stuck up in every direction. "I don't know where to start."

How about exactly what you told your mom about us, and why you told her about Waitrose. And how many other people you've mentioned it to. And what you're doing here in my garden after eleven at night. And that note you sent me.

"No one is charging K—Prince Everson."

"What?" That hadn't even crossed my mind, selfish as I was. Marcos had been at the trial? For how long? It had been going on for almost three weeks now. Had he been there this whole time? Why hadn't Father mentioned it? Father had been there, as had Kenna, who'd also had ample opportunity. Or Queen Galielle, when she'd come? Why hadn't Marcos himself come to see me earlier? *Would you have let him in if he had?*

"Witness after witness has been brought forward but not one single one of them wants Everson punished. By their own admission, he wrenched them from their lives and labeled them criminals, but none of them even seem to care. They're all saying the same thing. 'I seek no justice. I forgive him. All will be well.' It makes no sense. He was wrong. He deserves to be punished. But, unless one of them actually charges him, he's going to walk away without a single consequence."

Wow. And yet, the news didn't surprise me as much as it should have. It was difficult to charge a man who was so broken, so remorseful, and so visibly changed. Every Follower I knew had been praying that King Everson would choose to surrender to God for the past twenty years. To see him make such a public declaration of faith, with nothing to gain and everything to lose, was cause for celebration. A new beginning. This was a time to show grace, love, and forgiveness. To show him with our lives what being a Follower truly meant. To celebrate the miracle.

But that would make no sense to Marcos. He didn't believe in God. He wouldn't see the grace and forgiveness behind such a move, only a lack of justice. But then, punishment came in so many forms. Something I was all too familiar with.

"You think K—Prince Everson has escaped consequence?"

"Hasn't he?"

"He's lived with the guilt of what he's done for longer than I've been alive." And he likely would still, for years to come. Every time he saw a Follower he'd exiled, even if they lovingly welcomed him into their lives and homes, he'd remember what he'd done. Even if he accepted God's forgiveness in all its vastness, the truth of what he'd done wouldn't change.

"Regret isn't a consequence."

"Isn't it?" I asked, thinking back to all the nights I'd lay in bed, staring up at the ceiling, wishing I could go back to those innocent days where the greatest regret I had was eating too much at dinner and paying in heartburn. Marcos had regrets too. Though he loved Ryan with everything in him, so much about his relationship with Rachana—both recently and that one night so long ago—was shaded with regret.

"They're forgiving him," Marcos said, "just like that. It's not fair."

"Grace never is."

"They should be furious with him. They should be demanding justice. I would be. He took so much from them. He destroyed their lives."

The ball slipped out of my hands. I watched it roll down the path and stop in a patch of grass. It was more effort than the distraction was worth to rescue it. I wrapped my arms around my middle and turned to face Marcos instead.

"No, he didn't."

"They were convicted as the worst of criminals and taken from their homes, never to return."

Yes…but— It was so much more. *God, please, give me the right words. Don't let me wreck this.*

"Tell me this," I tried. "If you had the choice again, would you have chosen to go to that party with Rachana and do what you did? If you knew then how many years of pain and regret it would cause—for you, Rachana, your family, even Hodenia—would you have made that choice?"

Marcos let out a short laugh. "No, of course not."

I watched him, waiting for the realization to hit. It didn't take long.

"But then I wouldn't have Ryan."

"No, you wouldn't. Your life changed that night. It brought about pain, consequences, and loss like you could never have imagined. But it also brought you Ryan. Good out of the pain. Just like the Rebels' lives.

"The pain of their trials and exile gave way to the lives they have now, which have brought them new joys amidst the pain. They are the people they are today, with the families they have, *because* of what Prince Everson did. Their choosing to offer Prince Everson grace instead of judgment is a choice to put the pain aside and focus on the joy—and give him the chance to do the same."

My heart pounded in the darkness as I waited nervously for Marcos to speak. The words had come effortlessly, filled with a passion that left me feeling somewhat shaky, but me believing them didn't mean he would.

Marcos nodded but stayed silent. More than ever, I wished I could read his mind. Was he still confused? More so? Slowly coming to understand? Wishing he'd gone to someone else to share his frustrations? Sitting in wonderment over the concept of grace he was only just now coming to understand? *You wish…*

"Do you think your God would forgive me for the way I hurt Rachana?"

"Yes." Without a doubt.

"Would you?"

If he kept looking at me with those hopeful eyes, I was going to cry. Or lurch myself into his arms and kiss him. Both of which were terrible ideas. I pulled my legs up onto the chair, wrapping my arms around them like a double shield to my heart before letting myself answer. "Yes."

Silence stretched, held tight by the tension radiating between us. I forgave him. It was so easily done. How could I not when he'd already forgiven me so much? But what did that mean to him? For us?

"Do you pray for me?"

"I…" Where had that question come from? "Yes. I do. All the time."

Was this where he told me not to bother? That he was done with this God once and for all?

"Keep praying. Please," Marcos said quietly. "I'm not ready to believe yet but seeing Everson… He's different. Unafraid. What he said in his public address, about God being a crutch? I thought that too. Or, not a crutch but certainly not something someone in power would need. But now, watching both Everson and Thoraben…I don't know. Maybe I was wrong about God. Maybe he's not only for the weak. Maybe he's real."

My heart thudded harder against my ribs, pulsing even to my fingertips. My toes. My elbows, even. But it was nothing compared to the way my spirit danced. No, not danced. Yearned. Hoped. Leaned forward to the point of falling over with anticipation. Marcos didn't believe, not yet. But, like Queen Galielle had said, he was close.

There were so many things I wanted to say—not the least of which was to scream that yes, God was real and Marcos was absolutely right in thinking God was the one who gave Thoraben and Everson their strength—but I held every one of them back. This was between Marcos and God. Not me.

"I'll keep praying."

"Thank you."

"Have you been in Peverell for the whole trial?" I asked, after a time.

"Most of it. I've gone home a few times to see Ryan."

The thought of Marcos making his son a priority made me smile. "How's he doing?" Was he adjusting well to Mrs. Graham being his governess? Did she know yet what each of his little smiles meant? Was Ryan smiling at all? Or had he gone back into the quiet shell he'd hidden in after Rachana's funeral? Would he forgive me for leaving without saying goodbye?

"He misses you."

I missed him too, especially his cute little face when he tried to talk Chef Meyer into making more pies, without actually coming out and saying it. "How is his arm?"

"Better. He told me if it doesn't heal properly, he'll get a hook like Pirate Pumpernickel. He seemed a little disappointed when I told him that wouldn't be necessary."

He'd make a cute pirate. I'd have to send him a new bandanna or something. Maybe an eye patch. Was that asking for trouble to limit the sight of a six-year-old who already sported a broken arm? Maybe a card would be better. Let him know I hadn't forgotten him. Or a book. I'd seen one on Eder's shelf last week that Ryan would love.

"How's his dad?"

I shouldn't have asked. It went against every barrier I was desperately trying to keep in place between Marcos and me. But it wasn't Ryan's face that came to mind every time I thought of him falling out of that tree. It was Marcos's.

"He misses you too."

My lips trembled with the effort of keeping them shut. *Be strong, Wenderley. It's for the best. You have to remember that.*

"I'm s—"

"Wenderley—"

Our voices crashed over top of each other. Both starting, both stopping, helplessness hanging in the air like an oversized balloon. One filled with water, threatening to drown us both any second.

FORTY

You didn't have to leave."

Marcos's statement did nothing to ease the tension. If anything, it held a pin to the balloon.

He's forgiven you already. Take him at his word. Otherwise—

Otherwise, I might as well say goodbye right now, because even friendship failed without trust.

Trust…

"I couldn't stay. I couldn't face…"

"Me?"

I nodded. "And what I'd done. You told me about your promise not to kiss anyone but your wife, and I ignored it. My own promise too. So much for integrity. I wish I could change what I did, but I can't. All I can say is I'm sorry."

He took a deep breath. "I'm sorry, too, for not protecting you better."

"You shouldn't have to—"

"Protect you?" His smile was wry. "But that's what we men do for the women we love."

The women we love.

My breath caught in my throat. Queen Galielle had said Marcos loved me. He himself had intimated it on a number of occasions, but to hear the words was like rain trickling over the heart that, ever since that night, had felt dead. But that rain, those words, brought life. Flowers, daring to poke their shoots through dry, cracked dirt.

"You love me?"

Marcos nodded, never taking his eyes off mine. "Why do you think it took me so long to send you away that night? I didn't want you to leave."

The living room light flicked off, pulling my attention toward the now dark window. Midnight. Or Mom had finally finished her book and was going to bed. The darkness around us seemed far too intimate, all of a sudden. Or perhaps it was the turn of conversation. There wasn't a balcony between us tonight, and we both knew how explosive the attraction could be if we let it ignite. I walked over to the gate.

"Marcos, I think it's time—"

"Wait. Please. There's something else you need to know."

He was right beside me, taking the air I couldn't seem to remember how to breathe. I looked down at his shoes, too scared of what I might say—or do—if I looked into his eyes.

"Marcos—"

He was too close. His cologne tortured me, just like it had done at Alina's wedding, turning logic to yearning. I wanted him to stay. Which was exactly why he had to go.

"Waitrose can't hurt you anymore."

I staggered back half a step, catching myself against the fence. Frowning as I tried, and failed, to comprehend what Marcos was saying. "What?"

"In the trial yesterday, Everson confessed to paying Waitrose to find and bring in Rebel leaders, as well as trying to ruin the relationship between Thoraben and Mackenna—both before and after their marriage. Waitrose himself confirmed it. Only where every word Everson says is filled with remorse and a promise to pay back everything he's taken from people, Waitrose has done nothing but incriminate himself further. You were right in thinking you weren't the first woman he's blackmailed. But you will be the last."

The last. Because now they all knew, I'd have to—No. I

couldn't. Wouldn't. No matter what they said. "They can't make me marry him."

"They won't. They can't, in fact. He's already married."

"What? No. I slept with a—" I put a hand to my mouth, gulping back a throatful of bile. *Wenderley, what have you done?*

Marcos put a hand on my arm, steadying me. "No. You didn't. He married six months ago, to a woman from Allegria."

"He's married." The idea felt so strange in my head, not quite sitting right. Married? Waitrose?

"Married, corrupt, and convicted criminal. Waitrose will be going to jail for a very long time. After he pays back almost all his wealth in compensation to the women he's trifled with. You included. But Wenderley…" Marcos moved his hand to my chin, turning my face gently until I had to look at him. My troubled gaze met his clear one. "You understand what this means, don't you?"

Waitrose was married. Waitrose was going to prison. His poor wife. Whoever she was.

"He can't hurt you anymore. And he can't hurt your girls either. You're free. All of you."

I dropped my gaze, the reality of what Marcos had pointed out hitting me so hard to the chest that I couldn't breathe. *Free.* Aimee, Rory, Milly Rose, Anna, Liz, Parker, Max, Evanse. They were safe. My mistake couldn't take away their lives anymore.

Marcos's hand fell to my shoulder before running down my arm and squeezing my hand. My breath caught. It took every bit of self-control I had to stand there and not throw myself against his chest and beg him to hold me forever.

"I'm not going to propose again tonight. I said I wouldn't, and I want to be a man who keeps my promises. But I want you to know, the offer still stands."

"Marcos…" He was almost there. His path to God so close he might as well have believed. He'd asked me to keep praying for him. That was faith enough, wasn't it?

No. I didn't need God's voice to thunder in the sky to answer that. I knew it already. No, it wasn't enough. No amount of wishing would make it so.

"Don't give me an answer now. I know you have a lot to think about but…soon?"

I nodded. There was no way I was managing words. He loved me. He'd finally admitted it. But there was someone else he needed to love more. Someone I loved too much to compromise again.

Marcos leaned forward and kissed my cheek, pausing barely a breath from my face for an eternal moment before stepping back. "Goodnight, Lady Wenderley. I hope you sleep well."

FORTY-ONE

That was quite a talk you had with a certain prince last night." The knife I'd been using to cut vegetables stilled as I looked over at my mom. "You were listening? I thought you were reading."

"I finished my book half an hour before Prince Marcos even arrived. I'd been sitting there praying for you."

"Why?"

"You seemed troubled, sitting out there all alone for so long. I was praying for wisdom for you. Well, up until Prince Marcos arrived. Then I was praying for self-control for you both."

"Mom!" Not that she was far off. I'd been praying for the same.

"You have a complicated relationship."

I cut the rest of that carrot and two more before deciding to confide in her. Complicated was a gross understatement. "He wants me to marry him."

She didn't seem surprised, which was probably a good thing since she also had a sharp knife in her hand on the other side of the kitchen counter. "And you don't want to?"

"Like you said, it's complicated."

"Because of Ryan?"

"Actually, Ryan's the uncomplicated part." My heart had been his from the first moment I saw him, and he seemed to like me too. I'd never replace his mom in his life, but I'd cherish the role of friend. "It's Marcos. Or maybe it's me. I don't know. He's not a Follower, so there's that. But even if he does choose to believe, how do I know what's between us is enough? He told me he loved me, and I know I love him, but it's only been four months. Is that really long enough to know for sure? What if the only reason I want to marry him is because he's the first man who's ever asked? Or because it would mean staying with Ryan?"

"Is it?"

I sighed. "No." Maybe they were reasons, but they weren't the only reasons, nor were they the biggest. Fear held top spot. Fear that *I* wouldn't be enough. Fear that, despite what Queen Galielle had said, I'd lose myself again in trying to make myself into the "perfect" princess. Fear that Marcos would realize Princess Celeste really was a better option. Fear that I loved him too much. That if I said yes, and something took him away from me, I'd have nothing left. I'd been through that once already, after Thoraben. I didn't know if I had the strength to do it again.

"Can I give you some advice?" my mom asked.

"Please."

She put her knife down before turning her attention solely to me. "Don't wait for a feeling. Make a choice." The corners of her mouth tipped up in a smile. "From the time you were born, you've felt things deeply and relied on your heart. I'm not saying that's bad at all—it's made you the most caring, compassionate person I know—but emotions come and go. They *will* still come and go, even after you marry, regardless of whether that person is Prince Marcos or someone else. Marriage, relationships…just like faith, they're a choice to keep believing even when the feelings aren't there anymore.

"If you love and respect Marcos, and believe he's the man who will love, encourage, and treasure you for the rest of your lives, and that the two of you can serve both God and Hodenia better together than apart, then marry him. Don't give away what could be a wonderful future because you can't see right now how it will work. Faith doesn't rely on feelings or our understanding every tiny detail. If it did, it wouldn't be faith.

"Look at what you know to be true, and make a choice. Fight fear with faith and the knowledge that all will be well."

Advice given, she looked down, picked the knife up, and kept cutting, slicing the chicken breast in front of her into strips, then cubes.

I watched her silently. Long enough for her to look up again. "Okay?" she asked.

I nodded, blinked, looked down, and promptly cut my finger along with the carrot. Mom sent me out of the kitchen until I could focus. I might have been offended if she hadn't been trying not to laugh as she did it.

Make a choice, she'd said.

As if it was that easy.

I spent a lot of time over the next five days once again wandering the Queen's Garden at the palace. With each step I prayed. Pleaded. Fought. For Marcos. For me. For us. I wanted concrete answers, but none came. All I could keep coming back to were the three things I knew for certain.

One, Marcos loved me.

Two, he and God had both forgiven me.

Three, I had a choice to make.

Maybe God's plan was that I walk away from Marcos, but I couldn't help thinking that wouldn't be the case. Marcos's questions in the garden, they weren't the questioning of someone indifferent to God anymore. It was only a matter of time until Marcos chose God for himself.

I didn't know exactly when it would be—weeks, months, maybe only days—but I felt in my heart that it would be soon. And when he did, I wouldn't be able to hide anymore behind the promise I'd made to Queen Galielle. I'd have to choose, once and for all, whether I could be the wife—and one day queen—Marcos needed. I loved him, without a doubt, but was it enough? Could *I* be enough?

I turned a corner to see Kenna embracing Ben on the ornamental stone bridge spanning one of the flowerbeds. Kenna spotted me and waved before I could tactfully backtrack. The decision of whether to simply wave and keep my distance or go and speak with them was also taken out of my hands when they walked toward me.

Kenna threw her arms around me in lieu of a greeting. Her husband was more reserved, taking my hand for a moment before dropping it.

"Wenderley, nice to see you. Enjoying Mother's garden?" he asked.

"Yes, of course, Prince, I mean, *King* Thoraben."

He grinned. "Just Ben is fine."

I smiled back. "Just Ben it is."

"Especially since we'll be equals soon. *Queen* Wenderley."

"What?"

"Don't worry, I won't say anything publicly of course. I only wanted to be among the first to offer my congratulations. I couldn't be happier for you and Prince Marcos."

Kenna squealed.

I was too confused by Thoraben's words to do the same. "You think I'm engaged to Prince Marcos?"

"You're not?"

I shook my head.

"But he told me he was going to propose to you. He came and asked if I thought it was a good idea. I told him yes, of course." Ben looked stricken. "Oh no. He hasn't asked you yet. I've ruined the surprise."

"No, he asked." Twice, actually. "Although I'm not sure I'm talking about the same proposal you are."

"Marcos *already* asked you to marry him?" Kenna's eyes were wide, her face disbelieving, maybe even a little hurt. "And you never thought to tell me? Wenderley, I've been here every day. One little 'by the way, Prince Marcos proposed' would have been enough."

"Except I didn't say yes."

"Why?"

For so many reasons, most of which they didn't need to know, especially when there really was only one that mattered anymore. "Because he's not a Follower."

Kenna's smile dropped, understanding and concern instantly taking its place. That and the hand she put on my arm said everything she couldn't find the words to get out. Ben, in almost direct contrast, was grinning.

"Are you sure about that?" he asked.

"About what? That I won't marry someone who doesn't share my faith? Yes. Absolutely."

I'd compromised once on something important to me, and I refused to do it again. I could live without Marcos. Walking away from him would absolutely wreck me and I doubt I'd ever stop feeling the crushing pain of it, but I could do it. Who I couldn't live without was God.

"No, that he doesn't."

Kenna looked at Ben, frowning. I couldn't look away from the way even his eyes were smiling. He couldn't be saying what I hoped he was.

"You know something."

"I know a lot of things."

"Ben!" Kenna slugged his arm. Actually slugged him. Ben laughed at her indignation before putting that same arm around her and pulling her close. I held my breath, waiting, only to let out a gasp when Ben finally spoke.

"Before Marcos went home yesterday, he asked me how to become a Follower."

FORTY-TWO

My stomach gurgled with fear, anticipation, and far too much bacon. Stress eating had never been my thing, but procrastination? Absolutely. After breakfast, I'd told myself. After breakfast, I'll go and see Marcos. How it was possible to even balance that much bacon on a plate let alone make it last over an hour...

But that was all behind me now, like the five-hour drive to Hodenia and the seventeen palace staff I'd passed on my way to Marcos's office door. Yes, I'd counted. And greeted every single one of them, checking in on their families, their homes, their pets. Half-hoping one of them would think me an imposter and send me away. Not that I could hear much of their replies over the deafening thud of my heartbeat in my ears. But still, it took up time. Not enough, though. I still wasn't ready.

Just knock. Go in. Get it over with.

"Wenderley?"

I spun around, banging my elbow on the still-closed door, berating the staff in my head. Seriously. Not one of them had thought to tell me that Prince Marcos wasn't even *in* his office? No, he stood outside it, a stack of papers in one hand, pen in the other, his eyelids the only thing moving as he blinked at me.

I didn't know what to think of the shock on his face. Was it a good shock? Bad? Merely surprised? I took a deep breath and silenced the fear and uncertainty threatening to take me under.

"You're here." He was looking at me like I was a ghost or something. In the long list of reactions I'd imagined on the way here, that hadn't even been last.

"Marcos? Are you okay?"

He shook his head. I wondered whether I should be offering him a seat or something.

"Should I get Luka?"

"No. I'm fine. It's just…" He shook his head again before letting a smile stretch across his face. "You're here. Really here."

"For the afternoon, yes." Maybe forever, although that would very much depend on him. "Do you have time to talk?"

"Even if I didn't, I'd make time. Let me just…" With another baffled shake of his head, he walked past me into his office, dropping the papers onto a side table before walking back out and closing the door. "How about a walk? Did you see the lily pond when you were here? We could go there."

Grabbing my hand, he all but ran through the hall and down the stairs, making me thankful I'd once again skipped on the heels and gone with flats.

"What's the rush?" I asked, breathless as we rounded another corner and raced to a side door.

"Can't have my sisters or Ryan spotting you."

"Are they angry at me?"

"Are you kidding? No. They're angry at me for 'whatever it was I did' to make you go away. They've been asking every day when I'm going to bring you home."

"Oh." I let myself smile at that. "Really?"

"Yes, and if they see you, I'll never get the chance to speak with you alone."

"Hence the running."

"Hence the running."

I picked up my pace, my legs far less encumbered in flats and a summer dress than Marcos in his dress shoes and suit. I giggled like a child as I raced him toward the lily pond, loving every moment of the crazy freedom I felt.

By all accounts, the lily pond was gorgeous, but its beauty escaped me today. All I wanted to look at in this moment was right in front of me, in the winded man standing there.

"Been a while since you raced?" I asked with a grin.

"Maybe." He raised his eyebrows, his mouth quirking up along with them. "Or maybe it's you who take my breath away."

Was Prince Marcos the So Shocked to be Teased actually teasing me back? He reached for my hands again, having let go at some point in our harried sprint.

"Wenderley, I have to tell you..."

My smile dimmed at his suddenly serious tone. His thumbs stroked the back of my hands, making it difficult to concentrate. He wasn't taking back his proposal, was he? Surely not. He'd been so happy to see me only minutes ago.

Was it happy? He'd been shocked, but it had been good shock. Right? He wouldn't have been smiling or teasing me like he had if he was angry at me.

"I made a decision last night."

God, tell me I didn't come all this way only for him to take it all back.

"I chose to be a Follower of God."

"Marcos!" The word was barely a word, more a sound escaping my mouth, without any breath behind to give it air. *God, really? Truly? He chose you?*

"I was sitting on the balcony staring up at the stars, missing the fact that you weren't there to talk to, when I remembered something Mother had told me once. That I was never truly alone because God would always be there for me. I'd scoffed at her words then, thinking them merely something she said to comfort herself. But, in that moment, there on the balcony, they seemed so real. I could have sworn I felt God's presence there beside me last night. I couldn't have ignored him if I tried. So, I didn't try. I surrendered.

"Of course, this morning, it all seemed like a crazy dream and my doubts stormed back in. Had I really imagined a being powerful enough to create the universe would not only know my name but care enough to sit beside me on a balcony when I'd spent my whole life ignoring him, even going so far as to claim he didn't even exist? And to think he'd forgive me? Clearly, I was delusional.

"But I wanted to believe, even though it made no sense. His existence, I was willing to accept. Even his love, in a 'parents have to love you even when you're horrible' way. But grace? A chance at happiness when I'd already failed so miserably?

"And then you came." His hand moved to my face, his palm warm against my cheek. "I looked up to see that chance right in front of me. My beautiful Wenderley. The woman who's brought life and color and hope back into my world. Do you have any idea what it's like to ask God for one thing, not even sure he exists, only to have that one thing turn up right in front of you?"

My mind struggled to keep up with everything he was saying, my heart too clogged with emotion to be any help at all. "You asked God for me?"

He shook his head. "A gift as valuable as you? I didn't dare. Not in my wildest dreams would I have asked for you. I just asked for something. A sign. Something to show me that maybe, *maybe*, there might still be a chance at forgiveness."

"You're forgiven."

"So are you."

The sobs came then, a weight I hadn't realized I was carrying lifted as I finally accepted it. Like a layer of rocks off the top of a spring, the waterworks exploded. I really was forgiven. Not only by Prince Marcos but by God. And, with the tears, came a washing. Cleansing.

A second chance. A third. As many as I needed for the rest of my life. Every time I made a mistake. Every time I ran ahead of God. Every time I chose fear over faith and selfishness over someone else. He'd be waiting there. One step behind, waiting for me to turn back and find him there. Arms open. Heart overflowing with love.

And, as if forgiveness wasn't enough, this man, a gift to remind me, every day of my life, that God knew me. Knew who I was. Knew what I needed. Knew I was far from perfect but loved me all the same.

Marcos pulled me into his arms, tucking me in against his chest, holding me there until the tears slowed.

"Wenderley."

His heartbeat pounded against my ear, his words stuck behind a swell of emotion. I was struggling to breathe myself, held in this moment so rich with possibility. Promise. And potential heartbreak.

I pulled back, just far enough to look up at him. His hand reached out to rest against the side of my face, his gaze never leaving mine. That gaze. I could stare into it for years and never plumb its depths. This man. The pain he'd been through—some of it his doing, some others', some mine—the love he offered... It would take a lifetime to thank God for what he'd done in both of our lives.

A lifetime spent with Marcos. I took a deep breath, pulled in my courage, and asked the question I'd come here to find out.

"Do you still want to marry me?"

"Yes." His voice cracked on the single syllable, but his answer was instant. He cleared his throat and tried again. "Yes, I do."

"Because?" *Please don't say it's because I "fit" into your life...*

He smiled, banishing my fear.

"Because I love you, Wenderley. Because you don't look at me like I'm broken. Because you make me smile. Because you make Ryan smile. Because you don't let me get away with ignoring those important to me. Because you're not like any woman I've ever known, and I love that. Because you have the most beautiful heart as well as the most beautiful eyes. Because you're not only creative but full of life and wonder, something you can't help but share with every person you meet. Because I can't imagine spending the rest of my life with anyone else."

He ran his thumb across my lips.

"Because those kisses you gave me that night will never be enough."

It was a good thing he was still holding me, because my legs weren't doing a very good job anymore. I held his hand against my face before kissing his palm and taking both his hands in mine.

Those kisses. I wanted more, just as much as he did, but this time, I was determined to wait.

"Please, marry me, Wenderley." He whispered the words. He might as well have shouted them, the way they echoed in my mind, fusing themselves to my heart.

There would be time enough for more kisses. Time enough for talking and details and wonderment and finding Ryan to give him the news. For now, all that was needed was one word. One promise for a lifetime.

"Yes."

EPILOGUE

I heard the reporters behind me, discussing the design of my gown, my hair, the veil, and which from the immense vault of crown jewels I wore. Not one of them had noticed my shoes yet. Was it weird to hope they didn't?

I wiggled my toes inside the yellow sunflower shoes. Flats. Not one bit of heel. Marcos's special request. "Forget the heels," he'd told me. "Wear your favorites. And can they please be the yellow ones?"

I'd smiled, not sure he was serious, until this morning when I'd gone to put on the heels I'd been dreading only to find them missing and these in their place. The nerves I'd been feeling disappeared in an instant, flung aside by the laughter I couldn't contain and couldn't possibly have explained to Kenna and Alina who were looking at me as if I was crazy. Joyous laughter. Marcos knew me. He loved me. Even my crazy shoes. Especially my crazy shoes. I'd never thought I'd find a man who did, certainly not a prince. I'd thought I'd have to change for him. Instead, he was the one who changed me.

Or perhaps we changed each other. Perhaps God brought the two of us together just for that. Two broken people, one beautiful hope.

"Still determined not to marry a prince?"

Kenna's whisper had me grinning as the cathedral doors opened. I stood on my tiptoes, almost but not quite wishing I'd gone with the heels after all, just to catch a glimpse of my groom that much sooner. He was there. Down the front of the cathedral. Waiting. For me.

The music of a full orchestra hidden in a large alcove up front swelled. Our cue to begin. My heart thudded, my face already aching from the smile I couldn't have hidden if I'd tried.

I couldn't see Marcos yet but in amongst the crowd were so many others I loved.

Queen Galielle, her smile almost as big as mine as she stood beside King Dorien, who, to my surprise and relief, had given his wholehearted support to Marcos's and my union. Kahra and Lucie, who'd screamed with excitement when Marcos and I had come back from the lily pond to announce our engagement. As Marcos had predicted, they hadn't let me out of their sight again for the rest of the day.

Alina and Kenna, walking down the aisle in front of me. Two friends I'd once thought lost, our lives now fused forever in the ever-growing world of faith and royalty. Their husbands stood beside the man who would soon become mine, Thoraben, Joha, and Marcos having formed a good friendship over the past eight months. Come April, our little group of friends would grow by one more, Kenna and Ben having excitedly announced to the world just last week that they were expecting a child. I couldn't have been happier for them.

My mother, brothers, Jade, Ashe, and Callan, standing proudly in the front row. My girls and their families took up the next three behind them. They'd been almost more excited than me at the thought of me marrying a prince and had decided as a group that they'd forgive me for leaving Peverell and them, but only if I let them sleepover at the palace at least four times a year. Given how much I already knew Kahra and Lucie would love them— not to mention Queen Galielle—it was an easy promise to make.

Then there was Prince Everson, sitting between Joha's parents and Mr. Grant-Hartley and his wife. A free man, having not had a single charge laid against him, though he'd given all the money he had to recompense those he'd exiled. Much of it had been sent back and donated instead to the rebuilding of chapels all over Peverell.

There were those who still called him a fool for giving up his crown like he did, but for many, his abdication, words, and the humility of his actions ever since, gained him a respect that could never be bought.

And Ryan, too short for me to see yet but who I knew was up there at the front standing alongside his father. The boy who, in so many ways, had brought Marcos and me together. A daily reminder of God's grace and the way he brought beauty from pain.

Ryan had been stunned when Marcos asked for his blessing to marry me. "You mean, she's not leaving again? We get to keep her forever?" he'd asked.

I'd knelt down in front of him, taken his hands in mine, and nodded, barely holding back tears. "Would that be okay? I don't want you to think I'm trying to replace your mom because I could never do that, but I love your dad, Ryan, and I really love you and—"

He'd bowled me over in a hug then, his tiny arms squeezing me tight as he spoke into my shoulder. "I love you, too. And yes, it's okay. Very okay. I think Mom would have liked it, too. She'd like you. You do fun voices when you read me books and you make Papa smile. I'm so glad you're back, Wenderley. I really missed you. Please don't go away again."

The tears had fallen then, dripping off my face onto Ryan's shirt as I held him. When Marcos handed me a tissue, I saw his face was wet too. As was Queen Galielle's where she stood, watching the three of us. We'd stayed there for some time before Ryan asked if this meant we could have apple pie and ice cream for dinner. "Because Wenderley's back, and everyone is going to be too excited to eat *vegetables*..." He'd scrunched up his nose in disdain, making us all laugh.

He'd gotten his wish. We'd celebrated the engagement with apple pie and ice cream. Then, later, Marcos and I had read to Ryan and put him to bed together before going out on to our respective balconies and talking long into the night. About Ryan, our hopes for the future, our plans for a short engagement, God.

I'd sat there, overwhelmed with a gratitude that went beyond words, as I'd realized that that balcony—where we'd shared so many conversations—had also been the place God had become real to Marcos for the first time. It somehow made it all the more precious.

My hand shook in my father's, the joy of it all too much to contain. Eight months on from that night, the day had finally come. I was marrying Prince Marcos. God really had done the impossible. There would be no more need for separate balconies after tonight, something I was as thrilled about as Marcos.

The crowd moved enough that I could see him now. All six-foot-plus of him. Dark hair combed back, dark gaze locked on me, expression of wonder on his face. I knew how he felt. How was this real? How could anyone have planned this? All the twists and turns and heartache and joy which had brought us together, not only in our two lives but in Kenna and Thoraben's, Alina and Joha's, Everson and Ciera's, Rachana's...

God, thank you.

"Ready?" Father asked, his voice gruff with emotion. I squeezed his hand before placing my hand in the crook of his elbow.

"Absolutely."

A singer's voice joined the orchestra, the words of the song Joha had composed for this moment swirling around us like a benediction as I took my first steps toward the man who I'd soon call husband.

There's a grace that goes beyond
A love that brought us here
A hope that carries us
A peace that calms our fears.
Because of him, we stand today
Because of him, we know
We don't face this world alone
All will be well.

ACKNOWLEDGMENTS

I've always loved being part of a team because every person brings their own individual skills and passions to achieving the goal. Publishing a book is no different. I love that I don't do any of this alone. You're holding this book today because of the many people who offered their gifts, passions, and time to see it—and me—from that first hint of an idea for a story to what it is today. I couldn't, and wouldn't want to, do any of this without them.

So, before I start getting too teary thinking of all the wonderful people in my life to see the words I'm typing, let me take a moment to publicly thank and introduce you to some of the amazing people on my team.

My mum, Jacqui. I've written and rewritten this paragraph ten times over already (probably more) trying to find the right words to express how much you and your endless support mean to me. I'm pretty sure I could write a hundred books and still not find the words. Thank you for the many little (and big) things you do, but mostly just for being there for me through all the ups and downs of being an author. I love that I get to do this journey with you.

Brett. You're amazing. You know that, right? I really hope so. I'm so incredibly thankful God gave me you as my husband. Thanks for all the sacrifices you make for me and our family. It means so much to me that you support my writing and are proud to have an author wife, even though you'd pick the movie over a book any day.

My three amazing kids. Life wouldn't be half as much fun

without you. Nor would my heart be as full. Thank you for pirate days and treasure hunts, crazy outfits, shared books, and many, many chats about multi-storied-treehouses. I love that I could write some of our adventures into this story. Thank you in particular to my oldest daughter, who came up with the character of Pirate Pumpernickel. I hope I did him justice.

Gabrielle. You inspired this story in more ways than you know. Maybe one day I'll tell you exactly how much, but for now, thanks for being the beautiful, creative, colorful, passionate, loyal, loving woman you are. I'm super proud of you and the fact that you're my sister. Thanks for being the very first reader of this series and for sharing every chapter of the journey with me. We should do this again sometime!

My dad, David. I love that you have an entire library (and now a Street Library too!) at your house, not because you're a big reader but because you love and value those like Mum and me who are. Thank you for always being the first to jump in and support our dreams.

Roseanna and David White. I don't know how you do all your do, and sometimes I feel guilty being one more thing on your list, but please know that I appreciate you, your help, your encouragement, your wisdom, and your time more than I could ever say. Especially these past few months when there's been so much else going on in your lives. Thank you for the way you not only believe stories change the world but put that into action every day. You inspire me and it's truly an honor to work with you.

Roseanna. I'm pretty sure there is a large percentage of people who pick up my books purely because of their gorgeous covers. I know I would! On behalf of all those who judge a book by its cover—whether or not we should—thanks for the time and skill you put into making mine look so beautiful. I love showing them off and pointing people your way.

Dina Sleiman and Janelle Leonard, my books' lovely editors. Dina, thank you for seeing the potential in my first drafts and for the wisdom, insight, encouragement, and suggestions you've offered each time to make the stories even better. I always appreciate getting your edits. Thanks for recommending WhiteFire give me a contract for these books too. I really, *really* appreciate that! And Janelle, thanks for—among other things—picking up on my Australian-isms and taking the time to help me figure out what the American equivalent would be. I love your excitement over books and life in general. It's been amazing to work with you both.

Katie Ganshert and Lisa Bergren, authors of two of my favorite Young Adult series – *The Gifting* and *River of Time*. Every time I read these series (which, according to Goodreads, has been five times each since I discovered them three years ago, ha!), I'm captivated all over again. Thanks not only for providing an escape when my own characters were driving me crazy and inspiring me as an author, but for reminding me how thrilling it is to be transported to another world and changed by a story and its characters. When I realized both series had a main character named Luka/Luca, I couldn't resist naming my Luka in honor of yours.

Many thanks also to *Paw Patrol* for keeping my young son occupied during his rest time each afternoon so I could write. You've been an unusual but fun writing soundtrack.

To you, my readers. Where do I even start? The fact that I have readers at all still blows my mind. To have you actually excited about things I write? So seriously cool. And incredibly humbling. I've loved meeting so many of you over the past year through the wonders of social media, and chatting about books—both mine and a thousand others. You truly are a passionate bunch and, despite the fact that many of you live on the other side of the world, I feel like I've found true friends. I love you guys! Thank you.

And to God—my rock, my strength, my hope. I know it sounds cliché but the honest truth is, I couldn't have done any of this without him. I wouldn't even have a story to tell.

Like Wenderley and Marcos, I struggle with accepting grace, purely because it's so undeserved. And yet, God keeps offering it, time and time again. Not when I've done enough to be worthy of it but when I'm at my lowest and absolute worst. Because that's what grace is. A second chance when we don't deserve it. A third. A fourth. As many as we need. Because that's who he is.

Writing this series has given me a greater view of that God, and reminded me time and time again of the truth which became the Rebels' catchphrase. Through it all—ups and downs, disappointments and joys, failures and successes, faith and doubt, and all those average days in between—God will still be God.

He's the one who offers a grace that goes beyond what I could ever imagine or deserve, a love that holds me here, a hope that carries me through the darkest days, and a peace that calms my fears. Because of him, I stand today. Because of him I know I don't face this world alone.

All will be well.

To God be the glory.

THE
DAUGHTERS OF PEVERELL
SERIES

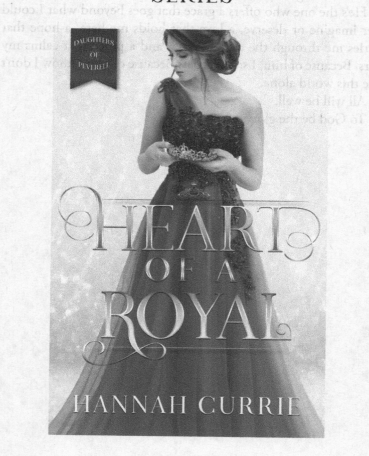

Heart of a Royal
Daughters of Peverell, Book 1

Everyone wanted her to be their princess…
except the ones who mattered most.

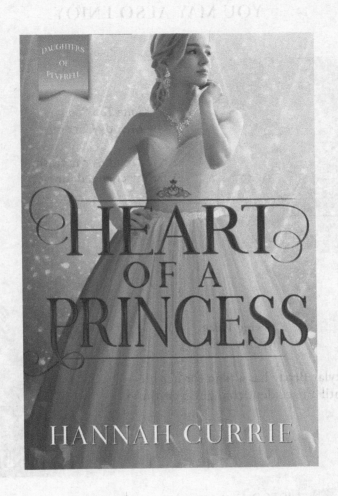

Heart of a Princess
Daughters of Peverell, Book 2

From the outside, Princess Alina appears to have it all...
But on the inside, she's barely holding it together.

YOU MAY ALSO ENJOY

Gone Too Soon
by Melody Carlson

An icy road. A car crash.
A family changed forever.

Seeing Voices
by Olivia Smit

Skylar Brady has a plan for her life—
until an accident changes everything.

Victoria Grace, the Jerkface
by S.E. Clancy

A sassy teen, a woman born before
sliced bread.
Just add boys...and homework.

CPSIA information can be obtained
at www.ICGtesting.com
Printed in the USA
LVHW041337280122
709583LV00012B/1764